BERNIE CHRISTENSEN

atmosphere press

Book Characters,
Made Up

- Mayor Bud Thorne
- Mayor Pete Ferrari
- KB, Kristian Bjornsen
- Officer Crystal Cobb
- Officer Reginald Bardouche
- Bell Star – Mustang Ranch, retired.
- Chief Hamper
- Detective Abel Sanchez
- Letitia Jackson
- Fran Tarter
- Director Milt Hershey
- Bobby
- Mathew (teenage boy)
- Pat Flynn
- Harold Washington
- Jessica Bang
- Dr. Dan Draper, Washoe County Coroner
- Coretta Draper
- Betsy Boggs
- Major General Harlan "Howlin Mad" Clark
- General Nate Arnold
- Captain Vickie Doolittle

- Lieutenant Barnes
- First Sergeant Smith
- Sergeant Nguyen
- Private Armbruster
- Brad Inouye
- Councilwoman Mandy Cockburn
- Juanita
- Melody and DuWayne
- Bob and Sally Sloan
- Moses LaBarge and Doug Finch
- Tiffany and Jenny
- Kam Ho and Su Lee
- Madam Zho, Jenny, wealthy woman from Hong Kong
- Mister Morley
- Donald Teeters and Bunny Bardot
- Kermit and Lucille
- Bubba, Gene and Dexter
- Nigel
- Jorge and Juanita

Book Characters, Real People

- Jim Sherman Oaks, head of the OSU Hatfield Marine Center
- Nicole Betzer
- Denise Burns, Dora, Dorothy, David, Darla, and Hunter
- Joe Fontana
- Roberta Gomez
- Henry Sims
- John Tyson TV personality
- Governor Bob Miller
- Bruce Breslow, Sparks mayor
- Tad Dunbar, TV announcer
- John and Karen Rickman
- Tony Spinelli
- Ron and June Rush
- Judge Reed
- Vern Robbler
- Cliff Brown
- Chuck Readen, A&P mechanic
- Melody Rogers
- Pat Hawkins

Chapter One

G-21 Grumman Goose, "The Gander"

Sparks, Nevada
July 11, 6:05 p.m., Friday evening

"Gawd, what a day," mumbles Sparks' mayor, Bud Thorne, as he gets comfortable on the end toilet.

"Now for a few moments of peace." *No phones. No one knows I'm here.*

On Victorian Avenue, just east of John Ascuaga's Nugget, the pumice-block city-restroom sits behind a retired *NCO* steam locomotive. The locomotive formerly belonged to the Nevada, California, and Oregon Railroad (fondly remembered as "the nasty, crooked and ornery").

Their elegant *NCO* depot and headquarters building still stands, next to the tracks, on East Fourth Street in Reno. Their goal was to build the NCO RR from Reno all the way to the Columbia River. The NCO erected a graceful headquarters building for their north end at Alturas, California.

Be that as it may, building the railroad farther north didn't work out. They only got as far as Lakeview, Oregon, where they again built another attractive headquarters building. (They are both still there.)

Mayor Thorne hears a dainty splash. He peeks between his legs.

Paralyzing pain penetrates his testicles. Bawling like a boar roasting alive, his reverberating scream jolts two-dozen toilet flies into looping flight.

Mayor Thorne's gonads, and a foot of vas deferens, have been ripped from his body.

As if from a blazing blowtorch, titanic torture tears across his rectum.

"*Good God,*" screeches Mayor Thorne.

His stall door crashes open.

He shrieks, "*Help me.*"

Mayor Thorne's colon hangs from his anus. His ankles tangle in his Macy's suit pants. Shaking in terror, he glances in his underpants at what appears to be a pair of root-bound baby potatoes. He screams bloody murder; then he screams some more.

Stumbling over his shiny black leather attaché case, the concrete floor slams his knees.

On all fours, Mayor Thorne scurries toward the light. He shrieks for rescue. His palms stick on the concrete as he scrambles past the urinals.

"For God's sake," he screeches. Warm blood swamps Mayor Thorne's thighs. He feels himself weakening.

"Help me," he screams. "*Help me.*"

Mayor Thorne's advance abruptly halts. Panic catches up with him. He pulls again.

"It's got me," he cries.

Mayor Thorne shudders at the sucking sounds spreading from the toilet bowl. "*For the love of God.*"

Faint-headedness overtakes him. "Save me," he gasps.

His face smacks the concrete.

Beat cops Crystal Cobb and Reginald Bardouche of Sparks PD, respond.

"Buck up, Reggie." Officer Cobb hands her trainee a Kleenex tissue. "You wanta be a cop, or not?" Officer Cobb stands short and enjoys a low center of gravity.

Officer Bardouche presses the tissue to his lips. He resembles a stork who repairs computers.

Officer Cobb drops her fist on her hip. "What didja think police work would be, Reggie? Strutting like a peacock among your adoring citizens?"

"Gimme a break, Crystal." Officer Bardouche swallows. "This isn't just some wino whose liver blew up. It's our mayor, Bud Thorne, for chrissake. He's really a decent guy. Who did *you* vote for?"

"We treat 'em all the same, Laddie Buck. This's a dead man with his pants around his ankles. I'll just make a wild ass guess here, Reggie, and suggest he bled to death out his heinie."

Officer Bardouche gulps and tries to re-swallow his last bite of Wendy's half-pounder. He mutters, "What're those?"

"I'm no anatomist, NG, but I'd guess his nards were torn out by the roots."

Officer Bardouche swipes the tissue across his brow.

Officer Cobb gives him a wry grin. "As soon as ya finish with our report, I'll call the ghoul squad to haul this mess outta here. Don't forget to mention that everything he had dangling . . . *disappeared*."

"Got to exit the building, Crystal, possibly evacuate my esophagus."

"Don't embarrass our beloved Sparks police force in front of the gathering citizens, douche bag. If you're going to heave your hamburger"—Officer Cobb jerks her thumb over her shoulder—"please have the foresight to do it in the other toilet."

Officer Bardouche takes a step toward the door. "The stench, Crystal. I'm—"

"Sure, Reggie, but, before you step outside, gimme your observation here."

Officer Bardouche's diaphragm spasms.

Officer Cobb points. "With all that gore blown out behind him, it looks to me like somebody shoved a hand grenade between his butt cheeks. Whata *you* think, Reggie?"

Officer Bardouche presses his lips together.

Officer Cobb flops her notebook open. "Do ya think he was tryin' to make it out the door? I suppose he would've made it, too, if his intestine hadn't got hung up in the toilet bowl."

Officer Bardouche upchucks his Wendy's half-pounder into his Kleenex tissue.

Reno, Nevada
6:20 p.m., Friday evening

Reno's mayor, Pete Ferrari, watches the clock ticking in his mother's room. A broken ankle has sent Rosa to the Washoe Medical Center Rehabilitation Hospital. Although Pete couldn't possibly know it, she only has minutes to live.

The 1940s rehabilitation building stands in downtown Reno near the Truckee River. Pete has just driven from city hall and still wears his suit and tie. He dabs a handkerchief on his brow. *Whew. Has the air conditioner broken down, or is it really that damned hot around here?* On his way over, Mayor Ferrari received a message on his car phone, stating that his fellow Truckee Meadows mayor, Bud Thorne, had just deceased.

Rosa, a mummified lady in the late stages of Alzheimer's, sits in her comfortable chair by the window. Her bed exudes that sour rest-home smell.

Pete's elbows rest on his knees. A robust forty-five-year-old Italian American, he appears tall and well proportioned.

"Eeew," says Nicole, Pete's twenty-one-year-old, and only,

daughter. "I totally hate it here, Daddy. Grandma doesn't even, you know, know we're here."

Pete nods. "I understand, precious. Grandma doesn't have a *goddamn* clue."

"*Daddy.*"

Pete raises his head. "Sorry, angel."

"It, you know, all stinks in here, Daddy." Nicole boasts dark hair and brown eyes, just like her father. "My clothes and hair all smell like this place." Dressed smartly in her business attire, she'd just left her city hall typing job.

"I don't wanta come here anymore." Nicole stands tall and possesses the knockout shape a trendy dress is designed for.

"I understand perfectly, Pussycat." Pete talks behind his hand. "It's all very depressing. Nevertheless, wouldn't you feel guilty if you quit visiting her—and then she suddenly died?"

"Big whup, Daddy. What's to feel all guilty about? It's like, oh my God, Grandma doesn't even—"

Pete sighs.

Rosa sits in her chair, grinding her gums on a long-ago goodie.

Nicole inches her chair closer to her father's. "Besides, you're the only one packing guilt around here. I don't believe in it."

Pete raises an eyebrow. "Packing guilt?"

"Uh-huh. You know. Over Mom."

Pete winces.

"Not only that, Daddy, I just don't happen to have your— pedal to the metal—need for power."

Pete grips the chair's arm and gazes into Nicole's eyes. "Now, where did *that* come from?"

"You'd be so totally better off if—"

"Why is it, Kitten, that we only seem to talk about serious matters in such inappropriate places?"

"Fer sure. You're all smart. *You* figure it out."

Pete studies the wall, which features a familiar print of Saint Peter's Basilica.

Nurse's aide, Letitia Jackson, breezes into the room. She sees Pete and gives him a warm smile; then she begins to fidget with Rosa's water glass.

Pete bumps Nicole's arm.

Nicole smiles. "That's totally rad, Dad. You're making this chick nervous."

Pete grins. "I guess that's just part of being locally famous, Sweetheart."

"Uh-huh. You gotta face it, Daddy. That chick knows—like every chick in town—that you're totally, totally single."

Pete smiles at Nicole. *Damn. I simply cannot start dating, yet.*

Letitia turns toward Pete. "I think your mother needs to go to the bathroom, Mister Mayor."

"I think you're right." Pete sits up straight. "I see her squirming. Do you want me to take her down the hall? And by the way, Letitia, you can just call me Pete."

"Oh no, Mister Mayor." Letitia shakes her head. "I couldn't do that." She gives Pete a fetching smile. "We won't be gone five minutes."

Pete glances up, smiling at Letitia, and nods. "All right, girl. We'll be waiting right here." Pete involuntarily wrinkles his nose at the room's vinegary smell.

Letitia places the aluminum walker in front of Rosa. "Come on, Rosa honey. Your loving family will still be here when you return."

Even though Rosa weighs next to nothing, Pete stands and helps Letitia lift her to the walker. Rosa shuffles into the hallway. In less than five minutes she'll be hideously killed.

Oregon Coast
6:25 p.m., Friday evening

"*Hjælp!*"

"What is it, fair maiden?" Sherm talks into his microphone.

Doctor T Sherman Oakes heads the Mark O Hatfield Marine Science Center in Newport, Oregon.

"*Se her!*" Kristian Bjørnsen, or KB, a doctoral candidate in marine biology from *Denmark*, points out the starboard window of the G-21 Grumman Goose. The ninety-five-year-old, eight-passenger airplane has been maintained in tip top condition.

"What is it, KB? What's Heidi barking about?" Fifty-six-year-old Sherm stands normal height, sporting sandy hair and matching walrus mustache. He wears a Hawaiian shirt and knee-high black rubber boots.

"The engine," KB says, in her honeyed alto voice. "It is the engine, Sherm."

The white-colored seaplane, with its merlot-colored trim, features *The Gander* painted on each side.

"What's wrong with it, KB?"

"There is smoke roiling out." KB had recently turned twenty-eight. She stands regular height and boasts Viking-blue eyes and light brown hair. She flaunts dangling silver earrings, silver rings on her fingers and her toes. Her most treasured trinket is her silver charm bracelet. In addition, she sports a navy-blue baseball cap bearing the words "Newport Marina," beneath which perches an embroidered rendition of the gracefully arched *Yaquina Bay Bridge*.

Sherm licks his upper lip. "What color is—"

"There is *fire*, Sherm." When KB enters a room, all eyes turn to her, especially the men's. "A tongue of flame just shot out."

"The tach's losin' RPMs, KB." The big 1937 seaplane turns right. "I'm gonna shut down the starboard engine. We don't want it to seize up.

"Kristian, can you persuade that goofy Heidi to desist barking?" Heidi, KB's white-and-brown terrier, became her constant companion four years before.

"Heidi. *Kem her.*" KB pats her thigh. Heidi jumps onto her

lap. "Can we make it back, Sherm?" KB uncorks her thermos bottle. She pours her coffee (which includes cream, sugar, and one-hundred-ninety proof lab alcohol) into her cup.

Sherm pulls back on the right throttle and centers the propeller blades. To counteract the push to the right, he holds the wheel to the left and turns the trim tab. Dried tideland mud flakes off his hands. Ten minutes earlier, they'd departed Siletz Bay carrying twenty-five ice chests containing live marine specimens.

"We're in no danger, KB, uh hum. Let's see, we're at a thousand feet and just off Yachats, which makes us only ten minutes from Newport. I don't think we should chance trying to make the airport, though. Let's put down in Yaquina Bay." Sherm sniffs. "Arrr, I'd say you got a good mix on your coffee this morning."

KB stares straight ahead.

"Anyhoo, there's absolutely no problem, my sweet."

KB peers hopefully at Sherm. She wears a snug white T-shirt and cut-off Levis.

Sherm's left hand squeezes the steering wheel. With his right he touches the dried mud on KB's cheek. "We're all right, KB. Trust me. I'll never let us get into trouble."

"Oh, I love you so much, Shermy."

"Aye, I know you do, me lovely." Sherm gives KB's cheek another pat; then he grips the wheel with both hands. "Now, get the checklist out and help me land this bucket of rivets."

"Oh, Shermy." KB smiles wide. "First, let us buzz Nye Beach and scatter the beachcombers."

Reno
6:30 p.m., Friday evening

Rosa pushes her walker across the polished linoleum. Letitia moves a wisp of white hair on Rosa's forehead.

The July sun seems to hang just outside the rehab building. Sweat beads on Rosa's skull. *My head's hot.*

"Oh look." Letitia points toward the window. "It's a chauffeur-driven limousine."

An elegant pink, majestically maintained, Rolls-Royce Phantom limousine glides by. Rosa's face remains blank; she doesn't know about automobiles. To be sure, she doesn't even remember that her son is Reno's mayor.

"All right now, Rosa," coos Letitia, "just a little farther."

Rosa glances up at a round metallic ceiling grille. Her face sags as *Lady of Spain* settles around her. *Why always the same song?*

A crack of summer thunder rattles the windows. *Lady of Spain* sizzles.

Rosa shuffles on. She peeks in Mister Skeleton's room. She sees him slouching in his wheelchair. She wrinkles her nose. Mister Skeleton endlessly scratches his crotch through his bathrobe. His mouth, resembling an empty French-fry sack, hangs open.

"Okay, Rosa. Let's hold up and I'll get the door."

Rosa snarls. Her right hand lets go of the walker. She steadies herself with her left and—though Letitia doesn't see it—takes a swipe at her nurse's back. *I need to go to the bathroom.*

The door swings open. The fluorescent lighting causes Rosa's eyelids to flutter. The odor of pine-scented disinfectant tickles the inside of her nose.

Rosa grips her walker with both hands and slides her feet forward. Letitia stops her. Rosa makes a low sound in her throat. *I need to go to the bathroom.*

"All right now, Rosa honey. No need to growl at me. Let me just get you turned around so you can sit."

Rosa begins to turn. Her image crosses the bathroom mirror. "Hah." *I see an ol' hag.*

For a moment, Rosa's eyes turn mean. *Oh, it's only me with my hair stickin' out.* Rosa can't remember that this same scene plays out a half-dozen times a day.

With Letitia's help, Rosa continues her rotation. Nonetheless, during the turning operation, the attractive nurse's aide keeps Rosa at arm's length.

"All right now, sweetie. I have you. You can let go of your walker." Letitia grips the fleshless shoulders. With her foot, she scoots the walker out of the way.

"You remember now, Rosa, don't you? We hike up your bathrobe. Then we pull your panties down."

Letitia squats. Muscles bunch in her thighs—ready on a moment's notice to spring away. Letitia slips the panties down Rosa's matchstick legs. "All right, Rosa honey. Let's sit down."

Rosa grabs a handful of Letitia's pink-and-white nurse's uniform. Letitia lowers Rosa onto the toilet.

A hint of a smile adorns Rosa's face.

"Sure, Rosa. You remember just fine." Letitia backs into the hallway and peeks around the door. "Now, Rosa honey. You just go about your business there. I'll be back in a few minutes. All right?"

Rosa gawks at Letitia's face.

"Okay, sweetie. I'll just close the door now, but I'm close by. Okay?" Letitia's fingers flip the wall switch. A fan begins to hum.

Rosa's eyelids blink.

The door closes.

Rosa hears a burbling in the water beneath her. A grin turns up the corners of her mouth.

Rosa suddenly straightens. *I haven't done nuthin' yet.*

The toilet water splashes. Rosa feels it moisten her bony behind. A perplexed expression covers her face.

A smooth shape, the size of a big tube of salami, slides effortlessly past Rosa's relaxed rectum. She feels lubricating slime dam up around her sphincter muscles.

Rosa's lips part. Her eyelashes flicker like mayfly wings. She hasn't thought this hard in thirteen years.

Sharp pain *rips* through Rosa's abdomen. For a moment she remembers a tormenting episode from her childhood—on a hot July afternoon, against all adult advice, she'd eaten nine green apples.

Agony cuts through Rosa's bowels. Quickly, as if twenty years younger, she yanks up her bathrobe. Astonishment leaps onto her face as she beholds her paper-thin abdominal wall heaving in and out.

"Hah." Rosa feels her insides disappearing in bite-size chunks.

"Hah." She hasn't talked in ten years.

Rosa's belly begins to pucker like a leaky inner tube. She struggles to remember how to scream.

Dark venous blood spills into the toilet bowl.

"Hah."

Rosa crumples closer and closer to the toilet seat. Her mouth is open as far as it can stretch—but no scream breaks through.

Rosa teeters on her seat. The salami slides out. Her body tumbles to the floor.

A last splash in the toilet flips up bloody water. The hospital-clean porcelain bowl has become a blood-streaked tureen.

Blood spreads across the white tile between Rosa's legs. Her mouth gapes. Her right slipper sits beneath the toilet paper holder. The fan continues to rid the bathroom of its pernicious breath.

"Rosa, honey." Letitia's fingers appear around the door's edge. "How're you doing?"

The door opens several more inches. "How're you doing, hon?"

Letitia peeks around the edge.

The hallway resounds from her bloody scream.

"Mister Mayor. Mister Mayor." Letitia backs into the hall. "It's your mother. Hurry. Get down here. *Puleeeze.*"

Pete bolts from his mother's room. Pete had just received a call from his office. His friend and fellow mayor, Bud Thorne, had just been savagely murdered in the pumice-block bathroom near the old railroad engine. Pete races down the hall. Nicole hurries after him.

Oregon Coast
6:35 p.m., Friday evening

"Sherm." KB points out the windshield. "There is the Yaquina Head Lighthouse.

"Aye, me pretty. Won't be long now."

"Shall we start down the checklist?"

"Arrr, when we're abreast of the lighthouse. We're maintaining good altitude and airspeed. We'll make Yaquina Bay, *no problema.*"

"The wheels are up and locked, Sherm. We are ready for a water landing."

"Excellent, me lass. Please work that right carb heat knob, KB. I think our difficulty was that new linkage I installed this morning; it simply got a little hung up."

KB takes a swallow of coffee and then pulls the knob in and out. "It works easy, Shermy."

"Just as I suspected. I think that rough engine problem's just fixed itself. Let's try restarting it."

KB discreetly wrings her hands. *He is smart, you bet you. But he is not the mechanic he fancies himself to be, that is for sure.*

"Ahhh, KB, gimme carburetor heat. Make sure both magnetos are on."

KB adjusts the knobs on the center console. "Should we not just land, Sherm? We are already past the place to start down the checklist."

"Don't concern yourself, KB. I just wanta get that starboard engine going—for added safety."

KB whispers under her breath, "Jiminy Cricket." She holds

her cup and pulls Heidi closer. The big seaplane zooms past Jumpoff Joe. "Oh, look, Sherm. There must be a hundred people on Nye Beach."

"Aaargh." Sherm depresses the starter switch. The right propeller begins to turn.

KB squints at the starboard engine. A puff of white smoke belches, followed by a shot of flame. Heidi barks.

The four hundred fifty horsepower engine roars to life.

"*Craperenski.*"

The steering wheel rips from Sherm's fingers. The Gander shoots up.

"Oh." KB clutches her stomach. She hears ice chests sliding back toward the tail.

"Aaargh." Sherm forces the steering wheel forward. "We have all our power back now, KB, so I'll take 'er up over the bridge."

Because Sherm had trimmed the seaplane to fly with only the port engine, the extra four hundred fifty horsepower pushes the seaplane assertively to the left. Sherm turns the wheel to the right and depresses the right rudder pedal to the floorboard. He furiously winds the trim tab.

His muddy right boot slips off the pedal.

The Gander makes a violent left turn . . . and rolls upside down. Twenty-five ice chests—each two-thirds full of seawater and living marine creatures—tumble onto the overhead.

KB shrieks. She squeezes her dog and releases her cup, spilling creamy, sugary, alcohol-laced coffee on the windshield. The checklist falls onto the ceiling.

"Yeow." Sherm works the steering wheel and the pedals to roll the seaplane back to upright and level.

"Sherm." KB points at Nye Beach. "They are running for their lives."

"Holy kee-rapp, KB." Sherm yanks the Grumman Goose back to level. "Do you think I possibly give an aardvark's patootie pile for those stampeding beachcombers?" Sherm adjusts the trim to bring the seaplane back to level. "What's that infernal clicking sound back there?"

"Shermy, I am getting sick."

Heidi dog jumps off KB's lap and hops back through the doorway into the former passenger space. Three months earlier, Sherm had removed all the seats but one, and converted the space into a cargo area.

Heidi barks and barks.

KB salivates and swallows.

"KB, *Grab a sick sack.*"

She jerks a sack from the map holder and whips it open.

"Now, look back and tell me what you see. Moreover, shut up that amoebae-brained dog. I can't hear diddlysquat over all that confounded yapping."

Holding her hand in front of her mouth, KB loosens her seat belt with the other. She peers into the cargo hold. "Sherm, Heidi is barking at all the baby crabs."

"Crabs? Kee-rapp. How many of the little scum suckers spilled out?"

"All of them, Sherm, hundreds, and all the sea cucumbers, anemones, sea squirts, starfishes—"

"Gazillions of crabs," Sherm mumbles through his clenched teeth. "I get the idea, KB."

"—barnacles, mussels, shrimp, all of them."

Sherm hisses into the mike. "KB, could you possibly convince that dog to desist from that accursed barking?"

"There is one crawling over the doorsill. Ugh. I am going mad." KB's voice grows shrill. "There are going to be hundreds of crabs in the cockpit with us, Sherm." She turns to face the front and throws up in her sack.

Heidi barks frenetically.

"Say what?"

KB dabs her lips on the puke sack. "The crabs are crawling into the cockpit."

The fir-covered hills speed by the port window. Sherm

holds the wheel steady. He speaks softly into the mike. "If you possibly can, KB, shove the inquisitive little crustaceans back into their skanky, slimy shitboxes."

KB yells, "The engine is trailing fire and smoke, Doctor T. *Shut it down.*"

Sherm mashes his jaw so hard it makes his cheek muscles bulge. He glowers at the tachometer and oil pressure gauges. "All right, KB," he mutters. "I'm shutting 'er down."

He pulls the right throttle back to idle and shuts off the magneto. The seaplane turns heavily to starboard and down. Down the aluminum deck slides ice chests, seawater, Heidi the dog, and four generations of crabs. Heidi yelps.

Sherm pushes the fire extinguisher button. Black smoke and fire transform into a trailing white cloud.

Reno
6:45 p.m., Friday evening

Nicole stands outside the bathroom and sobs. Letitia holds her and pats her back.

Pete yanks the cell phone off his belt and pushes a button. "Lyle. Pete here."

Chief of Reno police, Lyle Hamper, appears wiry, and he sports curly black hair streaked with strands of silver. "Well, hello, Pete. What is it?"

"My mother's dead."

"For goodness' sake, Pete, I'm really sorry to hear that. What was she, seventy—seventy-five years old?" The first thing you notice about Chief Hamper is the over-decorated Christmas tree that serves as his uniform. Five gold stars ornament each shoulder of his blue ensemble, accompanied by a great gold badge, a bag's worth of brass buttons, and myriad patches and awards.

"Lyle"—Pete peers at Nicole and shakes his head—"she's lying in a spreading pool of blood. There's gore all over the toilet. She's been *eviscerated*."

"I'm, uh, dreadfully sorry that your mother is suffering a massive hemorrhage, Pete. Do you know that Belle and I are at the Scottish Rite dinner and dance out at Kerak Temple? There's nothing I can do about your mother. Why aren't you here for the social? Did you forget?"

"Dammit, Lyle. My mother didn't simply have an old-age hemorrhage. Her goddamn guts are lying between her legs. Somebody's *killed* her."

Two other couples, and his new wife Belle Starr, sit at Chief Hamper's table. He turns in his chair and cups the telephone in his hand. "Frankly, Pete, I know this is a bad time for you. Honestly, just let the authorities follow their established routine. Maybe you should take a tranquilizer."

"I have to go. By the way, Lyle, have you heard about Sparks and Mayor Bud Thorne?

"No, what's up?"

"I received a quick message from Bud Thorne's office. It said that he died a horrible death in that public bathroom near the stationary railroad locomotive."

"What a terrible thing."

"Affirmative, he was a very good person, and a good friend. I have to go. So long for now."

Pete disconnects the call. "Jesus H Christ," Pete hisses through his teeth. "What a feckin' dildo. Oops, sorry, Letitia. I usually don't talk that way."

Letitia pats Nicole's back. "That's okay, Mister Mayor. I understand."

"Lyle's not going to do anything." Pete clutches his necktie. "He thinks Mother died from a hemorrhage."

Red rims encircle Nicole's eyes. "I'm so sure, Daddy. That's no hemorrhage." She points at the bathroom door. "*Please*, do something."

Moisture reflects in Pete's eyes. He blinks it away. *First, she didn't want to come here ever again. Now, she's bawlin' her head off.*

Pete catches Nicole and Letitia watching him. He pushes another speed-dial button. It rings at Reno burglary detective Abel Sanchez's home. Denise answers.

"Hello, Denise. This is Pete."

"I knew it was you. Do ya wanta talk to my man?"

"Yes, please."

"What's the matter? Something wrong, Pete? We just, this minute, got back from wedding rehearsal and dinner."

"Oh crap. Wedding practice. I'm sorry to bother you, Denise, with everything going on at your house, but—"

"That's okay, Pete. That's what friends are for. I'll get 'im."

Pete gives Nicole a nod.

With the aid of her cane, Fran Tarter hobbles around the corner. She stops, stares at the three people in the hallway, then aims straight for the bathroom.

Letitia releases Nicole.

"No, no, Missus Tarter." She holds her hands up and hurries toward the old patient. "You *mustn't* go in there. Please go to the other end of the hall."

Missus Tarter frowns. "Letitia, I can't *make* it to the other end."

Letitia pats Missus Tarter on the shoulder with one hand and points down the hall with the other.

Pete can't make out their conversation, but he sees Missus Tarter emphatically point at the floor between her legs. "Oh, Abel. Thanks for being home, partner."

"We jus' got home, my friend. What's up?"

"Nicole and I are at the rehab center. My mother's just been killed. Poor Nicole is beside herself."

"You call homicide?"

"Not yet, *tío*. I called that"—Pete turns his back to Nicole and puts his hand over the cell phone—"dildo chief, but he's too busy to help because he's dining and dancing with the lodge brothers."

"He's too busy drinking and partying to respond to duty, huh?"

"I effing guarantee you, Abel, Lyle's *not* drinking."

Abel bursts out laughing. "What about his ol' ho-bag—Miss Belle Starr? I bet she knows plenty how to drink and party."

"Now, Abel, you remember the chief's claim on that. Belle was *not* a working girl; she was only the *madam* out at Mustang Ranch."

Abel snickers. "You mean, boss, she madam *after* she got too effin' old to, how you say, cut the ketchup."

Pete bursts out in a huge guffaw. "I hear you, partner." Pete chuckles. "Ordinarily, around here we say . . . cut the *mustard*, but ketchup works just fine."

Abel laughs uproariously. "I bet she got in forty good years cuttin' the . . . *mustard*."

Pete chuckles, nodding his head.

"What I do for you, *mi compadre*?"

"I know you're neck deep in family responsibility with Dora's nuptial Mass wedding tomorrow, but . . . could you possibly come down and take a quick look?"

"Yes, my friend." Abel sighs. "Wedding not 'til eleven tomorrow. It's a big day for Dora and her mother. You know how is with *Mexicanas* and their daughters. If father, in any way, mess up ceremony, he in deep *caca*."

Pete laughs. "That's similar to a gringo wedding."

"Similar, *si*. I not in homicide, Pete, but I see plenty homicides when I walk the beat. I just five blocks away. I walk, that way I don't have to hunt parking space."

Nicole dabs at her nose with a tissue. "Daddy, tell Abel some sick psycho caught Grandma in the bathroom and cut her up with his butcher's knife."

Oregon Coast
6:50 p.m., Friday evening

"Aaargh." Attempting to maintain altitude, Sherm wrenches the steering wheel to the left and pulls back. He rewinds the trim tab.

"We are flying by the little Yaquina Bay lighthouse, Sherm." KB sets the sack between her legs. "We have not done our checklist."

Sherm turns his head toward KB. "Please believe me when I say this to you, KB, and please forgive me in advance for the crusty language that I know disturbs the delicate nature of your sensitive gender, but—*we ain't got no feckin' time*. We're losing altitude. I don't know if we can *get* over the bridge."

KB screeches, "*The bridge.*"

"Holy feckin' *shit*."

The structural elements of the Yaquina Bay Bridge fill the entire front view.

Sherm rips off his headset and yells. "Gimme full feckin' flaps, and make sure yer seat belt's on tighter than feckin' duct tape."

Sherm bangs the steering wheel forward into the dashboard. To avoid the bridge's north pylon, he twists the wheel to the right, full stop. He kicks the right rudder pedal to the floor. Unfortunately, a baby crab had sought refuge under it. KB hears the crunch.

Sherm's eyes bloom big as goose eggs. "Holy kee-feckin'-rapp."

The Yaquina Bay Bridge not only fills the entire windshield, it fills the left side window as well. Sherm pounds the rudder pedal—all the way to the floorboard. The seaplane dives under the bridge, missing the north pylon by a whopping fifteen feet.

KB sucks in a breath and fights the burning urge to urinate.

The steep plunge accelerates the Grumman Goose twenty-five miles per hour past maximum safe speed.

"Holy Crap," Sherm yells. "We're makin' two hundred twenty-five miles per hour. It'll rip the feckin' covering off. If I try to touch down now, we'll skip across the bay like we're a blazing meteorite."

Sherm, ever so slightly, nudges back on the wheel. The seaplane hurtles into the air like it was a South Carolina carport.

"Release the flaps, KB. *Release the flaps.*"

With the starboard engine dead, and the prop feathered, *The Gander* streaks past Bay Boulevard at two-hundred-five miles per hour. "Arrrbeedarrr."

Oh, we made it. "Sherm, look at all the people on the street." *I do not care what happens now.*

Sherm steals a quick peek forward and then it's back to the gauges.

"We are going very fast, Doctor T." *Maybe I do still care.* KB clutches Heidi. "Hang on, little Heidi. Hang on."

A pure-white male seagull hoves into view.

KB shrieks. "*Bird.*"

"Holy kee-*rapp.*"

Before Sherm can react, the seagull tucks his wings and dives. *The Gander* whistles over the plunging bird at one hundred seventy miles per hour. The seaplane's backwash rolls the bird up into a ball. A white feather flutters bay ward.

KB squeezes her shaking dog.

Sherm executes a highly inclined turn over the Mad Dog Saloon. The maneuver dumps another fifty miles per hour off the airspeed. The Gander straightens out for the final glide.

"Flaps, KB."

In front of Bay Boulevard, Sherm drops the seaplane closer and closer to the water's surface.

"Floats, KB." The floats, which stand in as wingtip extensions while in flight, rotate down to become the stabilizing wing floats.

"How's your guts, KB?"

KB glances at the sack sitting between her feet; she reaches down and twists the top closed. She smiles valiantly.

"All right now, KB. We're just about to touch down. Hold Heidi in your lap and wave at Admiral Fontana." Sherm waggles the wings.

The commander of the Thirteenth Coast Guard District, Rear Admiral Joe Fontana, watches from the headquarter building's front porch.

As gracefully as a Canada goose, *The Gander* dips its boat-like hull into the bay—squarely in front of the Newport Coast Guard Station.

A smiling pedestrian, walking north on the Yaquina Bay Bridge, leans over the railing for a better look.

Sherm clenches his teeth. "Whoopee."

Admiral Fontana shakes his head and saunters back into his office.

The Gander finishes its run-out under the bridge.

Sherm guns the left engine, making a spraying right turn. The propeller blows spindrift seventy-five feet behind the tail. Then he motors the seaplane toward the South Beach Marina's fuel dock.

"KB, what time is it?"

Reno, Nevada
7:05 p.m., Friday evening

Pete hears the familiar march of Florsheim wingtips on the linoleum tiles. He smiles and nods to Nicole.

Abel hurries around the corner. He wears a thin-line mustache, and his hair shows shiny black as a new Chevy. His tan-colored double-breasted suit appears sharply pressed.

Nicole wraps him up in her arms. "Oh, Abel, I'm so glad to see you."

Abel stretches his neck to see over her shoulder. "You been cryin'." He rubs Nicole's back. With the other hand he pulls a pressed white handkerchief from his suit coat, and gently dabs at Nicole's eyes. Then he presses the handkerchief into her hand.

Pete grips Abel's shoulder. "Thanks for coming down, my friend. I know you have a lot on your plate this weekend."

Abel steps back from Nicole and squeezes her arms. "You my friend, Pete. You call, I come."

Pete pats Abel's shoulder. "Thanks."

Abel glances at the ceiling.

"What is it, Abel? Are they playing your favorite song?"

"Is *La Cucaracha*. Not my favorite."

Pete laughs. "That's not what they taught us in grade school."

Abel snorts. "Is gringo song. No play *La Cucaracha* in hospital."

"Why's that, partner?"

Abel peeks at Nicole. Pete recognizes the twinkle in Abel's eye.

"La Cucaracha is . . . *the cockroach*."

Letitia smiles and shakes her head. Nicole grins.

Pete slaps Abel on the back. "You look as if you just stepped out of a Macy's catalog."

"Thank you, Pete." Abel cocks his head at the light shining into the hallway.

Pete gets a serious look and gives Abel an affirmative nod.

Abel rubs his nose. "What that smell?"

Pete snorts. "Sick people and disinfectants."

Abel rolls his eyes. "Come on, boss."

Letitia guides Nicole down the hall and around the corner to a bench near the entryway.

Abel steps into the bathroom.

"¡*Por Dios*!"

Pete looks over Abel's head. "It's more than you expected, huh?"

24

Abel turns toward Pete. "Forgive me, my friend. I must inspect scene. I no disrespect your beloved mother."

"I know, Abel. Moreover, I know that ordinarily you'd hustle me out of here before you inspected the crime scene. You're going to let me stay because I'm a former prosecutor, right?"

Abel nods. "I not sure it crime scene, Pete. I look first. Please forgive me." He pulls a gold pen from inside his coat. Abel kneels beside Rosa's corpse.

Pete unconsciously fingers his gold square-and-compass ring. It soothes him.

Abel sticks the gold pen under Rosa's bathrobe hem and pulls it up, exposing her trunk.

Pete gulps.

Without turning around, Abel asks, "She always this skinny?"

Pete leans over Abel's back. "Jesus Christ, *no*."

"She skinny as a mummy."

"Whew." Pete straightens. He spins around—"I need fresh air"—and hurriedly exits.

"I understand, Pete. I stay here."

Pete rushes down the hallway, around the corner, past Nicole. "Need air. You stay. Gotta hurl." He stampedes out the front door.

Newport, Oregon
7:15 p.m., Friday evening

KB rubs Heidi dog's back. "It is fifteen minutes after seven, Sherm. It is sure good to be back floating on the water."

"Aye, me lass, that it is."

The fuel dock is located just inside the South Beach Marina breakwater. As the seaplane enters the protected water, the port-wing float rotates inward and down into the water.

Bobby, a gangly teenage boy wearing coveralls too big, stands by the fuel pumps. He holds the tie-down rope.

The port engine coughs and dies. Its three-bladed propeller comes to a stop. The acrid scent of aviation gasoline and engine exhaust, mingled with the biting smell of barnacle-encrusted creosote-soaked pilings, tells you with your eyes shut that you're home. A pure-white male seagull circles and squawks.

The Gander's wing silently passes over Bobby's head; the hull gently bumps the dock. Bobby neatly ties the craft down fore and aft. Then he positions himself at the floatplane's small portside door located at the hull's rear. He wears a sheepish grin.

The door handle dips down, and the little door opens. Bobby tucks his head down but maintains his gaze on the entrance.

A suntanned feminine leg casts over the high threshold. KB's silver ankle bracelet glistens through the Siletz Bay mud. Her rainbow-colored rubber flip-flop searches for the wooden dock.

Bobby unconsciously gives his lips a lick.

Holding a twisted paper sack in one hand, KB grasps the seaplane's upper door frame and boosts herself out onto the dock.

Bobby takes in KB's T-shirt and sighs. "Good, uh—"he coughs—"evening, Miss Bjørnsen."

KB flashes Bobby a dazzling white smile. "Hello, Bobby," she says in a voice rich as Scandinavian honey. She appreciates that Bobby probably practiced his greeting all afternoon. She replaces her blue baseball cap and nods at Bobby, causing her silver earrings to tinkle. "Thank you for tying the airplane down." *Jumping Jiminy, I wish I had a stick of spearmint gum.* "You are a very conscientious young man." KB holds her hand over her mouth.

From inside the seaplane erupts a ferocious barking. Little Heidi wriggles over the door flange and drops onto the dock. Scrambling to her feet, she hurls her snarling self toward the young man.

Bobby drops to one knee and opens his arms. "Hi there, Heidi. Did you have a nice flight?"

Heidi's stub of a tail wags so fast it's a blur. Bobby rubs her head.

KB smiles and holds the sack behind her.

Sherm crawls out, his rubber boots dropping dried mud. "Howdy, Bobby." Sherm replaces his white straw hat on his head.

Bobby stands up holding Heidi in his arms. He stretches his neck while Heidi tries to lick his face. "Hello, Doctor T."

"How're you doing? Bobby," Sherm asks, smiling and taking in a full breath of the fresh air.

Heidi's tongue darts for Bobby's mouth. Bobby steps back grinning and lengthening his neck—and *runs out of dock*.

"Yeow," Bobby yells, and falls into the bay.

When they surface, Heidi has abandoned Bobby, and is single-mindedly dog paddling for the dock.

Bobby flips his head, throwing wet hair off his face. He calls, "I'm sorry, Miss Bjørnsen."

KB drops to her knees, sets the paper sack beside her, and reaches for Heidi. Her charm bracelet brushes the wharf. "That is okay, Bobby." She laughs. "It is just one of those days."

Sherm kneels beside KB and steadies her. "Aye, Bobby, absolutely fer sure, it's just one of those cockamamie days."

KB sets Heidi onto the dock. Heidi gives her coat a good shake. Water sprays out six feet.

Sherm ducks his head and holds his hand out to Bobby. "I guess we're all going to get a little wet today. Here, gimme your hand." Sherm pulls Bobby up onto the dock.

Bobby stands on the wooden surface in a puddle of briny water. "Sorry, Doctor T."

Sherm grabs Bobby's shoulder and shakes it. "You're doing just fine, Bobby. Do you think you ought to run home and shower? There's no tellin' what kind of dangerous critters live in this ocean water. You don't want some slithery creature biting your . . . tender-most parts." Sherm guffaws.

"That is for sure," says KB. "I'm going to bathe Heidi, right now."

Bobby nods. "I'm gonna take a bath in the employee's shower—put on some dry coveralls. Be back in a few minutes."

"You're a good laddie, Bobby, that you are." Sherm slaps him on the back. "When you come back, will you please top off the tanks and check the oil?"

"Yes sir, Doctor T. I know that you want to keep 'er ready to go at all times."

Sherm smiles.

"And, I also know, sir, that if the tanks are kept full, no condensation takes place."

Sherm gives Bobby's shoulder a squeeze. "You show fantastical grasp of the mechanical treasures I've laid before you." Sherm tosses his head back and snarls, "Arrrbeedarrr."

Bobby grins.

"Hey, KB," says Sherm. "What time is it?"

Bobby steals another peek at KB. He gulps.

KB glances at her wrist. "It is seven twenty-five, Sherm."

Sherm gestures at *The Gander*. "We still have some daylight, KB. I guess we'd better muck out the seawater and lab specimens, especially the squished one under the rudder pedal."

"Oh, Shermy. Let us do it in the morning. We have experienced a harrowing afternoon. Let us hurry to the *Hana Hou* and share a large glass of wine."

Sherm's home is a fifty-two-foot, Cross-designed trimaran named *Hana Hou*, which in Hawaiian means, *Let's do it again*.

Sherm grows a serious look. "I . . . I suppose that would be okay, KB. I just hate to think of that saltwater corroding the electrical connections."

"It will be okay until morning. Let us sit down and relax."

Sherm shrugs. "Okay, KB." He smiles. "Let's head fer the barn." He reaches into the floatplane's door and pulls out a plastic grocery bag. He pats the bag on the bottom and peeks inside. "Uh hum. Bit wet on the outside, but the goods appear to have survived."

Sherm supports the sack from the bottom. A loaf of French bread protrudes, as well as the tops of two bottles of red wine, and the corner of a one-pound bar of Belgian chocolate.

"Okay, Bobby," says Sherm. "Thanks be to you, me little shipmate, for taking such good care of the ol' *Gander* here. You shall surely receive your reward in a briny paradise. Until then, here's a little token for being such an assiduous lad." Sherm hands Bobby a twenty-dollar bill.

Bobby accepts, grins, and looks down at the dock.

Sherm nods at KB. Heidi spins in circles, making the medallions on her red collar jingle. "Come on all you ladies. Let's tie 'er up for the evening."

They tread up the ramp and step again onto solid dry land. Bobby watches with a starving stare.

Throwing a tremendous thick wake, a 36-foot Coast Guard cutter approaches. KB turns toward the bay. From the cutter's mast flutters the US flag, Coast Guard ensign, and the sinuous Coast Guard pennant. KB bumps Sherm's arm and points.

Sherm looks. "Oh, it's the 36-footer. They're headed straight for us."

"Oh, Miss Bjørnsen." Bobby hollers from the dock. "Don't forget yer sack."

7:35 p.m., Friday evening

Pete ambles back and forth in front of the rehab building, puffing on a Tinder Box Panatella cigar.

Abel steps out of the main entrance. "Hello, Pete. Fresh air help?"

"Affirmative, partner. Along with my cigar"—Pete indicates the lighted globe hanging above the door—"and my new pals."

Abel glances up. "Must be hundred bugs."

"I heard thunder cracking over the Sierra Nevada," says Pete. "There's a storm approaching."

Abel pats Pete's back. "Thunderstorm take care bugs, yes?"

"If this cigar smoke doesn't get 'em first." Pete nods. "What do you think, Abel? Obviously, no human did this to Mother, right?"

"I no think so, Pete. Why someone go so much trouble jus' to kill somebody?"

"Oh. Look at that, Abel." Pete points. "A chauffeur-driven *pink* Rolls-Royce."

It slowly glides by on Gould Street.

"The driver. He a mountain."

"Could you see who was riding in the back?"

"Window too dark."

Pete sucks in a fresh breath. "It's a beautifully maintained old limousine."

"Yes, it beautiful. Maybe, someday."

"Maybe so, Abel, someday. Well, all right, my friend. What do your guts tell you happened in there?"

"Something attack from toilet."

"Hell." Pete shrugs. "This ain't no homicide. This's just a starving grain-elevator rat trapped in the sewer. No need to bother Reno's finest, over that. We'll simply call Milt Hershey at the sewer department. His team is skilled at dealing with troublesome animals in the sewer pipelines."

The front door gently swings open. Nicole and Letitia step outside and down the concrete steps. "Excuse me, Nicole," says Letitia, "but I need to ask your father something kind of sensitive."

"Okay," Nicole nods. She absentmindedly bats at the moths.

"Mister Mayor," says Letitia. "The people are here to take your beloved mother away and clean the restroom, that is, if it's not a crime scene."

Nicole sobs again. Pete glances at Abel.

"I no think crime scene"—Abel shrugs—"unless a citizen knowingly turn loose dangerous creature in sewer pipe. That constitute reckless endangerment."

"Do you think, Abel, we could prove that a human being threw a common wharf rat down the sewer?"

"I not know, Pete. What if not rat? What if rat is tropical snake citizen got for Christmas?"

Pete sneaks a look at Nicole.

"When too big"—Abel rolls his palm up—"citizen drop him down manhole."

"I don't know, Abel. Don't snakes have to throw coils around you and squeeze you to death?" Pete tips his head toward the building. "Snakes don't eat out your body like that, do they?"

Letitia steps away from Nicole. "I remember seeing a show on the *Discovery Channel*. It was about a kid in New York City who got an alligator for Christmas."

Pete frowns at Abel.

"Well,"—Letitia raises her eyebrows—"apparently the alligator grew and grew until he couldn't stay in the apartment any longer. So, the kid somehow lifted a manhole cover and stuffed the gator down the storm drain."

Nicole blows her nose.

"Well," says Letitia, "the neighborhood's dogs began to disappear."

"Cripe sakes, Letitia." Pete scowls. "A dad-blasted gator making a living under our streets?"

"Yeah, Pete," says Abel. "Big lizards *eat* people."

"You mean," says Letitia, "those monitor lizards living on the tropical islands?"

Abel vigorously nods his head. Pete glares.

Letitia opens her hands. "I saw a program on the *History*

Channel about crocodiles in Africa. They bite the wildebeest and"—Letitia's hand makes a circular motion—"twirl until its innards twist out."

Abel clears his throat as if he were a professor. "Tropical creatures live in sewer, stay warm. I wonder if city losing dogs."

Nicole bursts out crying. Letitia grows a horrified look.

Pete sighs. "What kind of a *jerkoff* would throw their pet down the sewer? Oops."

Pete turns to Letitia. "Sorry."

Newport, Oregon
7:45 p.m., Friday evening

KB sits close to Sherm at the dining room table on board the *Hana Hou*. "Is that the part you worked on earlier today?"

"Hmmm, yes, it is, me lovely." Sherm holds a screwdriver. The carburetor lies on a newspaper.

"Ugh, it makes the boat smell like gasoline. What made the engine malfunction?"

Sherm wipes the back of his hand across his mouth. "Uh hum. A cotter pin fell out."

"Is that the pin you put in at lunchtime?"

"Aaargh, you wound me to the quick with your cogent observations, me pretty."

"I know about Shermanomics." KB laughs. "You are not made out of money. You have to save dollars on airplane repairs."

Sherm grins and shakes his head.

KB leans against Sherm. "I was glad that Admiral Fontana was simply inviting us to his party tomorrow night."

Sherm peeks at KB over his reading glasses.

"After we dove under the bridge," says KB, "I was afraid the cutter was coming to arrest us."

Sherm sets the screwdriver down. "Yes, when I saw those

flags fluttering my heart skipped a beat as well. You may rest assured, me pretty, I would've been the one arrested. After my trial the FAA would've confiscated *The Gander*, rescinded my flying license, fined me an amount I could never've paid, jailed me with a three-hundred-pound sex-starved able seaman, and threw away the key."

KB giggles. "Shermy? May I bring you a glass of merlot?"

"Zip-a-dee-doodah, zip-a-dee-ay, bring me a quart of chamripple, what a wonderful day."

"I'll bring you a glass—a full glass—and I will have one, as well."

"Yes, KB. That *was* a harrowing trip back from Siletz Bay."

"*Ja.* I was a bit scared when I saw the flames. We will have a little wine and then I will prepare the *middag.*"

"Ahhh, we'll have a little soup, followed by steak, potatoes and green beans?"

"Yes, Sherm." KB walks into the galley and pulls a wine bottle from the sack.

"After our repast, me lass, do you have a little dessert prepared?"

KB poured wine into two glasses. "I have prepared my own self for the dessert, Shermy, that is, if you are up for performing some homework."

"Arrrbeedarrr. Yer a fine wench, that you are. What time is it?"

"It is almost time for you to perform your homework."

Sherm screws the tiny bolts on the aluminum cover. "God, I love it. Let's put on some Jimmy Buffett."

7:55 p.m., Friday evening

Pete, Nicole, Abel, and Letitia stand in front of the rehab building. Two hundred moths circle the hanging globe. Across the lawn looms the multistory Washoe Medical Hospital.

Pete sniffs. "Smells like rain."

"I heard thunder earlier," Letitia says.

Abel gazes at the full moon making its way to its zenith.

A lone automobile cruises west on Mill Street. Its tires thump on the uneven concrete.

Nicole dabs at her eye. "Daddy, check out that radical car."

Pete squints at the vehicle passing under the streetlight. "Hey, Abel. Is that the same Rolls we saw on Gould Street?"

"*Por cierto.* No *two* pink Rolls-Royces."

"I saw it, too," Letitia said. "We saw it when I was taking your . . . that is, when . . ."

Pete pats Letitia on the shoulder. "That's okay." Pete drops his other hand on Abel's shoulder. "Thanks a million for coming down, my friend."

Abel's lips form a thin line, as if he were thinking of all the demands for Dora's wedding—just fifteen hours away. Then his face brightens. "Hey, Pete."

Pete turns.

"I was jus' thinking about the alligators under New York City."

"Yes?"

"I bet when story got in papers, citizens plenty upset, no?"

Pete stares at Abel.

"If story get out *here*"—Abel circles his finger—"it cause citywide panic, no?"

Pete scowls. "If there's a gator under our streets, Abel, it won't cause a panic. Our water employees will simply trap it."

Abel grows a serious look. "I 'member from television news New York have citywide panic. What if too big to trap? What if he *eat* city employee?"

Pete clenches his teeth.

From up Mill Street wails a distant siren. Abel turns his head and cups his ear. "*¿Qué es eso?*"

Pete shrugs.

"It's getting closer," says Letitia.

Nicole cocks her head. "I hear two sirens."

Down Kirman Avenue the boxy REMSA ambulance races. Strobe lights light the cottonwood trees. Sirens caterwaul. Dual tires screech as the ambulance guns around the curve onto Mill Street.

The foursome stand like statues. Their long shadows stretch behind them.

"Look," Nicole says. "There's a black-and-white following the ambulance."

Pete shoves his hands in his pockets. "That's odd."

Abel shrugs. "*Yo no sé.*"

Green clad nurses spill from the emergency room. The orange-striped ambulance bounces over the corner of the sidewalk and into the lot. Close on its bumper chases the black-and-white. The ambulance cranks hard left until the flat rear end faces the emergency room door.

Nurses charge the ambulance. They yank the door open and grab the gurney.

The patrol car pulls in beside the ambulance and slams to a stop. Its front dips down and returns to level. Rubber-smelling white smoke drifts forward. The uniformed driver steps out. His partner plucks up his notebook and opens the passenger door.

Abel points. "Hey, Pete. That look like Pat Flynn and Harold Washington."

Pete nods. "That's a pair to draw to."

"They been together long time."

Pete dons a crooked grin. "Is that because no one else'll work with 'em?"

Abel snickers.

Pete addresses his three companions. "What do you say? Shall we wander over there and see what's happening?"

"Outta sight, Dad." Nicole smiles. "Reno's mayor in the emergency room on Friday night. Totally outta sight."

"I've got to check on my patients," says Letitia. She pats Nicole on the shoulder.

Nicole gives Letitia a big hug. "Thank you."

"Yes, Letitia," says Pete. "You've been absolutely wonderful. Thank you from the bottom of our hearts."

Letitia squeezes her hands. "Thank you, Mister Mayor. I'm so sorry for what happened." Then she turns and hurries toward the rehab building.

Pete, Nicole, and Abel walk across the Washoe Med Hospital's lawn.

Abel yells, "Hey, Pat. Harold."

Officer Flynn—the wiry, highly-strung, patrol car driver—halts. He sports curly-blond hair. He faces the lawn area and hollers, "Who's that?"

Officer Washington, the big man wearing an Afro, says, "It kinda sounds like Abel." He pushes the bill of his patrolman's cap up, with the aid of his notebook.

The threesome step under the light.

"Yo, Harold." Officer Flynn bumps Officer Washington on the arm. "Who's the necktie there with Abel?" He talks from the corner of his mouth. "Check out the split tail."

Officer Washington flops his notebook closed. "Straighten up, Pat. That's the mayor. It's Friday night and he's—"

"Taking his secretary out to dinner," says Officer Flynn, "in, you know, appreciation for services rendered. Do ya suppose he'll take us out for dinner and dancing?"

Officer Washington chuckles.

The green-garbed nurses hurry the gurney through the emergency entrance doors.

The threesome walk up to the two patrolmen.

"How goes it, Abel?" asks Officer Flynn.

Abel nods. "Jus' fine."

Abel introduces everyone.

"It's a pleasure to meet you," says Officer Washington. He jerks his head toward the building. "Excuse me, but I need to see about the victim." He opens his notebook and briskly walks toward the doors.

Officer Flynn surreptitiously cruises Nicole from her ankles up to her neck. Then he glances at Pete and Abel. "What's up?"

Abel shrugs. "We jus' investigate problem in rehab building."

Officer Flynn grows a skeptical look but says nothing.

"Why you follow ambulance?" asks Abel.

Officer Flynn licks his upper lip. "A neighbor of mine called tonight on my private cell phone. They were preparing for an evening at the Atlantis Casino, you know, Friday night and all.

"She said someone had tried to *bump off her husband*."

Pete glances at Nicole.

"You know how it is," says Officer Flynn. "I advised her we'd have a look. I'm here to tell ya, Abel, Mister Mayor, we arrived at the scene of what looks like a particularly ugly attempted murder."

Abel pulls his tie. "¡*Por Dios* It no worse than—"

Pete quickly clears his throat.

Officer Flynn's eyes dart between Pete and Abel. "This victim was sprawled out on his bathroom floor, in front of his toilet."

Pete and Abel's eyes meet.

"His wife found him with his pants down below his knees. Blood and meat strips hung out of"—Officer Flynn peeks at Nicole—"his bottom area. There is blood everywhere."

Nicole's eyes open wide.

Pete drops his arm around her and pulls her tight.

Officer Flynn shifts his feet. "It was, you know, somebody attempted to ice him by employing a particularly gruesome method."

"¡*Dios mio*! What perpetrators use for murder weapon?"

"Well, detective," Officer Flynn says. "It was *attempted* murder. The sucker's still alive. And, we didn't see any weapons.

But, just between you and me, I think it was one of those Mexican gangs."

"Why you say that man?"

"Well, you know, Abel, the viciousness of it. Whoever committed that attack means to send a message."

Pete scowls. "In what part of town did this assault occur?"

"Not far from here," says Officer Flynn. "It was, you know, my neighbor's house on Stewart Street, right across from the park."

"What's the matter with you, Abel?" asks Pete. "You look as if you've just received a kick in the *huevos*."

"Stewart Park jus' four blocks from *my* house."

Newport
9:05 p.m., Friday evening

"Do we have to get up early in the morning, Shermy?"

Sherm and KB lie in the after bedroom. The full moon shows through the boat's skylight.

"Arrr. Not on your life, me little chickadee. We've worked hard all week, not to mention, we've experienced some minuscule airborne stress today. However, we're treating ourselves to an abundance of libation and lovemaking tonight." Sherm rubs KB's naked arm. "We'll sleep in so late they'll find us immobilized by cobwebs."

"Ugh."

Sherm lifts his glass to KB. "That was fabulous steak you cooked up on the barbie, KB."

"Barbie?"

"Uh hum. Yes, my little Danish flower—the barbecue."

KB smiles. "You, Doctor Oakes"—KB hoists her wine glass—"performed yeoman service getting the barbie fired up."

"KB, yer a fine lass, that you are."

"Oh, Shermy, I love you so much. Do you love me?"

"Ahhh, right back at you, fair maiden. Would you like some more chamripple?"

KB snickers. "Yes, and fill my glass to the top this time, please."

"Uh hum, that will be a pleasure. We'll be sure to drink some water and swallow a vitamin B12 before we go to sleep. A person needs to hydrate after drinking alcohol. We don't want to wreck our late-morning sleeping with a head-banging hangover."

"I know how to drink responsibly, Sherm. I've been doing it for . . . a long time."

"You're the sexiest woman, KB, and the horniest I've ever known."

"Horniest?"

"Horny means desirous of sexual activity."

KB cocks her head.

"Hmmm," says Sherm, "yes, a horn is an ancient symbol for an erection."

"I understand." KB reaches under the sheets. "Do you mean like this horn?"

"Hi ho and up she rises. Mister Winkie is about to erect his renowned winkie tent."

"Do you love me more than the other young women who have lived on your boat?"

"Aye, but you are causing me some confuzzlement. There's only been . . . a couple of others, way back, in the past."

"That is not what the women at the Science Center say."

Sherm rubs KB's back. "Aaargh, what do they say, me little Danish dumpling?"

"They say you run young female students through the *Hana Hou* like it was an assembly-line floozy factory."

Sherm freezes.

"They say you entertain a girl six months, then, after that, you find an excuse to expel her. When the coast is clear you bring in the next one—whom you have preselected."

Sherm's face flushes. "Uh hum, you have me at a distinct disadvantage here, KB. Perhaps, we've had enough wine for the evening."

"Is my time up? Is it time for me to be replaced?"

Sherm takes a sip. "Naaa, I'm not *about* to move you out, KB. I assure you of that."

"Then you love me? You want to make a life with me?"

"Here, have another swaller." Sherm splashes wine into KB's glass. "We're just living together—getting acquainted. It's a wee bit early to be considering a long-term commitment, don't you agree?"

KB begins to sob. She pulls the sheet up. "I have *never* had a long-term relationship. What is wrong with me?" She pats at her eyes with the sheet.

Sherm hands her a Kleenex tissue.

She gently bats it away. "Why can't I have a strong, loving relationship like other people?"

"My little maiden, maybe it's because you're not like other people. Something in your past, perhaps?"

"There is nothing wrong with my past," says KB. "My grandfather was a schoolteacher—a pillar of our community." KB bawls. "I was a vamp of a girl. I was born seductive. My mother told me so." Her shoulders shake. "It was not my grandfather's fault." She falls prostrate across the bed and weeps.

Sherm lies down beside her and gently lowers his arm across her shoulders.

Chapter Two

Rolls-Royce Phantom Limousine

9:10 p.m., Friday

In the Reno foothills, a thunderclap rattles the windows.

"*Madame Chiang Kai-Shek has just been killed,*" Doctor Chan, in his white lab coat, hollers from the patio. "*Come quickly.*"

Madam Jenny Zho wails. She rips the cigarette from her mouth.

"No, no, Madam Jenny," shouts Doctor Chen, the taller and thinner of the two Chinese researchers. "Not come out. You no want to see."

Seventy-seven-year-old Madam Zho, a tailored black Chinese pantsuit gracing her tiny frame, pushes herself off her hassock. She hurries toward the French doors that open into the pool area.

Mister Morley, her big butler, steps in her path. "No, Madam. Please. First, let me have a look."

Using her left hand, Madam Zho takes a long drag from her Virginia Slim cigarette.

"As you wish, Mister Morley." Her right arm had been

paralyzed ever since a street beating during her ragamuffin childhood days in Hong Kong. "You're a good bloke." Her hair appears as glossy black as a Ming Dynasty enameled table.

The huge Mister Morley, who keeps his head shaved and wears plain, but tailored, black suits, ducks his head and steps through the door into the pool area. He closes the door behind him.

Madam Zho had moved from Hong Kong, prior to the British transferring the colony to the People's Republic of China. She had moved her money—and Mister Morley—to Vancouver, British Columbia.

A trembling Madam Zho creeps up to the French doors. Through the venetian blinds she sees the two researchers and Mister Morley hunkered at the pool's edge. She has a little cough and takes another drag.

After settling into her four-story Canadian château, Madam Zho had purchased this sixteen-bedroom, twenty-two baths, ranch-style mansion on University Ridge Drive in Reno; now she can get away anytime she pleases to indulge in her passion for gambling.

Paving tiles cover the expansive automobile parking area, as well as the patio surrounding the pool. The mansion boasts a stunning downtown view of Reno. Local residents insist that Marilyn Monroe stayed in the guest suite during the filming of *The Misfits*.

Through the gate, separating the swimming pool from the parking area, her little Shih Tzu, Mao Tse-tung, scampers toward the three men at the pool's edge.

Twenty minutes earlier, Madam Zho, Mister Morley, Mao Tse-tung and Madame Chiang Kai-Shek had returned from downtown Reno in Madam Zho's cherished old pink Rolls-Royce Phantom limousine. Mao enjoys sleeping on the cushioned rear seat. Madam Zho had left him undisturbed with the door open.

"*No.*" Madam Zho yanks the French doors open. Her cigarette falls from her lips. She cries, "No, Mao. *Stop.*"

42

Mister Morley spins around.

Madam Zho screams.

Mister Morley is holding Madame Chiang Kai-Shek's pink collar and her dripping fur . . . it's all that was left.

Reno
12:30 a.m., Saturday morning

"Okay, sugar," Abel calls out. "Bathroom yours."

An hour earlier, while the summer thunderstorm cracked and rumbled, and with lightning striking on Mount Rose, Abel had trotted home from Washoe Med.

Denise swishes past Abel rustling her nightie. He watches the scanty nightie and smiles.

Stopping at the doorway, Denise delivers a come-and-get-me smile. Abel nods his head and grins. She executes a passable pirouette and gently closes the bathroom door.

Sighing, Abel muses on how Denise's black hair frames a still pretty face, even after being married to him for twenty years.

Abel scans his .38 Smith & Wesson police revolver hanging in its shoulder holster on the back of his chair. He glances at the box containing his army medals. The box sits on top of the chest of drawers in front of a multitude of Denise's ceramic angels—next to his old bayonet.

Abel hears water running in the bathroom. He reflects on what a sexy body Denise still displays, even after giving birth to their five children.

"It take me time for wind down tonight." Abel sits on the side of their bed. He reminisces on Denise crawling into bed with her nightgown riding up over her hip. Abel smiles as he remembers how she dresses for bed like an angel, but—when the mood is right—she makes love like a she-devil.

Abel shrugs. "Hey. I no work *mañana.*"

A scream, as shrill as if Denise's foot was being crushed in a vise, pierces the bathroom door.

Instantly, Abel assumes his old Army Special Forces crouch. "Abel," she shrieks.

Abel leaps to the bathroom door. He glowers at the doorknob.

Denise cuts loose with another earsplitting screech of pain.

Snapping a lightning-fast kick to the door, Abel splinters it clean off its hinges.

He crashes through the falling remains, landing on his feet in the middle of the bathroom.

Abel's eyes widen. "¡*Madre Mía!*"

Denise leans against the wall. She holds the hem of her nightie tight against her knees. Her mouth opens as far as it will stretch—her window-rattling scream vibrates the house.

Something splashes in the toilet bowl.

Abel's hands spread as if to tear a man's throat out.

The bottom of Denise's nightgown flutters like sparrows trying to escape.

Then he sees it—a slick brown side. It resembles a large stick of quivering sausage. *It drapes from the toilet to under his wife's nightie.*

"¡*Madre de Dios*! What *that?*"

Abel whirls and bounds back through the shattered door, his vision grazing his six-shot pistol.

He shakes his head, *no.*

A sound causes Abel to glance up. Their teenagers— Dora, Dorothy, Dominic, and David—stand at the bedroom door. Eight-year-old Darla struggles to see around them.

"Papa," says Dora, "we heard—"

"*Go to bedrooms.*"

In ten hours, nineteen-year-old Dora will be the bride having a nuptial Mass wedding at *Saint Thomas Aquinas Cathedral,* followed with an outdoors grandiose Mexican reception at *Rancho San Rafael Park*.

"*Now*," says Abel.

Abel spots his bayonet.

He lunges.

In one motion he grasps the scabbard, jerks the bayonet loose, spins back toward the bathroom pulling the tablecloth and fifteen ceramic angels off the chest.

Abel springs back through the door.

Her eyes mashed shut, Denise screams.

Abel slashes his blade halfway through the creature. "You *sonofabitch*."

The tube thrashes.

Abel's left-hand clutches at the animal, but he can't get a hold on the slimy surface. He furiously saws the blade back and forth, *cutting all the way through*.

Blood trickles from the exposed meat.

Denise bawls uncontrollably.

The tube's long end retreats back into the toilet. The tube splashes, then disappears down the drain, leaving the bowl's insides-streaked red.

The severed rear end drops out of Denise's nightgown. It vibrates and shudders. The rear end appears to be about the same length as his bayonet.

Abel stares. "*¿Qué es eso?*"

Denise weeps openly. She stands frozen, her eyes closed.

The creature's twitching motions begin to die down.

Denise continues shaking.

Keeping clear, Abel circles to his wife. Shifting the bayonet to his left hand, he slips his right around Denise's waist. He draws her away from the wall.

"Come, my beloved," whispers Abel. Denise whimpers. He steers her to the doorway.

Abel kicks the remaining door fragments clear and guides

Denise through the splintered wood into their bedroom.

Denise is sobbing.

Abel shepherds her to the bed. He sits her down. Abel drops the blood-smeared bayonet on the throw rug and sits beside her. He tenderly places his arm around her.

"Everything be all right, my pretty wife." Abel clenches his jaw, making his mustache go crooked. *Sonofabitch move fast. He crawl from Stewart Park to Washoe Med, to my house, in jus' one hour.*

"I take you to emergency in jus' a minute," Abel whispers. He glances up and sees their five children *still standing there.*

Earlier, the wedding party had held a rehearsal and then enjoyed dinner at their favorite restaurant, *El Adobe Café on Arroyo*. Dora had just returned from a ribald shower and party.

"It okay, *me hijos*. Come. Embrace your mother."

The five hijos stream in and surround Denise. She reaches out to hold them. Tears gush down her cheeks.

"Mama," asks Dora. "What happened?"

"We heard so much . . . racket," Dorothy says.

Abel peeks at the nightie's hem. *No blood.*

Sporting white hair, white walrus mustache, and a bathrobe dragging the carpet, Grandpa Ricardo shuffles into the doorway.

Abel spreads his hands. "*Buenos días, papá grande Ricardo.*"

Grandpa Ricardo dips his head. "*Buenos días, me hijo politico.*"

Little Darla pulls on her father's sleeve. "English, Daddy."

"Darla, you know Grandpa Ricardo speak only Spanish."

"No, Daddy." Darla stares at Abel. "*You.*"

Abel wraps his daughter in a bear hug.

"Honey," says Denise quietly smiling.

"Yes, my beloved."

"The bathroom door wasn't locked."

Reno
12:50 a.m., Saturday morning

Mayor Pete sits on the edge of his bed rubbing his temples.

Thunder makes Nicole's Siamese cat, Fiddle, whip its tail back and forth.

Pete can't help thinking of his mother bleeding on the bathroom floor. He shakes his head to make it go away, and then he sees his wife, Maria, floating face down from their waterskiing accident on Pyramid Lake, five years earlier. Then he sees Mayor Bud Thorne torn apart in the Sparks public lavatory.

Pete clutches his chest. He and Maria had enjoyed a couple of beers. At ten o'clock at night they'd decided to take advantage of the glass-smooth water. At twenty-five miles per hour, Maria had slammed into the side of an eighteen-foot Glastron boat. Two lovers had anchored it a hundred feet offshore. To keep from being disturbed, they'd switched their anchor light off.

Then, Mayor Pete remembered his notice that Mayor Bud Thorne's funeral would be held Wednesday at 1:00 p.m.

Pete's loosened necktie hangs down his front. *I could sure enjoy a drink, but I have too damned much to do this morning.* He saunters toward the master bathroom. Fiddle bumps into his leg. Pete hears a nearby splash. "Fiddle, did you hear that?"

Fiddle flattens her ears and lowers her body. The hairs on her back bristle up.

"What is it, girl?"

Pete turns the light on.

Fiddle treads onto the tiled floor. Pete hears his leather shoe squeak.

The furry pink toilet lid lies closed. For the last five years Pete has left Maria's house decorations just as they were.

Fiddle approaches the porcelain stool. She sniffs.

Pete feels his pounding heart. *What'm I afraid of?* He licks his lip. *For crapsake, I'm afraid of being gutted by a sewer-sucking crocodile—that's what I'm afraid of.*

Pete imagines Nicole padding into the master bedroom and spotting him and Fiddle staring at the toilet. Pete reaches for the toilet lid. He clenches his teeth . . . and flips the lid up.

Fiddle places her paws on the porcelain rim, stretches her neck, gazes in the toilet bowl.

Pete looks in.

Nothing.

What a dip shit. Pete straightens. *I must be getting goddamned senile.*

Pete frowns, wait a minute. *Fiddle heard it too.* He hears footsteps on the carpet.

"Like, what are you two doin' in there?"

"Oh . . . Fiddle and I were just playing African safari."

"*Geddoutahere.*"

Pete smiles and shrugs.

"Well, I'm all tired, Daddy," says Nicole. "I need to, you know, get some rest."

"I know, precious. Come here." Pete wraps his arms around her.

"I love you, Daddy."

"I love you too, Nikki. Do you think you may need to take something to help you sleep?"

"I, fer sure, could use something. But I don't want to take any drugs."

"You're a good girl, angel. See you in the morning."

Nicole kisses her father on the cheek.

Pete picks up Fiddle. "Here's your kitty cat."

The telephone rings.

A scowl grows on Pete's face. *What dip shit calls at this effing hour? Undoubtedly one of Nicole's obsessively needy friends.* He hears Nicole talking. In a few moments there's the tap on his door.

"Daddy. It's Abel. He sounds, like, kinda hyped up."

Pete opens the door. Nicole hands him the cordless receiver.

"Thanks, Nicole. Yes, *tío*. What's up?"

"Hey, Pete. You *not believe* this."

"Huh?"

"Denise attacked in toilet. It tropical snake."

"Chrissake, Abel. You're shitting me. I mean . . . is Denise all right?"

"*Si, mi amigo.* I not shit you. And yes, Denise okay."

"What happened?"

Abel describes Denise's screams, the fracas, and the sawing off of a foot-long sample.

"My God, Abel. It sounds like your tropical snake picked the wrong toilet to dine from. Good work, my friend."

"Pete. It late. But you can come, look at *este cosa?*"

"You got it, partner." Pete reaches for his wallet and car keys. "I'm ten minutes away. Be right there."

Pete thinks of Nicole. *I'd better warn her about the toilets.* Then he decides that she's experienced enough stress for one night, and that nothing could possibly happen before morning.

Reno
1:20 a.m., Saturday morning

Pete crouches in Abel's bathroom, three feet from the severed specimen.

Abel rests his knee on the tile. He is still wearing his well-pressed suit, but his necktie hangs askew. A strand of black hair uncharacteristically droops across his forehead.

Behind Pete and Abel, Officer Washington, from Reno PD, stands with his yellow pad. Officer Flynn scowls.

"I don't think," mutters Pete, "that it's an alligator."

Abel prods it with his pen.

"I don't see any scales, tío." Pete rubs his chin. "Doesn't an alligator have scales like a big lizard?" He glances up at the two patrolmen. "I mean, the skin on this specimen is as smooth as an Oscar Myer Weiner."

Officer Flynn shrugs.

"Damn." Abel squints at Pete. "It got to be *something*. Maybe it tail off big snake."

"I think even a snake has scales, Abel," Pete says.

"Okay, boss, but maybe so small, you no see."

"Cripe sakes, partner," says Pete. "I don't know. I'm, sure as to hell, no dad-gummed biologist."

Abel shrugs. "It right color for snake."

Pete nods.

A shuffling at the bathroom door makes Abel glance up. "¡*Dios mio*! I no want you to see this."

"Children," Abel says, full of patience and love. "Go back to bedrooms. I be with you in few minutes."

The four teenagers, and little Darla, stare at the specimen. "Okay, Papa," says Dora. She herds the younger ones down the hall. "We're waiting for you in *my* bedroom."

Abel places his hand on his chest.

Pete pats him on the arm.

"Pardon me, detective," says Officer Washington, "but, isn't that a *fin* on the rear end there?"

Abel runs his ball point pen around the tapered end. He catches his pen in the folded skin and spreads it. "Holy mother of God. It a sonofabitch'n fin."

"For chrissake," mutters Pete. "You're right, Harold."

"Maybe," says Abel, "we take evidence in. Get Doctor Draper look at it."

"*Right*." Pete grasps Abel's shoulder. "Let's get the ol' county coroner out of bed right now."

Pete and Abel stand up. Pete looks into Abel's eyes. "What

50

is it, my friend? You're worried about Denise?"

"What if she *infected*? What if she bleeding inside and we jus' no see it? What if my five children lose their mother?"

Pete indicates to the two patrolmen to place the exhibit in an evidence bag and hustle it back to headquarters.

Abel sighs. "Dora's wedding in jus' eight hours."

"I'll help you any way I can, buddy."

"I know. Thank you, Pete. What if story get out about citizens attacked on toilets? There be citywide panic, no?"

Pete's face sags. "Whew."

Abel raises his eyebrows. "What Reno do?"

"We'll deal with it, Abel," says Pete. "For the time being, concentrate on getting your family through this marriage ritual."

"Excuse me, Mister Mayor," says Officer Flynn. "Does this evidence"—he holds up the bag—"you know, have anything to do with the victim that Harold and I escorted in?"

Pete shrugs. "We'll gather the evidence, Pat, and go where it leads us. I assure you; we're going to get to the bottom of this."

"You got it, boss."

Officer Washington says, "You can count on us, Mister Mayor."

"Thanks, men," says Pete. "I'm calling Doctor Draper, right now. He'll identify the creature and then we'll figure out how to kill the sons of bitches. Should have 'er under control by the end of the weekend." He draws a breath. "Abel." He places a hand on Abel's shoulder. "How's Denise doing, emotionally?"

"She really shook up. Ambulance took her jus' before you got here. She worried about monkey wrench in Dora's wedding. But, funny thing, Pete."

"Yes?"

"Even though she in shock, no bloodbath like on your sainted mother."

Newport
1:25 a.m., Saturday morning

The full moon shines through the skylight, casting the two naked bodies in silver. Candles extinguished. KB's empty wine glass stands on her bedside table.

KB smells the varnished-wood fragrance permeating the aft cabin. Through the open porthole she hears the moan from the far-off whistle buoy. A gentle wind makes the boat's rigging hum.

KB senses the familiar smell of Sherm's hair. *At least, he is my man for now. Perhaps he loves me. For sure, he really cares for me.*

She sniffs the briny air. *My life is good. What could be finer?*

For a moment, KB entertains the idea that, without warning, it could all come tumbling down. *There are no guarantees in this world; that is for sure.*

KB reminisces on the lovemaking they had engaged in immediately after her crying jag. Now, Sherm lies beside her, softly snoring. *Sherm has had lots of women, always much younger. I know he is really interested in me. Of course, I was with many men, but that was different.*

The partial memory of her maternal grandfather slipping into a helpless little girl's room in the middle of the night, disturbs KB's spirit. Once again, she pushes the recollection way down deep. She entertains the impulse to spring from bed, grabbing a bar of soap and splashing into the bay.

From beyond the jetty drifts the buoy's mournful sigh.

I am glad we get to stay in bed in the morning.

Reno
1:50 a.m., Saturday morning

"Holy shit." Pete blinks. "It looks like the Mall of America."

Pete stands inside the police dispatching room at the headquarters building on East Second Street. All three dispatcher stations are filled. Fresh coffee aroma pervades. Every overhead light blazes away.

Red flashing dots speckle the dispatcher's boards. It looks like a bad case of electric measles.

Behind dispatcher station number two, Pete spots Chief Hamper. His bespangled uniform coat hangs open.

Pete's suit coat is draped over his arm. He has rolled his shirtsleeves up, mid-forearm. His necktie creates a bulge in his left pants pocket.

Chief Hamper turns as Pete approaches. "By golly, Pete. I see dispatch finally found you."

"They didn't find me," says Pete, displaying a puzzled look. "I was on my way down here already."

"You don't say," says Chief Hamper, turning toward the dispatcher's board.

"Yes, I do say." *Jesus Christ, I hate it when he says that.* "What're *you* doing here in the middle of the night?"

"Well, Councilwoman Mandy Cockburn called me a half hour ago. You're well acquainted with her, I assume?"

Pete half closes his eyelids.

"It seems, starting around midnight, our citizens began calling our area police forces, fire departments, and ambulances. She said I should get down here, quick."

Pete grimaces. *No shit Sherlock. Having your posterior munched on while sitting on your personal toilet can cause a guy a shit load of distress.* "The way those boards are lighting up, Lyle, it appears we may be on our way toward a citywide panic."

"Frankly, Pete." Chief Hamper shakes his head. "I wouldn't go so far as to say that."

"Chief Hamper." Pete sweeps his hand at the room. "What in Christ's name *would* you call it?"

Chief Hamper sets his teeth.

Pete drops his face to within a pistol's length of Chief Hamper's. "I see we have dozens of calls for police and ambulance services." Pete backs away. "I just called Spark's mayor Bud Thorne's private line. They would like it if we could send over a couple of detectives to help them out."

Chief Hamper's eyelids blink. He nods.

Pete spreads his hands. "He bled to death out his asshole."

Chief Hamper swallows.

"I'll send over a couple of good ones, but I'm going to hang on to Abel."

Pete leans in until his Roman nose almost touches Chief Hamper's face. "Now, godamit, Lyle. You're going to mess things up good if you keep on kissing those whales' asses instead of getting serious with your police work."

"Oh, my heck, Pete," sputters Chief Hamper. He takes a step back. "To be honest, the people of Reno put me in this job to make better lives for all our citizens, not to create a panic that'll run business off."

"Don't feed me that sound-bite horse hockey, Lyle. The *people* didn't put you in"—Pete's index finger slices in front of Lyle's nose—"the *wealthy casino owners* put you in."

"To tell the truth, I won fair and square and above board."

"Don't lay that platitudinous bullshit on *me* of all people. Those dildos vote the way the big money tells 'em. You know as well as I do the majority of our citizens can't think for themselves. They need duplicitous radio personalities to *tell* them how they feel."

Chief Hamper's mouth falls open. Nothing comes out.

"We don't have a government *of* the people here in Nevada,"

Pete continues. "We have an *oligarchy*. This state's run by a handful of the wealthy and all you had to do, to advance your exceptional political career, was kiss their collective gold-plated asses."

"By heck, Ferrari, I've heard enough of this unfair criticism. Frankly, I love this city at *least* as much as you do. I know you're bigger than me. You can out shout me, and you have a big lawyer vocabulary. But, dang it, Pete, I want what's best for this city, too." Chief Hamper shrugs. "Being a conservative, I just don't want to start a panic that could get important people hurt."

"Here you go again, bragging about being a conservative. If the human species had always chosen conservatives for their leaders, we'd still be sitting in front of the cave chipping out arrowheads."

Chief Hamper glares.

"Maybe you just can't see it yet, Chief, but we have a damned big problem breaking here." Pete waves his arm. "This may be happening all across the country. It's crucial we discover the cause, then move forcefully to eradicate it."

Chief Hamper's eyes furtively sweep the room. The relief dispatcher has disappeared. The three sitting dispatchers keep their backs to the mayor and chief's discussion. Pete mashes his lips together to discourage a face-splitting grin.

Wearing a worried face, Abel enters the room.

"Chief Hamper," Pete loudly announces. "Detective Sanchez and I have something we need to talk to you about. It's urgent."

Chief Hamper peers up at Pete as if staring at Benedict Arnold. He glances at Abel and his face softens. "Let's go upstairs to my office." He catches Abel by the arm. He hollers over his shoulder, "Are you coming, Brother Pete."

Reno
2:05 a.m., Saturday morning

Pete, Abel, and Chief Hamper march into the chief's thick-carpeted office.

"How're your sea serpents doing, Lyle?" asks Pete. He bends down and peers into the aquarium.

"They're moray eels, Pete, from the Muraenidae family. See them hiding in the rocks? The thunder scares the poor things."

Abel bends down beside Pete. "Eels live in salt water?"

"These moray eels, Abel," Chief Hamper says, "live their entire lives in salt water. There are, however, freshwater eels from America and Europe, that live in lakes and rivers, but spawn in the open ocean—the Sargasso Sea."

Pete and Abel look at each other.

"Hey, Lyle," says Pete. "Sorry about going off on you down there. I guess I'm a little upset."

Chief Hamper shrugs. "That's all right, Pete. I guess anyone would be a little edgy after being rousted out in the middle of the night."

Pete frowns. "Rousted out? My mother was just killed in a bathroom at the rehab center. Abel's wife was brutally attacked by *something* in her bathroom. My friend Bud Thorne was butchered alive. What if *your* wife had been attacked, Lyle? Wouldn't you be a little upset?"

"Sorry, Pete," says Hamper. "What've you got?"

Pete glances at Abel.

"I make call, Pete," says Abel. "Go ahead. Tell 'im."

"Here," says Chief Hamper, indicating with his hand. "You can use this phone, detective."

"Thanks, Chief." Abel hurries to the large desk and picks up the telephone receiver.

Pete summarizes for the chief: what had happened at Washoe Med Rehabilitation Hospital with his mother, Harold Washington and Pat Flynn's Washoe Med Emergency Room case, and the incident in Abel's bathroom, as well as covering Mayor Bud Thorne's demise. He explains how Abel, with his army knife, had acquired a foot-long piece of the creature and that the specimen now waited on the autopsy laboratory's dissection table. Doctor Draper has been called.

Reno
2:10 a.m., Saturday morning

A REMSA ambulance squats under the ten thousand twinkling lights roofing the concierge area. Its backdoors stand open toward the Silver Legacy Hotel's guest entrance.

Roberta Gomez and Henry Sims rush a gurney toward their waiting conveyance. Something, under the sheet, lies tied to the gurney.

Channel Four newswoman, Jessica Bang, thrusts a microphone at Sims. "What did you find in there, sir?" She hustles to stay abreast.

Sims shakes his head, as if Bang didn't want to know.

"Where did you make this pickup, sir?"

"We were called to the ground-floor main lavatory."

"Was it another—?"

Sims nods.

The ten thousand lights flicker, followed by the rumble of far-off thunder.

The gurney nears the ambulance's back end. Gomez prepares the front wheels for the push.

"Sir, if you could just tell me. How does the victim look?"

Gomez nods at Sims, who then initiates the shove. He tosses a glance toward the newswoman. "The man looked as if he'd been gutted out."

"Do you mean his front was cut open?"

"No, miss." Sims shoves the gurney all the way in. "I mean he looked as if he had been gutted out, *from the inside*. Here, excuse me while I get the door."

"Well, sir, where did he appear to have been gutted from?"

Gomez and Sims close the doors. "Look, miss. We got to get under way here."

"Well, is the patient still alive?"

Sims stops at the driver's door. "No, ma'am."

"Why are you in such a hurry, then?"

"We"—Sims indicates his partner by jerking his head—"have dozens more calls."

"You say"—Bang shoves the microphone under Sims's nose—"his front was not cut open. How did he appear?"

"There're no visible marks on him. His pants were down around his ankles." Sims sighs. "But there's *nothing* left inside him. Yet, his skin is unbroken. I'll leave it to your imagination to guess which opening his guts were pulled through."

Bang gulps, but the microphone remains in Sims's face.

"Girl, he looked like a collapsed wedding tent."

Reno
2:25 a.m., Saturday morning

Pete whispers, "Abel." They stand off to one side as Doctor Dan Draper, the county coroner, examines Abel's specimen. The morgue, autopsy room, and Doctor Draper's office occupies part of the basement at Reno police headquarters on Second Street. "What did you find out about Denise?"

At the far end of the room, an ambulance crewman delivers another loaded gurney.

Wearing his surgical gloves, Doctor Draper, a taller than

average man with a professional appearing mustache and graying hair at the temples, feels the specimen's sides. He's ten years older than Pete, and has a wife named Coretta. They enjoy two grown children and a granddaughter. In addition, they support a big black lab named Jesse in their exclusive Caughlin Ranch home in the foothills below Mount Rose.

"It funny thing, Pete," whispers Abel. "They find no injury"— Abel tips his head toward the gurneys—"not like those poor *paisanos*."

Pete nods. "How's Denise getting along though?"

"Hospital sedate her. Keep her till morning. She in bad shock." Abel peers up at his old pal. "Who the sonofabitch'n hell wouldn't be?"

Pete nods. "No shit, Sherlock."

"I think," says Abel, "it be long time 'fore my sugar baby feel like sitting her cute little Latina behind on commode again, no?"

Pete stifles a snicker.

"Yo, gentlemen." Doctor Draper speaks from behind his clear plastic facemask. "If y'all insist on whispering, I must insist you step outside. It's quite distracting, you know what I'm sayin'?"

Pete and Abel look at each other.

Doctor Draper takes a step back and pushes up his face-mask. He strips off his gloves. "First, gentlemen, please allow me to congratulate you on your exquisite dress this morning."

Abel glances at Pete's necktie-bulging pants pocket. Pete brushes imaginary lint from Abel's suitcoat.

Abel laughs.

"Thank you very much, Dan," Pete says. "My esteemed partner and I are eager to perform our part in upgrading the decor here in your, otherwise drab, room of doom." Pete raises an eyebrow at Abel.

"Feckin' A," says Abel.

Doctor Draper guffaws. Then he frowns. "I've never seen

anything like this, man. My best guess—it's some kinda fish."

Pete tentatively nods.

Doctor Draper points at the specimen. "It has a fishlike tail fin, but no scales. I can take a slide and begin to examine it under the microscope. I mean, it may have scales so small we can't see them. On the other hand, I think our city may be in the first throws of a major catastrophe; therefore, we simply don't have that kind of time."

Pete expels a breath. "Whew."

"At least, that's my instant opinion, Pete. I suggest we fetch an expert. Let's find out, posthaste, what the hell we're dealing with here, then lay plans to kill the sons of bitches."

"We can call Nevada Fish and Game," says Pete. "However, from what you've just told me, Dan, they probably can't be much help."

"Uh-huh," says Doctor Draper. "And I could get hold of the biology department here at UNR, but I suspect this creature is beyond their field of knowledge, as well. I think we need a first-rate *marine* biologist, man."

"Hey, Pete," says an excited Abel. "You tell me 'bout your vacation last month."

Pete squints at Abel.

"You 'member"—Abel brushes Pete on the arm—"at Newport? You 'member."

Pete's face brightens. "Yes. Yes, *indeed*, Abel." Pete wrestles Abel's shoulder around. He turns toward Doctor Draper. "Last month I was sucking up the seacoast atmosphere in Newport, Oregon. While there, I visited Oregon State University's marine laboratory. I have some stuff on it at home."

"I hear ya, man," says Doctor Draper. "I'm aware of that institution. Let's figure out how to get hold of the top scientist there. And, Pete, let's get in touch with 'em like—*yesterday*."

"The only one home is Nicole." Pete sighs. "I don't want to wake her. I'll just drive home and locate the materials. Should be no more than twenty-five minutes."

Doctor Draper winks at Abel. "That is, unless he gets tied up in his toilet."

Reno
3:05 a.m., Saturday morning

On the burglary squad's conference table, Pete, Abel, and Doctor Draper push through vacation souvenir pamphlets.

The door squeaks. Chief Hamper strolls in. "Well, how's it going?"

"Good morning, Lyle," says Pete, without looking up. "We're searching for the name of the director of the marine research facility up at Newport, Oregon."

Pete notes the silent response. *That Hamper's gotta be the boil, on the butt of life.*

"Why," asks Chief Hamper, "are you trying to find a fellow from Oregon, Pete?"

"Doctor Draper determined that the piece of evidence brought in from Detective Sanchez's house was some kind of a fish. We think a top-notch marine biologist could tell us exactly what kind it is and the best way to go about eradicating them."

Chief Hamper furrows his brow. "Frankly, Pete, Denise wasn't even *hurt*. What if your specimen isn't the creature causing our difficulties?"

Pete glares up at Chief Hamper.

"I mean," Chief Hamper says, "we don't want to create a panic over some harmless non-game fish."

"For fecksake, Chief," says Pete. "We've already been down this time-worn path." From the corner of his eye, Pete sees a grin pushing its way onto Abel's face.

"You bet, Mister Mayor," says Chief Hamper. "And I told you before, I was elected to *protect* the good citizens of this town. That protection includes not causing an unnecessary panic."

Pete rolls his eyes.

"If we needlessly scare our citizens, why, we could get ourselves a mass evacuation. Out-of-state gamblers would get wind of our problems and cancel reservations. Some of our biggest events, such as next month's Hot August Nights, could be canceled. Because of *your* imprudence, we'd have *you* to thank for our local economy racing toward a train wreck."

Pete gestures. "What if, Mister Chief of Police, we end up with a bunch of *dead citizens*? Do you think, possibly, such a disaster just might make the headlines across the whole feckin' nation? What do you suppose'll happen to your precious Hot August Nights then? Do you think that their ladies might be a little upset when slimy serpents slither up their legs into their poodle skirts?"

Pete risks a look at Doctor Draper. Pete looks away quickly when he spots Dan's shaking sides.

"Dang it, Pete," says Chief Hamper. "You act as if you don't even care whether this city grows and prospers."

"That's just the point, Chief Hamper. I *do* care."

"Well," says Chief Hamper, "I guess what we've got here is just a good old honest difference of opinion."

Pete glances at the ceiling. "Yes. Perhaps you're right, Lyle." Pete extends his hand.

Lyle accepts.

"I still think," says Pete, "that we should bring an expert in here, straight away."

Lyle withdraws his hand.

"What I mean is, don't you think it would look good if you and I tried *everything possible* to get to the bottom of this . . . *incident?*" Pete cocks his head. *Not only that, you little pip-squeak, but I'm the goddamned mayor and I'm calling in the experts no matter what you say.*

Chief Hamper drops his gaze. "Maybe so."

Pete drops his hand on the chief's shoulder.

Chief Hamper glances at the table. "Have you found any-thing?"

"Oh, yes. We discovered that the head of the Newport lab is a real marine expert, not just an administrator."

Chief Hamper nods.

"However, the literature doesn't say how to contact him at home."

Doctor Draper grins. "I know how to find 'im."

Pete raises an eyebrow.

"Uh-huh," says Doctor Draper. "I just happen to be an astonishingly high-quality computer wizard."

Pete grins and nods. *Do it.*

Reno
3:15 a.m., Saturday morning

Doctor Draper sits at the computer in his basement office. Pete yawns. Abel sips potent instant coffee from a paper cup that Doctor Draper had prepared.

On the computer screen, Pete sees divisions of the Oregon State University, available classes, research centers, and labo-ratories that appear, roll down and disappear. Doctor Draper then scrolls through the registry displaying Oregon State University's professors. Most appeared in Corvallis, but some instructors listed Newport.

"Ah hah," says Pete.

"Sure enough," mutters Doctor Draper. He leans back and waves his hand, inviting Pete and Abel to gaze upon the screen.

"Yes," says Pete, giving a victory-fist salute.

The cursor sits beside a *T Sherman Oaks, PhD* in Marine Biology, *Director of the Mark O Hatfield Marine Science Center in Newport, Oregon.*

Doctor Draper waves the printout from his computer. Pete shrugs. "I don't know if this'll prove profitable."

"Be cool now, Mister Mayor," says Doctor Draper. "Would y'all please try to call that Doctor Oakes posthaste?"

"You want me to . . . what?"

Doctor Draper points to his telephone.

"Doctor Draper," says Pete, "is this not scientific work? Shouldn't you—doctor to doctor—be the man to request his services?"

Doctor Draper rises. "There ya go, man." He takes a sip of coffee and grimaces. "In this city, you decidedly outrank me. Not only that, a request from the mayor of Reno has much more weight than an appeal from the county coroner whose office resides in the basement next to the morgue. Don't y'all agree, Pete?"

Pete swipes the paper from Doctor Draper's hand. "Would you be so kind as to allow me to use your official coroner's telephone, or will you require me to use the pay phone in the hall?"

Abel snickers.

Doctor Draper waves his hand at his chair.

Pete drops into the well-worn leather seat. He lays the printout on top of the ink blotter and pulls the telephone closer. "Does this relic have a speakerphone, Dan?"

Doctor Draper leans over and pushes a button.

"Shall I bill this call to my office?" Pete asks.

Doctor Draper snorts.

Pete punches in the numbers. The telephone rings.

"Er . . . aaarrrrggg." From the telephone's tiny speaker rasps a sound resembling a dried-up wheel bearing on its last hoo-raw.

Pete scowls. "Doctor Oakes?"

"Good Gawd," mumbles a far-off voice. "Is the marine center on fire? It better be if someone's calling me in the scum-sucking middle of the night."

"Doctor Oakes?" asks Pete.

A dry swallowing sound follows. "Yes."

Pete glances up at his cohorts, nodding. "Doctor Oakes, I'm sorry to call you at this hour but we're experiencing an urgent situation here in Reno."

The little speaker remains silent.

Pete looks at Doctor Draper and catches him smiling. "I'm Pete Ferrari, mayor of Reno." *This dip shit's gone back to sleep.*

"Try again, boss," says Abel.

"Doctor Oakes, if you can hear me . . . we've had several people seriously injured here in Reno this morning"—he peeks up at Abel and shrugs—"by what we think is some kind of a *fish.*"

A honeyed alto voice flows from the speaker, followed by the deeper voice grumbling like a grizzly bear grouching over a case of thorn-berry hemorrhoids.

"Forgive me, Doctor Oakes. I'm sorry to have awakened your, ah, wife."

"That's not my wife."

Doctor Draper's sides quake.

Pete bites his bottom lip. "Doctor Oakes, I'm so sorry to call you at this ungodly hour, but can you possibly see your way clear to advise us through our life-and-death emergency?"

"Sure, Mister Mayor. I've enjoyed visiting 'The Biggest Little City' on several occasions. I'd love to show my graduate assistant your lovely city, Lake Tahoe, and its environs."

Pete leans back, smiles, and rolls his palms up. "Do you mean to say, sir, that you're willing to motor down to our fair city?"

"Yes. Yes, of course." A dry licking sound issues from the speaker. "KB. What time is it?"

The alto voice says something indecipherable. Pete frowns at the telephone. From the speaker escapes the sound of a voice mumbling, as if working a math problem.

"Uh hum, Mister Mayor. Have your representative at the

Tahoe City pier by 5:45 a.m., to chauffeur my graduate assistant and me."

And with that, Doctor T Sherman Oakes terminates the call.

Newport
3:50 a.m., Saturday morning

The seaplane's dashboard vibrates, making the needles bounce in their gauges. A tremendous white cloud, like someone had started five hundred rotary lawnmowers, blows out the starboard engine's rear.

KB talks into the mike. "There is much smoke."

"Uh hum, what color is it, my Danish dumpling?"

Even though the sun hadn't risen in the east, the full moon in the west and the harbor lights allowed KB to see. "White."

"It's just that dry chemical blowing off from our emergency engine shutdown last night, KB. It's nothing to concern yourself over. I put a brand-new cotter pin in the linkage; we won't have any more engine trouble. Trust me."

KB gives Sherm an adoring smile. *Jumping Jiminy. I hope he fixes it better than he did last time.* "I am sorry, Sherm. Maybe we should have cleaned the bilge last night."

"Aye, me pretty one. Don't worry about it. I dug the baby crab out from under the rudder pedal."

"What about the others?"

"The alive and dead marine creatures are floating in the bilge."

"Will it cause us trouble?"

"Aye, me Danish flower. If it's hot in Reno, this seaplane's interior could blossom into something quite odoriferous—not to mention, the saltwater causing mischief with the electronics."

KB presses her lips together. *Please, look after us dogs, professors, and silly fools.*

KB keeps her finger on the airplane's checklist. Through the trembling windshield she takes in a glorious sight. Straight ahead, the majestic Yaquina Bay Bridge arches over the harbor's entrance. The full moon appears ready to settle below the Pacific horizon.

Testing the magnetos and carburetor heat, Sherm revs up first one engine and then the other.

KB's earphones crackle. "What's next, me little chickadee?"

"Gas."

Sherm touches his finger on the left-hand fuel gauge and then the right.

"Remember," says KB, "when we flew up to Seattle for that meeting at the University of Washington?"

Sherm laughs.

"Altimeter," calls KB. She moves her finger down the checklist.

Sherm leans forward and dials in 30.01, the current barometric pressure.

"Remember," continues KB, "when we walked into the conference room, you wearing your flip-flops, and me—"

"And you," hollers Sherm, "with your boobs preceding us?"

They both guffaw.

"Radio," says KB.

Sherm reaches forward and sets the dials for the Newport area's transmitting and receiving frequencies. "Do you recall the first words from the university president's mouth, when we sauntered into that august assemblage?"

KB chuckles. "Yes."

As if rehearsed, Sherm and KB sing out together, *"Oh, my God."*

Sherm laughs uproariously. He wipes a tear from his eye.

"They were dressed so pompously," KB says, "in their tufted puffin three-piece suits, and here you walk in wearing your Hawaiian shirt."

"And you," says Sherm, "with those bare legs sticking out of your cutoffs."

KB gives Sherm the thumbs-up; then she secures the checklist.

"Arrr," says Sherm. "Let's see if we can get this bucket of rivets airborne."

KB smiles. "I am ready."

"All right, KB. *Heads up.*"

The seaplane floats in the channel's middle, directly in front of the Coast Guard station. KB and Sherm peer high and low looking for any boats and aircraft.

"I see no boats," hollers KB.

"I see no aircraft," answers Sherm.

KB gives Sherm another thumbs-up.

Sherm drops his right hand on the two throttle levers.

"Gimme a little mixture, KB."

Sherm shoves the throttles ahead. The engines hesitate, then roar. "*Unpeel those eyes.*"

KB hollers into the microphone. "Aye, aye, skipper."

Sherm shoves the throttles all the way forward.

Thunder roars from the exhaust pipes. The propeller blades bite off slabs of air. Sheets of water spray back. The seaplane begins to move, slowly at first. Straight ahead the Yaquina Bay Bridge spans their course.

"Full flaps, KB."

KB grasps the flap lever and wrenches up on it.

The airplane accelerates—faster and faster.

Sherm's feet pump the pedals. "Get on the radio. Announce that we're on our way."

KB reaches for the mike.

The galloping seaplane's bow begins to intercept the waves.

The Yaquina Bay Bridge looms overhead.

The seaplane now skips along on top of the waves.

In the moonlight, KB sees foaming rollers beyond the Yaquina River's bar.

On the step, the seaplane appears to dance. Sherm, ever so lightly, eases back on the steering wheel. The plane's hull breaks free and *The Gander* swoops up into the sky, right out from under the Yaquina Bay Bridge.

"Flaps, KB."

Standing in the ground-floor corner office of the Thirteenth Coast Guard District Headquarters, Rear Admiral Joe Fontana shakes his head.

The seaplane aims straight at the orange-colored setting moon. The last of the bay water blows off the hull. The powerful seaplane accelerates faster and faster.

"Mixture," calls out Sherm. "Floats."

KB flips the levers, and the floats begin their ascent to again become wingtips.

On the Yaquina Bay Bridge's seaward side, the chubby little seaplane suddenly pulls up and to the right. Its twin Pratt & Whitney radial engines report off the seaside cliffs.

"Carb heat, KB." The seaplane buffets as it encounters wind rising off the coastal bluffs.

KB shoves the two carburetor heat levers, then glances out her side at the harbor and its early-morning lights. She gazes down on the low-lying evergreen cypress growing in patches on the sandstone headland. On top sits the historical white-and-red-colored *Yaquina Bay lighthouse.*

As the seaplane comes around, KB sees the first gray-colored lightening in the east. Sherm grins at her. She smiles back. *This really is a quite satisfactory life I have.* She senses a swelling in her heart.

She peeks down at her T-shirt. *On the other hand, I wish I'd had time to take a shower and put on clean clothes.*

Reno
4:10 a.m., Saturday morning

In his top-floor office Chief Hamper explains that July, August, and September—with their Hot August Nights, Great Reno

Balloon Races, and The Championship Reno Air Races—are top tourist months.

Abel stands near the door, maintaining a noncommittal look.

Pete's white shirt grows more wrinkled. He yawns. He sips his coffee. He waits for his turn to speak.

Doctor Draper saunters into the room and makes for the coffee pot. "I think that summer thunderstorm has passed." He bends down and peers into the darkened moray eel aquarium. "Are they asleep for the night?"

Chief Hamper halts in mid-sentence.

Pete works to stifle a yawn but doesn't succeed. *Dawn is always the worst.* "It often happens that way, Dan. The thunderstorms build up in the evening, but by morning we again have blue sky."

Pete turns toward Chief Hamper. "Listen, Lyle. I respect your viewpoint on Reno's need to keep tourism up. Nevertheless, on my authority I requested a so-called marine expert. Heck, I don't know if he's going to help us or if he's simply destined to become an unholy embarrassment."

Chief Hamper gives a nod.

"If I may, Chief," says Doctor Draper. "I determined that the creature's some kind of a fish. I also determined that there's probably no expert in the area who can identify it. I suggested to Pete that we get hold of a marine expert as soon as possible; you know what I'm sayin'?"

"Yes," says Chief Hamper.

"Thanks, Dan," Pete says, "nonetheless, if there's any fall-out, I'll take the heat."

Chief Hamper smiles and glances out his window.

Pete follows his line of vision. Red dawn appears in the east. Red and blue strobe lights flash up and down the tree-lined streets. An orange light flashes in the middle of Second Street. Sounds of several sirens intrude. "Omigod," he whispers. *What's happening to my beloved city?*

"Look, Lyle. It may prove that I've made a colossal blunder. Nonetheless, Doctor Oakes said he would help. He asked me to have someone standing by the Tahoe City pier at five forty-five a.m."

Abel manages to suppress a grin.

Chief Hamper scratches his nose. "Abel, why don't you leave here within the next twenty minutes, so as to be positioned at the Lake Tahoe pier by"—he glances at his watch—"five forty-five."

Abel turns his palms up. "Chief, I glad to do whatever you tell me. But, my daughter, Dora, getting married in jus' six hours."

Chief Hamper takes another sip of lemon water. "Frankly, you'll be back in plenty of time, detective."

"Okay. But what I look for?"

Pete shrugs. "He was in bed when I talked to him, Abel. He simply told me to have someone at the Lake Tahoe pier by five forty-five, and *then he hung up*."

Abel gives up a huge yawn. "What if I wait on pier all morning for lab geeks and they no show?"

Doctor Draper lifts his cup to his smiling lips.

"What I look for?" asks Abel. "White lab coats?"

Pete shakes his head and stifles a big grin.

Abel stammers, "I happy drive to Tahoe for lab geeks. But do I look for ten-speed bicycle, smoking Volvo, or duct-tape skateboard?"

Pete snickers. "All I can tell you, Abel, is the marine biologist is a man and his name is Doctor T Sherman Oakes. I suggest you look for a nerd wearing black horn-rimmed glasses with a piece of white adhesive tape wrapped around the bridge. Look for one, possibly two, pocket protectors."

Abel shakes his head.

"In all seriousness, Abel. I can't even tell you if his lab assistant's a man or a woman."

Chapter Three

Nicole's Siamese Cat, Fiddle, Checking Out the Toilet

Tahoe City
5:45 a.m., Saturday morning

Tahoe City.

The lake lies smooth as a glass tabletop.

Abel yawns.

The morning sky backlights the far away ponderosa pines.

Abel strolls out to the pier's end. He sips tepid coffee from his paper cup. He shivers. He pulls on the lapels of his double-breasted suit. Abel worries about Denise undergoing examination at Washoe Med. He pulls his lapels tighter. He adjusts his shoulder holster.

Abel listens to the chirping of a thousand awakening birds. He tries to peer into the lake's legendary clarity, but the sun hasn't yet peeked over the ridge.

He squints to the south, searching for the town of South Lake Tahoe. The south shore lies twenty-two miles away. Due to the earth's curvature, he only sees the top floors of the Stateline casinos.

"Thunderclouds gone," he whispers. Abel glances at the lightening sky. "¡Caramba! Be hot for Dora's wedding." He checks his watch. "Jus' five hours." Must get tuxedo on. Will hospital let Denise go home? "Hope lab geeks get here *pronto*."

Abel exhales. He sees his breath. "Why I not bring overcoat?" He shoves his hands deep in his pants pockets.

A mile and a half away, at the public boat launch, an outboard motor wheezes into life. Abel looks to the left and spots a man standing in his skiff, bent over his outboard motor. A small white cloud dissipates toward the United States Coast Guard Station next door to the public launch.

Tahoe City's streetlights begin to blink off. Several automobiles brandish their headlights as they navigate Highway Twenty-Eight, the sole road encircling the lake.

Abel tips his head back to suck in an invigorating breath of fresh Lake Tahoe air.

Twin, bellering, radial-aircraft engines shatter the stillness. Exploding at treetop level, nine hundred belching horsepower roars over the Tahoe City water master's gate.

Abel whirls to face the ambush. He observes a charging, high-winged, white-and-purple seaplane. His eardrums rattle from the two Pratt & Whitney engines bawling like nine hundred castrated steers.

As if lining up the crosshairs, the seaplane locks on Abel. In three heart-pounding seconds the one-hundred-ninety-mile-per-hour aircraft closes. Abel crouches. He makes out the pilot and copilot's faces.

"¡*Hijo de puta!*"

Abel dives. His right knee skids on the weathered wood. A long thin splinter jabs deep into his right thigh.

Overhead, the airplane hull rushes past. Abel flattens out as if he was a puddle of olive oil.

Double cyclonic thunders shake the dock. Eighteen exhaust

blasts ripple the lake's surface. Abel sniffs hot engine oil. He risks raising his head and sees oil streaks running under the nacelles.

The seaplane then rockets into the sky, popping into the sunlight. Its dual three-bladed propellers throw off sword-flashes of silver.

The aircraft gains altitude, flying east toward Incline Village. The G-21 skirts the shore as if the pilot might be showing the copilot Lake Tahoe's magnificent beachside residences.

Glaring at the shrinking apparition, Abel pushes himself to his feet. His palms wear red marks from the dock's snaggle-toothed surface.

At one hundred ninety miles per hour the airplane reaches the far shore in three minutes flat.

Abel glances at his suit pants. "*Alocado.*"

He jerks the sliver from his thigh. The rip in his pants runs from his knee to his underpants. The splinter hole bleeds. Abel presses his white handkerchief onto the wound.

Abel locates the seaplane far to the east, banking in a right turn directly over Marlette Lake, the source of Virginia City's water supply.

White smoke blows out of the starboard engine's back. "*¿Qué es eso?*" Abel sees the smoke dissipate. A few moments later black smoke belches, followed by two blasts of fire.

"Holy Mother of God. Those numb nuts in world of *caca*."

The seaplane pulls up, then dives to the right, rolling on its side.

"Pilot awful darn good—or awful damned bad."

Abel watches the seaplane plunge on its side toward the lake. Then it twists upside down.

"*Sonofabitch.*"

At the last moment, hurtling to the granite boulder strewn shore, the seaplane snaps back to level.

"*¡Caramba!* It gotta be doin five hundred miles an hour." Abel crabs a couple of steps closer to shore.

"*¡Maldito sea!* It come back. They *bestia*."

Zooming across in front of Lakeshore Drive's mansions, the seaplane re-enters the shadow. Abel hears the engine revolutions reduce. He sees the plane hike up its rear end as if the flaps had just been applied.

A white cloud suddenly trails from the starboard engine.

"*¡Por Dios!*"

The seaplane draws nearer and nearer to its skimming reflection on the surface of the six-thousand-foot elevation lake.

"They not know plane on fire."

Abel presses the handkerchief to his thigh. "You *bruja*." He backs away from the pier's end.

Directly in front of Abel, the boat-like Grumman hull touches the lake's surface. White powder puffs from the starboard engine. The aircraft slows and settles into the water. After a momentary roar, it turns toward Abel. White dust coats the starboard nacelle. The starboard engine coughs then dies. The starboard wing tip descends until it's floating in the water.

To Abel, the triple-bladed fan looks like a colossal margarita blender.

He back steps to the dock's far edge.

The port wing tip descends until it's in the water. The port engine sputters, then dies.

In the abrupt silence, Abel hears the sloshing sound of the approaching hull.

The Gander gently nudges the pier.

Abel glances at his watch. It shows six-thirty a.m., four-and-a-half hours until the wedding.

The small door at the airplane's left rear opens.

"*What that stink?*" Abel growls.

From within the seaplane's interior, barking erupts. A little white-and-brown colored blur, sporting a red collar, drops from the airplane's door. Toenails click on the wooden surface. Snapping and snarling, the terrier lunges straight for Abel.

Abel ducks down on his good knee. He thrusts his hands out.

Little Heidi sniffs. Abel gives her a pat on the head, and she clickety-clacks toward shore.

A woman's bare leg dangles over the airplane's doorsill. A flip-flop clad foot feels for the dock.

"Madre mía." That leg make two of my Denise.

A feminine hand wearing a jam-packed charm bracelet grasps the handhold above the door. In the other hand appears a paper sack with its top twisted shut.

"Whew." Abel frowns. He hears the cooling engines producing that tink-tink-tink sound. He wrinkles his nose.

From the seaplane's door issues a most sexy-looking woman. Abel unconsciously licks his lips, as if feasting on birthday cake.

KB reaches inside and picks up her overnight bag. Then she ducks her head, steps around the engine, and emerges from under the wing. She straightens.

Abel looks up.

"Hello," says KB.

Abel smiles, admiring KB's poise. She behaves as if a gorgeous woman, flying in an antique seaplane, puts on an air show and ties up to the Tahoe City pier every Saturday morning.

"Hello," says Abel, bowing his head. "Welcome."

"Your leg is hurt."

"It nothing."

"Here"—KB points at the handkerchief—"let me tie that for you." She kneels down and makes a bandanna. Then she knots it on top of the wound.

"Thank you. You kind."

KB smiles. "You are welcome." Then she gazes at the legendary lake.

"Perdón, miss," says Abel.

"Yes?"

"You lab geeks—oops, *perdón*"—Abel coughs—"scientists from Newport?"

KB giggles. "Yes."

Further movement at the airplane's door summons Abel's attention. He chuckles. He ducks his head for a better look.

A male hand grabs the handhold. An apparition emerges onto the dock that commonly only graces the gringo-covered beach at Ensenada, Mexico.

"Arrrbeedarrr," the apparition snarls.

Abel's eyebrows arch.

Sherm wears an outrageously loud yellow Hawaiian shirt, boasting globs of bright red blossoms. He clasps a backpack in his left hand and a brimmed white straw hat in the other.

Abel discreetly shakes his head. These *definitely* the lab geeks.

Sherm ducks under the wing. Then places the straw hat on his head. He tips his head back and closes his eyes. "God, I love this place."

"Welcome to Lake Tahoe," says Abel unobtrusively.

Sherm grins and sticks out his hand. "How do you do, sir? I'm Doctor T Sherman Oakes, head of the marine laboratory at Newport. Are you the gentleman assigned to pick us up?"

"Yeah," says Abel, grasping Sherm's hand. "I Detective Abel Sanchez, Reno PD."

"It's a pleasure to meet you, sir," says Sherm.

Abel clicks his heels and gives a little bow. "*El gusto es mio.*"

"*Muy bien,*" answers Sherm. "Did you recently hurt your leg there, Detective?"

"De nada."

Sherm gives Abel a questioning look. "I could look at that for you."

"It nothing."

"Very well, Detective Sanchez. May I present Miss Kristian Bjørnsen."

Abel nods.

"She's my laboratory assistant and a graduate student attending Oregon State University. She's working on her PhD in marine science."

KB thrusts her hand toward Abel.

Abel grips her hand, clicks his heels together, and elegantly bows. "Miss Bjørnsen, I at your service."

KB smiles graciously and then gives Abel's hand a firm squeeze. "You may call me Kristian, or KB, if you prefer."

Sherm saunters to the airplane's bow. He begins to tie the seaplane to the dock.

KB stares at the seaplane and emits a cleansing puff of air from her nose. "You may call that sedately dressed fellow," she says, pointing her hand toward Sherm, "Doctor T." She leans closer to Abel. "His good friends call him, simply, *Sherm*."

Clicking toenails approach from the shore. Abel turns to see Heidi approaching on the run. "She look like she smiling."

KB nods. "Yes, she is." KB kneels down. "Little Heidi, are you ready for our ride to Reno?"

Heidi hurtles into her mistress's arms. KB stands, holding her wriggly companion.

Abel picks up KB's overnight bag and the twisted paper sack. "You call me, Abel."

"Hello, Abel. Here, I will take the sack."

From the seaplane's after end, Sherm calls out, "Arrr, before we depart for Reno, I need to make a fast repair on that carburetor linkage."

Abel gulps. He senses the strongest urge to glance at his wristwatch—but that would be impolite. "You want I help you repair airplane *tomorrow*, after you meet mayor and see specimen?"

"Yer a fine man, that you are, me hearty, but you need not concern yourself. It'll only take me a fraction of a second. Besides that, these overpaid airplane mechanics don't know diddlysquat about these old carburetion systems."

Abel's mustache ripples.

KB leans close to Abel. "It will take him more than one second, that is for sure."

"I bring you up tomorrow?" Abel spreads his hands toward Sherm. "Bring plenty tools."

"Uh hum, you're a prince, that you are, Detective Sanchez, er, Abel. Nonetheless, I'll fix this minuscule problem, post-haste, with me trusty needle-nosed pliers. Then we'll hurry down to Reno and tackle your unfortunate fishy problem. How much of a drive is it, anyway?"

"One hour." Now Abel can look at his wristwatch. "Unless there car troubles, or too much traffic. Happen all the time." *Wedding starts in four hours.*

"I've been a bit confuzzled over that erratic performance on the starboard engine, but I just flashed on what the problem's been. Therefore, prior to my displaying some cognitive dysplasia, and consequently observing my brainstorm evaporate, I'll just fetch my toolbox and repair the recalcitrant carburetor."

Abel's jaw drops. He sets KB's overnight bag back down on the wharf.

KB mashes her lips together and gives Abel a shrug.

Sherm sets his backpack down and places his straw hat on top. He crawls back into the seaplane. "Hey KB, what time is it?"

Reno & Sparks
7:00 a.m., Saturday morning

"This is John Tyson, KOLO Channel Eight News," announces the resonant voice into the microphone. "I'm standing in front of the Twin City Surplus store on East Fourth Street." His silver mustache accents his suntanned face.

Above the announcer's right shoulder, the July sun is beginning to peek over the store's roof. "Behind me you see the long line of early-morning shoppers purchasing portable toilets." His western shirt and solid-silver belt buckle proclaim to the television audience—this is cowboy country.

"Here comes a lucky shopper now." Behind Tyson a man holds a determined grip on his portable toilet. He raises the rear gate on his sport utility vehicle.

Tyson ambles over to the lucky shopper. "Say there, buckaroo. What's *your* name?"

Lucky shopper glances up and smiles. "Snoopy Fumento."

"Whataya have there, Mister, ah, Snoopy?"

"Well, John. I got the last of the Thetford Porta Pottis." He nods toward his beer-keg-sized purchase.

"What're you doing out shopping so early, pardner?"

"Well, John, usually these surplus stores don't open at five in the morning." Tyson pushes the mike closer to Snoopy's mouth. "But because of *the pending disaster*, the stores selling portable toilets opened themselves up as soon as we could get ahold of somebody."

"So, you would classify Reno's toilet problem as a potential *disaster*?"

"Well, what would you call it, John?" Snoopy squints at Tyson. "I mean, you can't dare to get your precious buns even *close* to your commode." Snoopy grits his teeth. "Something will jump up and eat your *bleep-bleep* guts out."

Tyson nods his head in encouragement.

"Possibly," continues Snoopy, "take your *bleepers* and *bleeper* for dessert."

Tyson chuckles. "I'll let you get that purchase on home there, buckaroo. Thank you."

Tyson faces the camera. "Well, there you have it folks, there's at least one citizen who thinks Reno is headed for *a disaster*. From the length of the shopper's line, I would, at the minimum, say we've got the makings for *a citywide panic*."

In the background a serious-faced shopper packing a portable purchase, shuffles toward the news crew.

"And you, sir," calls out Tyson. "What's your name and what've you purchased this morning?"

"Name's Tiny Colón. They were out of the Thetford Porta Potti"—Mister Colón glances suspiciously from side to side—"so I bought me the SeaLand SaniPottie. Should be just as good, though."

"Why, Mister Colón, are you down here at Twin City shopping so early?"

"Well, young fella, the daughter called the wife at five thirty this mornin'. Said there was hysteria breaking out all 'round the Truckee Meadows. People bein' attacked from outta their very own *toilets*."

Tyson urges Colón with his beckoning microphone.

"I thought my womenfolk were crazy, 'til we flipped on the TV and saw the breakin' news. My God! People waitin' in line on gurneys, waitin' to get into the emergency room. Ambulances bringin' in more."

Tyson nods.

"The wife tells me"—Colón shakes his head emphatically—"don't even think for a second that I'm goin' *near* that bathroom. You go get us *a campin' toilet*."

Tyson brings the mike closer.

"The daughter and son-in-law already have a campin' toilet. I got down here 'bout an hour ago." Colón jerks his head toward the lengthening line. "Those poor citizens are gonna be outta luck—you know—SOL. They may as well go home and dig a friggen hole. Hell! For all I know even a *latrine* ain't safe. The bastards might live in the gol-darned *mud*."

Tyson turns to face the camera lens. "I don't see any signs of panic yet," Tyson says. "Of course, the toilet stocks are not yet sold out."

Behind Tyson, a late-morning shopper shuffles by. He grasps a flat furnace-filter-shaped box.

"And you, sir. What's your name?"

Late-morning shopper glances up. "Shorty Biddle."

"What've you purchased this morning, Mister Biddle?"

"Ah hum. A toilet seat that you hang a see-through clear plastic bag underneath." Biddle sighs, as if already anticipating Missus Biddle's coming diatribe. "It's all they had left."

Reno
7:40 a.m., Saturday morning

The morning sun beams into Chief Hamper's office. He sprinkles fish food in the aquarium. The moray eels pick up their food and retreat. Then they turn around and peek out from their rock crevices.

On the side shelf the coffee pot gurgles. A homey aroma pervades the room.

Chief Hamper sets the food package down. "To tell the truth, Pete, with the help of the good Lord we're going to handle this little incident and *not* mess up the geese that lays the golden eggs."

Pete and Chief Hamper had both been up all night. The chief's coat hangs open. Pete wears his suit coat. His necktie still bulges in his pocket.

Pete yawns. "I sincerely hope we do, Lyle."

Reno city councilwoman, Mandy Cockburn, pushes her way between the chief and the mayor. She is blocky built, wears white rhinestone glasses and sports pure black tightly curled hair. "If you blubber all over the airwaves that we've got a little plumbing problem in our sewer department, Pete, you're going to *harm* this city."

"You mean, Mandy," says Pete, "if the word gets out to *the whales.*"

"The whales?"

"The fat cats."

Councilwoman Cockburn frowns. "Listen, Pete, you're coming up for election soon. You may be in for a rude awakening when you discover how *few* friends you really have."

Pete produces a wicked grin. "Are you planning to run against me, Mandy?"

Councilwoman Cockburn looks at Chief Hamper. The chief is studying his desktop ink blotter.

"I care about what's best for the long run health of our city," Pete says. "In addition, I care *most* about the welfare of Reno's common citizens—of which I'm proud to be one."

Councilwoman Cockburn jams her fists on her hips. "Oh, *puleeeze*, spare me the violins, Mozart. Pull your head outta your fantasyland. Wake up and smell Reno's growing economy. If you had half—"

Pete sits down on the corner of Chief Hamper's desk, which lowers his head to the same height as the councilwoman's.

"Mandy. Let's get real. You and Lyle are bought and paid for by the casino interests, the outdoor sign companies, the—"

"Now, hold on, *Brother* Pete." Chief Hamper is fastening a new button on his bespangled coat.

Councilwoman Cockburn pushes Chief Hamper aside. "I know all about you and the chief harp player being fraternal brothers, but Lyle just isn't getting through to you.

"Now, you listen here"—she jabs her finger at Pete, as if spoiling for a sword fight—"come next election you're gonna get *steamrollered*. The city fathers are backing *me* with the biggest financial war chest in Reno's history. On the other hand, your hope chest is destined to trickle in from the misfits, intellectual snobs, gays, and Neil Road Mexicans."

Pete slowly stands. "Now, Mandy, that's a curious statement for *you* to make. Everyone knows that you're of Mexican—"

Almost stomping her foot, Councilwoman Cockburn fumes. "I'm *not* Mexican. My mother was . . . *Spanish*, and my father was a—"

"*Wino and a whore hound.*"

The chief's secretary, Sergeant Sandra Goodnight, flutters in behind Belle Starr, Chief Hamper's new wife. "I'm so sorry,

Chief Hamper. I tried to call you on the intercom, but—"

"Carry on, Sergeant." Chief Hamper dismisses her with a wave. "Good morning, petkins. You're up awfully early."

Belle Starr appears to be a good ten years older than her fifty-year-old husband, but she still boasts a crash-dive neckline on her red-and-black Virginia City "entertainer's" dress. She perches a black hat atop her Marilyn Monroe blond hair and has selected matching black high-heeled shoes. She wears long black eyelashes and resplendent red lipstick. "He was a wino and a whore hound. I served him plenty when I was madam out at Mustang Ranch."

Belle Starr threatens Lyle's nose with her parasol. "I'm up early? How could I sleep after listening to your early-morning strumming on that celestially stringed harp?"

"But, honey bun, I brought you juice and fruit. I thought—"

"Where's my cigarettes? Did ya throw 'em away again?"

"By golly, my precious lamb, our bodies are temples—"

"Screw it. You knew *all* about my fabulous temple when you, so-called, rescued me from the ranch. Now, where the hell're my cigarettes?"

"Oh, petkins, I wish you wouldn't talk that way."

Councilwoman Cockburn slips over to the window.

Belle Starr looks down on Chief Hamper. "You knew all about my mouth, before we started . . ."

Chief Hamper pats the air in front of him. "You bet, honey bun, you mean, before I rescued you from the ranch. Here. Here's your cigarettes. I saved them for you, for when you really needed them."

"I'm still not sure I needed saving. That was your idea. I think you just wanted a little free . . ."

Pete jiggles, bundling his urge to laugh.

Councilwoman Cockburn glares out the window.

Belle Starr lights her cigarette and takes a long drag. A great cloud of smoke billows out. "Now, where'd you ditch my ashtray?"

"By golly, petkins, I just wanted what was best for you. That other, that you mentioned, is just God's gift that naturally happens between two people who really love each other. Here's your ashtray."

Belle Starr sets the ashtray on the desk's corner next to Pete. "Or between two people where one has the goods and the other has the goodie."

Pete stands and removes a six-inch-long cigar from his suitcoat inside pocket. Belle Starr hands him her lighter. "Thanks, Belle." Pete lights up.

The intercom on Chief Hamper's desk crackles. "Chief Hamper, Doctor Draper's on his way into your office. I couldn't stop him."

Pete glances at the door. From the thunderstruck look on Doctor Draper's face, it appears that he heard Belle Starr and Chief Hamper's entire conversation. Pete peeks out the door at Sergeant Goodnight's station.

Sergeant Goodnight files her fingernails. She slowly turns her head toward Pete and bestows upon him a coy smile.

Pete guffaws.

In the sudden silence following, Chief Hamper turns toward Pete. "We, ah, we should've heard from Abel by now."

Pete attempts to rub the smile off his face. "Didn't he take his cell phone?"

Reno
8:20 a.m., Saturday morning

Pete had just driven his dark gray Jaguar XJS sedan from the Reno police station to his South Center Street, city hall office.

He steps to his bookshelf, opens a wooden cigar box, and pulls out a Panatella. He lights up as he dawdles back to his desk. He drops into his black leather chair. Leaning back, he places his shoes on the inkpad and folds his hands behind his head. *God, what a dick-suckin' sycophant that Lyle is.* A heavy cloud begins to grow above his head.

"*Mister Mayor.*" Juanita calls from her desk. "Mister Mayor, *open your window and close that door.*"

"Holy shit," Pete mumbles. Then he hollers, "You got it. Sorry, Juanita." Pete swivels and opens the window behind his desk. Smoking like a little steam locomotive, he walks toward his carved wooden outer doors. He leans through, his cigar clinched between his teeth. "Hey, Juanita. You can just call me, Puffing Pete."

Juanita grants him a glare. "Okay, Mister Puffing Pete. You'd better get started on your telephone calls. Everybody, including the governor, wants an update. And here's a couple of important messages." Juanita hands Pete two slips of paper.

Pete nods.

"And, sir, are you *really* sure that you want me to call you . . . *Puffing Pete?*"

Pete's eyelids blink.

"That particular nickname," coos Juanita, "can easily be, shall we say, misconstrued."

Pete hesitates. "Juanita, I accede to your superior grasp of nickname nuances."

Juanita smiles and nods.

"And thanks a million for coming in on your Saturday."

"You're very welcome, Mister Mayor. It looks like Reno's having a bit of a problem and I'll help out any way I can."

"Thanks, kid."

"Oh, and boss." Juanita points at Pete's face. "You're developing a bit of a five o'clock shadow."

Pete touches his chin. "Yes. I feel what you mean. I'll get to it pretty quick. Thanks." Pete pulls the double doors shut and he walks to his desk. He drops into his chair and pushes the speed dial button. It rings and rings. "Dammit."

Pete ends the call and rings the outer office. "Juanita, has Nicole called this morning?"

"I'm sorry, sir."

"When she calls, please push it through immediately, no matter who I'm talking to."

"You got it, boss. And don't forget Dora's wedding at eleven."

"Are you going?"

"For the love of Pete, Pete, of course I'm going."

Pete laughs and pushes the disconnect button. He checks his first message. Chief Hamper had called at 8:05 a.m. saying Abel had reported by cell phone.

Pete pushes the speed dial button for Chief Hamper's office. "Say, Lyle. Did you get your wife taken care of okay?"

"To tell the truth, yes, I did. Thanks for asking. She's got such a big heart. Underneath that brash exterior is a truly sainted woman."

"I'm sure you know 'er better than I do, Lyle. Did you hear from Abel?"

"Oh, my lord. Detective Sanchez reported that the son of a gun insisted on working on his airplane before coming to Reno to help us."

Pete glances at his floor-to-ceiling bookcase. *First, the dildo didn't want me to call him, now he wants him to report immediately.*

"To tell the truth," says the chief, "he sounds like a flake to me."

"You're probably right, Lyle. Thanks for the message. I can't seem to get hold of Nicole."

"If it'll help you, Pete, I'll put out an APB on her."

"I, uh, I thank you, Chief." Pete shakes his head. "If she doesn't show up pretty soon, I may call you back on that offer."

"That's what fraternal buddies are for, Brother Pete."

"Yes. Well, I'm quite busy, as I know you are also. I'll get back to you later." Pete pushes the hang-up button.

Immediately, the speakerphone crackles. "It's Abel, sir, line one."

"Thanks, Juanita." Pete pushes the button and lifts the receiver. "What's up, Abel? Where are you?"

"I still at Tahoe City. Doctor Oakes insist on repairing carburetor. His assistant say he jus' cheap, don't know diddly squash."

Pete touches his forehead. He thinks of Dora's wedding just three-and-a-half hours away, the message from Governor Bob Miller, his mother's funeral on Tuesday, the undelivered warning to Nicole, and now Mayor Bud Thorne's funeral.

"If I no get back in time for wedding, you can give Dora away?"

"Huh? Denise will come unglued, ol' buddy."

"You have tuxedo?"

"I do, from my Masonic work."

"I not want to call home, see if Denise released from hospital."

"Why's that?"

"Women's wedding-day madness."

Pete laughs uproariously. "I hear you, Abel. I'll call over there and see how things are going. Moreover, if everything goes to shit and you can't pry that fish doctor loose, I'll stand in for you. Nonetheless, you must realize, if you don't make it to the wedding on time you'll *never* be forgiven."

Abel gives up a resigned laugh. "Pete, I hear static sound. I am losing you."

"Better conserve your battery, *tío*. I'll call as soon as I find out something. Convince that numb nuts fish mechanic that he needs to get down to Reno, *pronto*."

Pete pushes the button to disconnect the call. Something makes him look up.

Reno
8:35 a.m., Saturday morning

The pink Rolls-Royce limousine eases into the mansion's parking area. Madam Zho speaks from the rear seat. "I say, Mister Morley, look at that van." Beside her snuggles the remaining Shih Tzu, Mao Tse-tung.

"Yes, Madam. It's got British Columbia plates. I think it may be your grandchildren."

"Which one?" Madam Zho laughs. "I have fifteen."

Madam Zho was so distressed over the death of Madame Chiang Kai-Shek that she gambled and smoked all night, and was now thoroughly knackered. On the way home she purchased a headstone and coffin from the Rock Boulevard pet store. She plans to hold a little ceremony and bury her beloved dog next to the patio.

A four-year-old girl, chased by a five-year-old boy waving a green-plastic dinosaur, rounds the right side of the house. "Oh look, Mister Morley, it's little Jenny and Robert. Those are my *great* grandchildren. How smashing. My oldest grandchild, Melody, and her husband, DuWayne, must be here."

Mister Morley places the shift lever into park. "It appears they brought their cocker spaniel as well, Madam."

Madam Zho laughs. "Everybody's welcome here, Mister Morley, *especially* Mister Jiggs. He and Madame Chiang Kai-Shek love to play."

"Yes, Madam, they certainly did."

Madam Zho hugs and kisses her granddaughter, Melody, her granddaughter's two children, Robert and Jenny, and Melody's husband, DuWayne. She embraces Melody's niece, Tiffany, a seven-year-old who looks as if she might grow up to be as tiny as her great-grandmother.

Madam Zho had invited Melody and DuWayne to stay for

as long as they wanted, whereupon they carried in a colossal stack of swaying luggage. Madam Zho bubbles with love and enthusiasm. Many times, she has invited her relatives and friends from Vancouver to come down to Reno and enjoy the mansion, whether she was there or not.

"Mister Morley," says Madam Zho, "bring me two of those boxes, one white set and one black."

Madam Zho calls Tiffany and little Jenny. "Come, girls. Here's a surprise for each of you."

"Oh, goodie, goodie," says little Jenny, clapping her hands. "What is it?"

"It's eel-skin boots, a belt, and a purse. One set is white and one's black. You're the oldest, Tiffany. Which color do you prefer?"

Tiffany smiles. "I like the black one, Great Grandma."

"Here you are, you precious thing. Try the boots on. We've got other sizes if these don't fit."

"Gimme the white ones, Great Grandma," says Jenny. She dances and claps her hands. "Gimme the white ones."

"Can you say, please?"

"Yes, Great Grandma."

Madam Zho grins. "Well, go ahead then, Jenny. Say please."

"Please, Great Grandma."

"What a polite little girl you are, lovey. I'm enormously delighted to give you this eel-skin gift."

"What about me, Great Grandma?" asks Robert.

"I'm afraid I've gone a bit bonkers, little Robert," says Madam Zho. "I overlooked my little man. Mister Morley, do we have wallets here?"

"Yes, Madam, we certainly do. All colors."

"Marvelous. Would you like to have your very own wallet, Robert?"

"Yes."

"Have you ever had one before?"

"No, Great Grandma. What is a wallet?"

"DuWayne," says Madam Zho, "show Robert your wallet."

DuWayne struggles to pull a bulging worn-leather billfold from his rear pocket. Robert's face sags.

Madam Zho laughs. "Now, little Robert, your wallet will be ever so beautiful, brand new, and shiny. In addition, it'll have a five-dollar bill in it. You may carry your new wallet in your pocket when you attend school this year."

"Oh, thank you, Great Grandma. You're the greatest."

"You're surely welcome, little Robert. Now, what color would you like? We have black, white, brown, green—"

"*Green*, Great Grandma, like Dino, my dinosaur."

"Smashing. Would you please fetch Robert a green wallet, Mister Morley?"

"And, girls, you just received a nice present. Why do you have such long faces? Do you each want a five-dollar bill in your purse, as well?"

"Yes, yes, Great Grandma," says Jenny.

"Yes please, Great Grandma," Tiffany says. "Thank you very much."

"What a dear you are, Tiffany. And, what about you, DuWayne? Could you stand a *new* eel-skin wallet?"

Reno
8:40 a.m., Saturday morning

Chief Hamper leans back in his chair talking on the telephone. "Mister Harrah—Bill—I'm doing the best I can with 'im. Frankly, he doesn't recognize what side of the bread his butter's on."

Chief Hamper nods as he listens to Mister Harrah. "I completely agree with you, sir. The casinos *are* the lifeblood of Reno, and, yes, we need more freeway signs to lure in cash-heavy gamers."

Chief Hamper looks up at the ceiling. "Yes sir, Mister, uh,

Bill, I'll try my best to get through to him. God bless. Bye-bye."

A light flashes on the telephone unit. Chief Hamper depresses the button. "Yes, Sergeant?"

"You got a call from your head of homicide and a call from Mister Harold Smith."

"Gimme Smith."

"Yes, sir."

Chief Hamper places his shoes on the desk and talks into the speakerphone. "Hello, Pappy. What can I do for you this lovely fine morning?"

"It would be a lot finer, Hamper, if the sun was blocked with signs declaring, '*Harold's Club or Bust*.'"

Chief Hamper drops his feet onto the carpet and leans forward. "Oh, I'm sorry, Mister Smith. I'm having a little trouble convincing the mayor of what side this city's bread is buttered."

"Do you remember, Chief, how much butter I spread on your bread?"

"To be quite honest, I sure do. Praise the Lord. I'm eternally grateful to you, sir."

"You can show me your gratitude, Hamper, by convincing the mayor and city council that we casino owners need to put up more and bigger freeway signs."

"Oh, yes sir, Pappy, I mean, Mister Smith. You've got my word. I'll try my best."

"I don't want you to simply try your best, Hamper. Get the goddamn job done."

Chief Hamper gazes at his aquarium. The black moray eel sporting the white spots peeks out from the rocks. The eel appears to yawn. "Hello, precious," whispers Chief Hamper.

"*What was that, Hamper?*"

"Oh, by golly, nothing, I mean, you bet, Mister Smith."

"You're still craving a run for the Governorship, aren't you?"

"Well, actually, now that you mention it—"

"If you want major backing from this area's big contributors, you gotta produce."

"Good enough, by golly. I understand completely, Mister Smith."

A pause ensues.

"Thank you for the chance to work for you, sir."

An audible click sounds from the telephone's speaker.

"Bye-bye, sir."

Reno
9:05 a.m., Saturday morning

A long-legged young woman wearing blue shorts and a skintight white top, stands with her hand on the doorknob. Dark circles show under her eyes.

"Nicole." Pete jumps up and embraces her.

"Daddy, I couldn't reach you at home. I've been hearing sirens all morning. I *figured* you'd be here at your office."

"Yes, angel. We've been up all night. Were you able to get any sleep?"

"I finally took something, Daddy. I slept maybe three hours."

"Denise was attacked in her bathroom by something living in her toilet."

"Eeew." Nicole wrinkles her face. "That's really gross. Like, I've heard of rats popping up in the toilet. Is that what it was?"

"Something like that, angel. We thought we were on the verge of clearing this up. However, now we aren't sure what the creature is, how many there are, or how to eradicate them. Nonetheless, we have a couple of top-notch scientists coming down from Oregon to help us."

Nicole frowns.

"I know it sounds bizarre, kitten, but just be careful around toilets until we get this under control—shouldn't be long."

Nicole smiles. "And you sure look all *elegant*, Dad"—Nicole throws her hands open—"in your mussed shirt and whiskers. Where's your necktie?"

Pete pats his pocket.

Nicole shakes her head. "Why don't you hang it over the back of the chair, so the wrinkles come out?"

Pete fishes the necktie from his pocket.

"And Daddy."

"Yes."

"If you get a chance, you might think about taking a shower."

Pete laughs. "I'm overdue, pussycat. I just have so much time—"

The speakerphone crackles. "You've got a number of urgent calls coming in, Mister Mayor, but Abel's calling from his cell phone. Says his battery's about dead."

"Thanks, Juanita. Go ahead, Abel."

"Pete. Doctor Oakes fix linkage. Engine still not start. It turns over, but—"

"Abel. You're breaking up. Dora's wedding starts in just two hours. Load up those two numb nut scientists and get your asses down to Reno . . . *pronto*. *That's an order.*"

"Okay, boss—"

"Whoa," says Nicole. "His battery's fryin', Daddy."

"If you can hear me, Abel, get down here quick as Speedy Gonzales."

"Bummer." Nicole shrugs. "I think his phone all died."

Pete pushes the button to disconnect.

"Like, I came to tell you, Daddy, me and my gang are gettin' out of town for the weekend. We're going waterskiing. Brad is—"

"Brad?"

"Yeah, you remember. This cool dude, Brad Inouye, is picking me up."

"Where did this fellow emerge from?"

"Like, not out from under a rock, if that's what you're all gettin' at."

Pete laughs. "No, no kitten, where'd you meet this fine young man?"

"When I was getting my car worked on at Intrepid on Linda Way, Brad works there. He's their best mechanic. He's got this awesome drag boat. It can pull eight skiers at one time, no problem. It's called *The Undertaker*."

"*The Undertaker?*"

"Uh-huh. It's totally rad, Dad. It's all totally black and the trailer's got old-fashioned undertaker lamps for taillights."

Pete raises an eyebrow. "Oh? What kind of boat is it, Nicole?"

"It's a flat-bottomed Sanger V-drive, with an outrageous big-block Chevy engine. It's all chrome air scoops and pipes. It's, fer sure, an outta sight unit. Whenever there's—"

Pete nods. "Are you going to make it to Dora's wedding?"

"Fer sure, Dad. Fer sure. We're packing up our gear, getting ready to go. Maybe we'll drive out and set up camp first. But I wouldn't miss Dora's wedding for anything."

"Just be extra cautious, angel, okay?"

"No problem, Daddy. Like, we're always careful. We've never had an accident. Maybe you'll get those sewer rats zapped by the time we get back."

"Where're you going to be camping, sweetheart?"

The desktop telephone buzzes. "The governor's still waiting for your call, boss. In addition, the chief's back on the line and he says it's urgent."

Pete looks up at Nicole and lets his face sag. He reaches out and pushes the button. "Put 'im on, Juanita."

"Pete, Mandy talked to *Harrah's* down in New Orleans. They've experienced a hurricane-caused flood. The sewer backed up and all kinds of tropical creatures took up residence in the pipes. The authorities simply poisoned them. Then the sewer department reintroduced the organisms needed to process the sewage. No problem. The Lord be praised. The crisis is over.

Mandy's getting all the particulars."

Pete hangs his head. "That's good news, Lyle. Nicole just walked in the office."

"Hi there, Nicole. Blessed be the Lord. We were just about to put out an APB on you."

Nicole throws her dad a scowl.

Pete rolls his eyes.

"Frankly, it's too bad that the scientists already departed Newport for Reno; otherwise, we could just thank them and dismiss them. Anyway, I'm awfully busy and I'll talk to you soon."

"Right, Chief." Pete pushes the button.

Juanita is on the speaker. "Governor Miller's on the line again, boss."

"I'll take it in a second, Juanita. Don't let 'im go."

Pete holds his finger on the button. "Well, Nicole, you shouldn't encounter any trouble, so long as you're not planning on water-skiing at the Sparks sewer ponds."

Reno
9:15 a.m., Saturday morning

Madam Zho stands in her living room. A cigarette smolders in her left hand.

"Great Grandma," says Robert, "can we go swimming in your pool?

Madam Zho coughs. "Oh, I'm sorry, lovey. Great-grandmother would like to let you, but the swimming pool is off-limits. In fact, you mustn't even walk through this door to the pool area. Can you promise me you won't go out to the pool?"

Robert's little face dissolves in disappointment. "Uh-huh, Great Grandma. I promise."

"That's a good boy. Why don't you ask Rachel to fix you some ice cream and strawberries?"

"Oh, thank you, Great Grandma," hollers Robert over his shoulder.

Madam Zho calls to her granddaughter. "Melody. Please come over here for a minute, dear."

When Melody arrives, Madam Zho points toward the swimming pool. "See those tanks out there? And those two men in lab coats?"

"Yes, Grandmother, I do."

"There. Did you see that?"

"Oh. What leaped out of the water?"

Madam Zho lowers her voice. "Those men are conducting some research on some little-known fish that live deep in the sea. We're afraid that the experiment may have to be called off because the fish have grown a bit aggressive."

"Grandmother, you've got fish living in your swimming pool?"

Madam Zho blows a cloud of smoke. "You know my income is derived from my leather and meat importing business. Furthermore, you understand that I need to acquire the absolute latest in developments to stay ahead of my competition."

"Grandmother, what could possibly—"

"It's no different, lovey, than if I was raising longhorn cattle for steaks and leather. It would be dangerous for your children to play around the bulls. Do you see?"

"I guess. I just've never—"

"You're welcome here at any time, my child, and you're free to do anything you want—only—don't let any of your family go near the swimming pool. Is that understood?"

Reno
9:35 a.m., Saturday morning

"This is Betsy Boggs, Channel Two News. I'm standing on top of the Boomtown Road overpass on Interstate Eighty West.

You can see below me the traffic at the onramp has slowed to a crawl as our residents flee to California."

The July sun stands close to meridian height.

"Ralph." Boggs motions with her hand. "Swing your camera toward town."

As the camera moves off Boggs, she wipes her forehead with the back of her hand. A curl of dark hair hangs over her forehead.

"You see bumper-to-bumper traffic leaving Reno," says Boggs into her foam-covered microphone. Beyond the automobiles the television screen shows the fabulous Reno skyline—including the Silver Legacy Resort Casino, the Reno Hilton, and John Ascuaga's Nugget.

"Excuse me, sir." Boggs pushes her microphone toward a black Jeep Cherokee's darkened window.

"Excuse me, sir"—Boggs hollers over the car's rumbling V-8—"could we talk to you for just a minute?"

The powered window drops down. A refrigerated puff of air escapes into Boggs's face.

"We're gettin' outta Dodge," the driver announces.

Ralph's camera shows a woman sitting in the passenger seat and two children in the rear beside a huge, red-colored dog.

"And, what's *your* name, sir?"

"Chuck, and this is the wife, May. Chuck and May Baggitt."

"Where're you headed, Mister Baggitt, and how long're you going to be gone?" Boggs swivels the microphone in front of Baggitt's mouth.

"We're headed for my sister's in Auburn."

The dog takes a step forward. He lowers his head between the two Baggitts. He begins to pant.

Baggitt grasps the dog around his neck. "How're you doin' Skippy, ol' boy? This's been quite a day, huh?"

"Well, Mister Baggitt," says Boggs. "To your knowledge has anyone been attacked here in Verdi?"

Baggitt glances at his wife. Missus Baggitt shrugs her shoulders.

"We don't know of anyone getting assaulted up here," says Baggitt, "but why take a chance? We saw the television report this morning from in front of Saint Mary's Emergency Room." Baggitt shakes his head. "I mean, those people were getting their guts ripped out, right through their—"

"Orifices," offers Missus Baggitt.

"Yeah." Baggitt nods. "Right out through their *orifice holes*."

Reno
9:40 a.m., Saturday morning

Pete sits at his desk talking on the telephone. "The last I heard from him, Denise, he was still at Lake Tahoe. Unfortunately, his cell phone has died."

"I'm almost hysterical, Pete. This's the biggest day in Dora's life. I was just released from the hospital. My darling husband, who's supposed to give Dora away in an hour, is nowhere to be seen."

"Please try to hold it together, Denise. Think of Dora, and all your family and friends who're depending on you."

Denise bawls.

"We'll get through this, Denise. Before Abel drove to the lake he asked me, simply as a backup plan, to fill in—"

"He's known about this wedding for *two years*," Denise wails. "How could he let us down like this?"

"Now, Denise. It's not Abel's fault. The chief—"

"I can't talk anymore." Denise sobs. "Hear, Dora. Take this."

"Uncle Pete, is Papa going to make it back in time to walk me down the aisle?"

"He probably will, Dora. I asked him to grab up those two scientists and haul their buns down to Reno, *at breakneck speed*."

"Pete," says Dora, "we don't know *positively* if he's going to make it in time. Is that right?"

"Well, yes, Dora, that's about the gist of it."

"Hi, Uncle Pete."

"Is that you, little Darla?"

"Yes, Pete. I love you."

"Darla. I love you, too."

Denise takes the phone. "If he doesn't get back here for the wedding, I'm never going to speak to him again."

"Gimme the phone, Mama." Dora seizes the telephone. "We're under an awful lot of stress here, Uncle Pete. Because of the attacks, many guests haven't decided whether to stay in town for the wedding or not. Please grab your tuxedo and get over here. Maybe you can calm the stormy waters."

"I have to call the governor back, Dora. He insists on driving up from Carson. Then I'll be right over to your house. Maybe your mama should drink some herbal tea, or something."

"You're such a good friend, Uncle Pete. See you in a few minutes. I'll try to get Mama to take something."

Truckee
9:50 a.m., Saturday morning

Abel stops on top of the Interstate Eighty and Highway Eighty-Nine overpass at Truckee, California. "It no good, Sherm and KB. No make it for wedding. I dead meat."

"Arrr," growls Sherm from the back seat. "Who would've guessed the eastbound lanes would be turned into westbound lanes? There are California Highway Patrol everywhere."

From the passenger seat, KB sits wide-eyed. "This is more automobiles than in all of Denmark, you bet you. Is there another way to Reno, Abel?"

"There old Dog Valley Road to Verdi, KB, then take old highway, Business Eighty, to Reno. Avoid freeway."

"Arrrbeedarrr. Then let's be on our way. We have a wedding to attend."

"No make it in time, Sherm. I dead taco meat, *forever*."

Reno
9:55 a.m., Saturday morning

From his office Pete talks to Nevada's governor, Bob Miller. "It appears we have it pretty well handled here, Bob. The chief thinks he's found a solution to the sewer problem. I certainly can't order you not to come up, Mister Governor, but—"

"I'm a little doubtful, Pete, that such a simple solution could be arrived at this easily."

"I hear you. I'm a little unconvinced over *anything* Chief Hamper puts on the collection plate."

Governor Miller laughs. "I know what you mean, pal."

"If Hamper's solution fails, Bob, we still have Doctor Oakes, the chief scientist at Oregon State University's flagship marine laboratory. If he can't come up with answers, no one can."

"And, if this Oakes character fails to come up with answers, what do we do then, Pete? Do we close Reno town? What about Sparks? Fernley?"

"Unfortunately, Bob, we've already experienced trouble in Sparks. Did you hear about Bud Thorne?"

"What about Bud?"

"Last evening, while taking a dump in that little public lavatory behind the steam locomotive, he had his intestines ripped right out through his asshole."

"Indeed, that's what I'm talking about, Pete. I'm jumping in the limo and heading your way."

"I think it'd be a waste of your valuable time to make a side trip to Reno, partner. I *absolutely* have to go to a wedding at eleven o'clock at Saint Thomas Aquinas Cathedral. After that, we're heading out to Rancho San Rafael for the biggest wedding reception you've ever seen—that is—if the caterers haven't fled."

"Listen, pal, if this little problem isn't completely contained, like yesterday, my political career's going to hit the fan. My aspirations will be the laughingstock of the national news. I'll have *plenty* of valuable time after Jay Leno finishes with me."

Reno
10:35 a.m., Saturday morning

Pete ambles up the walk to Abel's house. *Damn, I failed to find out where Nicole was camping this weekend.* In one hand he carries his patent leather shoes and in the other a garment bag containing his tuxedo. *God, I'm sleepy.*

Before he can ring the bell, the front door swings open.

Denise throws herself into Pete's arms. "Pete, you handsome hunk." She pulls his head down and plants a long wet kiss.

Pete's eyes grow big as shot glasses.

Denise strokes Pete's cheek. "Oh, I love that rugged stubbly feel."

Crowding behind their mother stands Dora—in her resplendent white wedding gown—along with Dorothy, Dominic, David, and little Darla. The house buzzes with the feminine voices of sisters and aunts.

"And I absolutely adore your manly smell. Grrr."

Dora unpeels her mother from Pete's body. "Mama, get your corsage on. We need to get to the church."

"Howzit goin', Uncle Pete?" Dominic's large rented tuxedo coat hangs open. "Dora found Papa's special *Patrón* tequila under the sink. Mom might've done one too many shooters, ya know what I mean? She's maybe just a little *Borracho*. Whataya think, Pete? Will she make it through the wedding okay?"

"Without a doubt, Dominic." Pete grins. *That ol' gal can pull off anything, no matter how borracho she is.*

———

Reno
10:45 a.m., Saturday morning

Standing by the stainless-steel tanks Madam Zho smokes her cigarette. She talks with Doctors Chen and Chan.

From around the corner drifts the sound of three children frolicking, accompanied by two dogs barking. Doctor Chan glances at the wooden gate. His face grows worried.

Madam Zho hears Melody shouting. Madam Zho places her hand on her chest.

The gate bangs open. Mister Jiggs bounds through, closely followed by Mao Tse-tung. Two squealing girls run after the dogs, chased by Robert and his plastic dinosaur.

Melody's voice shrieks. "Robert, Jenny, Tiffany, get *out* of that pool area."

"Mister Morley," rasps Madam Zho around her cigarette. "Get those dogs away from the pool."

Mister Jiggs, his tongue hanging out and a smile on his face, makes a splendid spaniel leap out over the swimming pool.

Madam Zho spits her cigarette out and screams.

Mister Morley grasps her around the shoulders. He whispers, "Oh, dear bloody God."

Doctor Chen drops his beaker.

The three children slide to a stop. Robert gapes at the soaring dog. "Wow."

Before Mister Jiggs reaches the apex of his arc, three-yard-long tubes of salami clear the water. In midair they slime their way in and munch on the screaming spaniel's organs. A furious frothing ball falls back into the pool. The water turns blood red.

From the driveway, the sound of a three-tone Cadillac horn sounds.

More aggressive than South American piranhas, the slippery beasts continue to slide into the squalling spaniel's orifices and gobble the still-living dog from the inside out.

As Mister Jiggs's collar settles to the pool's bottom, two richly dressed elderly Chinese couples step through the pool gate. Madam Zho's sister and brother-in-law, Jean and James Wu, smile and wave. Her brother and sister-in-law, Kam Ho and Su Lee, follow them, giving a little bow.

"Oh, dear Jean." Madam Zho hurries around the pool. "We've just experienced a bloody catastrophe here."

They embrace. "What is it, Jenny? What's wrong with your pool?"

"Oh, it's just a wee experiment the two scientists and I have been working on. The results seem to be all cocked up. We may have to bin it. Be that as it may, dear sister, I desperately hope you didn't drive all the way down to Reno to go swimming."

Melody screams.

Mister Jiggs's black-and-white fur has just bobbed to the surface.

Reno
10:55 a.m., Saturday morning

A thundercloud is beginning to form over the Sierra Nevada Mountains.

Dorothy pulls Pete's garment bag and shoes from the car. "I don't care what you say, Pete, we don't have time for you to shower and shave. We're *starting* in five minutes." She shoves the clothes at Pete. "Just get inside and get that tux on."

"I'll help Uncle Pete get dressed," says a happy Darla.

Dorothy shakes her head. "No, Darla. Thank you, but you must go in and check on Dora. That's a very important job. She's the star of the show, you know."

"Okay, Dorothy." Darla skips up the sidewalk to the church's back door.

"David," Dorothy says, "help Uncle Pete get into his clothes. And, one other thing, Pete—after you escort Dora down the aisle, the priest will ask you *one* question. All you gotta say is, 'Her mother and I.'"

Pete yawns.

"You'll be okay, Uncle Pete." Dorothy pats him on the arm. "Now, get going. And David." She grabs David by the sleeve. "If Papa shows up before Dora and Uncle Pete start down the aisle, switch 'em out."

David nods and follows Pete into the church.

"Dominic," says Dorothy. "You're escorting Mama down the aisle. Hold 'er steady. Don't let 'er stop and talk. We don't want any embarrassing moments that we'll have to hear about for the next forty years. I don't know where she's getting it, but *absolutely* don't let her have any more tequila."

———

The church sits nearly full. Father O'Leary and the wedding party stand at the front. Pete has just handed Dora to her soon-to-be husband, Hunter Burns.

Denise pats the pew beside her. Pete strides over and sits. Denise leans against Pete. "Isn't Dora beautiful?"

"Yes." Pete glances into the row behind him, coming face-to-face with a scowling aunt.

"Here." Denise opens her beaded purse. "I brought a little flask of encouragement."

"Put that away, Denise, and keep your voice down."

"Oh, Pete, you're so handsome in that tux"—Denise pushes her shoulder under Pete's arm—"especially with that stubbly chin."

"Here"—Pete points at the wedding party—"gaze upon your beautiful daughters and your good-looking new son-in-law."

Denise bumps Pete with her elbow. "What's the matter with Dorothy?"

Instead of watching the ceremony, Dorothy is gawking at the back of the church. Her mouth has fallen open.

Denise sits up straight. "Check out Dora."

Even though a veil covers Dora's face, Pete sees her blush. He grows aware of droning voices in the church's rear. He distinctly hears, *Oh, my God.*

"Sit still, Denise," Pete whispers. "I'll take a look."

Pete stands and peers toward the back doors. He sees Abel in his brown suit, the blood-stained handkerchief still around his thigh. Pete sees that Abel's jaw has darkened from his growing five o'clock shadow. Behind Abel stands a pair who appear to have arrived directly from a Jimmy Buffett concert. KB holds an overnight bag and her squirming terrier. Sherm wears his white straw hat, his backpack hanging over his shoulder.

Pete swallows. *Have I just entered the goddamned "Twilight Zone," or am I, in fact, witnessing the swan song of my political career?*

Halfway to the back, Nicole gives Pete a little wave. Beside her sits a handsome black-haired young man. Pete forces a smile on his face.

On the other side of the aisle, boasting the tallest hat in the room, sits Belle Starr. Beside her, Chief Hamper luxuriates in his resplendent full-dress police chief's uniform.

Pete sighs. *Maybe the chief can get me a job sweeping tumbleweeds from the vacant casinos.*

Heidi wriggles free from KB and trots down the aisle, collar jingling.

Pete whispers to Denise. "You can look now."

Denise pushes herself to her feet. She bursts out laughing and slaps her thigh.

Abel dons a timid smile.

A grinning Father O'Leary looks at Pete and shrugs.

Denise wobbles, then waves her arm. "Honey . . . come on down."

Pete spots Belle Starr beaming as if she was a tourist holding a fistful of free-drink coupons.

Denise hollers, "And bring your friends."

Reno
12 noon

Summertime thunderclouds build over Mount Rose.

Outside the large pavilion at Rancho San Rafael Park, Grandpa Ricardo superintends the men operating the smoking barbecues. Under the pavilion's roof a keg of Pacifico beer sits in its ice-filled tub. Two hundred family and guests mill among the salads and desserts, sitting bowl to bowl along the table. English and Spanish voices mix with the clang of pans and the clink of utensils. Soda pop, beer, bottles of wine, and spirits crowd the counter.

The public restroom sits fifty yards east of the pavilion. Across the vast lawn, escapees on North McCarran Boulevard create bumper-to-bumper traffic.

A seven-piece mariachi band slowly moves among the guests. The musicians wear black outfits highlighted in silver. Besides the two trumpets and four guitars, Linda, a raven-haired woman with a strong clear voice, belts out Mexican *ranchería* songs.

Two-dozen children run, screeching and playing on the lawn.

Leaning on the railing of the pavilion's entrance bridge, Pete quells a yawn. Then he takes a sip of his paint-peeling wedding punch. Denise prepared it for him and forced the plastic glass into his hand.

Nicole introduces her new boyfriend, Brad Inouye, to Pete, Belle Starr, and Chief Lyle Hamper.

Under the pavilion's roof the new couple, Hunter, and Dora Burns, greet a line of well-wishers.

Abel leads his charges toward the mayor's group. "Mister Mayor, this Doctor T Sherman Oakes. He head of Newport lab."

"Thanks, Abel," says Pete. "This city treasures your dedication, my friend."

Pete sticks his hand out to Sherm. "Thank you, Doctor Oakes, for coming down. I can't tell you how much we appreciate it." Pete's eyelids flutter. He sniffs aviation gas and the pungent drift of Oregon tidal flats.

"Arrrbeedarrr," growls Sherm. "Hullo, Mister Mayor. The pleasure is mine, that it are." He grasps Pete's hand and pumps it vigorously.

"Heck, Doctor Oakes, you can just call me Pete."

"As you wish, matey, um, Pete. My students and staff simply call me Doctor T." He glances at KB. "Some people just call me Sherm."

Nicole turns her back to Sherm and whispers in Pete's ear. "Whoa. Outta sight, Daddy. This is the scientist who's going to save Reno?"

"Pete," Abel continues, "this Kristian Bjørnsen. Or jus' KB."

Her purse hanging on her shoulder and Heidi in her arms, KB thrusts a hand toward Pete. He releases Sherm's hand and accepts KB's. For a *long smoldering* moment, he looks into KB's blue eyes. He feels his heart surge. Marvelous warmth invigorates his palm. He manages to stammer, "Welcome, KB, to the biggest little city in the world."

From inside the pavilion, Denise hollers. "Abel, get your *campesino* ass over here."

"Dora give Denise tequila." Abel looks at Pete and shakes his head. "You talk. I attend to the mama."

"Absolutely, *amigo*," Pete says, "and thank you for performing above and beyond the call of duty."

"*De nada.*"

"Better get that wound attended to, Abel."

"*De nada.*"

KB flashes Pete a brilliant white smile and tenderly and reluctantly removes her hand. "And this is Heidi."

"Well, hello little Heidi."

From the south end of the city, the air-thumping sound of a Bell UH-1E Huey helicopter grows louder. Pete squints at the approaching craft.

"Oh, look at that." KB touches her fingertips on Pete's arm. "Somebody very famous just drove in, that is for sure.

A black Cadillac stretch limousine, bearing the silver-colored great Seal of Nevada on its rear door, eases into the pavilion's parking lot. Blue Nevada State flags flap from the front fenders.

"It's the governor," says Belle Starr. Following closely, a dark blue Chevrolet sedan displays the silver Seal of the Nevada Air National Guard. Two flags, each exhibiting a single star, flap from the Chevrolet's front fenders.

The approaching din from the olive-green-colored helicopter drowns the pavilion's voices. The chopper prepares to settle on the lawn. The wedding guests cover their faces from the whirlwind of dust, dried grass, and stinging little pebbles.

KB points at the helicopter. "Oh, look, Sherm. The name."

Sherm had been surreptitiously studying Pete. "Aye, KB. *The Gutsy Lady.* Do you suppose she'd like to meet *The Gander*?"

The governor's limousine makes a deluxe stop. The driver, a Nevada state trooper wearing an official Nevada blazer, rushes around the back of the automobile and opens the right rear door. Six-foot-seven Governor Bob Miller pulls himself out the door. He wears a light summer sport coat and tie.

"Thanks, Todd. Good job." He bends down and looks in the car. "Come 'ere, girl." His big golden Labrador, Abby, hops out. Governor Miller straightens, spots Pete, and walks straight toward him. "Come on, Abby." Governor Miller waves. "Hiya, Pete."

Nevada Air National Guard, Sergeant Hoover, hustles to the Chevrolet's rear door. Brigadier General Nate Arnold, too tall to be a jockey but just right for the cockpit of an F-4 Phantom, steps onto the asphalt saying, "Thanks, Sarge." He follows the governor. General Arnold wears his Air Force flight suit, which bears a single silver star on each shoulder. He unfolds his dark blue campaign cap and pushes it on his head.

Before the Nevada National Guard chopper has touched the lawn, Major General Harlan "Howlin' Mad" Clark has alighted. A big man wearing a big face, he obviously enjoys serving it. He wears two silver stars on his dress army uniform and an officer's cap whose bill boasts a double helping of scrambled eggs. He acknowledges Governor Miller's head above the crowd and makes a beeline for him and Mayor Pete Ferrari.

Chapter Four

US Coast Guard Cutter, Lake Tahoe, Munson boat

Reno
12:10 p.m., Saturday afternoon

Madam Zho, her family, and the two scientists sit at her formal dining room table.

Mao Tse-tung, the remaining dog, huddles on Madam Zho's ankle. Tiffany and little Jenny bear red-rimmed eyes.

Ordinarily, Madam Zho doesn't serve alcohol until after five. However, due to Mister Jiggs's fully observed dismemberment, she ordered an exception.

Rachel opens the kitchen's swinging door. "Mister Morley. Would you please assist me in serving?"

"Be my pleasure, Rachel."

Robert squirms in his chair. "Mum."

"Yes, Robert," says Melody. "What is it?"

"May I use the restroom?"

DuWayne sets his wine glass down. "You just came from the bathroom, Robert. Why didn't you go then?"

Madam Zho laughs heartily. "We all know the answer to that question, DuWayne, don't we? I remember my father asking me, time and again, why didn't you go to the loo when you were in there?"

DuWayne snickers. "Five minutes ago, Robert, you didn't have to go, correct?"

Robert vigorously nods.

"Go ahead," says Melody. "If you gotta go, you gotta go. Hurry back, so you can finish your lunch."

Robert scrambles from his chair and skips toward the hallway.

"He's a great little boy," says James. "Say, Jenny, when I was standing out on your patio, I noticed quite a gathering at that park."

"That's Rancho San Rafael," says Melody. "It could be a wedding reception or a family reunion."

"Hear music," says Doctor Chen, "like bullfight."

Doctor Chan nods. "Yes, I hear the trumpets playing."

"It is probably a mariachi band," says Melody. "They play Mexican music."

Tiffany discreetly clears her throat. "Doctor Chan . . . did you see any kids at the park?"

"Yes, little Tiffany," says Doctor Chan. "There appeared to be dozens playing on the lawn."

"Maybe," says Madam Zho, "after lunch we can drive down to the park. Our children might enjoy playing with the others."

"Yes, yes," says Tiffany, swinging her feet back and forth beneath her chair.

James hoists his gin and tonic toward the kitchen door.

"Excellent *do* on the drinks, Mister Morley."

"Thank you, sir," says Mister Morley. "I cherish your appreciation."

James takes another sip. "Did any of you notice all those cars heading west on North McCarran Boulevard?"

Kam Ho nods. "I watched Channel Eight this morning. There are lots of citizens leaving the valley."

Madam Zho delicately clears her throat. "I don't think you're cosseting Robert, DuWayne. All children are like that, especially little boys. They simply live in the moment."

Doctor Chan finishes pouring beer into his glass. "You're so right, Madam Jenny. Little boys often forget the simplest life-saving instructions."

Madam Zho laughs. "Yes, I remember a certain *brother*"— with her left-hand Madam Zho pats Kam Ho on the arm— "who couldn't learn to stay out of the street. Remember?"

Kam Ho beams. "I remember honorable parents resorting to physical measures in their attempt to teach me to play in a safer place."

Madam Zho grins. "Even after your baby duck was run over, you still didn't learn."

Su sets her gin and tonic on her placemat. "Yes, Jenny, but Kam Ho was so young then."

"Yes," says Madam Zho, "five years old, the same as little Robert."

"*Robert.*" Melody glances at his chair. "I haven't heard a door close or water running."

Kam Ho smiles. "He take it on the lam."

Doctor Chen sips his gin and tonic. "He see open door—he make a run for it."

DuWayne stands. "Well, I better go check on him."

DuWayne walks down the hall to the nearest bathroom. The door stands open. Then he walks to the end of the hall and Madam Zho's bedroom. He peeks in.

"Robert?"

DuWayne strides across the bedroom toward the master bathroom. The door stands open.

"Robert, are you in there?"

Shaking his head, DuWayne peers about the bedroom and notices the curtain twisted in the sliding door—the door that leads to the patio and the swimming pool. He scowls. He pulls the curtain aside.

"Robert." DuWayne slides the door open. He yells. "*Robert. Goddammit*, get away from that pool."

Little Robert, a good seventy feet away on his hands and knees beside the pool, trails his green dinosaur back and forth in the water.

DuWayne rips the curtain clear and rushes toward Robert.

Before he had moved a half-dozen strides, the entire dining room company has spilled out of the house.

Reno
12:20 p.m., Saturday afternoon

Against a stark blue sky, thunderclouds stack up over the Sierra Nevada Mountains.

Under the pavilion's roof, guests file by the wedding party. The row of barbecues produce prodigious, meat-cooking aromas. Linda and the mariachi band play lively Mexican tunes. Two-dozen kids frolic on the lawn. The bumper-to-bumper traffic has . . . mired. Two hundred guests talk faster, and louder and **louder**. Through the hubbub slips the sounds of sirens and automobile horns.

Governor Bob Miller shakes hands with Pete. "Hiya, pal."

Pete clutches his wedding punch solidly so that it doesn't spill. "Hi, good to see you, Mister Governor. And how about you, Abby?" Pete bends down and gives Abby a good butt rub.

Governor Miller gestures. "Pete, this is General Nate Arnold, head of the air guard."

"Hi, Nathan," says Pete. "Good to see you again."

"And this is General Howlin'—I mean—Harlan Clark, head of the Nevada Guard."

Howlin' Mad works the candy-bar-sized cigar in his plump lips. "How do ya do, Mister Mayor."

Sounding like a railroad track foreman, Denise hollers from the pavilion. "Hey, you kids. There's a bazillion Canada geese out there. Watch your step. No nasty shoes allowed in *my* car."

Pete glances at Governor Miller. "Whataya think, Bob?"

Governor Miller shrugs. "I don't know about you, pal, but ... I'm staying off that lawn."

The Gutsy Lady has shut down her whining turbine engines. The gathering wind pushes the rotor blades in lazy circles.

Captain Vickie Doolittle, a well-built woman sporting short blond hair and tiny silver earrings, wears a khaki-colored flight suit. Lieutenant Barnes, her second in command, holds Howlin' Mad's leather briefcase. First Sergeant Smith, Sergeant Nguyen, and Private Armbruster mill about the Huey helicopter—prepared to respond in an instant.

Howlin' Mad pulls the cigar from his lips and spits on the concrete pad. "Mister Mayor, I been followin' your goddamn developments from my office in Carson. Hell, if yer plannin' on needing the services of the National Guard you gotta notify the governor here."

"General," says Pete, "the situation here in Reno would have to worsen significantly before we would call state services for rescue. I've invited two scientists—"

"Hell, Mayor, why don't we just napalm the sons of bitches?" Howlin' Mad jerks his thumb toward North McCarran Boulevard. "Look at that exodus. You got a mass evacuation under way, or hadn't you noticed?"

Pete quietly speaks. "I know we do, General. However, I didn't order an evacuation. We actually think—"

"Now, Pete," says Governor Miller. "We're not butting into your business. We're simply here to assist."

"Bob, I appreciate that. Thank you. We think we have it pretty well—"

Chief Hamper fingers his coat buttons as he insinuates himself into the group. "Hi, Mister Governor."

"Hello, Chief Hamper."

"Frankly, sir, I'm afraid the television reporters have over-reacted. By golly, Pete, here, is absolutely right. It's not as bad a situation as it first appears on TV. If we throw too much importance on this strictly municipal situation, we're going to scare off Reno's lifeblood. You can surely see our viewpoint."

"In other words, Chief," says Governor Miller, "you feel the casinos should be kept open at all costs—no matter what kind of crisis is unfolding?"

The top of Belle Starr's hat reaches the same height as the governor's head. "Hello, Bob."

"Hi there, Belle" says Governor Miller. "How're ya enjoying retirement?"

Chief Hamper squints at the governor and then at his wife. "You know each other?"

Nicole and her boyfriend, Brad Inouye, slip up behind Pete.

"I don't want you to get the wrong idea here, Bob," says Pete. "The chief and I don't quite see eye to eye on this situation. I think we should *publicize* this serious problem, full bore. Lyle, here, wants to keep everything hushed up so as not to scare off business."

The happy sounds of two-dozen children chasing each other intersperse the conversation.

"Indeed, Pete," says Governor Miller. "I doubt that you, I mean Reno, have the means to combat this situation. I don't say that as a personal attack. It's just that the state can handle it better because we have so many more resources—including money. Why don't you declare an emergency, step back, and let the big boys handle it?"

General Arnold holds up a finger. "In other words, Pete, your number-one goal is to save as many citizens as possible."

Pete gives up a cautious nod.

Chief Hamper waves his arm at KB and Sherm. "Doctor Oakes. Miss Bjørnsen. Please be so good as to step over here. I want to introduce you to the governor and the generals. Chief Hamper gestures an open hand at KB and Sherm. These are the two scientists *Pete* invited down."

"Now, Lyle," whispers Belle Starr. "Don't say anything you're gonna regret later."

"My golly, petkins, I'm simply following Emily Post's rules of etiquette."

Belle Starr throws him a doubtful look. "And, Lyle, why is it you got *five* stars on your shoulder, while these two generals only get a couple?"

Chief Hamper's face pinches together. "That was . . . is . . ."

A sudden flurry of horn honking erupts on North McCarran Boulevard.

Chief Hamper makes a display of graciously introducing the two scientists.

Sherm wears his white straw hat and KB her Newport baseball cap. Sherm carries his backpack. KB shoulders her purse—the one containing her flask—and holds Heidi in her arms.

"Oh, my God," mumbles Howlin' Mad around his cigar.

"What'd you expect, General?" asks Pete. "Two lab rats wearing starched white coats?"

Hiding her smile behind her hand, Belle Starr takes a drag off her cigarette.

"How do you do, Doctor Oakes and Miss Bjørnsen?" Governor Miller bends down even with Heidi dog. "And, who's this little cutie?"

"This is Heidi, Governor Miller," says KB.

"Would you like to meet Abby, little Heidi?" asks the governor.

KB sets Heidi down and the two dogs circle and sniff, sniff and circle.

Pete gestures toward the jam-packed traffic. "I admit, General Clark, that we have a worsening situation here. Moreover, I agree with *you*, Bob. We absolutely can't operate like the government did after the hurricane hit New Orleans. We need to save *all* our citizens. We don't have the marine expertise here in Reno; we *had* to go afield."

Heidi and Abby slip away from the group and trot toward the squealing children.

———————

"Daddy," says Nicole. "Like, tell 'em what Doctor Draper found."

"Thanks, kitten." Pete calls out, "Dan, please get your bones over here."

Doctor Dan Draper and his wife, Coretta, join the group. Pete introduces them.

Pete puts his arm around Doctor Draper's shoulder. "Please explain to the governor and generals, Dan, what you found in your lab this morning."

Abel saunters up to the growing group.

Doctor Draper explains how he has surmised that the specimen is the tail end of some unknown species of fish.

"Arrrbeedarrr," says Sherm. "Doc, you did the right thing calling me, that you did. If my assistant and I can't figure out what kind of fish that is, well then . . . it *ain't* no bloomin' fish."

A Latino trumpet duet soars through the conversation.

"It fish," Abel says. "Live in toilet water."

Pete introduces Abel.

"Detective," asks General Arnold, "did you actually see the specimen swimming in your toilet bowl?"

"It jus' tail, General," says Abel. "I cut off. Whole fish maybe meter long."

"That's right, Nate," Pete says, "and I guess you know my mother was gutted out at the rehab hospital last night, by what we think was the same species of creature."

Pete hears Nicole sob. He turns toward her; however, Brad already has his arms around her.

"Frankly, gentlemen," says Chief Hamper, "we don't *know* that it was the same creature. Your mother, bless her soul, was mutilated. Denise wasn't—"

"What you mean, Chief?" asks Abel. "Denise in shock. She go to hospital in ambulance. She may have—"

"Honey," says Denise. "Take it easy. Watch your blood pressure. You're no spring chicken, you know. Here, have a sip of punch."

Abel drops his arm around Denise's shoulders and pulls her tight.

"*Doctor* Oakes"—Howlin' Mad blows a cloud of cigar smoke—"what the hell do *you* possibly think you can do for the people of Reno?"

"Ahum, General Clark," says Sherm. "You wouldn't be judging my abilities by the criteria of my rather unorthodox appearance . . . would you?"

Howlin' Mad spreads his legs and crams his fists on his hips. "Now that you bring it up, *Doctor*, you've got the look of an overaged peacenik."

Sherm develops a barely perceptible grin. "Alas, General Clark, I'm not a medical doctor. I merely have a PhD in marine biology. Therefore, I'm never referred to simply as . . . Doctor."

KB glances up at Sherm with glowing admiration.

"Now, you listen up, Oakes." Spit bubbles around Howlin' Mad's cigar. "Don't you lecture . . ."

Sherm steps up nose-to-nose and quietly speaks. "You listen to me, General. I deduct from your artless and coarse manner that you've advanced through your ranks by manifesting brutish and uncompromising behavior. Furthermore, I suppose I've more education in my little finger than you have in your entire monumental body. How'm I doin', General? Pretty close?"

Howlin' Mad yanks the cigar from his lips and shakes the

soaked end. "You people—livin' on welfare, wearing peace signs and smokin' pot—while the rest of us defend your country. Why, I've broken men in two that would've made *ten* of you."

KB places her hand on Sherm's shoulder.

Sherm pats KB's hand, smiles at her, and then gently removes it.

"Aye, General, I'll bet you've jammed your heel into the backs of many a good man on your climb through the ranks. You're a perfect example of that old saying: If you can't be a *thoroughbred*, you can always be an *ass*."

Pete looks at Nicole and shakes his head. "A crisis always brings out the best in some people, and the *worst* in others."

Governor Miller lays his hands on Sherm's and Howlin' Mad's shoulders. "Now, gentlemen, we're under a lot of stress here. If this situation deteriorates further, we'll have an awful lot to do, and we *must* work together."

Sherm nods. "Aye, Governor. Whataya say, General Clark? Do ya want to start over?"

Howlin' Mad is now busy, attempting to relight his cigar.

"Just give me the word, Pete," says Governor Miller, "and I'll call in the Feds."

"By heck, you can't do that. I mean"—Chief Hamper pats the air in front of him— "sorry, Governor, the problem isn't that big and we don't want to kill the goose who lays the golden egg. To tell the truth, Governor Miller, the casinos are the *lifeblood* of this state. Without them we'd all be paying a *lot* more in taxes. Boy oh boy, I think Pete and his liberal constituents need to realize what side their bread is buttered on."

"Dammit, Lyle," says Pete, "you have your nose so far up their collective fat-cat asses you couldn't tell the butter from the—"

"All right, *Lodge Brother*," says Chief Hamper, "why can't we just have a civil conversation? I didn't come here to—"

"You're right, Lyle, I'm sorry I got a little salty there. Nevertheless, I simply cannot go against my voting base on this subject. They'd crucify me."

Chief Hamper opens his hands. "Frankly, you'd be so much better off, Pete, if you *helped* the local businesses. In return, they'd help *you*. To be quite honest, Governor, forgive me for being so forward, you could take a lesson here as well. If the casinos do well, the whole state does—"

"That goddamned goose *owns* your ass, Lyle." Pete glares at Chief Hamper. "They say, 'kiss it' and you shove your nose right up through their butt feathers. You collect votes from the have-nots while ass kissing the 'have-mores.'"

"Now, see here *Brother* Pete—"

"Your motto is the motto of *all* your breed"—Pete waves his hand—"I got mine, *fuck* you."

"By *heck*, Pete—"

"Excuse me, ladies," Pete says, waving his hands. "I don't usually talk that way."

Belle Starr guffaws.

"Gosh darn, Pete, from the bottom of my soul—"

"Is that the soul of your heart, Lyle, or the sole of your well-heeled shoe?"

"Atta boy, Pete," hollers Denise. "Here, let's have another swallow. KB, do you—oh—you brought your own."

"Pete," says Chief Hamper, "that was totally uncalled for."

Pete swipes his finger underneath Chief Hamper's nose. "It's the warmed over ol' trickle-down theory, huh, Lyle? Dole out a tidal wave big-tax-cut to the rich and perhaps a droplet trickles down to the working class."

"Oh, my heck, Pete," says Chief Hamper. "Frankly, I don't see where it would harm Reno to put up some more roadside signs. Reno isn't like a regular city; its main source of commerce is gaming."

"For chrissake, Lyle, haven't you figured it out yet? If you

place all your eggs in one basket, you're headed for an eco-
nomic train wreck. Pardon the mixed metaphor, but Reno's
future depends on us finding some nonpolluting businesses to
move into our area. Reno, and for that matter the whole state
of Nevada provides legalized gaming, that's a fact—but more
importantly—they also provide favorable breaks for business.
We should capitalize—"

"You don't say. I realize the necessity for extending our
hand to other types of businesses, Pete, you bet I do, but we
absolutely cannot abandon what is currently the lifeblood of
the city. We're here as their servants to—"

Governor Miller shakes his head. "*Gentlemen.*"

"For crapsake, Lyle, I've no *intention* of abandoning the
goose that lays the golden egg. I simply can't side with the
forces who want to place more signs within the city limits.
Open your goddamn eyes, Lyle. There are miles of freeway
aimed at Reno from all four directions. The casinos are free to
put their big ass feckin' signs in Washoe County until it blocks
the very goddamn sun. Their advertising ability won't—"

Abel places his arm around Pete's shoulder. "Easy, *amigo.*
Remember blood pressure. You no springy chicken, you know."

Pete pulls a cigar from his pocket and lights up.

"Here, Pete," says Denise, "you need a recharge." She pulls
the flask from her purse and pours a generous splash into
Pete's glass. "How 'bout you, Governor Miller, you ready for a
man's drink?"

Governor Miller laughs uproariously. "Indeed, Denise,
you're some kind of woman. It's a genuine pleasure to meet
you." He holds up his hands. "You bet I'll have a drink with
you. But, if it's okay, I'll do the mixing myself."

Sherm laughs.

"Pete." Abel points. "Look at car. Is that . . .?"

Pete feels himself calming down. "Yes, that's the Rolls limo we saw next to—"

"Lyle, don't you let that highfalutin Mister Mayor, there, get away with that." Councilwoman Mandy Cockburn elbows herself into the group's middle.

Pete whispers from behind his hand. "Denise, did you invite that Kewpie doll?"

"Kewpie doll?"

"Yes"—Pete nods toward Councilwoman Cockburn—"that overpainted Barbie doll."

Denise laughs. "You can take it from me, Pete—that skank is no *doll*."

Pete turns toward the councilwoman. "And to what do we owe the dubious pleasure of your visit, Miss Cockburn?"

Councilwoman Cockburn stretches to her full short height. "This is my district, Mister Mayor. I saw the helicopter. I—"

"And you just couldn't keep your nose out of it, huh, councilwoman?"

Councilwoman Cockburn glances at the governor, the generals, and other guests.

Belle Starr hits Chief Hamper in the arm. Chief Hamper clears his throat and introduces her.

"Chief," Councilwoman Cockburn says, "you *care* about your citizens, tell 'em ."

Pete holds up his hand. "Mandy, you and Lyle are cut out of the same hunk of rotting wood. You don't give a *damn* about your working-class citizens; all you care about are your big-moneyed, campaign-contributing cash cows." Pete glances toward the pink limousine. Three children and a Shih Tzu bound from the limo and roll on the lawn.

"That is totally, totally uncalled for," says Councilwoman Cockburn.

Pete nods and smiles. "But true."

Newlyweds Hunter and Dora Burns, and the rest of the wedding party, have edged up to the discussion group. The mariachi band is taking an unscheduled break and eases up behind the wedding party. Several dozen guests hold plates of food; the ones in the back stretch their necks to see.

General Arnold catches Pete's attention. "What's your plan of action, Pete?"

"First, Nate, we need to determine what kind of creatures are attacking our citizens."

General Arnold nods.

"When we know, then we must decide on how to neutralize them without harming our citizens, or the ecosystem."

"You're thinking you may have to use poison?" asks General Arnold.

"Quite possibly, Nate. At this point, we don't know how many there are. We don't know if they're a breeding colony or how far they've spread."

"I hear ya, Pete." Doctor Draper shrugs. "I'm storing that specimen in the refrigerator. It looks to me like it could be a fish—but I can't even detect scales on it, you know what I'm sayin'?"

"Arrr," Sherm says. "I hear you, Doc, and the mayor's correct. The first step is to determine which creature is maiming our citizens. I mean, is the specimen Abel brought in actually harmless, while the real culprit dwells undiscovered in the sewer pipes? Solving this question logically leads to the second step, which is to come up with a plan to preserve the citizens and environment, while at the same time *eliminating* the suckers."

Howlin' Mad yanks the cigar from his mouth. "That sounds like one hell of a good goddamn plan to me." He thrusts his ham of a hand toward Sherm. "Doctor Oakes, with all respect, let's start over."

Sherm grasps Howlin' Mad's hand and gives it a hearty shake. "Arrrbeedarrr. Yer a fine general, that you are. If this situation worsens, you and I will undoubtedly be working together. I welcome the confabulation."

Pete smiles and gives a nod.

Sherm now takes up a position in the eye of the storm. "Governor Miller, Generals, Mister Mayor," Sherm calls out loudly to the dignitaries present, while nodding to the others in the crowd. "For myself, I should *immediately* inspect that specimen in Doctor Draper's laboratory. Secondly, since every eyewitness account places these attacks at the toilet-seated inlets to the sewage system, I'd like to have my assistant, doctoral-candidate Miss Kristian Bjørnsen, hurry to the sewage treatment plant and see what she can discover there. I understand that the plant serves both Reno and Sparks."

"Excellent," Pete says. "Sherm, you go with Dan, *immediately*, and look that specimen over. Okay?"

Doctor Draper nods.

"Next, I'll call Milt Hershey, the director of the sewerage plant and set up an inspection tour of the Truckee Meadows sewerage system, for *you*, KB. Both the city of Sparks and Reno use the same facility."

"Yes," KB says, "I will inspect the screens, aeration and settling ponds for creatures and their eggs. In addition, I will search for any traces of their victims."

"Outta sight, Dad," Nicole says. "I was like, all worried. But I think you and the scientists have the problem totally, totally under control, you know what I mean?"

Pete nods. "Thanks, pussycat."

Nicole gives Pete a hug. "Me and my gang are like going waterskiing now. See you tomorrow night. I love you, Daddy."

"I love you too, precious." Pete pats Nicole's back. "See you tomorrow."

"I'll take good care of her, Mister Ferrari," Brad says.

"I'm sure you will, Brad. Just keep that ski boat under a hundred, okay?"

"Fer sure, Mister Ferrari," says a grinning Brad.

Pete turns toward the governor, the generals, and Chief

Hamper. "And one other thing." He gestures toward the slow-moving traffic. "I don't want to *mislead* our citizens, nonetheless, for their sakes I'd like us in authority to *assume a role of assurance.*"

Chief Hamper energetically nods. "By golly, that's exactly what I was saying, Pete. Frankly, we don't want to start a stampede—"

An *earsplitting shriek* erupts from the women's side of the public restroom.

"*No.*" A look of utter fear contorts Pete's face. "Not again. Not here. *Not now.*"

"¡*Por Dios!*" Abel slaps his hand over his heart.

Pete rips the cigar from his mouth and drops it in the little creek. He takes off running as fast as his feet will carry him.

Abel follows on his heels.

Halfway to the restroom, Pete notes a finely tailored older Chinese lady, helped along by a tall, enormously wide-shouldered manservant, hurrying to the same location.

Pete and Abel arrive first.

Melody bursts from the door pulling her pants up. She screams as loud as only a completely traumatized woman can scream. Pete and Abel glance at each other, then plunge inside the ladies' restroom.

A minute later Abel steps outside. In his paper-towel-wrapped hand he presents a dripping green plastic dinosaur.

Sparks
1:00 p.m., Saturday afternoon

The *black Lincoln Continental limousine* cruises toward Sparks on East Fourth Street. Its rear door boasts a graphic of Reno's famous arch proclaiming Reno as The Biggest Little City in the World.

Abel yawns. "Thank you, Pete, for getting me to drive." He takes a sip of coffee.

"You're welcome," says Pete. He and KB ride on the rear plush seat. Heidi lies between them. KB keeps her purse close by her side.

"Did Denise chew you out for showing up late," asks Pete, "needing a shave, and wearing a torn suit?"

Abel chuckles. "She feelin' no pain, Pete. Maybe later. I jus' glad to get away from chief."

Pete sips his coffee. Earlier, they had created a stir when the limo pulled through a coffee kiosk. In addition, KB had created a stir in the limousine when she splashed laboratory-grade alcohol into her cup.

KB pats Pete's arm. "Your wife sure did a first-class job picking out your tuxedo."

Pete rubs Heidi's head. "I don't have a wife."

"Interesting," says KB, smiling from ear to ear.

"Look." Abel sets his to-go cup in the dashboard holder. "Sparks patrol car sitting under city limits sign."

"Jumping Jiminy," says KB. "He just turned on his red lights. You have a big gangster car, Pete; let us make a run for it."

Pete bursts out laughing. "You're a wild young lady. I like you, KB. Nonetheless, Abel, you're *not* authorized to *make a run for it*."

For a long moment, KB gazes adoringly at Pete.

"Okay, boss, I not run for it. But look." Abel points. "He not pull us over. He pull *ahead*. And he turns on his siren."

"Well, I'll be a son of a bitch. We have an escort. Oh, excuse me, KB. I usually don't talk like that in front of ladies."

"That is okay, Pete. They are only words."

"Where he taking us?" asks Abel.

"As long as he's going in our direction, let's follow."

"He is speeding up real fast, boss."

"Let's see what this baby'll do. Stay with 'im, Abel."

"Turn on siren?"

"Ahhh, better not." Pete snickers. "You might pull our escort over."

Police siren caterwauling and the light bar flashing, the two automobiles speed down Victorian Avenue – right past John Ascuaga's Nugget, and the retired NCO steam engine, and the pumice-block restroom, where the Sparks mayor recently lost his life.

Abel laughs. "Hang on."

The two cars cut across the wide intersection at Pyramid Way and turn hard left onto East Nugget Avenue. "Won't be long now, KB," says Pete.

KB swigs her coffee. "By golly, this is fun, you bet you."

Abel turns the wheel to the right. "*Por cierto.*"

The two automobiles turn off the frontage road onto a gravel driveway. They churn up a cloud of dust. Two blocks ahead stands a pink concrete building. The structure's left wing sports a glass-brick window, giving the Sparks Sewer office a fifties look.

"We are lucky the director is here on a Saturday to give us a tour," says KB.

"Milton Hershey doesn't *have* much of a life, KB. He's pretty much on the job, all the time."

Abel laughs. "*Si*, since his ho-bag wife run off."

Pete clears his throat. "That is *very* unkind, Abel."

"Ho-bag?" asks KB.

Pete snickers. "Abel, could you please explain to KB what a ho-bag is?"

Abel laughs, while vigorously shaking his head—*No*.

Pete adjusts the air-conditioning knob. "It's a seamy drama, KB. Milt's wife was a schoolteacher out in Wadsworth. She was caught in the teacher's room having a close relationship with a student, a male student, and was fired. Afterward, she took up with a distressed fellow twenty-five years her junior and kicked Milt out of their spacious home." Pete points at an old house trailer. "Milt now resides in that singlewide next to the office."

KB giggles. "I think I know what ho-bag means now, Abel."
Abel laughs raucously.

"Does Mister Hershey have a lady friend," asks KB "or any pets, hobbies?"

Pete shakes his head. "Just the spiders he allows to live inside his trailer."

"Ugh. That is disgusting, that is for sure."

The Sparks police car parks in front of the pink building.

"Jumping Jiminy, why did Mister Hershey not stay in his fine house and throw his ho-bag wife out?"

Abel snorts, "Mouse *huevos*."

The Lincoln Continental limo slows, and the gravel makes a crunching sound under the mammoth tires.

"All right now," says Pete. "That's Milt's little white pickup truck, so he's here. He's an odd duck—"

"Yo," hollers Officer Cobb. "*Mister Mayor.*"

Pete drops his window.

Abel pushes the gear selector into park. "Hey, Crystal."

Officer Cobb bends down. "Oh. Hello, Detective."

"Crystal Cobb, she a pistol, Pete," says Abel.

Pete reaches for the door handle, but Officer Cobb quickly opens it for him. "Your office called ahead, Mister Mayor. Bruce Breslow, our acting mayor, ordered me and my NG, Bardouche, there, to escort you to the Sparks sewer ponds."

"Good old Juanita. Thank you, Crystal. I appreciate it. You can just call me Pete."

"Naw, I couldn't do that, sir."

Pete, KB, and Abel slide from the car's cool interior into the July heat. Pete notices that the storm clouds over the Sierra Nevada have grown darker.

Heidi bounds out and a heretofore-undetected black-and-white cat makes its escape toward the single-wide trailer house.

"You stay, Heidi," says KB. "That pussy cat will bloody your nose, that is for sure."

"And this," says Officer Cobb, "is my FNG, the incomparable Officer Reginald Bardouche."

Pete reaches in the car and grabs KB's coffee cup. He grins and hands it to her.

"Thank you, Pete. We are all in need of coffee, you bet. What is FNG?"

"Ah . . . let me put it this way, KB," says Pete. "It more or less stands for *new guy*."

KB wrinkles her brow.

From the office's front door, steps a lanky septuagenarian wearing a white shirt and white linen slacks. A fire-extinguisher-red bow tie and matching suspenders completes his ensemble. He sports a full gray beard and wears round gold-rimmed glasses.

"Jumping Jiminy," says KB. "He looks just like my chemistry professor from the university."

"Howdy, Pete," says Director Milton Hershey, "or, I mean, Mister Mayor. What're ya all dressed up for, and didn't ya have time to shave?"

"Just came from a wedding, and . . . no. Just call me, Pete, Milt—or are you trying to impress this beautiful young woman here?"

"Thank you very much, Mister Mayor." KB flashes her dazzling smile. "I was not sure you had noticed."

Pete shakes hands with Director Hershey and makes the introductions. To their backs traffic whizzes by on Interstate Eighty. To their front, an enormous three-unit diesel freight train departs Sparks Yard, heading east to Lovelock and on into the Great Basin Desert. Exhaust columns blast straight into the sky.

Director Hershey's prominent Adam's apple bobs up and down when he shakes hands with KB. "Watch yer dog there, KB. We wouldn't want 'er to fall in the sewer ponds." He waves his arm. "Come on. Follow me."

After a short walk through the dust, they stop in front of a set of weathered wooden stairs leading up the side of an earthen bank.

"Follow me, one at a time," says Director Hershey.

They tread up the steps. The old slats creak. At the top, Heidi darts ahead.

"Heidi," calls out KB. *"Get back here."*

Heidi hurries back to her mistress.

Director Hershey gestures. "This is pond number one." In the pond's middle a fountain creates a rainbow. Director Hershey faces the group. "Now tell me what're we lookin' for?"

Reno
1:10 p.m., Saturday afternoon

"I'll start the coffee," says Coretta. "It appears none of us got any sleep last night."

Doctor Draper skims his hand down the wall. Banks of overhead lights blink on. He yawns and tosses his suit coat on the autopsy room's coat tree.

"This is it, Sherm," calls Coretta from the office. "Welcome to 'Dan's Dungeon.'"

"Arrr, the underground secret dungeon where the mad doctor performs his arcane research."

"Be cool now, Sherm." Doctor Draper laughs. "Y'all rile me up and I'll surgically turn you into a *real* fish doctor."

"In furtherance of thought," says Sherm. "I shall desist from questionable observations of the good doctor's noble endeavors." Sherm spots the medical doctor's degree from the University of Alabama framed and hanging on the wall. He points. "Arrr. So, you're a bona fide doctor, Doctor Dan. I shall henceforth treat you with the dignity that you have earned."

Doctor Draper peers at Sherm through half-closed eyelids.

The trio had just arrived at police headquarters on East Second Street in Doctor Draper's black *Cadillac Escalade SUV*.

On the way, Coretta had asked Sherm about KB. He'd

131

explained that while KB was bright, she was also clinically depressed—and had probably been so all her life. She also experiences low self-esteem and all that goes with it.

Doctor Draper had asked if Sherm knew the cause of KB's depression. Sherm told them that KB was sexually molested by her maternal grandfather, over and over again. KB felt betrayed by her mother for not protecting her. Her father was mostly absent. Because the mother had repeatedly told KB that she was no good and would never amount to anything, KB feared success and made certain she didn't quite achieve it.

Sherm had observed that KB was unsure of her abilities, impulsive, and romantically attracted to older men.

Doctor Draper rolls up his sleeves and walks to the stainless-steel refrigerator doors.

Sherm glances at the dozen sheet-covered gurneys parked at the room's far end. They create their own gruesome gridlock.

Doctor Draper pulls his reading glasses from his shirt pocket and perches them on his nose. He slides the drawer open. It contains a flat tray the size a restaurant uses to bake scalloped potatoes. A soaked towel lies over a lump that could've been a summer squash.

Sherm hears the coffee pot in Doctor Draper's office perking.

Doctor Draper places the tray on the end of the closest autopsy table. Sherm and Coretta gather around. The overhead lights brighten the table. Sherm leans forward, pressing his abdomen against the table's edge.

Dramatic as a Reno Hilton magician, Doctor Draper draws the towel's end toward him. A brownish-colored smooth-skinned tapered tube appears.

Sherm pulls off his hat and glances around.

Coretta reaches out and takes it. "Arrrbeedarrr, yer a fine lass, Coretta, that yee are."

Sherm bends his face down close to the specimen. He pokes the exposed flesh with his finger.

"Want some latex gloves?" asks Doctor Draper

"Uh hum. No, Dan. Thanks." Sherm holds the specimen with one hand and brushes his fingers up and down its side with the other. "Ahhh. It seems fishlike, but I feel no scales."

"I hear ya," says Doctor Draper. "I kinda had the same experience. Check out the tail."

"Uh-huh." Sherm sticks his fingernail under a fold and lifts. "Hullo. Check it out." It unfolds like a fan. "That is most definitely Mister Fish's tailfin."

"Sure enough," says Doctor Draper. "So, what do we do now?"

Sherm straightens. "Aaargh. I'm confuzzled, Dan. It's a kind of fish, a member of the Vertebrata phyla, of that I'm certain. Nonetheless, with all my background in marine biology I simply don't recognize the species, genus, or even the family."

"I'm afraid I can't be of much help to you either, Sherm," says Coretta. "I didn't retain much from my high school biology class. But, just let me get that piece of meat into my kitchen and before you've enjoyed your first cocktail, I will have cooked that sucker up for you."

Doctor Draper laughs. "There ya go, honey." He puts his arm around Coretta's waist. "And she sure enough would do it, Sherm, and with all the fixins."

Sherm grins. "Aye, maybe when we retire this specimen ..."

"Uh-huh, perhaps. Now, if you two can get your mind off the fish and chips, ya need to get back to work. Sherm, if *you* can't figure out what this is, we're up that creek without a paddle."

"And, you better remember, honey," Coretta says, "not to hang your butt over the side of that boat without a paddle."

Sherm grabs his rear and dances a jig.

Doctor Draper cracks up.

"Aye, you're a fine one, Coretta, that you are," Sherm says. "On a more immediate note, Dan, I felt the spine where Abel cut it. It's not bony—it's cartilaginous. Therefore, this creature is *not* in the class Osteichthyes. However, since we only have the tail end, I can't tell whether it's in the class Agnatha—fishes without jaws—or Gnathostomata—fishes with hinged jaws."

"I hear ya, Sherm. Like I said, if this is as far as we can go, we're up that *shit* creek without a paddle, you know what I'm sayin'?"

"Correctamundo, my friend, I sure *do* know what you're saying. And, if that weren't enough, try this one on for size: As I understand the story, Detective Sanchez's wife wasn't even physically *harmed* by this creature."

"Sure enough, Sherm. The chances are better than good that this strange creature is not even the one eviscerating our citizens."

"If what I *suspect* is correct," says Sherm, "I do know of an expert who could possibly help."

"How long would it take for your expert to get with us?" asks Doctor Draper.

Sherm glances at his watch. "Oh, say, 'bout fifteen minutes."

Coretta and Doctor Draper, wide-eyed, look at each other.

"It's KB," says Sherm. "She did her undergraduate work at the University of Århus in Denmark. They're the world's leading experts on certain kinds of little-known, deep-dwelling fishes."

"Yeah?" says Doctor Draper. "Let's hustle KB over here; that is, if we can talk her into abandoning her breathtaking tour at the sewer ponds."

Sparks
1:25 p.m., Saturday afternoon

"Milt," Pete says, "we're not sure what we're looking for. KB's a marine biologist. She simply wants to nose around and see if she can discover anything that might lead to the creature that's evidently inhabiting *your* sewer pipes."

"Yep," says Director Hershey. "If we don't find anything in the settling ponds, maybe we wanta explore under the streets in the storm drains, or maybe in the sewer's main trunk line."

Pete squints at Director Hershey. "I know I look a little scruffy, Milt, but there's *no way in Hell* that I'm crawling around underneath the city in a storm drain. What about you, Crystal?"

Officer Cobb plants her fists on her hips. "Only if I can order Officer Bardouche ahead of me to shoo the fricking rats out of the way. How 'bout you, KB?"

KB snorts. "By golly, crawling in a dark smelly sewer pipe is definitely not what I had in mind when I elected to study our beautiful oceans."

Officer Cobb chuckles.

"Let's continue our tour," says Director Hershey. "We think it's better if I go first. Officer Bardouche, why don't you bring up the rear and make sure we don't lose anybody."

The troop begins to file around the levee's top.

"Heidi, you stay near me," KB says. "Reggie, please help me keep an eye on her."

Officer Bardouche grins and gives KB the *okay* sign.

Director Hershey halts. "Now, everybody, when we cross from one pool to the next be very careful walking on these old wooden planks. No more than two people at a time. Soon, we'll move our operation out to the state-of-the-art facility at Vista. We're no longer *maintaining* this facility."

Director Hershey starts across the parallel boards. They sag and squeak.

Pete follows.

"Better watch it there, Mister Mayor," shouts Officer Cobb. "If that board gives way, you're going to get yourself a surprise bath."

"I could use a bath." Pete glances at the ditch fifteen feet below and grimaces.

Officer Cobb advances next.

"Come on, little Heidi," KB coaxes. "Stay by me."

Out in the middle, Officer Cobb abruptly freezes on her plank.

Pete slowly turns and asks quietly. "What's the matter, Crystal?"

Officer Cobb mashes her lips.

"Is it too far up for you?"

Officer Cobb imperceptibly nods.

KB picks up Heidi.

Pete shuffles back to the middle. When he reaches Officer Cobb, he gently grasps her arm and slowly guides her off the boards.

Safely on the far bank Pete gives Officer Cobb a pat on the shoulder. "I was kind of scared myself, Crystal. Those planks are bouncy; not to mention that they're *way up* in the air."

"Oh, that's so silly of me, sir," says Officer Cobb. "I'm not usually afraid of heights, and"—she shakes her finger at Officer Bardouche—"and, don't you say a word, Reggie, if you wanta good report."

Pete bursts out laughing.

"You say you're going to level this joint, Mister Hershey," says Officer Cobb. "*Can't be too soon.*"

"Now, Officer," Director Hershey says. "Where would this city be without its efficiently functioning sewer system?"

"Yeah, I know," says Officer Cobb. "We'd be knee deep in—"

"*Effluent?*" suggests Director Hershey.

Officer Bardouche grins.

"Well, come on gang," says Director Hershey. "We have many miles to trudge before we sleep."

"Yeah," says Officer Cobb. "We shall trudge through the sludge and hope we don't fall in the deep."

Pete laughs heartily.

Little Heidi picks her way onto the board. She resembles a newborn calf trying to walk on a trampoline.

KB shuffles to the middle.

Officer Bardouche brings up the rear.

"Oh, this is springy." KB bounces the planks up and down. Heidi makes a run to the far side and hops off.

"Be careful there, KB," hollers Director Hershey. "We wouldn't want to fall in."

KB slips. She catches herself on one knee.

Without hesitation Officer Bardouche shuffles out and grasps her shoulders. "Please be careful, Miss Bjørnsen. You can't trust these old boards."

The troop continues to walk around pool number two's dusty rim.

Pete looks ahead over the next set of weathered planks. They lead to the third pond. He catches Officer Cobb's eye and gives her a shrug. With her fingers and thumb, Officer Cobb gives him an Okay sign.

KB squints at the morning sun. She pulls the bill of her cap down. "Heidi, I cannot see a thing with the sun reflecting in my eyes."

When Director Hershey reaches the third set of boards, he holds up. "All right, KB. Have ya seen anything of interest yet? Do ya wanta get closer to the water's surface?"

"I would dearly love to know what is living in that skanky liquid, but I do not see what we can gain by crawling and slipping down the dirt sides." KB shrugs. "We need to see into the water with an underwater window or use a net—something like that."

"I agree, KB," says Pete. "It would simply be *too* fortuitous to catch a glimpse of the creature lollygagging on the surface."

"Yeah," Abel says, "unless it *alligator*."

Pete snorts.

A mile away sirens sound. Flashing red lights ascend a hill to the northeast.

"That's Sparks Family Hospital, KB," Director Hershey says. "Another victim going in. Shall we finish our tour?"

Pete follows Director Hershey to the boards leading to the third pond. Resembling a diving board, these boards hang over pond number three. Twenty seconds later, on the other side, Director Hershey and Pete step off. Pete turns to watch Officer Cobb.

Reno
1:30 p.m., Saturday afternoon

"We break into this program," says television announcer John Tyson, standing in front of the Reno police headquarters building on East Second Street, "to show you the seriousness of Reno and Sparks' sewer problem."

Tyson gestures with his thumb. "Behind me you see portable toilets being delivered for the use of Reno police personnel."

Reno's television screens show a low trailer featuring JOHNNY ON THE SPOT imprinted on its side. It's backed into the police employee's parking lot.

"These units were the last available transportable toilets in the Truckee Meadows. We also checked with Sani-Hut, Shamrock, and Nev/Cal Porta-Potties. There are no more available."

Behind Tyson, the trailer's ramp drops to the parking lot. Two coverall-clad men inch the green fiberglass units to the asphalt.

"Earlier today," Tyson says, "we did a piece on the early-morning rush to buy up all the portable camping toilets. The last of the supplies sold out three hours ago from the area's RV, camping, and marine supply stores."

Behind Tyson the first two portable toilets sit on the pavement. The camera moves in closer.

"We've not been successful yet, in getting an interview with the mayor or the chief of police. Nevertheless, it's this investigative reporter's view that the city is fast approaching a panic situation. A vicious creature is attacking our citizens when they sit on their toilets.

"And even though the authorities have *not* found it necessary to make a formal announcement, most of Truckee Meadow's citizens know that—*something fishy's going on.*"

The camera moves in closer still.

"All I can say is: Take care of *yourselves.* We don't know what we're up against. We do not, at this point, know what the authorities are planning to do about it. It's best to figure that you are on your own.

"What we *do* know is that several dozen citizens, mostly from the low-lying regions of town near the river, have been rushed to emergency rooms at Saint Mary's, Washoe Med, Northern Nevada Medical Center, and the Veterans Administration Medical Center on Locust Street.

Even more mysteriously, while some unfortunate citizens have been eviscerated, other victims have apparently not been hurt at all.

"This is John Tyson, News Channel Eight, reporting from the Reno police headquarters' building."

***

Sparks
1:45 p.m., Saturday afternoon

Pete and Director Hershey mosey to the berm's edge and stare into pond number three. Officer Cobb walks up behind them, then Abel.

KB sets Heidi down. "Go ahead, Heidi. Go across."

Heidi dashes across the boards and immediately begins sniffing the weeds growing around the third pond. When KB approaches the far end, Officer Bardouche starts off.

Rather than stepping off, KB edges closer to the plank's end—out over the liquid discharge.

Director Hershey hollers. "Be careful there, young lady. We

understand those planks resemble a diving board but that's one pond you don't wanta do a swan dive into."

KB waves at Director Hershey. "I am an Olympic gold medal diver, you bet you." She slides her feet farther out on the planks. She squints into the pond. Behind her, Officer Bardouche continues across.

KB inches closer to the end.

Officer Bardouche shuffles past the halfway point.

KB stands on her toes. "Uncle Milty," shouts KB. She springs up and down on the board. "Look. I'm bouncing on an Olympic diving board."

Officer Bardouche reaches the earth rim and prepares to step off.

"Douche bag," yells Officer Cobb. "Don't you dare—"

Officer Bardouche steps off the board—the weight on the fulcrum shifts—and he quizzically looks at Officer Cobb.

"*Help!*" KB shrieks.

KB, her purse, coffee cup, baseball cap, pair of flip-flops and the two bouncy planks, plummet toward the stinking swill. KB smacks the water hard, and sinks. Expanding rings locate the spot where she went under. Her purse lies in the water's edge. Her flask has slid out.

Heidi barks and jumps up and down on the dirt rim.

"Stay, Heidi," commands Pete. He slides down the bank. His left foot slips out of his black patent-leather dress shoe.

Abel begins a pebble-rattling slide down the bank, brown wingtip dress shoes stirring up a dust storm.

KB surfaces. "Ugh." She spits. "This stuff *stinks*."

Director Hershey starts down the bank.

"You ain't shittin', KB," Pete says. "That stuff stinks."

Abel grasps Pete by the arm. Pete kicks off his remaining shoe. It falls in the pond.

"Hey, KB," hollers Pete. "*Don't make a wave.*"

Abel shakes his head. "Pete. You sick sonofagun."

Director Hershey slides to a stop at the shoreline.

"Yes, Pete." KB rubs her eyes with her knuckles. "You are a sick son of a gun."

Pete bursts out laughing.

Up on the rim, Officer Cobb picks up the straining terrier.

Pete hunkers by the fluid's edge. "Can you get close enough to grab my hand?" He stretches his hand out.

"The bottom is so slippery," says KB.

Pete reaches out farther. Abel and Director Hershey now steady him.

KB shrieks.

The pond's surface erupts in a swirling splashing melee. KB beats the water with her hands. She screams. *"Something is in here with me."*

Pete's mouth falls open.

KB flails in the water, as if she can't decide whether to fend off attackers or make a lunge for shore.

"Ow." KB screeches. *"It bit me."*

Little Heidi struggles as Officer Cobb grips her with both hands. "Hang on there, Heidi." She yells, "Bardouche, do something."

Officer Bardouche reaches for his service revolver.

"No," screams Officer Cobb.

"They are after me," shrieks KB. "Help me."

Pete steps into the liquid sewerage. His black stockinged feet slip on the slimy bottom. "Son of a . . ." He falls and slips under.

KB shrieks. *"Get me out of here."* Her frantically splashing arms appear to be an attempt to prevent something, or things, from attacking her in the crotch area.

Pete surfaces. He seizes KB's arm. KB's baseball cap and Pete's shoe float nearby. The coffee cup has disappeared. Pete lunges, attempting to pull KB to shore. Her feet keep slipping. Pete thrusts his hand toward shore.

Without hesitation, Abel places his right foot in the sewage. With a strong grip he grapples on to Pete's flailing hand.

"Hurry," KB screeches. *"They are taking mouthfuls."*

Director Hershey throws a bear hug around Abel's waist. The two of them labor to drag Pete and KB onto the bank.

The soupy sewer water continues to churn where KB was standing as if something still senses her presence.

Pete lies panting in the shore-side weeds. Then he props himself up. He stares at KB. His eyes grow wide. "Holy shit, KB." Pete points. "Look. From your waist to your knees, you're covered in . . . *goo.*"

KB shoves herself to a sitting position. Her abdomen and thighs appear as if someone has dumped a case of clear-colored apple jelly on them. Bits of grass and rabbit brush pepper the slime.

"And look," Pete says. "You have bloody bite marks next to your shorts."

A white-and-brown bundle, stirring up a mini dust cloud, charges down the bank.

"Oh, Heidi," says KB. She labors to scoop up her dog.

Heidi sniffs the goopy mixture, then she growls at it.

"Come on, Heidi," KB says. "Get away from that . . . *stuff.*"

"Here, KB," says Pete. "I'll help you up the bank. Let's get those wounds attended to."

Abel grasps KB's other arm. They struggle to the top. Abel's wet shoe gathers a layer of dust.

"A lot's happened in the last couple of minutes, KB," Pete says. "Do you have any idea what kind of creatures you've encountered?"

KB shudders.

"Never mind," Pete says. "Let's take 'er slow and easy."

"Believe me," says Director Hershey, "this isn't the first time we've fallen in. We're equipped here for just such a mishap."

KB glances at Abel's right pants leg. It bears a green cast. Then, she checks out Pete's feet. "Pete. What happened to your shoes?"

Pete jerks his head toward the still churning water. "I sacrificed one of them, as a diversionary tactic."

KB glances at Pete with a puzzled look. The trio arrive at the bank's top.

Officer Cobb throws her arms around KB.

"Oh, Crystal," KB says. "You are going to get your uniform all slimed up."

"Not to worry," says Officer Cobb. "Are you all right?"

"While we're showering up," says Director Hershey, "we'll wash and dry your clothes. And let's get some first aid on those wounds, KB. We think you should probably get professional medical attention on them. No tellin' what you mighta picked up in there."

"Yes, KB," says Officer Cobb. "I suggest you take Mister Hershey up on his offer. You're bleeding and, you don't smell very good either."

KB bursts out laughing.

"Yeah," says Pete. "I'm worried for you, KB. Let's get you cleaned up, patched up, and have a doctor check out those wounds."

KB hugs Heidi and nods.

Pete glances down at his tuxedo. "Abel, do you think our suits should maybe go to the cleaners?"

"They'll probably demand you burn 'em," offers Officer Cobb.

Pete laughs heartily. "Do you have anything here we can wear?"

"And *you* don't smell very good either, Mister Mayor," observes Officer Cobb.

Pete pats her on the shoulder. He glances at the pond and sees that his shoe has sunk. The other one still lies in the brush. KB's Newport baseball cap slowly circles, as if moving by something coiling and uncoiling beneath it.

"There's no way, KB," Pete says, "no matter how much you value your precious cap that I'm going back in after it."

"And even if you were successful, Pete," says KB, "there is no way that I would place it on my head."

Reno
3:00 p.m., Saturday afternoon

Doctor Draper calls Pete and asks him to rush KB to the autopsy room, ASAP.

Earlier, Director Hershey had directed KB to a deep sink where she'd given Heidi her bath. Then, KB showered, and Officer Cobb had bandaged her bite marks.

KB dresses in her freshly laundered T-shirt and cutoffs, while Pete opens his limo's trunk and retrieves a brand-new baseball cap from a box. Then he presents KB with her brand new "*The Biggest Little City in the World*" baseball cap, featuring Reno's famous arch.

Pete and Abel stuff their tuxedo and double-breasted suit into a sack. Following their showers, they each don Reno/Sparks Water Department white coveralls and hurry back to the Reno police station.

They still haven't shaved.

Little Heidi trots down the police station ground-floor hallway. She hears her toenails clicking on the polished linoleum. She is thirsty. Thunder cracks and rumbles over the mountains, making her shake. She needs a nap.

The mistress now wears different flip-flops.

The old human who lives at the sewer-smelling place gave the flip-flops to KB. They formerly belonged to a man; they are too big and slap the floor. They have a strong rubbery smell. Heidi blows a puff of air from her nose to clear her nasal passages.

Heidi's tongue hangs out. All that dust at the human-excrement plant has dried her mouth. The mistress had offered her a drink from the cat's water bowl. But Heidi wasn't having that. Everyone knows that she prefers refreshing, cool, new water—directly from the toilet bowl.

Heidi's nose wrinkles from the smell of the cleaning fluid and floor wax. She sniffs. She detects a restroom ahead. She realizes that if she needs to make a quick getaway, it will be hard to get traction on the polished floor.

The humans hold up.

Heidi sniffs. She watches them talking and waving their arms.

Stealthily, Heidi takes a few steps down the hall.

"Oh, what a cute little doggie," says a passing parole officer.

Heidi freezes, then hangs her head. She endures the comments about how utterly adorable she is.

Ordinarily, Heidi thrives on this kind of attention. She recognizes the often heard and drawn-out story about how she'd been the mistress's constant companion since the mistress was nineteen, and on and on and . . . on.

The parole officer bends down to pat Heidi's head. Heidi releases a quiet little growl.

The parole officer jerks her hand back.

Humans animatedly talk, point, and wave their arms. Heidi remembers how humans claim that dogs are stupid because they occasionally bark a little. On the other hand, humans couldn't talk if their arms weren't flapping like a buzzard's wings.

Nonchalantly, Heidi tries strolling down the hall. After gaining a little distance, she trots. She hears her toenails tapping on the linoleum. She wills that her mistress won't look up and see her.

Heidi sniffs. The water source is now close.

A door just ahead of them swings open. A set of human feminine legs swish by Heidi's nose.

This is it.

Quickly, before the door closes—her feet slipping on the smooth surface—Heidi skids around the door's end and into the ladies' bathroom. Heidi's feet form a blur as she rushes past the garbage can. She peeks under the first door.

A pair of ankles are sitting in there.

Heidi checks the second stall. No ankles. Under the door she scampers.

Heidi prefers *public* facilities: there is never a lid stopping you from getting your tongue into the water. In addition, she desires the ladies' bathroom to the men's; the porcelain rim is not as sticky.

Heidi rears up on her back legs. She drapes her front feet over the rim. Her dog tags scrape over the porcelain. Heidi sniffs. The water smells acceptable. She stretches her neck until her muzzle just clears the water.

Heidi laps the water. It refreshes her dry throat.

She sees movement. Heidi jerks her head back. She barks.

Heidi sees a long brown thing. She doesn't remember seeing it before. She moves her head back and forth attempting to see below the water's surface, but the overhead fluorescent lights create too much surface glare.

All at once, Heidi sees it. It waves stubby little fingers around the gaping mouth hole. She can't help herself and cuts loose with a furious yapping.

She quits barking. Nothing happens. Everything seems calm. Heidi again stretches her neck nearer the water. She moves her head to and fro.

Heidi makes out a large hole in the beast's upper end, surrounded by short waving fingers. The hole is enlarging. It can't be the head end; there are no eyes.

The brown tube abruptly thrusts upward.

Heidi yelps.

The thing splashes water as it breaks the surface.

Only Heidi's lightning-quick reaction averts the creature's

attempt to make a meal of her face. Heidi flings her head back and drops to the floor. She discharges a ferocious barrage of barking.

The woman in the first stall jumps to her feet and yanks up her pants.

The entrance door bangs against the wall. The mistress calls out. "*Heidi.* Are you in here?"

Now, Heidi growls with a purpose.

"By golly. There you are, Heidi. What is going on in here?"

Heidi barks at the toilet bowl.

The mistress peers in.

The mistress shrieks.

The woman in the third stall rushes out, pushing her skirt down.

"Pete," KB shouts. "Abel, get in here."

The two men charge into the bathroom—bumping into the woman adjusting her skirt.

"Sorry."

They crowd into the stall behind the mistress. Heidi presses against the wall.

Heidi cannot quit barking. She knows the creature in the toilet is the same kind of ogre that slimed her mistress.

A splash sounds from the toilet bowl. Heidi places her front paws on the rim. She peeks in. Rings expand in the water—but the creature has disappeared.

Heidi hears her mistress and the two men talking.

"Jumping Jiminy, did you see that?"

"I no get good look."

"Holy feckin' shit that is one ugly bastard. Sorry, I don't usually talk that way."

Chapter Five

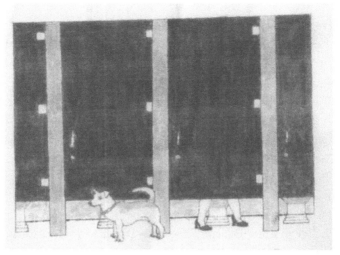

Heidi dog at Ladies' Bathroom, Reno PD

Reno
3:10 p.m., Saturday afternoon

Pete walks with KB and Abel to the police department ground-floor elevator.

From there, KB and Abel descend to the basement and the Washoe County coroner's office.

Pete ascends to the top floor and Chief Hamper's spacious office. Still wearing the water department's white coveralls and thrift store elephant-ear-sized flip-flops, Pete enters Chief Hamper's office. He glances at the moray eels.

"Chief, I'm here to bury the hatchet. There's just too much . . . going on . . . to . . ." Chief Hamper is hunched over in his leather chair.

Goddamn, the dumb shit's gone and shot himself. "Lyle."

Pete flies across the room and around the desk. He kneels down. "What's the matter? What happened?"

Pete sees Chief Hamper blink. Pete waves his hand in front of the chief's face.

"*Lyle.*" Pete lays his hand on Chief Hamper's knee. "Talk to me."

Chief Hamper's voice rasps, "My wife. Belle. They got 'er."

Pete pats Chief Hamper's knee. "*Who* got her, Lyle?"

"The fish," says Chief Hamper. "The sewer fish."

"Jesus Christ, Lyle." *Didn't he warn her?* "How bad is it?" Pete clears his throat. "I mean. Is she going to be okay?"

Chief Hamper bears red-rimmed eyes. "No, Brother Pete, she's *not*"—his voice breaks—"going to be okay."

Pete fights the urge to break eye contact.

The desk telephone rings. Pete touches the response button.

"Hi there, Lyle," says the telephone's tiny speaker. "This is Tad down at Channel—"

"Mister Dunbar," says Pete. "This is Pete, I mean, Mayor Ferrari. The chief can't—"

"Yeah, Pete, how are ya? I need—"

"The chief can't come to the phone. I'll tell 'im you called." Pete pushes the button.

Chief Hamper stares at the carpet.

Pete talks softly. "How did it happen, Lyle?"

Chief Hamper manages to glance up. "I'd just fed the eels, the ones at home. I was getting ready to play my harp and wondered if Belle cared to listen."

"Then what happened?"

"I called her name. Not getting a response, I went looking for her."

"Where was she?"

With a shudder, Chief Hamper sighs. "I saw the door closed on the ground-floor bathroom. I tapped on it and called out. Not hearing anything I slowly opened it." Chief Hamper shakes and starts to cry.

Pete grasps him by the shoulders. "Take your time, Lyle."

"I, that is, she ...

"Go easy, old boy."

"It looked like she'd tried to reach the door. There is blood, lots of blood." Chief Hamper sobs and shakes uncontrollably.

"Ground floor, hmmm?" Pete marches toward the door. He leans around the corner. "Sandra. How're you doing?"

Sergeant Goodnight glances up and smiles. "You just asked me that a minute ago, Mister Mayor." She grins. "I'm still fine."

Pete nods. "Sandra. Don't allow any more calls into the chief's office."

"What's up, Mister Mayor?"

Pete leans down and talks tenderly. "His wife's been *killed*"—Pete tilts his head toward Chief Hamper's chair and desk—"by them."

Sergeant Goodnight stares at Pete.

"The *fish*," says Pete. "The late Belle Starr-Hamper has been gutted out by those damned sewer fish."

Reno
3:15 p.m., Saturday afternoon

Heidi the dog darts into the room and sneezes. Abel, still wearing his white coveralls, rolled up at the legs, leads KB into the autopsy room. KB's purse hangs from her shoulder.

"Okay. She here, safe an' sound."

"Arrrbeedarrr. Thanks be to you, Detective. Yer a fine police officer, that you are. Moreover, I compliment you on your choice of functional wearing apparel."

"Coretta," asks KB, "is that coffee I smell?"

Coretta smiles. "One cup coming up."

Sherm places his arm around KB's shoulders. "Arrr, you sure smell good, but what's happened to your thighs? What're all those Band-Aids covering up?"

"After my little mishap at the sewer ponds, I had a relaxing steam shower with antibacterial soap. At the same time, Mister Hershey washed my clothes. After the shower, Officer Cobb applied the bandages."

Doctor Draper asks, "KB, may I look at those wounds for you?"

"Yes please, Dan. I am afraid of infection."

"Sit up here, girl," says Doctor Draper patting the ink blotter, "and I'll have a look. What happened?"

KB sits on the ink blotter, which is on the oak desk, and places her feet on the old office chair's seat. "If it is okay, Dan, I will explain in a minute. Sherm, why did you call me?"

"Try to hold still, KB," says Doctor Draper.

"Arrr, me little chickadee. You've replaced your Newport hat with a fine 'Biggest Little City' one."

"Here's a cup of coffee, KB," says Coretta. "What we all *really* need around here is a good night's sleep."

Doctor Draper sips his coffee. "Amen, *Sister*. KB, I'll clean these bite marks up and get some Polysporin on 'em."

Coretta says, "Look at those flip-flops. Are you planning on taking a skiing trip?"

KB giggles and spreads her arms to give Coretta a hug.

"Hold still, girl," says Doctor Draper.

"Excuse me, Doctor Dan. They are *men's* flip-flops, Coretta. It's all that they had. I could ski like a Norwegian on these two platforms, you bet you. Why did you call me, Sherm?"

Sherm gestures toward the towel-covered tray. Doctor Draper sets his gauze and alcohol down and again ceremoniously uncovers the specimen.

"¡*Caramba*! That creature from my bathroom," says Abel.

KB nods.

Again, Sherm motions toward the tray.

KB hops down from the desk and stands next to Doctor Draper. She clasps her hands behind her. *It appears to have a notochord*. KB bends down to within a one-foot's ruler's length. She frowns. "Jumping Jiminy."

She grasps the specimen with her left hand. Her right index finger pokes the sliced flesh and the dark spot where the backbone should be. She wiggles her finger in, then extracts it. Bloody smear garnishes her fingernail.

KB runs the ball of her finger down the creature's side. "I am feeling for bumps or tiny holes," she mumbles. After a few moments she stands up straight. She clears her throat. She gazes at her cohorts. "Gentlemen, Coretta, your specimen is—get ready for it—a *hagfish*."

Sherm nods and presses his lips together.

Doctor Draper squints at KB. "A . . . hagfish?"

Sherm glances at his watch. "I'm calling Admiral Fontana, KB. We'll not make the party tonight. Probably won't make the one next weekend either."

The double doors swing in. Pete enters the room.

Reno
3:20 p.m., Saturday afternoon

"How are you two doing with our clever little project?" asks Madam Zho. She has slipped away from her family at the park to meet Doctors Chan and Chen at the poolside. Mister Morley drives the Rolls-Royce limo.

Doctor Chen holds herring bait over the stainless-steel tank. "Please to watch, Madam Zho." Three fish—each the size of a large tube of salami—hit the stainless-steel mesh on the tank's top.

Madam Zho falls back into Mister Morley's stomach. "Oh, pardon me, Mister Morley. Those fish scared me to death. My heart is fluttering."

"So is mine, Madam."

"You've just observed the problem with this clever project, Madam Zho," says Doctor Chan. "We've successfully back bred these California hags, the Eptatretus deani, so that they're able to live in freshwater. In addition, we've been successful breeding for fast growth and large size. The meat and leather's superb. The downside is—this hybrid species is *intensely* aggressive."

"I certainly see that, Doctor Chan." Madam Zho draws a deep drag on her cigarette. "My heart's still pounding."

"I afraid," says Doctor Chen. "Possible more than Mister Jiggs to suffer death."

Madam Zho coughs. "Very well, gentlemen. As soon as my family drives back home, we'll bin this batch."

Reno
3:25 p.m., Saturday afternoon

"What the hell's a *hagfish*?"

"An excellent query, Pete." Sherm waves a hand toward KB. "There stands the expert. She's studied eels and hagfish at Oregon State for her graduate studies, which includes studying the several species of Pacific hagfish."

"What the matter, Pete?" asks Abel.

"Yes," Coretta says, "you look like you've just lost your best friend."

Pete nods. "It's kind of like that. I just came from the chief's office. I'll explain in a minute. What've you found here?"

KB wipes her fingers on a moist antibacterial wipe. Her face grows a frown. "In my opinion, gentlemen, Coretta, this creature could not be the beast causing the alarm here in Reno. You see, hagfish *only* live in salty water. They cannot even *survive* in brackish half salty, half fresh water."

"Yeah?" cried Abel. "I slice tail off that '*monstruo*' It attack my *Denise*."

Pete motions at the specimen. "*Tío*, nonetheless, *this* creature didn't actually *hurt* Denise."

"Pete, I tell you. It *attacked* her." Abel jabs his finger at the specimen. "I saw it." Abel appears as if he might cry. Then he drops his sight to the table. "It inside her . . . her nightie," he mutters.

"Jesus H Christ," says Pete. "Nevertheless, *amigo*, she wasn't *injured* like the others."

"I know, Pete." Abel's eyes display a hurt look. "That true. But, when I slice end off sonofabitch, it still . . . up her nightie. That the truth."

KB shakes her head. "I do not know what to tell you, Abel. It is like nothing I have ever seen before."

"Yes, Abel"—Sherm shrugs—"KB here is probably one of the *top thirty experts* in the world on hagfishes."

"Hagfishes do not only live exclusively in briny water, Abel, they also do *not* live in shallow water. I know I am looking at a hagfish tail here. There are nearly sixty species of these blind sea creatures. They inhabit every ocean but the two arctic seas. Nevertheless, they do *not* live in sewers. In addition, they do not leap from the water to attack their victims."

Abel shakes his head.

"Do they have victims, KB?" asks Doctor Draper. "I mean, are hagfish predators, or do they eat plants, or plankton, or krill, you know what I'm sayin'?"

"Oh, they are predators all right, Dan."

At the chamber's far end the doors burst open. A sheet-covered gurney plunges through, pushed by a woman donned in a blue uniform. Hair strands have fallen across her face.

KB's face contorts. "We are wasting our time with this, gentlemen. This hagfish avenue is a dead-end."

The woman pushing the gurney peers at the assemblage gathered beneath the bright lights. After warehousing her burden, she scurries off.

KB furrows her brow. "Hagfish attack dead or moribund

fish by crawling through any of the victim's orifices. They also have a knot-tying technique for chewing directly through the victim's side. Once inside, they gulp down prodigious mouthfuls of flesh using a tongue with sharp teeth growing on it."

"¡*Madre Mía!* What moribund?"

"A moribund creature, Abel, is one approaching death," says KB. She nods toward the specimen. "What we have here is a lot of guesswork on their feeding and reproduction activities. For instance, in the hagfish guts we have recovered not only many kinds of bony fish, but shark, mammalian flesh, birds and feathers—and even *whale* flesh."

"Uh-huh," says Doctor Draper, "I presume the whale was dead when the hagfish attacked it."

"We presume so," says KB. "However, not long ago a fisherman brought up a large and very alive Pacific spiny lobster. Embedded in his abdominal segments a full-grown *Eptatretus longipinnis* lived undisturbed. Sherm, I need to talk to you for a second."

Doctor Draper gestures toward his office. "Y'all are welcome to use my facilities, such as they are."

"Um, thank you, Dan," says Sherm. "Come on, KB." He closes the door behind them.

"It was slime worms, Sherm," blurts KB. She begins to sway. "I saw them. I felt them. I sensed their fleshy feelers. And *they bit me*."

"Here, KB," says Sherm. "Sit down. Want me to bring your purse?"

KB shakes. "I have seen underwater videos of them. The pictures show them aggressively swarming and writhing around bait in a trap. Nevertheless, I never considered they would be *that* forceful around a large vigorous organism, such as myself."

"Your information is profoundly troubling, KB," Sherm says. "It absolutely doesn't fit with anything we thought we knew."

"They covered me with slime, Sherm, from my waist to my knees."

"Were they trying to eat you ... or was it something else?"

"I do not know. I was very scared."

"I'm truly confuzzled, KB. I don't want to panic Reno's citizens unnecessarily. Let's keep this knowledge to ourselves for just a little while, until we've had time to let this information ... ferment."

Reno
3:30 p.m., Saturday afternoon

"Auntie Melody," says Tiffany.

Melody sips her wine. "In a minute, sweetheart." The adults are standing around in the dining room. "I'm talking to your great-grandmother."

"Tell Mum again," whispers little Jenny.

Tiffany pulls on Melody's sleeve. "It's Robert, Auntie Melody."

"Excuse me, Grandmother," says Melody, peering about the room.

"He's not in here, Auntie, he's—"

A little boy's heart-rending screech stabs the post-lunch ambience.

DuWayne jerks one of the sliding doors open.

Robert's shattering scream skewers the air.

The adults pile through the door, followed by the two girls. The green dinosaur lies on its side, next to the pool. The swimming pool's water agitates, looking like it is an insane washing machine.

Robert's little hands thrust above the surface. He shrieks, "*Help me, Mum.*"

Mao Tse-tung barks and barks.

Long brown shapes coiling and diving around Robert,

make the water's surface boil.

He screams and screams, as if his little body is being consumed while still alive.

Mister Morley suddenly leaps forward to dive in. Madam Zho grabs his arm with both hands. "*No.*"

Robert frenetically smacks the water with his tiny palms. The frothing water suddenly turns red. His last cry gurgles from beneath the waves.

Melody wails and falls to her knees.

"DuWayne," Madam Zho shouts. "The pole. Grab the pole."

DuWayne yanks the aluminum safety pole off the fence and shoves its hooked end into the water. He frantically sweeps back and forth. The turbulent frothing ball moves to the far side of the pool. Shreds of Robert's T-shirt float to the surface.

Melody begins to yowl.

James, Doctor Chen, and Doctor Chan spread out along the pool's far edge.

Kam Ho drops to his knees beside DuWayne.

Mao Tse-tung barks at the pool's edge. Kam Ho grabs him and hangs on.

"For the love of God, Grandmother," screeches Melody. "How bloody goddamn hell could you?"

"Get to grips with it, my dear. You're obviously a bit overwhelmed."

"Excited? You insatiable *bitch*. Your goddamned greed has just *killed my son.*"

"Yes, my dear, something has gone terribly wrong. Nonetheless, it's simply an accidental—"

"When'll you have enough, Grandmother?" shrieks Melody. "You've got more money than you can possibly spend, yet you bloody well want more."

"Codswallop. It's all for you, my precious. I'm leaving my wealth to you, my family."

Melody screams, "I don't give a good God damned about

the money, Grandmother. You've martyred my Robert to
your insatiable avarice. I *hate* you. You'll never lay eyes on me
again."

"My heart." Madam Zho clutches her blouse and faints.
Mister Morley catches her.

Reno
3:40 p.m., Saturday afternoon

KB returns to the autopsy room from Doctor Draper's office.
"When I first started at the university, we learned that hags
were merely scavengers. From their rich densities we now
know that they are predators as well. In the first underwater
camera studies, where bait was placed in a trap and lowered
to the sea floor, the hagfish swam en masse *from every direction.*
Inconceivably, it did not matter which way the current, and
therefore the scent, flowed. Within minutes the trap writhed
in a swarm of slime worms." KB peers at her five companions.
"They covered the trap with buckets of slime."

Coretta grimaces.

"Where does the slime come from?" Doctor Draper asks.

KB points. "See this little row of holes down this specimen's side?"

Doctor Draper nods.

"That's their slime holes. For example, a hagfish curled up
in a pail of water can, if disturbed, fill the whole pail with
slime in . . . *one second.*"

"That's absolutely nauseating, KB," declares Coretta.

"Why do they slime on everything?" asks Pete.

"Slimed food tends to keep the competition away."

"There ya go," chuckles Doctor Draper. "Works for me."

Abel laughs.

"Say, KB," says Coretta. "How did these creatures ever get

the name of—hagfish?"

"My Denise had slimy stuff on her thighs," reveals Abel.

KB stares at Abel.

"You mentioned, KB," says Doctor Draper, "that they're drawn to food despite which way the current's flowing. Just how *are* they attracted to their prey?"

"Hagfish don't have eyes," KB says. "Nonetheless, they are able to locate their prey with an exquisite smelling system, located in the fleshy feelers growing around their mouths."

"They squirm into orifices?" asks Coretta.

"Hags do not have a jaw, Coretta. Their only bone is their skull. However, where eels attach to the *outside* of the victim's body and eat in from the outside—hags slip *into* the body and eat it from the *inside* out. Which is why commercial fishermen abhor them. They occasionally hoist a large fish from the ocean, only to have a stuffed and sated hagfish fall back into the sea from their fish's anal vent."

Abel shakes his head.

"The anus?" asks Doctor Draper. "Hagfish must be small if they can slither up a fish's vent."

"An average-sized full-grown hagfish," says KB, "has a much smaller circumference than the one here. I am puzzled by the girth of this one. Generally, they grow two-feet long and are as big around as a stick of German sausage. However, I would guess—"

"Arrr, KB. Tell 'em about the biggest one ever found."

"Yes, Sherm, although it is easy to get the wrong idea from this. Off Hawaii an *Eptatretus carlhubbsi*, brought up from three thousand feet, measured three feet ten inches."

"¡*Por Dios*! That *four feet long*." Abel points at the specimen. "It stretched from toilet to—"

"Yes, Abel," KB says, "from the size of this tail sample this hag may have been four, maybe even five feet long—an unheard of length. Nonetheless, normal-sized slime worms slip quite effortlessly into tight openings by possessing a boneless, very flexible body, and by covering themselves with extraordinary amounts of high-quality slime."

"KB," says Coretta. "That's positively repulsive. Why on earth did you ever choose to study a creature with such revolting dining habits?"

KB chuckles. "I don't know. I didn't start off wanting to study them. Nevertheless, they are a big part of the deep ocean biomass. Just looking at them, I understand why a person wouldn't choose to study them. But I saw that my revulsion of the hagfish was causing me to miss an especially important part of the picture. Hags actually do perform a function in the ocean, and they possibly may even become an important resource for human beings to harvest."

Coretta arches an eyebrow. "Anyone for more coffee?"

KB laughs. "Yes, please, Coretta, thank you. Here is my cup." She reaches into her purse and produces her flask. "Would you please stir in a drop?"

Coretta nods and takes the flask.

KB continues. "The hagfishes are a separate group from the *bony fish* with which we are all familiar—for instance, the *salmon.* In addition, hagfish are a separate group from *the chordates,* that is, the *sharks.*

"Hagfish look like an *eel,* but *eels make up the third separate group.*

"*Hagfish* constitute the *fourth* and *final fish group.* Within this group there exist sixty species in five genera."

"Here's your coffee, KB," says Coretta. "I'll drop your flask back in your purse."

KB takes a sip. "That is good, Coretta. Just right."

"Y'all said they only live in deep water," says Doctor Draper.

KB says, "One of the Pacific species, *Eptatretus deani,* a common hagfish found off the North American Coast, has been recovered from as shallow as three hundred fifty feet, and all the way down to nine thousand feet.

"I hear ya, KB," says Doctor Draper, "but is there any place in the world, or an earlier era, where hagfish show up in more shallow water?"

KB swallows a sip of coffee. "By golly, Dan, I am reluctant to mention it because it is easy to jump to erroneous conclusions. A healthy *Eptatretus bischoffli*, found off the coast of Chile, was captured at only *twenty-six feet*. This is an extremely unusual—"

"Uh-huh," Doctor Draper says, "I see why y'all were reluctant to mention that fact. That is a worrisomely shallow depth."

Pete shakes his head. "Do you mean to say, KB, that there's absolutely no way on earth that it's hagfishes attacking our citizens? Even when you know that Abel cut this piece from one of them while it was in the process of doing *something* to his wife?"

"I cannot even *imagine*, Pete, how a hagfish could get into the city's sewer system and even stay *alive*, let alone attack human beings."

"There ya go," says Doctor Draper. "I bow to your superior knowledge on this fishy subject, KB, ya know what I'm sayin'? Nonetheless, it's irrefutable that the head end of *this* particular hag has escaped into Reno's sewer system."

Pete slowly nods.

"Maybe," says Doctor Draper, "we should err on the side of caution. Even though we're not certain which creatures are actually taking our citizens for food—perhaps it's freshwater toads—we should seriously consider killing *all* creatures living in Reno's sewer system."

Reno
3:50 p.m., Saturday afternoon

"Godammit, Milt." Pete talks into his mayor's limousine telephone. "Can't you just flush the sons of bitches out?"

Pete has retreated to his Lincoln limo, parked behind police headquarters. He's changing into his emergency pinstriped suit that he keeps in a garment bag in the trunk.

Water Department Director Milt Hershey frowns at his desk speakerphone. "That would be difficult, Pete. I mean, we'd have to divert an enormous cache of water to another reservoir, connect it to the sewer system—"

"Holy shit, Milt, the city's in a whole bunch of trouble here."

"Yes, Pete, we know. We were with the young lady when she fell in."

"All right then." Pete looks in the mirror and works to get his necktie adjusted. "Then you know just how nasty these little suckers can be."

"We sure do, Pete."

"Well then, why in hell don't you come up with a plan for getting these haggy monsters out of *your* sewer system?"

"Pete, we've called in several teams of our most experienced men. And, this is Saturday, you know."

"Milt, I don't give a good goddamn how much overtime your department pays out. Just between you and me, we're in danger of losing our whole feckin' city."

"Ah, now, Pete." Milt tugs at his red suspenders. "We don't think it's as bad as all that."

"Damn it, Hershey. We have several dozen citizens who've had their son-of-a-bitching guts drug right out through their assholes, and you say you don't think it's too bad? Listen, if we don't get this bastard under control, I won't have a job around here. Not only that, but a lot of other people are also going down the shit hole with me. Hell, if we don't find a way to eradicate these horse-dick monsters, there may not be a town council to even hire people like you and me."

"We know we've got a problem, Pete. We weren't trying to tell you any different. The water department has a number of ways for getting rid of sewer intruders. But there *are* strategies that're simply not workable—too dangerous. We assure you, Pete, we at the water works will do everything possible to clear the sewer system of this infestation. Just be glad, Mister Mayor, that these creatures are contained within the sewer pipes and that they're not out in the city's *freshwater* supply."

"Holy shit, Milt. What're the chances these slime worms can wriggle into the freshwater supply?"

"Not to worry, Mister Mayor. The sewer system is completely separate from the city's freshwater supply, including the freshwater rivers and streams. We've got very good safeguards in place to ensure that the two systems can never, ever mix."

"All right, Milt. That'll give me something positive to say when I hold a press conference later today. I need to update the citizenry on what the prognosis holds for our future. As it stands now, Milt, I don't have enough positive material to even go on the boob tube. That's why I'm laying low. All I would accomplish now is to scare the absolute shit out of our citizens.

"Yeah, you're probably right, Pete. I'm still of the opinion that we're going to get this problem under control fairly soon. Those two scientists know what we're up against. They'll surely come up with a poison or a natural predator."

"Taking a reasoned approach, Milt, to ridding ourselves of these ass-hole diving worms is all well and good. However, I'm afraid of a citywide full-blown panic if we don't come up with a plan in a good goddamned hurry."

"Well, Pete, from what you've told us, these hagfishes are a true fish. They've got gills and need water to live in. KB says they need *salt* water. From my standpoint, I can't figure out how fishes can swim up the main trunk line, then get into the laterals and into individual resident lines. The laterals are ordinarily dry. They only load up when there's actual sewage flowing down them, for instance, after a flush. You've got a few rats running around in those pipes, but fish? That's why I'm sending crews down. What we're afraid of is these fish might have a lung like a lungfish or be able to live out of water for a time like catfish. If that's true, they could easily swim up the trunk lines, then squirm their way up the laterals to get to the individual toilets."

"Oh, *thank you*, Milt."

"Hold on there, Pete," says a chuckling Milt. "KB assured us that what I just said's not the case. Hagfish *cannot* live out of water. I'm not a biologist. We were just wondering though. For instance, Miss Bjørnsen also said hagfish must live in salt water and here they are living in sewer water. Something's mighty fishy."

Pete grits his teeth, smiling at Milt. "As soon as your inspection crews discover something, Milt, let me know. We desperately need to move on this—like *yesterday*."

"Will do, Mister Mayor."

Pete slips his emergency dress shoes on. "As a word of advice, Milt. I'd be a little selective about which toilet seat I plunked my precious cheeks upon."

"Yeah, I know, Pete. At least the devils can't get through a urinal."

Reno
4:00 p.m., Saturday afternoon

Pete, KB, Sherm, Abel, Doctor Draper, and Coretta sit around the Reno police headquarters' conference table. Officer Washington stands beside the Truckee Meadows map that he and Officer Pat Flynn had pinned to the freestanding bulletin board. Earlier, Officer Washington had contacted Pete and invited him to view their findings.

"At two this afternoon," says Officer Washington, "General Arnold sent this map to police headquarters. It's a topographic map of the Reno area produced from a highly detailed U-2 photograph."

Pete notes that the map features green pushpins, red pins, and a smattering of white pins. "Look, Abel. There's a green pin stuck right in your house."

"That's likely significant," says Officer Washington. "All the attacks have occurred in the bottom land of the Truckee Meadows, near the river."

"Harold," says Doctor Draper. "What do the three colors signify, or did you simply run out of your favorite colors?"

Officer Washington grins. "I didn't run out, sir."

Doctor Draper winks at Officer Washington.

"We found," says Officer Flynn sitting in a chair near the wall, "that some attacks, you know, caused victims to be gutted out. Those we represented with red push pins. Green pins indicate where victims were attacked but the ER physicians couldn't find physical damage.

"Yeah," says Abel, straightening up in his chair, "except scare *caca* out of them."

Pete tugs on his necktie. "I guess you've all heard by now what happened to Belle Starr. Do you have a pin for her?"

Officer Washington silently points to a red pushpin on California Street.

Pete presses his stomach and mumbles, "We have to get this son of a bitch under control."

Sherm looks across the table. "Um, Pete. It always seems darkest just before the dawn. Please forgive that platitudinous-sounding phrase. On the other hand, please believe me. We'll come up with a way to eradicate these beasts, *whichever* ones are the guilty ones." Sherm turns toward KB.

KB sets her coffee cup down and licks her lips.

"You know," says Pete, "I've argued with that big-business oriented top cop, but in a pinch, Lyle will do the right thing. Belle Starr being killed really upsets me. She was a great character and a great woman. We *must* do something."

"Uh-huh." Doctor Draper's index finger wags at the board. "I'm intrigued by your pattern of pins there, Harold. Do you have any idea why the attacks, both brutal and benign, are confined to the lowlands of the Truckee Meadows?"

"No, Doctor, I do not."

Officer Flynn leans forward. "Harold. Tell 'em about, you know, what we discovered about ground floors."

"Yes, Pat and I discovered that *all* attacks originated in ground-floor or basement bathrooms."

"Arrrbeedarrr. Yer discoveries there, me hearties, are significant indeed. The attacks, both brutal and benign, have occurred in the lowlands near the river. In addition, they've taken place exclusively in basement and ground-floor bathrooms. These two key facts will surely narrow the scope of our search. I predict that with your significant clues, Officers Washington and Flynn, you'll be recognized as the two investigators who broke this case. I further predict that we shall soon have this crisis nipped in the ol' pectoral fin. On behalf of my colleagues here, I congratulate you both."

Doctor Draper peers over his reading glasses. "Harold, what information do the *white* pins convey?"

"They show where 'sightings' have occurred. This white pin stuck in our police headquarters' building is where KB's dog, Heidi, spotted the creature in the ground-floor ladies' room."

At the sound of her name, Heidi—from beneath the conference table—gives a little growl.

Pete glances under the table. "Go get 'em, tiger." Then he gives KB a warm smile.

She warmly smiles back.

The room stands silent.

After a few moments, KB squirms. "Something diabolical is happening here."

"Uh hum," says Sherm. "Whatever do you mean, my little chickadee?"

"I mean, it does not make sense that these voracious meat eaters would enter an orifice and then *not* begin to energetically eat."

"Pete," says Doctor Draper. "How sure are you that Belle Starr was killed by these same creatures?"

"Pretty sure, Dan. They're delivering her remains to your morgue. You'll be able to determine for yourself. Nevertheless, Lyle said he found her in the downstairs bathroom sprawled out in front of the toilet. There was blood everywhere. He said it looked like she'd lost fifty pounds."

Reno
5:00 p.m., Saturday afternoon

Pete and Chief Hamper sit side by side at the KOLO Channel Eight news desk.

"Ladies and gentlemen." News manager Tad Dunbar looks into the camera. "We break into our regularly scheduled five o'clock news program to bring you this important breaking news. In our studios we've got Mayor Pete Ferrari and Chief of Police Lyle Hamper. They're prepared to brief us on the very latest developments—that is—on the disaster that has befallen the biggest little city since last night. Mister Mayor. Chief. Welcome."

"Thanks, Tad," says Pete, as he looks at himself in the TV monitor. He appears fresh in his pinstriped suit. "A lot has happened since last night. While we're not out of the woods yet, Lyle and I want to bring you up to date on what we're up against and what we in authority are doing to alleviate the problem."

Chief Hamper, adorned in his dress-blue uniform, appears haggard in the monitor.

Pete looks back into the camera. *Holy shit, keep it together, Lyle.*

"The *problem*"—Chief Hamper shakes his head—"has gotten a whole lot worse since last night."

For chrissake, Hamper, don't screw the pooch.

"Last night"—the camera dollies toward Chief Hamper's face—"I made the argument with Pete here that we haven't got much of a problem. Frankly, I'm sorry to say we've got a *real big* problem."

Pete steals a glance at Chief Hamper. *For crip-sake, Lyle, don't go all maudlin on me.*

"It's not going to do us any good to ignore it," says Chief Hamper. "To tell the truth, we've got the potential of a *city-wide disaster.*"

Pete crunches his teeth together. Suddenly, he catches the side of his glaring face in the monitor. *Oh, for the love of Pete.* He toils to put on a more encouraging look.

"Our priority now," says Chief Hamper, "is to save the people. Isn't that right, Pete?"

"The chief is absolutely right." Pete swallows. "Before daylight I called in a pair of experts. They flew in this morning."

"And" asks Dunbar, "what've these professionals told you, Mister Mayor?"

"I think we have the top marine researchers on the entire west coast, Tad," Pete says. "Miss Kristian Bjørnsen from the University of Århus in Denmark has tentatively identified the attacking creature as some aberrant variation of the hagfish species."

"Ah, Mayor Ferrari," says Dunbar, "what on earth is a hagfish?"

"As I understand it," Pete says, "the hagfish is a deep saltwater sort of shy fish that ordinarily people never see or hear about.

"They apparently perform an important—"

Chief Hamper slams his hand on the table. **They killed my wife.**

Oh, shit. Pete mashes his lips together. *Here goes the goddamned citywide panic.*

"They killed your wife?" asks a stunned Dunbar.

"Just a few hours ago." Chief Hamper looks squarely into the camera. "I found her in the bathroom sprawled out in front of the toilet."

The camera dollies in. Pete glances at the monitor and sees red-rimmed eyes filling the screen. He feels a rush of sympathy.

Dunbar draws himself up. "How do you know, Chief Hamper, that these creatures are the ones who, ah, harmed your wife?"

Chief Hamper looks at Dunbar. "There is blood all over the bathroom floor, Tad. It came out of her"—he makes little circles with his right hand—"her lower end area."

Pete sees Chief Hamper's bottom lip trembling.

"Well, Chief," says Dunbar. "How do you know, sir, that she didn't hemorrhage or something like that?"

Chief Hamper appears to grow agitated. "My heck, Tad, there was nothing left inside her." He seems to struggle to maintain his composure. "Her body looked like a birthday balloon that had suddenly deflated." He drops his head on his arms. His sides shake.

Pete leans over and drops his arm over Chief Hamper's shoulders. He gives him a squeeze. Pete sees Dunbar give a signal to the control booth. The red light on the nearest camera blinks off.

In a flash, Dunbar and three other studio personnel surround the table. Dunbar gently pats the chief's back. "Mister Mayor."

"Just call me Pete, Tad."

Dunbar jerks his head toward the studio dressing rooms.

Pete nods in the affirmative. "Come on, Lyle. Let's go back to the dressing room. Okay, partner?"

Chief Hamper struggles to stand.

Pete escorts Chief Hamper past the cameras and over the cables toward the dressing room. Dunbar follows, placing an arm on each man's shoulder.

"As soon as you feel a little better, Lyle," says Dunbar, "come back out and join Pete and me in the program."

Silver Creek Campground
5:05 p.m., Saturday afternoon

Bob and Sally Sloan, from Sacramento, camp in the Tahoe National Forest. Bob stands average height, but he towers over Sally. He has thick dark hair and a full beard just starting to turn gray over the chin. Sally features suntanned skin and sports short blond hair.

Their longtime friends John and Karen Rickman from Tracy, camp with them. John boasts a deep-booming voice and appears normal height with a good build. He sports graying hair and a gray mustache. Karen appears tall and attractive with short salt-and-pepper hair.

The foursome had been fortunate, on this Fourth-of-July weekend, to pitch their tents at one of their favorite spots, the Silver Creek Campground. It stretches between Highway Eighty-Nine and the Truckee River near Tahoe City.

John stirs the "vittles" in the two railroad men's secret caboose stew. "Boy, it's sure good to get away from that valley heat, huh?"

Bob sits opposite John on one of the logs encircling the fire pit. "You got that right, good buddy." He pushes his fingers through his hair, as if to comb out stray pine needles. With his other he tips up a Heineken beer—fresh from the ice chest.

Sally watches the two men sporting their knives on their belts. She shakes her head, her little diamond earrings flash. Sally glances at Karen, who is leaning against a cedar tree growing next to the parking lot.

Earlier that morning the two women had been summarily banned from the kitchen area. John and Bob assured the two ladies that they would, in due course, be allowed to partake of a unique and never-to-be-forgotten campfire dinner.

A light breeze brushes Sally's cheek. The campfire's errant smoke spices the high-mountain air. She hears the summertime songbirds chirping in the ponderosa pines. Sally senses the week's stresses draining from her body.

The Truckee River—which flows from Lake Tahoe, through Reno, and ending in Pyramid Lake—tumbles over granite boulders just behind the Forest-Service-provided public toilet.

The two couples wear shorts and colorful tee shirts. In addition, John wears his backyard barbecue apron. The foursome's flip-flop clad feet have gained a layer of the forest floor's granitic brown dust.

John peers up at his three companions. "Do you realize it's fully twenty-five degrees cooler here at Tahoe than it is in downtown Sacramento?"

Bob nods. "Yes sir, this's a great way to beat the heat." He gives the pine needles a push with his flip-flop.

"Yeah," says Karen. "This is the life. Beautiful surroundings and the men preparing supper."

"Yes." Sally speaks to Karen from behind her hand. "And drinking beer, stirring up a perpetual dust cloud, and no telling *what* revolting ingredients they're dumping into that percolating mixture they call, 'secret conductors stew.'"

Karen smiles and delivers a knowing nod.

"Hey," calls out John. "At least we're not eating *Bambi*."

"You know, Karen," says Sally, "I wouldn't put anything past those two. There could be tainted Bambi hunks in their stew, earwigs, or rattlesnake tongues."

"Eeew." Karen rolls her eyes.

Sally peers toward the outdoor toilets. "Well, I can't put it off any longer, Karen. I've *got* to use the facilities."

"*Ugh.*" Karen pushes herself to a standing position. "Gross." She folds her lip in the universal feminine expression of repugnance. "Aren't those the most *disgusting* toilets you've ever sat upon?"

"Yes," agrees Sally. "No matter how nice it is for our tax dollars to provide free bathrooms, that thing over there is nothing more than a *glorified outhouse*."

Karen wrinkles her nose.

"But" says Sally, "at least we're not experiencing the trouble they're getting down in Reno."

"Oh, isn't that just awful, Sally? I kinda wish we hadn't turned on the radio and heard about those attacks in the toilet."

Sally shakes her head. "Yes, but we had to find out why there was all that westbound traffic."

"For sure." Karen nods.

"At least we're safe up here. Reno's mayor, Maserati, or whoever, said the hagfish problem's wholly contained within the Truckee Meadows drainage area."

Karen pushes her bottom lip up. "Well, that's one thing you can say about the Forest Service's glorified outhouse."

Sally glances up at her chum.

"It hasn't *got* a sewer pipe," says Karen. "It's revolting, but it's just a completely safe nauseating hole in the ground."

Sally sighs and begins her march down the pea-gravel path toward the bathrooms.

"Hey, Sloan," hollers John. "You headin' for the dry holer?"

"You just mind your stew, Rickman," shouts Sally. "Are *all* you chefs just nasty perverts?"

"Gawd," Karen says. "They get more disgusting with every beer."

Sally nods. "You got that right."

Bob's sides quake.

"Here," whispers Karen. "Don't forget to take some toilet paper."

"Thanks."

"Yeah, half the time there's none in there."

John glances up from the picnic table, where he's whacking up carrots.

"Don't fall in, Sloan. Even though they call it a 'dry holer', *it ain't dry.*"

Reno
5:10 p.m., Saturday afternoon

"I assure you, my fellow citizens," says Pete, looking into the television camera. "We're *not* headed for a citywide disaster. I'm profoundly sorry to hear of Chief Hamper's tragedy. Lyle told me he'd instructed his wife not to use the ground-floor toilet."

"What's the significance of that instruction, Mister Mayor?"

"Our research has shown that the attacks have occurred in the low-lying lands of the Truckee Meadows."

"In other words, Mister Mayor, there've been no reported attacks at the upper elevations?"

"That's correct, Tad."

"And why exactly did the chief ask his wife not to use their ground-floor bathroom?"

"The police department has discovered that attacks have only taken place in ground-floor or basement lavatories."

"I'm not familiar with how sewer systems work, Mister Mayor, but are you saying that it's safe to use a toilet if it is *above* ground-floor level?"

"That's exactly what I'm saying, Tad. In addition, it's safe to use any toilet located *away* from the river. If you live near the river, simply use an upstairs bath."

Dunbar takes an audible breath. "That is, if you've *got* an upstairs bath."

"It appears," continues Pete, "that we have these mysterious fish wholly contained within the lowest elevation of the Reno and Sparks sewerage system. The way I understand it, the sewage pipes connecting to upper-story bathrooms do not contain liquid; fish can't swim up them."

"So, you're saying," says Dunbar, "the problem is contained and there doesn't seem to be the threat we thought earlier."

"That's right." Pete nods. "An interesting point though,

Tad. According to the head of the sewer plant, there shouldn't be any water in the small sewer pipes exiting the individual houses either. Director Hershey's baffled by how the fish gain access."

"What," asks Dunbar, "does Mister Hershey guess might be happening?"

"He suggested that a catfish or lungfish could crawl in the damp sewer laterals and reach the ground-floor toilets."

Dunbar nods. "I see."

"No. *No.*" Pete waves his hand. "Our marine experts say that hagfishes *cannot* crawl in open air like a catfish or a lungfish." He glances at the monitor and sees his eyelids blinking. *Son of a bitch, I've said too damned much about laterals and lungfish.*

"*We about have this problem licked.* Follow the simple instructions I've given or use the portable toilets that've been made available."

"And, Mister Mayor, does that include the row of toilets in the police department parking lot?"

Pete laughs. "Absolutely, Tad."

"Fine," says Dunbar. "How do the marine experts figure they're going to wipe out these fiendish fishes?"

Pete narrows his eyes at the news anchor. "We've brainstormed poisoning—the same procedure used over at Lake Davis in Plumas County, California. However, there's controversy over that idea. We've discussed the use of natural predators which these hagfish already have. In addition, we've talked about breeding sterile mates, such as is done with harmful insects."

Dunbar nods. "That sounds reasonable."

"Human beings are very adaptable, Tad. We'll soon learn how to live with this threat."

Silver Creek campground
5:15 p.m., Saturday afternoon

"John, you're genuinely *disgusting*," declares Karen, giving her hair a shake.

Amidst a torrent of male laughter, Sally pads down the path to the public toilets. She hears her sandals crunch in the pea gravel. Behind the toilets, the Truckee River rushes around the big boulders in its riverbed. She wrinkles her nose and steps around the privacy partition. "Oh, that's ripe. I'd almost rather squat behind a bush."

Dozens of flies the size of raisins buzz the little building. She hears them hitting the screen that runs around the roof-line. "There're so many spider webs, how can there be any flies?"

Sally stands in front of the door with the "women" sign. She glances at the partition, knowing the men's door stands just on the other side. She touches the doorknob. *Is anyone in there? Worse yet, is there a man on the other side?* She remembers that both toilets dump into the same common hole. She clenches her teeth and turns the knob.

Sally peeks around the edge. *Good.* No one here. She closes the door behind her and locks it.

Sally stands in the middle of the concrete floor, mesmerized by the looping flies and the toilet's sour emanations. She listens to determine whether a man occupies the other side. Only a cobwebbed fly screen at the top separates the two compartments.

"Why do the toilet's builders waste the effort to put up a screen; the flies simply fly down the men's toilet hole, drone over the lake of sewage, and then buzz up through the women's hole. Men are so lucky."

A stainless-steel cone bearing a black toilet seat stands in the concrete floor's center. *Is that someone's twisted idea for a throne?* "Darn. There's no place for my toilet paper." Sally delicately places her little package on the concrete beside the stainless-steel cone.

She lifts the lid. The smelly greeting burns her sinuses. *It's almost full.* "Yuck." *What a revolting picture.*

Keeping her lips together, so no flies can gain entrance, Sally drops her shorts. She turns her backside around and carefully places her cheeks on the seat. Her short legs prevent her feet from reaching the concrete. *I gotta hurry and get the hell outta here.* Almost at once a dainty stream trickles onto the foul surface.

Sally hears a splash. "Oh, no." *Someone's on the other side.*

Two more splashes follow. *That's weird.* She unrolls her toilet paper. *Sounds like it's getting closer.*

Sally yelps. She'd just felt soft fingers brush her bottom. Something satiny gently presses on her anus. Instantly, her reflexive muscles slam that orifice shut.

Every fly takes to wing when *Sally screams. Something,* the circumference of a beer bottle, *has attempted to shove into her orifice.*

Sally leaps to her feet. A brown-colored tube hangs from the folds of her skin. Its three-foot length dangles down through the toilet's opening.

Slime oozes from the fish's skin.

"Bob," Sally shrieks. "Somebody help me."

Gripping the slimy fish's sides, Sally tries to remove it. She finds the creature too slippery to hold on to.

"Help," shrieks Sally.

She shuffles away from the toilet. The creature's tail drags over the stainless-steel rim. It leaves a slime trail as if it was a giant slug.

"*Help me,*" Sally screams.

The doorknob wiggles. Then the door blows open with a crash. The latch hangs askew.

Bob, gasping for breath, fills the entrance. His eyes grow round as eggs. "What the . . ."

He leaps forward and grasps the writhing fish with his powerful hands.

Sally feels the organism's teeth tearing her sensitive skin. She shrieks.

"Oh, my God," Karen hollers. "What *is* that?"

At that instant, John pokes his head into the ladies' bathroom. He holds his carrot-cutting butcher's knife.

"John, I can't get it," yells Bob. "It's too slippery."

"It's hurting me, Bob," sobs Sally. "Get it off."

The creature takes another bite. Sally shrieks and grabs at it.

"*Do something*," yells Karen.

Bob reaches for the camping knife on his belt.

John plunges through the doorway, his knuckles white where he grips his butcher's knife.

"Here, Bob," bellows John. "I'll get the son of a bitch."

Bob struggles to hold the squirming creature for John's blade.

Karen grabs Sally's shoulders and steadies her.

John's knife slices the beast's back. A bucket of goo oozes from the lateral slime glands. Blood trickles. The fish splats onto the concrete.

Blood trickles down Sally's leg. She shrieks. "The son of a bitch took a hunk out of her," Bob yells.

Karen wads up toilet paper and crams it into Sally's crotch. "Here, Sally, hold this." Pushing Sally's sobbing face against her chest, Karen urges her to step outside. Shorts around her ankles, Sally shuffles from the buzzing room.

The fish flops on the concrete floor as if it was searching for a place to burrow.

John mutters through clenched teeth. "What an *ugly* motherfecker."

Bob glances at John. "Let's cut this bastard up so it can't get anyone else."

"Okay." John places the knife's edge just above the gill

holes. He leans forward, preparing to behead it.

Bob looks up. "*Wait.*"

John hesitates.

"Wait," Bob says. "This donkey-dick son of a bitch's still alive. Maybe we should take it down to Reno so that the scientists can examine it. We heard on the radio that they're trying to figure out a way to kill these bastards. They can practice on this piece of shit."

John peers at the hagfish, then at his butcher's knife. He nods in agreement. "Well." He stands up. "It shouldn't take long to drive to Reno."

Bob looks up quizzically.

John spreads his hands. "All the traffic's headed the other way."

Reno
6:20 p.m., Saturday afternoon

"Where is Doctor Draper, Sherm?" asks KB. She and Sherm had just arrived at "Dan's Dungeon." Heidi scampers under an autopsy table.

"Ahum. Maybe he's in his office, KB." Sherm then points toward a blue-colored five-gallon plastic water jug, displaying a Sharpie hand-printed *J&K RICKMAN* on the side. "Might be the specimen Dan called about."

Illuminated by a bright single overhead light, the container sits on an autopsy table. The rest of the room remains in the dark.

KB hears a thump inside the water jug. She makes out a dark eel-like shape slowly coiling and uncoiling.

Sherm grasps the water jug's molded handle with his left hand and the white plastic cap with his right.

"No, Doctor T," declares KB. "Do not unscrew that cap."

"Arrr." Sherm begins to slowly untwist the cap.

KB clasps her hands in front of her chest.

Sherm glances at KB. "Let's see what we have in here. Come on over, KB."

KB's eyelids blink. "What do you want me to do, Sherm?"

"You're the slime worm expert here, kid." Sherm clenches his teeth. "When I remove the cap, take a peek and tell me whether we have a hagfish, an eel, or a baby Loch Ness monster."

KB runs her tongue along her upper lip. "All right, Sherm. Get the opening right under the light and I will take a quick look."

"Atta girl."

KB shakes out her hair and moves her head to the side, out of the way of the light.

Sherm slowly lifts the plastic cap.

A brown apparition, the circumference of a potato, jambs its eyeless face out of the opening.

KB screams and falls back.

Sherm claps the cap on Mr. Potato head. Six stubby tentacles comb the air. The rasping toothed tongue aggressively flails from its grapefruit-sized mouth.

"Gawd *damn*." Sherm squeezes the fish's head between the cap and the jug's rim.

It instantly slimes. The goo oozes out the top.

"Yeow," Sherm bellows.

KB hears the powerful tail thrash the inside of the container.

Sherm groans. "Damn it, Kristian. Help me *can* this slippery son of a bitch."

KB stares at the spectacle. *By golly, Sherm never curses, and he never calls me Kristian.* She wrings her hands.

Sherm's hat falls to the deck.

"Godammit, KB. *Help me.*"

"What do you want me to do, Doctor T?"

"Find something to help me jamb this son of a bitch back into this jug."

KB hurries to a cloth-covered cart. She yanks the white cover back. She sees rows of stainless-steel instruments. She tentatively plucks up a forceps.

"Aye, KB. *Hurry.*"

Working the instrument, KB cautiously grips the creature behind the flailing tentacles.

"*Harder,*" Sherm grunts. "Grab that damned thing harder and shove it, the hell, back into this container."

KB grasps the forceps with both hands. She squeezes. Cartilage crunches. The floundering fish straightens as if electrified.

"Aaargh," Sherm gasps. "*Shove it in.*"

KB shoves the head in until the forceps hit the plastic rim. Clear slime oozes out.

Sherm slaps the cap over the flesh-ripping tongue and pushes. "*Pull the forceps.*"

KB jerks the instrument away.

Sherm forces the head back into the container.

A lone tentacle still sticks out. Sherm commences screwing the cap down. With each turn the flagellating member inches around the rim, sweating blood. Sherm twists the cap until it won't go any farther.

"That oughta hold 'er."

"Jumping Jiminy."

"My little Danish dumpling," Sherm says softly. "You're the expert here. Have you ever known them to be so strong and bellicose?"

KB shakes her head.

"Ahhh. Do you have any idea how we're going to eradicate them?"

KB presses her lips together. *Why can't I just lead a quiet life, maybe teach a quiet class?* "What were you saying, Sherm?"

"I said there are people dying out here, KB. The citizens of Reno called us because they're in deep trouble."

"I know, Sherm, but when I decided to go into hagfish research, I did not think it would have so much tension to it."

Sherm's lips form a hard line. "I know, kid. Nonetheless, you possess intelligence. You have education. You *owe* something. Even though you've made it a lifetime's endeavor to avoid hard work and total commitment, now there's a new game in town. The cards have been dealt. And you, my dear, and you alone, hold the best hand for getting this unfortunate town out of its ever-increasing difficulties."

KB squeezes her hands. She hadn't noticed but Doctor Draper had halted in the hallway outside the morgue. He quietly peers through the windows.

"Ahum," Sherm says. "Sometimes we, especially those with gifts known or hidden, are thrust into situations we never asked for. We either fail to rise to the task, or we gather our courage and plunge ahead for the good of all mankind and, ultimately . . . ourselves. *This* is your opportunity, KB."

KB takes a breath.

"You know more about hagfishes than probably anyone in the western United States. It's for sure you know more than anyone here in Reno. We didn't ask for it, KB, but we're involved in a life-and-death crisis here. Let's *take the bull by the horns* and try to save these people."

"I-I do not know that much, Sherm."

"Arrr." Sherm grits his teeth. "Quit hiding behind your boobs."

KB's lips part. "What?"

"Aye," says Sherm. "You've spent a lifetime hiding behind your mind-boggling figure rather than getting out there and fully using your God-given, rather formidable, mental talents. Now, KB, you either *help these people*, or *catch the next bus back to Newport*."

Reno
6:30 p.m., Saturday afternoon

Pete talks to Governor Miller on his office speakerphone. "So, you see, Bob, by warning everyone who lives in the low-lying areas, we'll have the immediate problem beat. We've also found that the attacks only occur from ground-floor toilets. For these reasons, we think we can simply poison the sewer system and eradicate them once and for all."

"I hope it's that simple, Pete," says Governor Miller. "You know how, in the fog of battle, things go awry."

"I understand. We just found out that Chief Hamper's wife was killed. Doctor Draper performed an autopsy and Miss Bjørnsen determined that the bite marks were indeed hagfish."

"I'm genuinely sorry to hear of his loss, Pete. I'll give him a call and thank him for all his help. This kind of brings it home, doesn't it, pal?"

"It sure does, partner. I thought we had a close call when Abel's wife was attacked, but—"

"Pete, this is your project then. From what you say, it appears the trouble is contained, at least for now. Therefore, why don't you, and the new Sparks Mayor Bruce Breslow, coordinate your activities to eliminate the beasts?

"Nevertheless, Pete, if you find your city assets overwhelmed just let me know. Anytime, night or day."

Chapter Six

Huey—"The Gutsy Lady"

Reno
7:00 p.m., Saturday evening

Thunderclouds assemble around Mount Rose. Pete's Jaguar
Sedan turns off South Virginia Street onto Walts Lane. Next, it
eases into the parking lot at El Borracho's Mexican Restaurant.

A *close* lightning flash, followed instantly by a thunderclap,
makes Heidi dive to the floorboard. She shakes.

Buckets of hail bounce off the asphalt. Pete parks against
the back fence. His is the only automobile.

"So, Pete," Sherm asks, "is this a good joint to dine in
privacy?"

"We'll slip in the back door," says Pete, "and head for the
bar. The customers in the restaurant part, will never know
we're here. Also, no one in this bar will complain about our Heidi."

"Will not the other patrons," asks KB, "rush out front and
tell everyone that Reno's mayor is eating dinner in the back
room?"

Pete turns the ignition off. "For some reason, KB, this spot remains a good hideout."

The trio trots through the rain toward the back door. Heidi runs alongside.

"Pete," asks KB, "what sort of restaurant is this, *Entrada?*"

Pete chuckles and points at the neon sign. "*Entrada* means 'entrance' in Spanish, KB. This's the back entrance to, *El Borracho.*"

"Okay," says a smiling KB, "what does *El Borracho* mean?"

"*The Drunk.*"

KB giggles, shaking her head. She steps into the cool interior.

A humungous crashing sound breaks the silence.

Heidi growls.

"You tell 'em, Heidi," says Pete.

Except for a red-haired young man wearing a tan baseball cap, the barroom stands empty. The red-haired bartender had just crashed a bucket of ice into a stainless-steel bin.

Empty stools line the length of the S-shaped wooden bar. Three tables with their chairs stand vacant.

"Yo, Pete," calls Tony. "You should've called ahead for reservations."

KB grins.

"Nevertheless, due to our years of friendship I'll squeeze you in as soon as something comes available."

"Thanks a million, Tony. You're the last true gentleman."

"Holy mackerel, Mayor Ferrari. That's the most gorgeous, sexiest, desirable piece of female on the hoof I've ever seen you with."

"You'll have to excuse the earthy observations issuing from our young host here, KB," says Pete. "He no doubt takes you for a *Lake Tahoe trophy babe.*"

KB smiles angelically and thrusts her chest out.

"Whowee," says a grinning Tony, vigorously wiping his hands on his white apron.

Sherm wanders in from the bathroom.

"Tony Spinelli, meet Doctor T Sherman Oakes," says Pete. "He's head of the marine science lab up at Newport." Pete indicates KB. "This luscious thing is Miss Kristian Bjørnsen. She's his personal laboratory assistant."

"I'm very pleased to meet you both," says Tony, flashing his wide white smile.

"And this," says Pete, pointing toward KB's ankles, "is Miss Bjørnsen's faithful assistant, Heidi, the terrific terrier."

"Well, hello," says Tony. He kneels down and extends his hand. "Welcome to the biggest little city in the world."

Heidi gives the bartender's hand a sniff.

Tony pats Heidi's head and stands.

"They're down here at the city's invitation," says Pete. "They're working to save us from this effing catastrophe."

"If they're successful they'll be famed heroes around here— *forever*. Doctor Oakes, Miss Bjørnsen, dinner's on me. I'm sure glad you're here."

"Thank you, Tony," says Sherm, as he doffs his hat and sticks out his hand. "That's very kind of you, sir."

Tony grasps Sherm's hand. "Yeah, look around, Doc. It must've looked similar when the black plague wiped out a bunch of Europe. There's only one occupied table out front. Ordinarily there's a waiting line stretching out onto the sidewalk. Half our employees called in sick this morning. I suspect they've left town."

Pete, Sherm, and KB seat themselves at the nearest table. Heidi sits at KB's ankles.

"Can I interest you in a nice Mexican beer?" asks Tony.

"Whataya recommend?" asks Sherm.

"*El Pacifico* is very good, so is a bottle of *Corona* with a wedge of lime stuffed in the top."

"Oh, I'll try the *Corona*," says a smiling Sherm.

"And I'll have a vodka martini," says KB. "In fact, make it a double." Then she looks down at Heidi.

"Heidi," says Tony, "may I interest you in a nice bowl of fresh water?"

Instantly, Heidi's tail is wagging.

"I'll take that as an answer in the affirmative," says Tony.

"Point of fact," says Sherm, holding up a finger. "Heidi *prefers* genuine freshly flushed toilet water."

Tony laughs. "Well, I shall just scoop up a brimming bowl and bring it to her ladyship."

"I'll have a coffee, Tony," says Pete. "I've already consumed Sanchez's wedding punch today and I'm so tired I can hardly function."

"One coffee comin' up."

After Tony fetches their drinks and sets a water bowl near KB's chair, the trio order tacos, burritos, and enchiladas.

Reno
7:05 p.m., Saturday evening

"Hey, Moses."

The stocky man sporting the white ring of hair glances back over his shoulder. "Whataya want, Doug?"

"This time-and-a-half pay for working on Saturday's great, eh?"

Moses LaBarge and Doug Finch have been called out in an emergency to inspect Reno's hundred-and-thirty-year-old main trunk sewer line and laterals.

"You bet, Doug," says Moses, adjusting the bill on his Reno/Sparks Waterworks cap. "I don't mind givin' up a Saturday night for *this* kinda dough. Heck, me and the missus was just gonna have a drink, eat some supper, and watch a movie anyway."

Black-haired Doug, lean and average height, shines his six-cell flashlight at the vaulted brick ceiling. His light reflects off the tunnel's perpetual drips. Next to his boots rushes the flowing sewer. The spiky smell makes the younger man's eyes moisten.

"Watch your step there," Moses hollers back at Doug. "One misstep on that slimy catwalk and . . . *in you go.*"

The masonry catwalk runs down the tunnel's right side.

"If you *do* fall in," continues Moses, "never mind them 'nasties.' Concentrate on trying to keep them hags from out of yer anus."

"Mose," Doug says. "You're about as appreciated as a hemorrhoidal bloom on a blue-assed baboon."

Moses guffaws.

The main trunk line stands eight feet in diameter. Ordinarily, in non-flood times, the effluent runs two feet deep. This Saturday evening it's reaching three feet. Its fecund surface laps at the catwalk's edge.

Doug wrinkles his nose. "Whew, that shit could gag a *maggot.*"

"What's the matter, Finch?" hollers Moses. "The recent Saturday night party smells getting to you?"

"You mean *potty* smells?"

Moses shakes his head, grinning.

"I tell you, Mose," says Doug, his foot feeling for its next step on the wet deck. "Sometimes I wonder why I went into this line of work."

"Fer the money, Doug. Did ya forget, all ready? It's the money."

"Oh yeah, LaBarge. I nearly forgot. The pay's so great it makes me put up with a whole lotta *shit.*"

Moses chuckles. Their two flashlights work the catwalk, the vault, and the fluid's flowing surface.

"What's that?" yells Doug.

"See something?"

"There's movement, Mose."

Moses directs his flashlight ahead. "That's rats, Doug. Dozens of rats."

"*Chrissake.* It stinks. It drips. It's frickin' crawlin' with rats. Shouldn't our union negotiate a decent raise?"

"Believe me, Doug, you'll come to love it in here. I consider these subterranean passages my second home."

"Yee Gawds. That just about makes me wanta *puke*. If I stay down here for the next forty years, do you think I'll become as peculiar as you?"

Moses laughs and slaps his knee. Then he wipes water drops off his flashlight's lens.

"What's the matter, Mose?"

"You know, from down here it's hard to believe we live in a desert."

"Hey, aren't you the one who told me the Reno area was nothing but a swamp when the European settlers arrived?"

"Yeah. That's right, Doug. I find it hard to believe that a young buck like you was payin' attention. Until the early settlers cut drainage channels in the Truckee Meadows, this valley floor was swamp. The early wagon trains found it necessary to skirt the swamp by making a trail around the eastern and southern edge of the Truckee Meadows. The remnants of the wagon train tracks are still visible in the eastern Meadows, by the way."

"Mose. You're an amazing man: a sewer rat who studies history."

"Whatever you do," says Moses, "protect your wallet from gettin' wet."

"*Now*, what the heck are you talking about, you old reprobate?"

"That eel-skin wallet of yours, young feller."

"Yes, Mose. What of it?"

"Well, I read in the Reno Gazette-Journal's travel section that the Asians make eel-skin wallets out of *hagfish* leather."

"Hagfish *leather*? What's a hagfish?"

"Yeah," says Moses. "As close as your wallet is to your vulnerable rear end, heed my advice. Don't let your wallet get wet."

"You know, Mose, sometimes I have a little trouble following your circuitous line of thinking."

"I mean, Finch. If yer wallet gets wet it's liable to swell up, elongate, and start nibbling its way toward your *bungus*."

"For crying out loud, LaBarge. I think you've been breathing toxic fumes for *far* too long."

Moses cackles.

Water drops spatter the bill of Doug's cap. "Lead on." He shines his powerful flashlight forward. It lights up the RENO-SPARKS sewn on the back of Moses's coveralls. Doug recalls how he and his family had almost left town with the afternoon's mass exodus. However, they'd watched Mayor Ferrari and Chief Hamper's television announcement at five o'clock and decided to stick it out. After all, they lived up at Mogul, well out of the danger zone.

"Hey, Moses," Doug hollers. "Is this how it felt when you were in Vietnam?"

"How's that, Finch?"

"I mean, we're trying to uncover a creature that'd rip our innards out in a second, if we fell into its domain."

"Yeah," answers Moses. His flashlight's beam sweeps ahead. He halts.

"Hey, Mose. Let me know when you're going to stop. I almost crashed into you."

"Look up there, Finch."

"Whoa. What's that?"

"That's *hundreds* of rats. We must be herding them ahead of us."

A dark shape snakes up out of the fluid, grabs a squealing rat, and yanks it under.

"Holy *shit*."

"I don't know 'bout the holy part, Finch. But I know that rat's in a world of shit."

Reno
7:10 p.m., Saturday evening

"Listen, Sherm," says Pete, "can you give me *anything* on how you might destroy these hagfishes?"

Sherm takes a swallow of beer.

KB sets her drink down.

"KB," Pete asks, "what could possibly *prevent* hagfishes from living in freshwater?"

"It is their *kidneys*, Pete. Hagfishes have a simple primitive kidney that restricts them to living in salty water. In order for a fish to live in brackish, or fresh water, it must have a big, complicated kidney that is capable of maintaining the creature's internal salt and water level. You see, in order for fish to enter fresh water, or, for that matter, for us land animals to crawl out onto dry land, we must be able to take the salty sea with us."

"Could hags have lived in fresh water in ancient times?" Sherm asks.

"Some researchers assume that hagfish have always lived in salt water. However, there are some present-day hagfish kidney characteristics that may indicate that they *once* lived in fresh water."

Pete nods.

"For instance," says KB, "the hagfish kidney's renal corpuscles are relatively *enormous*, resembling those of freshwater fishes and amphibians. It is in the *renal corpuscles that the reabsorption of salt from the urine takes place*. This feature is *crucial* for freshwater or dryland life."

"That's right," says Sherm nodding.

"In addition, hagfishes have a prominent *pronephros*."

Pete snorts. "KB, what in God's name is a pronephros?"

KB swirls the olive in her martini. "The pronephros is a kidney-like organ that occurs in the higher vertebrate *embryos*.

It disappears as the embryo develops. However, in simple vertebrates, such as the lamprey eel, it functions as a kidney."

Pete shakes his head.

"It appears that the hagfish pronephros may be a vestigial water excretory structure, although the pronephric duct in the modern hagfishes has shrunk in size."

"Is that because they no longer live in fresh water?" Pete asks.

KB nods. "That is the theory."

"Could hagfishes live for just a little while in fresh water?" asks Pete.

"No, Pete. They would quickly lose their vigor and die within hours."

"What about hagfishes in ancient times?" Sherm asks.

"Do you recall, Doctor T? A single hagfish fossil was found from the Pennsylvanian Period of two hundred ninety million years ago. The fossil revealed well-developed *eyes* and a *huge kidney* just like today's freshwater fishes."

Reno
7:15 p.m., Saturday evening

"Moses. Let's get the hell outta here."

"Hey, new guy. We *hafta* finish this inspection. Now, follow me."

Without warning, Moses's foot skids out from underneath him. His shoulder smacks the brick vault. "*Oomph.*" His six-cell flashlight strikes the bricks. His light beam extinguishes.

"Hang on," yells Doug. "Don't move." He drops on his knees and grasps the back of Moses's coveralls.

Doug shines his light at the catwalk's edge. Moses's left shoe lies inches from the running fluid. The light beam strays onto the effluent's surface. There appears to be something lurking below the foam. Doug squints. He can't be certain whether there are long tapering "nasties" or long tapering fish.

"Dad-burn it."

"You all right, Mose?"

"Yeah, I'm all right. Now, get the hell off me, you pervert. I think my damned flashlight's busted."

Doug shoves himself up. He illuminates Moses's flashlight and observes the broken glass.

"Hand me your flashlight, Mose."

Moses rolls onto his right side and hands the flashlight back.

Doug lights up the shattered lens and broken filament. "Son of a gun. Do you have a spare bulb with you?"

"Of *course* not. We gotta continue with yours. Now dad-gummit, help me up."

Doug steadies Moses as he struggles to his feet.

"Gimme yer dad-burned flashlight."

"Hey, Mose, why don't you let me go first—"

"No," says Moses. "I'm the senior man here. I've been crawling around in these sewer lines for forty years. I know my way 'round better than you or any of the rest of you young whippersnappers. Now, gimme yer danged light."

"Here, 'Oh Great One.'" Doug hands over his flashlight. "Will you please accept this humble offering?"

Moses grabs the flashlight and looks it over. "After I retire next month, you can lead the NG's through these caverns. Until then, rookie—"

"Is my immaculately maintained illuminating instrument to your liking, 'Oh Great One?'"

"Yeah," mutters Moses. "This seems satisfactory. Now back off. Don't stand so close."

"Well," Doug says. "Just don't drop *that* light or we'll both be in a world of hurt."

"No shit, Sherlock. Just don't let your immense clumsy carcass fall on me and knock me in. Those damned sewer fish will rip yer guts out before you can sing, 'Ring Around Yer Rosy.'"

Doug hears a splash. "What the heck's that?"

"Oh, there's always strange sounds down here. You'll get used to it."

"Well, Mose, let's finish this inspection so we can get the hell outta here. I could really use a breath of fresh air."

"What? You don't like breathing this shit?"

Doug pats Moses's shoulder.

"Come on then," says Moses. "I'll go slow so you can keep up."

Doug shakes his head. "Yes. Us FNG's got a lot to learn."

"What was that?"

"Oh nothing, Moses. Just don't go so fast that this poor rookie gets left behind."

"If you fall in you could *lose* your behind."

"Thanks, LaBarge, *that* really gives me a big shit load of confidence."

The two men continue single file. The single light beam sweeps from side to side. Again, Moses halts.

"What is it, Mose?"

"The effluent's rising. It's beginning to lap over the top."

"Might be a cloudburst somewhere?"

"Yeah," says Moses, "or possibly everyone just got home from dinner."

Doug blows a puff of air from his nose. "Lead on, Mose. Let's finish before the dreaded *Banzai Pipeline* opens up."

Moses snorts. "Come on then, NG, but step carefully. These bricks are slicker than *owl* shit."

The two men pick their way along the ancient, uneven, slippery walkway. The evening's fresh fetor fills Doug's nose. He feels his mouth brimming with spit.

Doug's shoe slips on a slimy brick. "Uh," he grunts. His left foot slides toward the rushing sewage. He stumbles, flailing with both hands.

Moses halts and twists part way around.

Doug topples against him.

Moses struggles to catch Doug's arms. "*Steady there, Finch.*"

As Doug tumbles into him, Moses throws his flashlight hand toward the curved brick ceiling. Struggling to get a handhold between the bricks, he barks his knuckles. "*Dang.*"

With his left-hand Moses grapples for his falling partner.

Doug strains to keep himself from shoving Moses into the stream. He feels nothing in the dark to grab on to—except his leader.

Moses's slick soles slip. His hip bone strikes the bricks. His flashlight hand misses the ledge and splashes into the stinking current. The flashlight plunges beneath the surface, creating a creepy green glow.

"Oh shit," cries Doug. He grabs for Moses's coveralls.

Moses's upper trunk splashes into the rushing sewage.

Doug reaches out in the darkness. Moses's work boot slams into Doug's lips. Doug grabs for the flailing leg. He misses.

"Damn," Doug hollers.

Moses slips off the ledge.

The flashlight surfaces in Moses's hand. He appears to be laboring to gain his footing on the bathtub-shaped bottom.

"Here, Mose." On his hands and knees, Doug reaches out with his left hand. "*Grab on.*"

Suddenly, Moses bawls like a bull calf feeling his testicles being ripped off. He beats the sewerage into a frothing boil.

"Moses," yells Doug. "Throw your arm over here. I'll pull you out."

Moses shrieks and slaps the water. He turns his back toward the onrushing current. *He transfers the flashlight to his left hand*, now closest to the ledge. He fights savagely underwater with his right.

"Doug," Moses screeches. "The bastard's biting the *Jesus* outta me." He slips again and sinks to his shoulders. The flashlight shows the sewer water turning blood red.

Only Moses's head sticks out. He screams and screams as if bite-size chunks of his body are vanishing. His right hand frantically beats the water. His left hand holds the flashlight above his head.

Crying in agony, Moses makes a last lunge toward the catwalk. He shrieks as another chunk of his body gets served up. He shoves the flashlight onto the ledge— then he lets go. His head goes under.

Doug seizes the flashlight. He scans the sewage.

An effervescent churning melee moves downstream.

Moses's bald head surfaces. He sounds as if he is experiencing the most excruciating pain humanly possible. He shrieks and shrieks some more.

Doug sees a profusion of slick arching brown bodies foaming the fluid around Moses's thrashing body. The last thing Doug hears of a disappearing Moses, is his vanishing screams echoing off the brick walls.

Moses's RENO-SPARKS baseball cap twists round and round as it hurries downstream on the pink sudsy surface.

Reno
7:20 p.m., Saturday evening

"Join us, Tony," says Pete.

Tony sits down with Pete, KB, and Sherm at El Borracho.

Pete leans back. "Tony just graduated from UNR. After he makes a little money, he's headed for Las Vegas to the William S Boyd Law School."

"Thanks for the intro," says Tony. "If I go on the road, you can be my warm-up man. KB, how do hagfish go about eating? I mean, what's their favorite fare?"

KB sets her martini down. "Hagfish are jawless creatures just like the *lamprey eel of the Willamette River in Oregon*. However, where an eel attaches its mouth to the outside of a fish, then parasitically sucks out the living body's ingredients, the hagfish plunges itself headfirst *through* the animal's side, then eats the victim from the inside out."

Tony makes a face as if a snake's head has just got stuck crossways in his throat.

"The hagfish has several rasping teeth on its protrusible tongue. These horny teeth are capable of quickly cutting through any fish's skin."

"God bless 'em," mumbles Pete.

KB pats Pete's arm. "With its circular mouth it sucks onto the victim's side. To gain leverage it ties itself into a half-hitch knot. The hagfish has no bones, except its skull, so it is *completely flexible*. It simply gnaws, tugs on the fish's skin, slimes, and pushes its head through and starts eating."

Tony looks down. "Phew."

"Hmmm, KB," says Sherm. "Kindly tell Tony about the hagfish's *preferred* mode of entering its chosen snack."

KB grins. "Forcing its head through the victim's side takes a measure of hagfish energy. It is much more expeditious to simply lay on a generous coating of slime and enter any of the victim's orifices."

"Orifices?" asks a suspicious Tony.

"Yes. The gills, the anus—"

"I think your order's ready," says Tony, shoving himself to his feet.

"Um, KB." Sherm cocks an eye at the retreating bartender. "Tell Mayor Ferrari how the haggy fishes get rid of their slime."

"Oh, *please* do," says a grinning Pete.

"The hag's slime can clog its row of gill holes and suffocate it. However, because of its flexibility it easily ties itself in a knot, then slips the knot down its body pushing the slime mass off its tail."

————————

Pete sets his coffee cup down. "Okay, you scientists, how're we going to go about killing these suckers?"

"There are several ways," says Sherm. "The fastest is poison."

"I talked to Milt," says Pete. "The fact that a hag was found near Lake Tahoe indicates that they somehow breached the barrier separating sewer water from the storm drain and freshwater."

"I understand, Pete," Sherm says. "We'd create a firestorm of protest poisoning the legendary Lake Tahoe."

Pete nods. "A few years back the folks in Portola, a tiny community over on the Feather River route, lit a statewide firestorm because the California Department of Fish and Game poisoned Lake Davis."

"Aye," says Sherm. "Weren't they trying to get rid of an unwanted trash fish?"

"Not a trash fish," Pete says. "Somebody turned Northern Pike loose. These top-of-the-food-chain game fish ate the preferred Rainbow Trout and Browns. The poisoning killed all aquatic life—that is, except, as it turns out, *the Pikes*. Then Fish and Game deposited an antidote to neutralize the poison. Only, it didn't work. The poison hung around in Portola's drinking water *for months*."

Sherm takes a swallow of beer. "Yes. I remember the article in *Scientific American*. It bothered me how arrogant the state officials were. They dumped sixty thousand pounds of Pro-Noxfish poison in the lake. Then, they poured in sixteen thousand gallons of Nusyn-Noxfish to neutralize it."

"Yes," says Pete, "the California Fish and Game spent two million dollars poisoning. Then they spent *nine* million dollars settling their lawsuits"—Pete leans forward on his elbows—"and to this day the Pike abound."

Sherm sets his beer down. "If the citizenry grows terrified enough, Pete, they won't care one swaller how much itsy-bitsy, teenie-weenie questionable chemical is plopped into their precious water supply."

Pete leans back. "You mentioned predators, KB?"

"Yes, sea lions, harbor seals. Apparently, some creatures have devised a way to get past the hag's disgusting slime production. For instance, Pete, if you were to grab a hagfish it would instantly produce a gallon of slime, tie itself in a knot, and slide your hand right off its tail. You cannot *possibly* hold on to it."

"Whew." Pete sips his coffee.

KB produces a wry smile. "As far as using natural predators, it may be difficult inducing a happy harbor seal to plunge down a manhole."

———

Tony sweeps around the corner, carrying a tray over his head. With a flourish he sets it on the table. Rich tomato and cheese aromas rise on the steam.

KB sets her martini on her coaster. "Oh, Tony, that smells positively heavenly."

"Thank you." Tony places a little bowl containing a mixture of beef and chicken cubes before Heidi. "Miss Bjørnsen. Your wee doggy appears to be nearly starved."

"Aye, guvnor," says Sherm. "That wee doggy is nearly starved every minute of its tiny little wee life."

Pete laughs. He, Sherm, and KB spoon green and red salsa onto their tacos and begin to eat. Tony sits down with them.

"Yes," says Pete, "it appears that the hag predator angle may prove difficult, what with trying to force a reluctant harbor seal through a manhole and all." Then, his face brightens. "What about this? What about breeding some sterile versions of the hagfish and turning them loose?"

KB and Sherm glance at each other. "Um, Pete," says Sherm. "With hagfishes, we don't, ah,—"

"We know hardly anything about their reproductive habits," says KB. "So far, we have been *unsuccessful* at breeding them in captivity. With the time constraints of the present crisis upon us, using their reproduction—"

"I kinda figured something like that." Pete sighs. "I mean,

this primitive creature really has the will to live." Pete places his face in his hands. "We *have* to come up with something, and soon."

"As the urgency worsens," says Sherm, "it'll become easier to choose what would ordinarily be an unpalatable solution."

Pete stares at Sherm.

KB sets her taco down. "The only thing good is, it is a *local* problem that just started yesterday."

"If we don't resolve this, KB," Sherm says, "and quick, we could soon have a *worldwide* problem."

"KB," Tony says. "Why are they called *hagfishes?*"

KB lights a twinkle in her eye. "Commercial fishermen, long ago, undoubtedly at sea for far, *far* too long, imagined that the hagfish face resembles an old hag's . . . *genitalia.*"

Pete's face freezes. Tony grows a self-conscious grin.

"The hagfish's face has no eyes, just a big round hole for a mouth," continues KB, "and above that large hole sits a small nose hole. *Four or six waving* fleshy *tentacles* surround the mouth area. What the ancient fishermen could *not* see, was the scraping teeth growing on the fish's tongue."

"Can you hear the ancient fisherman trying to explain his bloody stump to the wife?" Sherm spreads his hands. "I don't know, Lena. I was just holding this adorable baby shark in my lap . . ."

Reno
7:45 p.m., Saturday evening

The trio, plus Heidi, finish eating at El Borracho. Pete's cellphone rings. He pulls it off his belt and pushes a button. "Yes?"

"Hello, Mister Mayor?"

"What do you have, Milt?"

"We found the problem."

"Goddamn, Milt, I mean, congratulations. Don't keep me in suspense. What'd you find?"

"A Christmas tree."

"That's not—"

"One of my inspecting teams found the explanation for the backed-up sewage."

"Listen, partner. What does that have to do with Christmas? Are you offering me a Christmas present?"

Milt laughs. "You could say that, Pete. You see, this formerly festive tree is blocking the downtown lateral that drains into the main trunk line exiting—"

"Whoa, Milt, whoa there. I prefer plain English, please."

"As you wish, Pete. Some dildo, after finishing with his Christmas tree last holiday season, rather than disposing of his holy icon in the usual manner that our good citizens are wont to do, slipped out in the dead of night, like any other common vandal, lifted a manhole cover and jammed his dead Douglas Fir—ornaments, fake icicles, and tree stand—down the city's manhole."

"Thank you, Milt. *That* I comprehend. I don't understand, but—"

"The tree, an eight-footer, became wedged in the main outbound sewer pipe, the one that drains the entire lower part of the Truckee Meadows. The main outbound pipe is located in a junction at the bottom of a ladder under a manhole cover. This junction's got three feeder pipes. From New Year until summer, the tree dammed up more and more debris, which consequently backed up sewerage into the three feeder pipes."

"For Christ's sake."

"Atta boy, Pete. That's the Christmas spirit. In time, we would've discovered the sewerage bubbling out from under the manhole cover."

"What kind of material is this *debris*?"

"Oh, you know, Pete, rubbers, toilet paper, ah hum—chunks."

"Hold it right there, Milt," says Pete. "That's more than I needed to know."

"Yep," says Milt. "You got the picture. Because of this Christmas grinch, you've got *ample* fluid for the slimy fishes to swim up to their ground-level toilets. At the same time, our citizens plunk their unsuspecting cheeks upon the waiting toilet seats, delivering the haggy fishes *ready meal* to their—"

"Thanks, Milt."

"—gnashing beaks. No problem, Mister Mayor."

"Now, I assume that your crews are, at this very moment, cleaning out this Christmas tree and its accumulation of . . . Christmas cheer?"

Pete hears . . . silence. "Milt. You still there?"

"Yeah, Pete. I'm here. It's just that we've experienced a tragedy."

"How bad?"

"We lost one of our best waterworks men."

Pete grimaces. "What happened, heart attack?"

"The haggies got 'im."

Pete sees newspaper headlines: Ferrari Elected Mayor of Nevada Ghost Town. At a roadside stand he sells Indian blankets made in China.

"Do you mean—?"

"Yeah. It was Moses LaBarge, a good friend of mine. He was on one of those underground patrols. He fell into the main trunk line effluent. The haggies got 'im. He was eaten alive from the inside out."

"God Almighty."

"Yeah, Pete. When my crew fished him off the screen, there was nothin' left but skin and bones."

"Were there any reporters there?"

"No, Pete. We lucked out on that score."

"Holy shit, Milt. I'm afraid of causing a full-blown panic."

"We can't keep the news from 'em forever, Mister Mayor. On the other hand, the effluent level will soon drop and that should mark the end of this damned crisis."

Another silence occurs.

"You still there, Pete?"

"Affirmative, Milt. We need to keep a lid on this next item, as well. This crisis is *far* from over."

"Whataya mean?"

"A hagfish was found at the Silver Creek Campground."

"Now, Pete. You know I'm not a member of the wiener and marshmallow crowd. Where the heck is the Silver Creek Campground?"

"Just outside Tahoe City, an apparently famished hagfish attacked a woman sitting on the outdoor toilet at the Silver Creek campground next to the Truckee River. Even though the bastard took a chunk out of his wife's crotch, the husband was able to catch the son of a bitch alive. The healthy specimen now resides in a tank in the basement of the Reno police headquarters building."

Another silence ensues.

Reno
8:15 p.m., Saturday evening

In the basement autopsy room, the overhead light turns the aquarium water green. A brown-colored three-foot long sinuous creature coils and uncoils. Its flank hits the glass with a thump.

This fish's skin is smooth as a wiener's. It has no face. Instead, it features a round hole surrounded by six, now five, waving tentacles.

Standing in the light's edge, Pete, KB, and Sherm peer at the specimen.

"Arrr, matey," Sherm says. "Whataya think of the creature, Pete?"

Pete leans close. "That's one ugly motherfecker." Pete stands. "Pardon me, KB, I don't usually—"

"That is okay, Pete. I have heard it all."

Pete shrugs. "Do either of you have any idea what the next step is?"

KB glances at the autopsy room's lab supplies. "I could get the materials to perform surgery on this hagfish and analyze its internal organs."

Pete mashes his teeth together making his cheek muscles bulge. "I suppose that's what any marine biologist would want to do with a newly discovered species, huh, KB?"

"No, no," KB says, waving her hands. "This is not a *scholarly* investigation. A peek inside might show us how these creatures have adapted to survive in freshwater. With that knowledge we possibly can figure out how to stop them."

"Aye, KB," Sherm says. "On the other hand, it's Saturday night. The apothecary shops are closed and we're six hundred miles from our lab." He taps the tank's metal corner. The hagfish arches its side and thumps against the glass panel.

From under a neighboring table, Heidi growls.

The double doors swing open. Doctor Draper and Chief Hamper stroll in. Pete notices Lyle's red-rimmed eyes. They resemble his eyes after his Maria had been killed.

Doctor Draper and Chief Hamper bend down and squint at the fish.

"Uh-huh," says Doctor Draper, "so that's what the ugly suckers look like."

Pete reveals the Christmas tree dam story. He also tells the story of Moses LaBarge being eaten alive. "All right, you scientists. What's this mean, finding this slime worm at the Silver Creek Campground?" Pete catches KB looking at him. When their eyes meet, she gives him a wide warm smile.

"We need to eradicate these horrible creatures," mutters Chief Hamper.

Pete drops his hand on Chief Hamper's shoulder. "Yes, Chief. We need to *destroy* these sons of bitches." Pete grimaces and glances up at KB.

KB nods.

Abel slips into the room and leans against the wall.

KB motions toward him. "There have been several cases where the hags have come into physical contact with a human being, yet they have apparently not harmed them. We need to find out what's going on with that and see if we can save some lives."

"Arrr," growls Sherm. "There's so much to be done, investigating, speculating, etcetera. Nonetheless, I think we need to *focus on our immediate problem* and then adopt a plan of action."

"Oh, dear Lord, yes," says Chief Hamper. "I agree."

"By golly," KB says. "I think we should come up with a plan to immediately *get everyone out of the danger zone*. If we could accomplish that, then we could declare a victory of sorts. Then, after our victory party, we could step forward with the strategy to *eradicate* these beasts."

Doctor Draper nods. "That's a reasonable plan, KB."

"I think we can live with that," says Pete. He points at the aquarium. "Nonetheless, what's the significance of finding this fish at Lake Tahoe?"

"Um," Sherm says. "We thought we had success within our grasp. Even though we didn't understand how these saltwater creatures came to live in Reno, or how they can exist in fresh water, we at least thought we had them *contained*. At first, KB and I figured we could simply poison them. What does it mean that the hagfish have reached the Truckee River? How did it happen? What is it that we don't understand? It appears *the hags are out of the bag*."

———————

Pete steps to the wall and lifts the telephone handset off the hook. He punches in the numbers. "Milt? Good, you're still there. We're in a quandary. Please tell me the significance of finding a hag at Lake Tahoe."

"Aye," hollers Sherm. "Ask 'im how the hagfish got from the sewer system into the freshwater system."

"Just a minute, Milt," Pete says. He pushes a button on the telephone, then hangs up the receiver. "Can you hear me?"

"Yep. We got ya fine."

"Milt. This is Doctor Oakes the—"

"Yeah, Doctor T. Go ahead."

"Ahum. Would you be so kind as to explain to us how the hagfishes escaped the Reno sewer system and gained the Truckee River freshwater system?"

Director Hershey leans back and gazes at the ceiling. He shoves his fingers under his glasses and rubs his eyes. "The two systems are separate, Doctor T. There's no *way* that the hagfishes could've gotten from one system to the other."

Pete frowns.

"When you flush your toilet," Director Hershey says, "or grind your cantaloupe rinds in the gobbler, the slurry goes directly into the sewer system. This sewage travels in underground pipes 'til it reaches the treatment plant here in Sparks. There the sewage is strained, filtered, and processed until it's pure enough to be reintroduced back into the Truckee River."

"Tell me, Mister Hershey," says Chief Hamper, stepping up to the wall phone. "Frankly, isn't it true that in certain circumstances pollutants can flow from the sewer ponds directly into the Truckee River?"

Officers Washington and Flynn push through the doors. A growl arises from under the neighboring table. Officer Washington shifts the paper to his other hand, kneels down, and pats Heidi's head.

"We work real hard, Chief Hamper," says Director Hershey, "to maintain the separateness of the two systems. Now, it's true that during an extreme flood, where the sewage ponds are inundated with a cloud burst or snowmelt, raw sewage *could* be washed from the ponds and end up in the river. This danger will be eliminated, by the way, when the new facility at Vista goes online."

Pete points at the paper in Officer Washington's hand and raises an eyebrow.

Milt continues, "But, ladies and gentlemen, we've not experienced this rare flooding situation this summer. There's been no inadvertent runoff from the sewer ponds into the river. Furthermore, there's no way that *anything* could get through the screens and filters that separate the sewage in the plant from the fresh water in the Truckee River."

"Now, Milt," says Pete. "I've seen a warning stenciled on Reno's concrete curbsides right above the storm drains. They say something to the effect that you should be careful what you allow to pour down the drain because it flows directly into the river."

"Yep," says Director Hershey.

"Well?" Pete opens his hands. "You just told me about the Christmas tree dam and your unfortunate employee falling into the sewage. For crying out loud, what's to keep those sons of bitches from simply swimming into the river?"

"Pete, what you're talking about is two separate systems. You're right; the storm drains *do* flow directly into the Truckee River. On the other hand, when you lift up a manhole cover, you're accessing the *sewer* system. They're separate."

"Oh." Pete glances at Chief Hamper and shrugs.

"Arrr," mumbles Sherm.

KB steps to the telephone. "Milt."

"Yeah, KB."

"How do you account for a hagfish being found *outside* the sewer system?"

"That's a mighty good question, young lady. We suspect something more is going on here than we realized."

Pete mutters, "No shit, Sherlock."

"Whataya got, Officer Washington?" asks Chief Hamper.

Officer Washington holds up a map of the Reno and Sparks area. It shows red, green, and white dots sprinkled across the middle. "Something peculiar's emerged, Chief. Look at this." He lays the paper on top of the fish tank.

The group gathers around.

The hagfish bumps the tank's side.

Officer Washington grits his teeth. "Here, in the University Ridge area. See these events?" He indicates two white dots.

"Uh hum," Sherm mutters. "Are those contour lines there, Harold?"

"Yes sir, Doctor Oakes. We thought the only attacks, and sightings, were occurring in the low-lying Truckee Meadows, but here are two sightings that have occurred way *above* the valley floor."

"Do you mean," asks Pete, "that there've been sightings on the *hills* surrounding the Truckee Meadows?"

"Well . . . yes, Mister Mayor."

"What were the times on those sightings, Officer Washington?" asks Chief Hamper.

"Actually, Chief, the first one happened quite a while ago."

"Why are we just now getting the report on this?"

"The first sighting transpired, you know, around five this morning," says Officer Flynn. "The subjects thought it was a rat swimming in the toilet. The victim screamed. The husband rushed in, slammed the lid down, and flushed it. However, as the citywide panic started, they surmised that what they'd *really* witnessed was a hagfish and called in the report."

Chief Hamper clenches his teeth. "How can we be sure that the sighting is of a hagfish?"

"We can't really," says Officer Washington, "but the second sighting is as good as it gets."

Chief Hamper arches an eyebrow.

"At thirty-four-oh-five, Socrates Drive, this afternoon," says Officer Flynn, "citizen Ron Rush proceeded to empty the sewage tank on his motorhome, preparatory to he and his wife, June, fleeing the area."

Pete flexes his jaw.

"Mister Rush called this in an hour ago," Officer Washington says. "We found this report as we prepared this map. When Mister Rush uncapped his sewer-dump pipe, a two-foot-long slippery creature *jumped* at him. He yelled, fell back, and kicked at it."

KB covers her mouth with her hand.

"Missus Rush screamed, dropping her dishes on the driveway. As Mister Rush scrambled to get away from the fish, Missus Rush plucked up her kitchen knife and took a hack at it."

Sherm shakes his grinning head.

"When the bladed instrument opened the suspect's back," says Officer Flynn, "the creature, you know, dropped back into the sewer. Both Mister and Missus Rush saw it really good. They were adamant that they know what a rat looks like, and this was definitely *not* a rat."

"Holy shit," says Pete. "What's this mean?"

"Listen, gentlemen," KB says. "I think I see a pattern that perhaps explains why there was a hagfish caught at Lake Tahoe and why they were spotted on the side of the surrounding Reno hills. Let us take this map and see if we cannot track down these *sons of a bitches*."

Pete guffaws.

Laughter erupts from the speakerphone.

"Atta girl, KB." Sherm pats KB's back. "Welcome aboard."

Reno
9:05 p.m., Saturday evening

The sun sets behind thunderclouds. Lightning drills the foothills. Thunder rattles Abel's unmarked city automobile. Windshield wipers labor to clear the hailstones and rain.

Abel drives KB and Sherm up Socrates Drive into Reno's University Ridge district. "Where are we?" KB twists and holds the map for Sherm to see from the rear seat.

Their tires rumble over railroad tracks.

"Arrr," says a grinning Sherm, pointing at the map. "I have determined that we're precisely at these railroad tracks, me little chickadee."

"Do you want me to pull over?" asks Abel.

"Yes, Abel," says KB. "There is a white dot near here." KB taps her fingernail on the white dot. "Where is this, Sherm?"

Sherm squints. "Achilles Drive."

"It jus' here on left," says Abel.

A minute later Sherm says, "That two-story yellow house is the right number."

"It look closed up."

"Correctamundo."

The summer shower suddenly shuts off. An inch of new hail lies on the lawns but it's already melted off the pavement. Runoff rushes down the gutters and disappears into the storm drain.

Abel pulls into the driveway and shuts the engine off. They crawl out of the air-conditioned car into the clean smell of the thundershower. Little Heidi runs to the bushes. KB feels the evening warmth surrounding her.

Abel pushes the doorbell button.

Somewhere back behind the house a train whistles. KB turns toward it.

Abel shakes his head. "No one home." He looks at KB and smiles. He jerks his head for KB to follow him.

The trio crunch through the hailstones around the house's corner. Heidi's whiskers brush KB's ankles.

"Oh," says KB, as she beholds the panoramic view. Laid out at her feet lies the whole of downtown Reno. A yellow-colored three-engined train pulling seven boxcars roars up the grade. It whistles at the Comstock Drive crossing. For a few moments, KB forgets the pressures.

Unexpectedly, Sherm begins to sing:

"Pardon me, Roy, is that the hag who slimed my new shoes?"

Abel chuckles and turns to KB.

"Yes," says KB. "Doctor T often feels the need to make up little ditties. I think he is trying to tell us that we should get on with our investigation."

The trio strolls back to the car.

"My little Danish flower," Sherm says. "Where do you want to motor off to now?"

"Let us see if we can locate the place indicated by the *second* white dot."

They pile into the car. To KB it feels as if she has entered a hot house.

Abel starts the engine, and in moments, cool air spills onto KB's lap. She brushes her fingers behind her knees and feels moisture.

"Where to, Doctor T?" asks Abel.

KB holds up the map and points to the second white dot.

"It's up on University Ridge Drive, Abel," says Sherm.

"That two blocks, then go right."

They drive on.

Sherm points. "There. That gray one. See? There's the RV sewer dump Officer Washington mentioned."

KB notices that there is no motorhome, or any other vehicles, for that matter.

Abel walks to the front door. The two scientists clamber out and stand in the driveway.

Sherm removes his hat and wipes his forehead.

Thunder rumbles down the mountains. Heidi quivers.

Abel presses the doorbell button, and then shakes his head. He catches KB's attention.

KB smiles and the trio troop around the house's side.

The University Ridge house perches several hundred feet higher than the one on Achilles. KB gasps as she turns the corner.

The biggest little city in the world, her lights just beginning to switch on, presents a breathtaking first impression.

Abel gestures. "This area where youngsters used to park."
KB furrows her brow.

"Aye, KB," Sherm says. "You know . . . where the couples parked their cars, admired the grand view, and necked."

KB wears a perplexed look.

"You understand," says Sherm. "They sucked face, swapped spit, and groped like flailing octopuses."

Abel guffaws.

"Abel," KB asks, "how is it you know so much about such a place?"

Abel shakes his head. "I already married to my sainted bride when move to Reno, KB. But I 'member patrolmen had a time educating young people to find new place for passion."

KB smiles and gives Abel a hug.

The sun disappears behind the saw-toothed mountains and the thundering thunderclouds. It appears that Reno's casinos are taking turns blinking on their lights. KB sighs. "Oh, this is simply beautiful."

"Indeed, it is, KB," says Sherm. "As soon as this calamity is over, I would love to park up here with you and suck face."

KB giggles and jabs her elbow into Sherm's ribs.

While KB stands enthralled, Sherm bumps Abel in the arm.

"Look at this, Abel," Sherm whispers. He unwraps a jeweler's tissue paper and shows Abel a *sterling-silver charm-bracelet* pendant representing the head of a *longhorn bull*. "I'm going to give this to her at the appropriate moment because she's 'taken the bull by the horns.'"

Abel smiles and nods his head in approval.

Although the trio stand above the downtown area, they hear no sounds. Not only that, they also don't hear a pink-colored, fully restored, Rolls-Royce limousine behind them, majestically motoring up University Ridge Drive.

Raindrops spatter Sherm's hat. Again, his baritone voice sings out.

"Hag me.

Hag me.
They gotta eat my shorts to snag me.
Snag me from this seat so fre-e-ee.
Oh, hagfish let my asshole be-e-ee."

Reno
9:35 p.m., Saturday evening

Thunder cracks and raindrops splash. The trio, and little Heidi, jump back into the car.

"Where to now?" asks Sherm.

KB glances at the map and shrugs.

"Where to now, Heidi girl?" asks Sherm.

KB points up the hill. "Let us drive up a little farther. I do not know exactly what we are looking for, but . . ."

"That's a good enough reason," Sherm says. "Let us proceed, *señor Sanchez*."

The car backs into the street. They ascend University Ridge Drive. Plush homes line both sides.

The road crests. On the right, a wide, low, single-story mansion—32,000 sq. feet, sixteen bathrooms and twenty-two baths—sprawls across a tip of land overlooking the entire Truckee Meadows. A brick and black-iron fence surrounds the estate keeping the property secure, but not preventing a passerby from admiring it.

The wrought-iron gate stands open, showing off a brick and stone courtyard.

"Jiminy Cricket," KB says. "Look at that pink automobile."

"That an antique Rolls-Royce," says Abel, bringing his car to a stop. "That car Pete and I see."

"Arrr," growls Sherm. "That's a five-hundred-and-fifty-thousand-dollar car, me hearties. Moreover, it appears some drama's taking place."

KB rolls down her window. She hears a woman shrieking, "Grandmother, you're *cracked*. You'll *never* goddamned see us again."

"Yes," says KB, "the young lady appears to be scolding the older lady."

"The young man," Abel says, "in hurry to load van."

"You're the policeman here, Abel," says Sherm. "These are the first people we've seen on this hillside. Do ya suppose we oughta investigate this domestic drama?"

"Yeah," Abel says, as he bounds from the car. KB, Sherm, and little Heidi hustle to keep up. Raindrops spatter the pavement.

"Hello, citizens." Abel holds up his badge. "There is trouble?"

Madam Zho removes the cigarette holder from her Corvette-red lips and smiles. "No, love, there's no trouble here."

Melody screeches, "Why don't you tell 'em, Grandmother?" Her face turns red. "How long can you keep this unbelievable horror secret?"

"Come on, Melody," DuWayne says. "We're all loaded up. Let's just go home."

Melody stomps her foot and screams.

DuWayne gently but firmly grasps her shoulders. "Just get in, sweetheart."

As if possessed, Melody wails and beats on DuWayne's chest. Tears drip off her jaw.

"Sweetheart," DuWayne says, "there's nothing we can do to make things right. Let's just go home."

Tiffany watches her aunt with eyes big as pool balls.

DuWayne indicates the car door. "Tiffany, Jenny, please get in the van."

"Excuse me, sir," says Abel. "Is trouble I can help you with?"

DuWayne shakes his head. "No sir, no help from any source can make this situation good again." He eases into the driver's seat.

As Abel watches them drive off, he writes down the license number.

Melody's inconsolable shrieking sounds for two blocks.

Abel turns to face Madam Zho. A huge manservant now stands behind her. Abel involuntarily takes a step back.

KB notices two older men and two older women placing luggage in a big Cadillac's trunk. She taps Abel's arm and points.

Abel saunters up to Kam Ho and Su Lee, James and Jean Wu. "Is there problem here?"

Kam Ho smiles generously. "No, no, Officer. No trouble at all. We've had a lovely visit with my sister and we're motoring back to our home in Vancouver."

"Is that Vancouver, Washington, sir?" Sherm asks.

"British Columbia, my good man," says Kam Ho.

"Very good, sir," Sherm says. "I wish you a pleasant drive home."

Abel gives a little bow. "Excuse me, sir, but young mother seem very upset." Abel gestures at the departing van.

"My sister-in-law simply had a small family disagreement with her granddaughter. These things happen."

Near the Cadillac, little Heidi finds Chairman Mao. They circle and sniff each other.

"Excuse me, sir," KB says. "Are you leaving because of the threat from the sewer system?"

Madam Zho and Mister Morley walk up from behind.

Kam Ho, wearing his smile like a "happy face" mask, spreads his hands. "Threat from the sewer system? We know of no such thing, young lady. Everything's fine. We've enjoyed a nice visit but it's time to go home. Thank you very much for being concerned."

KB, Sherm, and Abel step in the clear as the big Cadillac maneuvers out of the parking area.

Madam Zho puffs on her cigarette. The two dogs line up taking turns watering the bushes.

"You've probably seen the news," Sherm says. "The city's in the grip of a serious problem."

Madam Zho grows a perplexed look on her face. "You're a cute one. No, I haven't seen *anything* on the news."

Mister Morley stays behind Madam Zho.

KB thinks, *you are as big as King Kong.* KB unfolds her map. Raindrops pelt the paper. "May we move onto your porch?"

"Of course, dears," says Madam Zho. "Right this way."

They step under the roof and stand in front of the immaculately carved wooden door.

Sherm asks, "Have you heard about the hagfish attacks, ma'am?"

"My name is Madam Zho." She holds out her hand. "Madam Jenny Zho. You can call me Jenny, young man."

Sherm shakes Madam Zho's hand and introduces himself, KB, and Abel. "Now, Jenny, are you not aware of the toilet-born attacks on humans?"

Mister Morley takes a breath, swelling his already enormous chest. Madam Zho maintains her impenetrable smile. "No, young man, I've not seen the telly."

"Jenny," KB says. "As Doctor Oakes said, I am Kristian Bjørnsen, a marine scientist. Look here please."

Mister Morley hands Madam Zho an ashtray. She stamps out her cigarette and hands the ashtray back. Then she nods at KB.

KB's fingernail moves up University Ridge Drive to the white dot. "This is your neighbor, Jenny. Just two blocks away."

KB looks directly into Madam Zho's eyes. "I do not think the hagfishes spread across the Truckee Meadows, then made their way up here. Rather, *I think their inception occurred on this hillside. Then* they made their way down into the low-lying areas."

Madam Zho glances up at Mister Morley. He produces a pack of Virginia Slim cigarettes. He shakes one up. She plucks it out. Mister Morley strikes up fire from his gold lighter.

Madam Zho draws the cigarette into life. A great cloud erupts as if it was her first smoke of the day. "Thank you, Mister Morley."

"Madam," says Abel. "You understand English okay?"

Madam Zho's smile fades. She stares at Abel, the only member of the trio who is the same height as her. She glances down at Heidi and her eyes soften. "Yes, Detective, I understand English perfectly well."

KB hears a strong Chinese accent; nonetheless, Madam Zho speaks English as well as KB does.

"We're not trying to get anyone in trouble, Jenny," Sherm says. "We simply need help finding the hagfish source."

"Yes," says KB. "This is an unusual species of hagfish. She notices Madam Zho's eyes blinking. *She knows something.*

Madam Zho takes a long drag off her cigarette. She turns and peers up at Mister Morley. His expression remains impenetrable.

"Madam Zho," Abel says. "City of Reno not looking for someone to prosecute. We grateful for assistance."

"I wish I could help you, young man." Madam Zho pats Abel on the arm. "Unfortunately, I cannot. Come, Mister Morley. Let's go in and clean up after our guests. Goodbye, Detective Sanchez."

———————

In front of Madam Zho's mansion, KB, Sherm, Abel, and little Heidi sit in Abel's automobile. Rain runs down the windows. The darkening sky intermittently lights up from streaks of lightning. Heidi shivers, giving the car that wet-dog smell.

"She lying," Abel says quietly. "I see her blinking and she look at ground."

"Arrrbeedarrr. You're correctamundo, Abel," Sherm says. "That's a fine observation you made. She indeed reveals excessive nervousness, and by glancing at the ground, she demonstrates that she wishes to make the symbolic dash for freedom."

Abel nods.

"You bet you," KB says. "She is a gracious lady, but . . ."

"We're in agreement then," Sherm says. "What're we going to do about it?"

"Call Pete," says Abel. "He know what to do."

Reno
10:15 p.m., Saturday evening

A cloudburst pounds the parking lot at Reno City Hall. Pete pushes his limousine door open. "Hurry," he hollers. "Get in outta the rain."

KB, Sherm, Abel, and little Heidi exit Abel's car, and dash for the Lincoln Continental limousine. They pile in the automobile's rear, dividing themselves between the backseat and the jump seats. Thunder rustles the cottonwood leaves. Pete pulls the door shut.

Little Heidi shivers. Pete pats the seat. Heidi hops up beside him.

"KB," Pete says, "I congratulate you for 'stepping up to the plate.'"

"Stepping up to the plate?"

"It's an idiom, KB, based on baseball. It means dealing with a problem directly and resolutely, which you have certainly demonstrated this afternoon. It has the same meaning as the expression, 'grab the bull by the horns.'"

KB sits up straight and smiles. "Thank you so much."

Pete pulls a paper from his inside coat pocket. "This is a search warrant for the University Ridge Drive residence. Pretty tough to get on a Saturday night, let me assure you. It's fortunate I was able to reach my old lodge brother, Judge Reed."

"Jumping Jiminy," KB says. "That will make Jenny talk, that is for sure."

"In addition, we have Officers Cobb and Bardouche meeting us there."

"Good," KB says. "Crystal, she is a pistol."

Abel smiles. "That good work, boss. Shall we go?"

Pete rubs Heidi's head. He looks first at one companion, then another. "Who's gonna drive?"

Abel twists in his jump seat and looks forward. He laughs. "*Yo no sé.*"

"Arrrbeedarrr," Sherm growls. "I'm a first-rate airplane pilot and a boat's captain, but I've never operated one of these big stretch limos. *I'll* drive us up to Madam Zho's mansion."

KB catches her breath.

Reno
10:25 p.m., Saturday evening

Madam Zho glances at Heidi and smiles. "Won't you please come in." She gestures to KB that it is okay to include Heidi. "Mister Mayor, it wasn't necessary for you to get a search warrant. If you wanted to look around all you had to do was ask."

"Thank you very much, Madam Zho," Pete says. "You're very courteous. You can just call me Pete."

"Thank you, young man. I would be pleased if you would simply call me Jenny. Come into the living room. Mister Morley, fix them something to drink."

"No thank you, Jenny," says Pete. "We'll only be here a minute."

Pete, KB, Sherm, Abel, Officers Cobb and Bardouche—and Heidi the dog—follow Madam Zho from the foyer into the living room. Chairman Mao and Heidi the dog replay their greeting ceremony.

Pete puts the back of his hand to his mouth and says softly, "Cool pad, huh, KB?"

KB flashes Pete an affectionate smile. "By golly, so this is how the American rich live."

Pete grins. "I think maybe she's Canadian, KB." Pete feels immeasurable affection swelling his heart.

"Won't you please sit down," says Madam Zho. She motions toward the nearest seating area, which includes two small plush couches and two overstuffed chairs. Madam Zho perches on the corner of an ottoman. She flicks off her ash into a huge orange-and-gold ashtray.

The foursome choose their seats. Officers Cobb and Bardouche unobtrusively begin checking for damning evidence.

KB settles herself across from Madam Zho. "Is it okay if Heidi runs around in your beautiful home?"

"Oh my, yes." Madam Zho motions with her left hand. "She and Chairman Mao seem to be getting along famously."

"Thank you, Jenny," says KB. "Now, what can you tell us please?"

"Among other things," Madam Zho says, through a cloud of smoke, "I own a leather-exporting business. I formerly lived in Hong Kong. However, with the communist takeover looming, I moved to Vancouver, British Columbia."

"Pardon me, Jenny," Pete says. "Are you a Canadian citizen?"

"Because I was born in Hong Kong, I've got a British passport. I bought eel leather in wholesale lots and sold them to companies in South Korea. They in turn produced wallets, belts, purses, and boots. However, when I moved to Canada, I found myself thousands of miles from the eel fishermen."

"What about hagfishes, Jenny?" asks KB.

Madam Zho takes a lightning quick glance in the direction of the swimming pool and then she draws a drag on her cigarette. She taps the ash into the tray.

Mister Morley crosses his arms.

Pete stands and stretches. Then he casually walks to a table near the French doors where Officer Cobb pokes through magazines. Abel nonchalantly follows.

"Crystal," whispers Pete. "I saw her take a furtive glance toward the swimming pool area. Slip out there and have a look."

"You got it, Mister Mayor."

"Pete," Abel says softly.

Pete places his arm around Abel's shoulders.

"Sherm bought KB silver bull for bracelet."

"Say again?"

Abel stealthily points toward KB. "Her charm bracelet. Sherm buy her longhorn."

Pete shrugs.

"For grabbing bull by horns. He give award at 'propriate moment to hang on bracelet."

"Ah hah." Pete nods. "Thanks, *tío*. I really appreciate you looking out for my ... interests."

"*De nada.*"

Pete and Abel wander back to their seats. At the same time, Officer Bardouche slips down the hallway.

"What you do in Reno?" asks Abel.

"I love to gamble, Detective, so I bought a house here. This is a popular place for my family to gather, as well."

Pete sees Mister Morley's jaw squeeze together.

Sherm removes his hat and places it on the seat beside him. "What are your activities in Vancouver, Jenny?"

"As I said, Doctor Oakes, I import eel meat and leather and I wholesale them to manufacturers and retailers."

"You know nothing about hagfishes?" asks Sherm.

"I've heard of them, of course."

The pool lights flick on. Jenny starts. She crosses her legs and takes a big hit off her cigarette.

"Uh hum," says Sherm. "Have you ever considered aquaculture as a source of meat and leather?"

"Now, young man." Madam Zho coughs. "We're in the desert. Where would I raise fish around here?"

From down the hallway drifts the Microsoft sound of a computer warming up. Madam Zho turns and peers up at Mister Morley. He sets his teeth—as if simply waiting for Madam Zho's order to throw the whole lot of them out on their duffs. She imperceptibly shakes her head.

Officer Cobb opens the patio door and leans in. She motions for Pete. He steps through the door, trailed by KB, Sherm, Abel, Madam Zho, and Mister Morley.

The rain has stopped but the patio stones still cup water. Pete notices that the free-formed-shaped swimming pool stands empty. Then he looks toward downtown. The clouds hang low over the casinos, their bottoms reflecting the lights.

"Oh," KB says. "That is the most spectacular sight I have ever seen, that is for sure."

"You pay the dough," says Sherm, "you get the show."

Officer Cobb gives Sherm a wry grin. "Come look at this, Doctor Oakes. There's a row of stainless-steel tanks on the edge of the patio."

Pete and Sherm walk over. Pete grasps one of the steel-meshed hinged lids and pulls it up. "Sherm, what do you think this was used for?"

"They're fish tanks, Pete."

"Oh, yes, of course," Pete says. "Jenny, what were you growing here?"

For a split second, Madam Zho glances at the pool's dressing room door. Then she turns to Mister Morley. He shakes a cigarette out of the pack and holds the lighter for her.

"Officer Cobb." Pete points at the dressing room.

Officer Cobb opens the door, turns the light on, and begins an inspection of the boxes, books, and equipment. In half a minute, she steps back out holding a stack of logbooks. She hands them to Pete.

Pete looks at the Latin words written on the top book: *Eptatretus deani*. He asks Madam Zho, "What do these words mean?"

She clutches the fabric on her chest.

"Sherm." Pete hands him the log.

Sherm grins and hands it to KB.

"Jumping Jiminy. That is the proper name of a hagfish species living just off the California coast."

Chapter Seven

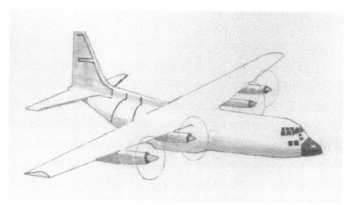

C-130 Hercules, Lockheed

Reno
10:40 p.m., Saturday Evening

Thunder is still rumbling around Mount Rose.

Rain pelts the patio.

From the hallway, Officer Bardouche walks into Madam Zho's living room.

"Mister Mayor, you might want to look at this. I searched the suspect's computer and uncovered records, contacts, and technical matters on *raising fish*."

"I'll write you up a good evaluation, Reggie," calls out Officer Cobb.

"Check out this computer screen," says Officer Bardouche. "It's in English and describes in detail how the fish were bred and fed."

"Good work, team," says Pete. "Jenny, we're not looking to prosecute anyone. We're seeking information that will save lives."

Madam Zho looks up at Mister Morley. His lips form a

firm line. He reaches in his pocket for cigarettes. Madam Zho shakes her head, *No.*

"I think you're a very nice lady, Jenny," says Pete, gently. "I don't think for one second that you meant to cause this tragedy. Nonetheless, I'm telling you, as Reno's former prosecutor, if you aren't forthcoming with helpful information, you and your manservant will be arrested, taken downtown, booked, and jailed—*tonight.*"

Madam Zho spins around and places her left hand on Mister Morley's arm. She looks up into his eyes. To Pete, it almost looks like the big man could cry. She pats him on the arm and turns to face Pete.

"This experiment went bonkers. I never intended to hurt anyone. I only wanted to develop a completely new way of harvesting meat and leather from the sea. But then, something went terribly wrong."

Pete nods. "Let's sit down, take a load off . . . and talk."

"Yes, dear boy, I experimented with raising a special breed of super hagfish. The world is familiar with eel-skin products. Millions of Asians eat eel meat. What is less known is that hagfish leather and meat is regularly substituted for eel."

"Do all species of hags make high-quality meat and leather?" asks KB.

Madam Zho slowly shakes her head back and forth. "Some of the Formosa Strait and South China Sea fishermen got to experimenting with catching certain kinds of hagfish. Some species produce leather as good as eel's. It's an unexamined and untapped market."

Sherm arches his eyebrows and looks at KB. KB nods in the affirmative.

"Well," says Madam Zho, "because I moved several thousand miles from the wholesalers, I wondered if I couldn't grow hagfish in a controlled fish farm."

"Looky here, Madam Zho," says Officer Cobb, rapping her knuckles on her logbook, "who are these guys who've signed off in here, Doctor Chen, and Doctor Chan?"

"I've got a remarkable lot of contacts in many countries, including the People's Republic of China," says Madam Zho. "Hong Kong's been an absolute hotbed of entrepreneurism. I found out, through the grapevine, that several pisciculturists were looking for a way to move out of Red China. I thereupon worked to arrange an escape. As it turned out, two extraordinarily brilliant young men were able to permanently and safely leave their families and escape to the west."

Pete labors to maintain a neutral face. "How did you get them out?"

"Well, Pete, I greased the skids." Madam Zho makes a hand motion as if dealing cards. "Then, I, well, I smuggled them in through San Francisco and brought them up here." She fires up another cigarette.

"What a pis-pisci-pisciculturist?" asks Abel.

Madam Zho gives Abel a big smile. "One who studies fish. One who breeds, hatches, and rears fish under controlled conditions. For instance, they are who you call when you're setting up a fish farm. Frankly, am I going to be in much trouble for, for—"

"For illegally smuggling communist scientists into the USA?" Pete asks. "For conducting scientific experiments in Reno and trying to set up a business venture without the proper licenses? For not putting in place the safeguards to prevent dangerous animals from escaping, which has now resulted in the deaths of a number of our citizens, including the wife of Reno's police chief?"

"I've got an awful lot of money, Pete. I can pay—"

Pete raises his hand. "*Not another word.*"

Mister Morley makes a movement toward Pete.

"*No.*" Madam Zho puts her hand out.

"I'm on *your* side, Jenny," says Pete. "Don't say another word about *money.*"

In Madam Zho's living room, Pete leans back in his chair. "Jenny, as a former prosecutor I can tell you that your cooperation in helping us to resolve this difficulty will go a long way in relieving you from criminal responsibility."

Madam Zho stands. "I can show you where the experiment took place."

"Ahhh, KB," says Sherm. "Would you like to view where the hagfish grew?"

Madam Zho walks toward the French doors. Mister Morley hurries to open them.

"Over there in those tanks," says Madam Zho, pointing, "is where the young ones were raised."

"They're empty," mumbles Sherm.

KB points. "So is the pool."

"Watch your step." Madam Zho coughs. "The grate's been removed from the terrace drain."

"Is cross a shrine to dearly departed?" Abel stands next to a small white cross in the flowerbed, reminiscent of the ones Latinos place beside the highway to honor their dearly departed.

Madam Zho sucks in a breath. Her left-hand trembles when she crushes her cigarette out. She turns to Mister Morley. He pulls a cigarette up for her and strikes the lighter.

"It's nothing." She blows a cloud of smoke. "A decoration, nothing more."

Abel lifts a dog's collar from the cross. "What meaning of collar?" He points to the tag. "There is writing."

Madam Zho clutches her blouse.

"It in Chinese," says Abel. He hands it to Madam Zho. "What it say?"

Madam Zho wads the collar in her hand. "It's nothing. Just an old memento."

"Yeah?" Officer Cobb says. "What about that fresh hole dug *beside* the cross, sister? Is that just a memento?"

Madam Zho glances at Pete.

Pete crosses his arms over his chest.

Officer Cobb picks up a shovel. "This hole was freshly dug. It appears you buried a pet under that cross. Did you have another pet die? Were you getting ready to bury it when we all showed up?"

Madam Zho shakes her head. "We were getting ready to plant a shrub."

"Where's the shrub, Missus Zho?" asks Officer Bardouche.

Madam Zho glances at Mister Morley. His lips appear chiseled out of granite. Madam Zho turns toward the officers. "The two scientists I brought in also brought in several live species of hagfish."

"Ahum," Sherm says. "You were able to successfully raise them here?"

"Yes, dear boy. I had these tanks constructed across town at Sierra Air. We worked through many generations of fish. In time, they outgrew the tanks. We expanded the research into the swimming pool." Madam Zho inhales a drag. "There were scores in there."

"Where are the two scientists now, Jenny?" asks Pete.

"They're presently in Vancouver BC."

"How," asks Officer Cobb, "did you get the scientists up there? Better yet, how'd you get 'em into the USA?"

"By ship, Officer Cobb." Madam Zho blows a cloud of smoke. "We, who've lived in a bustling entrepreneurial colony hanging on to the side of a stifling communist state, have grown adept at smuggling people. And, if we find the borders of The People's Republic porous, how do you think we find the borders of *this* great country?"

Pete smirks and gives up a knowing nod.

"The breeding experiments got off to a marvelous start," says Madam Zho. "The pisciculturists told me that they'd discovered, from fossil studies, that ancient hagfish lived in fresh water. Consequently, Doctors Chen and Chan brought in several special hagfish. And they began to back-breed them."

KB and Sherm edge closer.

"In time, the two young men seemed to resurrect, out of the generations, an earlier freshwater breed of hagfish. Not only that, but this earlier breed also turned out to be much more *predatory* than today's hagfishes. We were extremely pleased to note that because the creatures ate so much more, they grew faster. It appeared we could raise the creatures in a freshwater fish farm, not much different from raising vicious mink in a mink farm."

"What happened, Jenny?" asks Sherm. "Where did the experiment go haywire?"

"Well, Doctor Oakes," says Madam Zho, "Madame Chiang Kai-Shek fell in the pool."

"*Madame Chiang Kai-Shek?*" stammers Officer Cobb.

"My Shih Tzu," says Madam Zho.

"I'm truly sorry to hear your little dog was hurt, Jenny," says Sherm.

"She wasn't hurt, Doctor Oakes. She, she . . ."

Abel points at the dog collar in Madam Zho's fist. "Is pet's name on tag?"

Madam Zho's sides tremble.

"I've heard enough of this 'sob sister' crap," says Officer Cobb. "Did you lose your pet to your little experiment here? Did you lose a *second* pet?"

Madam Zho drops her cigarette, coughs, and stumbles. Mister Morley catches her.

"What else have you lost here?" Officer Cobb persists. "Were you going to dig a third hole? Or a fourth?"

Madam Zho begins to bawl. "Please. I can't—"

"You can't what, sob sister?" asks Officer Cobb. "You can't come clean with your sneaky little caper? You can't come clean so we can save some lives around here?"

Officer Bardouche asks, "Why were your relatives in such a hurry to leave when we drove up? What're you trying to cover up? Do you want us to dig up what's under that cross? Crystal, hand me that spade."

"No," Madam Zho cries. "*No.*"

Mister Morley holds Madam Zho from collapsing. "May I have your permission, Mister Mayor, to escort Madam Zho to her sitting room? I don't think you're going to get much more out of her, at this time."

"All right, Mister Morley," Pete says. "I'll give her a little time to get a hold of herself. However, *you* need to think about what I've been telling your mistress. *We're not leaving until we get to the bottom of this.* As a former prosecutor, I'm informing you, if Jenny doesn't come completely clean, she's looking at hard prison time. As for you, Mister Morley, only time and your cooperation will determine whether you escape incarceration."

"Thank you, Mister Mayor," says Mister Morley. "You're most kind, sir. I'll conduct Madam to her sitting room and get her whatever she needs. I shall return presently. Please, make yourselves at home."

———————

"I left her with cigarettes and a large glass of brandy, Mister Mayor," says Mister Morley. "She's absolutely knackered. I think it'd be better if we let her compose herself for a little while."

"Unfortunately, Mister Morley, we don't have time. Our citizens are being killed at this very moment."

"I understand, sir. Because of her ancient cultural upbringing, Madam was simply unable to confess to you. She came into this world in a good family. Unfortunately, they got crossways with the ruling communists and Madam became a throwaway kid existing on Hong Kong's mean streets. Every abhorrent act you can think of she performed to survive. Nonetheless, she not only survived, but she also thrived. She's ashamed of many things she's done. Nonetheless, she gave me permission to fully disclose to you what's happened here."

Sherm clears his throat. "Ancient Chinese proverb say, when you bury head in sand, you show yer ass."

"Madam is desperately sorry indeed," says Mister Morley, "for her reluctance to face the negative aspects of the experiment. She truly wants to cooperate in order to save lives and will make any monetary amends, that are lawfully *allowed*."

"Very well, Mister Morley," Pete says. "Let's start with that white cross and the dog collar."

"That's Madame Chiang Kai-Shek. It happened just yesterday afternoon. The unfortunate dog blundered near the swimming pool and the hagfish drug her right off the side. Before we could rescue her, there was nothing left but fur and bones."

"What was next accident?" Abel asks.

"Mister Jiggs."

"Mister Jiggs?" asks Officer Cobb. "Is that another of Madam's dogs or was that the pool boy?"

Mister Morley nods. "It was her granddaughter's dog, Officer Cobb."

"Well," says Officer Bardouche, "no wonder your accomplices were so upset when Detective Sanchez drove up."

"Whataya holding back, Buster?" says Officer Cobb. "Out with it, or I'm going to slip these bracelets on your big-ass wrists."

"I fully intend to cooperate with you, Officer," says Mister Morley. "Melody's husband not only loaded Mister Jiggs, but they also drove away with Robert."

"Yeah, and who's Robert," asks Officer Cobb, "the family gerbil?"

"He was Madam's great-grandson."

"Great-grandson's body in van?" asks Abel.

Mister Morley nods. "Both bodies are packed in ice. But there isn't much left of either one of them."

Pete rolls his eyes at Officer Cobb. "I'm blown away here, Crystal. They just keep racking up the violations."

"Did Robert jump into the pool," asks KB, "or was he pulled in?"

Sherm mutters under his breath. "It sounds like a frolical fish-feeding frenzy at hagfish Foodland."

Mister Morley frowns. "We don't know. I *did* witness Madame Chiang Kai-Shek being pulled in. When people walked near the pool, the fish leaped up out of the water."

KB picks up Heidi and hugs her. "What did you finally do, Mister Morley?"

"Madam talked it over with Doctors Chen and Chan. They decided to bin the experiment."

"Aye," Sherm says. "How did you figure to abandon the trial?"

"Doctor Oakes, this is where they seriously miscalculated. The two young scientists assured Madam that if they simply dumped the hagfishes into the city's sewer system the fish would die."

Pete glances at KB and Sherm.

"Doctor Chen and Doctor Chan lifted the grate in the bottom of the pool and removed the drain plug. The pool water and hagfish disappeared."

Mister Morley points to the removed grate and square hole in the patio. "They dumped the younger hagfishes from the stainless-steel tanks into *that* drain."

"That explains," says KB, "how the hagfishes got into both water systems."

"Correctamundo, KB." Sherm points to the pool's bottom. "I suspect that, *that* opening, drains directly into the sewer pipes." Sherm indicates the opening in the patio. "This hole evidently dumps into the storm drain."

"And, I bet," KB says, "the storm drain empties directly into the Truckee River."

"Aye, KB," says Sherm. "It's truly a citywide disaster."

"Christ Almighty," mutters Pete. "We're really in for it."

Sherm drops his hand on Pete's shoulder. He guides Pete

to a glorious city view. KB, Abel, Officers Cobb and Bardouche, Mister Morley, Heidi, and Chairman Mao follow them. They line up, facing the downtown lights. After a short time, Sherm's voice begins to recite:

"The time has come, Mister Hagfish said,
To speak of many things,
Of a brown round eye and screaming cries,
Then up the hole he fled.

He sucked and slithered and slimed away,
Until too pooped to advance.
Reno's mayor screamed in total grief,
'I think there's one in my pants.'

Pete jumped and cried and danced and hollered,
Until shake, no more he dared.
That nasty, dirty, slimy hag,
Had made a city scared."

Come bedtime, Mister Morley enters Madam Zho's chamber. He turns down her bed and lays out a warmed bath towel. He exits just before dawn.

Reno
12:05 a.m., Sunday morning

"Would you like to go somewhere and get something to eat?" asks Pete. The mayor, KB, Sherm, and Abel talk in front of Madam Zho's mansion. "We need to talk strategy."

"I go home, amigo," says Abel. "Check on Denise."

"Hey, Crystal," hollers Pete. "Will you please drop Abel off? And thanks a million for your and Reggie's excellent work."

Officer Cobb waves and slides into her patrol car.

"I cannot stuff anymore into my mouth," KB says.

"Me, likewise, ol' boy," says Sherm.

"Then let's stop off at George's Den, one of my favorite local watering holes."

"Yes," KB says. "Let us have a nightcap."

The trio, plus Heidi, ride in the mayor's Lincoln limousine to George's Den. It's located on the old Three-ninety-five North Highway. All three ride in the front, with Sherm driving.

"Hi Vern," Pete says, as they step through the green door.

"Be right with ya, Pete. Sit at the counter, or take that table."

"KB, Sherm," says Pete, "this is Vern Robbler. He's the friendly proprietor of *George's Den*, my favorite ol' watering hole."

"Greetings, Mr. Robbler," says Sherm as he extends his hand. "'Tis indeed a pleasure to know ya."

"Likewise," says KB. "I am glad to meet you, Mr. Robbler. I hope you serve more than just water—from the old watering hole."

Vern laughs. "*Mr.* Robbler is my father's name. I, on the other hand, can serve you *any* kind of drink, as long as there's alcohol involved."

"Sounds like we came to the right place," says a grinning Sherm.

"Vern is quite a guy," Pete says. "He's actually a working conductor on the railroad. I guess he just enjoys being a bartender."

"Let us sit at the table," says KB. "We can talk easier."

Pete holds the chair for KB, and they all sit down.

"Thank you, Pete. Something is bothering you?"

"It's Nicole." Pete sighs. "I don't know where her gang chose to water-ski. They go to different places every weekend."

Sherm says, "let's formulate a plan to find Nicole's party."

"What'll ya have?" asks Vern.

"I will have a double," KB says.

Vern makes a face at Pete. "*Excellent choice. A double . . . what?*"

"A double gin and tonic," says KB. "Let's have a drink, get a good night's sleep, and start fresh in the morning."

"That's a brilliant idea," Sherm says. "I'll have the same."

Pete glances up at Vern. "I'll just have a glass of draft, Vern. Thanks." Pete looks at KB and feels his heart grow. *I need to be with this young woman.* "When this is all over, KB, what do you hope to end up with?"

"You mean like an award?"

"I mean, what do you really want out of life? What are your innermost desires?"

"Oh, I want to get my PhD, teach a class, maybe lead some research."

Pete steals a glance at Sherm and then smiles warmly at KB. "I mean personally, KB. What do you want in your personal life?"

Sherm leans back in his chair.

"By golly." KB glances at Sherm. "I guess I want what everyone else wants; I just haven't been very successful at getting it."

Pete leans forward and looks into KB's eyes. "A bungalow in the suburbs, a soccer-mom van in the driveway, two point five adorable children?"

KB stares at the tabletop. "Something like that."

"Do you think you'll achieve it?"

KB shrugs.

Pete asks softly, "Don't you think you deserve it?"

KB sucks in a breath. "I-I am having a struggle with that."

Pete peeks at Sherm from the corner of his eye. "You're a lovely young woman, KB, both outside and inside."

KB blushes.

"I think the world of you," Pete says, "and I think you

deserve whatever in the depth of your heart you feel you deserve."

KB reaches into her purse for a handkerchief.

"Arrr," says Sherm. "KB's experienced a traumatic childhood, Pete. She's still learning to cope with deep-seated encumbrances."

"I figured something like that," says Pete. "You're a good-hearted person, KB. A lot of people really care about you."

Without a doubt, Pete now knew that this flashy, trashy, impulsive, disorganized young woman had hijacked his heart. He understood, right then and there, that he *must* try for a relationship with her.

KB wipes her eyes.

Sherm tips back in his chair. "What did you want to strategize about, Mister Mayor?"

"Arrr. At the risk of sounding like a doomsayer, I hope we haven't gone past the point of no return."

"What do you mean, Sherm?" Pete asks.

"It's happened many times before, sisters and brothers." Sherm shrugs. "A catastrophic change occurs. This forces all surviving organisms to live in a different way—or expire."

"I understand what you're saying," Pete says. "Whether it's killer hurricanes stoked by global warming or mushrooming Nazi-inspired terrorism stoked by ignorance and hate, our lives have changed forever. We're forced to live another way."

"Yes," KB says. "We can never go back."

"Aye, mateys, you're correctamundo. What about our problem tonight?"

"Because this is a life-and-death situation," KB says, "we could probably get authorization to use a very toxic poison."

Vern places their drinks on the table.

"There are longer range plans we could develop," KB says, "such as trapping the hagfish, setting natural predators after them, developing sterile adults to turn loose among them, and maybe even coming up with a type of hagfish bearing a genetically engineered 'suicide gene.'"

"That's good, my little chickadee," says Sherm.

"We have a more immediate problem, however," Pete says.

"Whataya mean?" asks Sherm.

"There're people being disemboweled as we speak."

"You bet, Pete," says KB. "At daybreak the disaster will worsen; that is when the vacationers head for the water. We should set an immediate and realistic goal."

"Uh hum. I quite agree with you," Sherm says. "We need to set a goal that we can accomplish quickly, and then declare ourselves a victory."

Pete nods. "What's the yardstick by which we measure our success? I mean, how're we going to know when we've achieved victory?"

"When no more patients are delivered to the ERs," says Sherm.

Pete sips his beer. "*Brilliant.*"

"What do you think, Pete?" asks KB. "Do you think we should immediately warn everyone to stop using their flush toilets and get them away from the area's streams and lakes?"

"Accomplishing *that* goal could signal the end of our initial phase," says Sherm. "You could order a celebration, Pete, after declaring a victory."

"Absolutely," Pete says. "I like the sound of it. After we warn everyone away from the danger zone, you two scientists can then work on a *permanent* solution."

"Yes, yes, hear, hear," Sherm says. They hold up their glasses.

"I know I should simply leave this alone until morning," KB says. "Nonetheless, I am really concerned that Reno's plight may grow even worse."

Sherm sets his glass down. "Why do you say that, me lass?"

"Since we arrived here in Reno, each time we thought we understood the problem and came up with a solution, the situation has always grown worse."

Sherm wrinkles his brow.

"I don't know," she says. "It just seems as if something diabolical is going on."

"What do you mean," asks Pete, "by diabolical?"

"Oh, I am just dismayed. I do not know what else to say."

"Do you think the devil is at work here, KB?" Sherm asks.

"Jiminy Cricket," KB says. "I do not know if I mean that or not, but I do believe there are evil people in this world. They do devilish mean things to satisfy their greed and need for power."

"Well spoken, KB," says Pete. He hoists his glass to her.

"Hmmm," Sherm says. "I don't have the sense that Madam Zho is evil, or that she developed these super hagfishes because of greed or because she sought power."

"She may not be evil, Sherm, but, by golly, she sure is greedy. I mean, she maintains this house here in Reno just so she can gamble. She has more money than she can possibly spend and still wants more. There is something evil about that kind of lust."

Pete grins. "Maybe she's found a way to take it with her."

"Arrrbeedarrr." Sherm holds up his glass. "The long sought-for formula."

After their nightcaps the trio pile into the mayor's limousine. Pete starts the engine. "Where did we put you up?"

Sherm fishes a paper from his pocket. "Um, it says *Eldorado*."

Pete raises his eyebrows. "That's the fanciest place in town. Good for the city of Reno."

Ten minutes later the limo pulls into the Eldorado's brightly lit entryway, making hundreds of sparkling lights move up the limousine's windshield. Stone paving and polished brass add to the elegance.

Pete places the shift lever in park. "I've never been in the rooms but I saw some pictures in the newspaper. They look exquisite."

"Now, Pete," Sherm says. "I'll wager the rooms you saw are

reserved for the high rollers. What the city's providing for us mere saviors will undoubtedly be considerably less ostentatious."

Pete laughs boisterously. "We don't want to break our budget."

Fifteen minutes later Pete walks into his University Ridge home. *Fiddle*, Nicole's Siamese cat, greets him. In the kitchen, the telephone is ringing.

Reno
1:45 a.m., Sunday morning

Pete peers through the window in the autopsy room's door. He's brandishing dark circles under his eyes. He still wears his pinstriped suit. He yawns. His breath smells like moribund beer.

A plastic shield covers Doctor Draper's face. A gutted-out female corpse lies on the stainless-steel table. The overhead operating light bathes her in brightness; the rest of the room remains in the dark. Between the body's legs sits a tray. Doctor Draper drops organic bits into it.

Pete pushes the door open. Chemical smells tickle the inside of his nose. He indicates that KB and Sherm should follow him. Heidi bounds in. Abel brings up the rear, rubbing his eyes.

Doctor Draper pushes his face shield up with his rubber-gloved hand. "Yo, Pete. Y'all look bright and bushy tailed."

"Good morning, Dan," says Pete. "Do you really need the overtime pay this desperately?"

Doctor Draper snorts. "Thanks for fetching the troops and coming on down, my man. There's fresh coffee in the office."

"I could use some," Pete says. "You *must* have something big to show the scientists."

Doctor Draper's eyes twinkle. "You don't appear to have made it to bed, Pete, you know what I'm sayin'?"

Pete shakes his head.

"Arrr," growls Sherm. "KB and I were just about to crawl into bed."

KB nods. "We are still in the clothes we flew down in. I *almost* made it into the shower."

"I hear ya," says Doctor Draper. "Nonetheless, y'all are dressed just fine for an early-morning meeting in the Washoe County morgue."

"Aye," says Sherm.

KB steps forward. "What do you have here, Dan?"

Doctor Draper stifles a yawn. "It's something I've never seen before." He pushes a rolling table toward KB. He indicates that she should pull on a pair of surgical gloves. Then he hands KB a magnifying glass. "All right. What do you make of this?"

Pete catches a glimpse into the tray and sees what looks like several white beans.

KB grasps the tray. She raises it to her face.

Sherm peers over her shoulder.

Pete sees KB's face take on a deformed look.

"What is it, KB?" asks Doctor Draper.

"*These are hagfish eggs.*"

Sherm mashes his lips together, nodding his head.

"Are you certain?" Doctor Draper asks.

KB faces Doctor Draper. "*One hundred percent.*"

"What this mean?" Abel asks. "Did eggs come from"—he points to the carcass—"from womb?"

"Not quite, Abel," says Doctor Draper. "They are attached quite firmly to the colon wall."

"Yes," says KB. "Hagfish eggs have filamentous anchors on their two ends. Here. Look at this."

Pete and Abel step up. Pete sees several three-quarter inch-long satchels.

"See these little filaments?" asks KB.

"Uh-huh," says Doctor Draper.

"Those are how the mother hagfish hooks the eggs onto things." KB sighs.

"What is it?" Sherm asks.

"It is just that"—KB shakes her head—"I never knew hagfish eggs could survive in an organism's gut. Maybe it's just this peculiar back-bred species. Maybe *all* hagfish lay their eggs in animal guts. Something really diabolical is going on here."

"You're right, KB." Pete's tongue feels as dry as a sunbaked carp. "Every time we think we're about to get this problem licked, something worse happens."

"Yes, by golly." KB forcefully nods. "We, at the least, thought we had the contamination contained within the Tahoe-Pyramid drainage system, and now look."

"What, KB?" asks Sherm.

"These eggs. They are laying eggs. Infected animals will *surely* transport fertilized eggs out of this drainage system. They could end up infecting . . . the *whole world*."

"They attacked my Denise," says Abel.

"I hear ya, man," says Doctor Draper. "When the hags attacked victims, but *didn't* eat their insides out, they were actually attempting to lay eggs."

"Yes. Jiminy Cricket," says KB. "That is it. They are trying to spawn."

"We're onto something," Sherm says. "Go with it, KB."

"Almost nothing is known about hagfish reproduction. We do not even know if they fertilize their eggs inside or outside the female hag's body. If fertilization takes place inside, then these are fertilized eggs. If fertilization takes place outside, then the male must swim up and fertilize them in place."

Doctor Draper picks up a specimen bottle and drops the three hagfish eggs into it. He seals it by pressing a plastic cap over the opening. He hands it to KB, and she drops it in her purse. "I will dissect and analyze these, Dan, the first chance I get."

"Abel, me good man," says Sherm. "Was a thorough examination performed on your dear wife after the attack?"

"Yes, Sherm. They find nothing, not even scratch."

"Probably didn't have enough time," says Doctor Draper.

"If the damned mama fish desires to use this poor woman as a brood chamber," says Pete, "then why's she been eviscerated?"

"Arrrbeedarrr," says Sherm. "That be a fine question, Pete, that it are. It would appear that the haggy fish do not respect each other's maternal efforts."

Pete arches an eyebrow.

"I mean, Pete," Sherm says, "when Mister Haggy's hungry he eats at the firstist opportunity. He doesn't give an aardvark's patootie pile whether Missus Hagfish has laid the next generation in there or not."

Except for the buzz of the overhead lights the autopsy room stands quiet.

KB sighs. "There is so much chance for failure here. After all, ninety-five percent of all species that have ever lived are now extinct. That is the natural order of things. When a species grows too numerous, too successful, too complicated—another species, more efficient, comes along and consumes them. It has happened thousands of times before. Quite possibly there is nothing we humans can do to control this infestation. We have here the possibility for human extinction."

Abel stares at the corpse. "What we do?"

"We *must* do all that we can," says KB. "That is how modern human beings have survived these past two hundred thousand years. We cannot simply roll over and let these creatures win. We have to be smart. We must fight this with everything we have."

"Thanks, KB," says Pete, "for stepping up to the plate and

swinging at the ball." He gently places his hand on her shoulder. "You're one heck of a woman."

"Pete," says KB, "do you think it is time to call the governor's bedside telephone?"

———————

Pete feels as if a thousand-pound millstone has been lowered on his shoulders. "All right let's get started. Abel, get the chief down here." Pete pulls his cellular telephone from his belt.

"Y'all may use my desk phone, Pete," says Doctor Draper.

"Thanks, Dan, but I have the governor's private number on speed dial." He pulls the antenna out and punches the button.

"Good morning."

"Good morning, Mister Governor. I'm afraid our worst fears have come to pass, partner. Oh, it's a little past two in the morning. I'm down here at Reno police headquarters. It's time to mobilize." Pete takes a sip of coffee. "I thank you very much, Bob. The police headquarters building can serve as our crisis center. Please order up Generals Clark and Arnold for me and have them report here. You're coming up? Great. Bye."

Pete looks up to see KB watching him. Then he notices Sherm hovering close by.

Abel leans out of the office. "Hamper on his way."

"Good," answers Pete. "Now KB, Sherm, what're we going to do to save our people?"

"Yeah," says Doctor Draper, "the last thing our citizens heard last night was 'everything's under control.' They went to bed with the idea that we had this sucker whipped. You know what I'm sayin', man?"

"That right, boss," Abel says. "In morning there be hundreds people swimming in Pyramid Lake, fly fishing in Truckee River, water-skiing on Lake Tahoe."

"Not to mention using the campground dry holers," mutters Doctor Draper.

Pete takes a long, large breath. "Let's hear some suggestions."

"Not only will there be multiple attacks when vacationers jump in the water this morning," KB says, "there is also the possibility of a worldwide disaster, that is, if a person infected with hagfish eggs leaves the area and deposits them outside the Lake Tahoe drainage system."

"How sure are you, KB," Pete asks, "that the eggs are fertile? You said yourself that reproduction might take place *outside* the female hag."

KB nods.

"It's likely," says Pete, "that those eggs haven't been fertilized. The male hag hasn't yet swum upstream and—"

"—washed the eggs in his slimy sperm?" offers Sherm.

"Precisely," says Pete.

"We cannot take a chance, Pete," says KB. "I can do an analysis on those eggs downstairs, but it will take time. We should err on the side of what is the safest course. I suggest that we assume, for the time being, that the female hagfish is laying fertile eggs. Can you imagine what would happen to the earth's animals if these creatures got loose in the world's water supply?"

"Hold on there, KB," says Pete. "I totally agree with you. What do you suggest we do here?"

"I think, for a first step, that we should get every citizen, from the top of the watershed to the final destination at Pyramid Lake, *away from all water.*"

Sherm nods.

"We should set that as our goal," says KB. "We should accomplish that goal and then *declare a victory.*"

Reno
2:25 a.m., Sunday morning

After stomping down the stairs from the roof, Howlin' Mad walks into the Reno police headquarters conference room. He has helicoptered from Carson City in *The Gutsy Lady*. He wears his fatigues, combat boots, and garrison cap. A stogie smolders in his lips.

General Arnold, wearing his threadbare flight suit and an Air Force hat, boasting lightning bolts on the bill, stands at the coffee table preparing himself a cup. Sergeant Hoover has just driven him over from Reno's airport.

Chief Hamper yawns and sips his orange juice. He bears dark circles under his eyes.

"Arrr," Sherm says. "My burnin' guts can't stomach any more coffee, yet I gotta drink it to chase the cobwebs from my mind."

Abel leans against the wall and yawns.

Pete asks KB if she's ready to deliver her plan. KB nods at the mayor.

"Gentlemen," says Pete. "Miss Kristian would like to deliver a suggestion for a plan to keep our citizens from being mutilated by the hagfishes.

KB looks at the generals. "Okay, I'll go first. Chime in whenever you wish.

"Use your soldiers, your airplanes, your radio and television news *to inform the citizens to get away from the area's lakes and streams*. This must be accomplished immediately. There may be someone taking a moonlight swim as we speak, or maybe even . . ."

Pete grimaces.

"Sorry, Pete. Anyone attacked must be promptly delivered to the area's medical facilities. Doctors will try to save their lives, as well as examine them for hagfish eggs."

Sherm sighs. "I suggest that your military forces quarantine the Tahoe-Pyramid drainage area. Let no one in, or out, until we determine that the crisis is past."

"We brought detailed maps of the area," says General Arnold. "We can lay 'em out here on the table. We'll formulate a plan of attack, concentrating on the lakes, rivers, and the low-lying areas of the Truckee Meadows. I've ordered the flight and ground crews of our C-130s to report for duty immediately. If ordered, they'll be airborne by dawn."

"Yeah." Cigar smoke leaks from Howlin' Mad's lips. "We're callin' up all Nevada National Guard personnel, as well. We're gettin' all troops, helicopters, trucks, and jeeps prepared, as we speak. We'll be ready to roll *before* dawn."

General Arnold rolls his eyes. "Sergeant. Come in here, please."

Sergeant Hoover carries a large tube containing a map. He and the general extract the map and unroll it on the table. It shows, in astonishing detail, the Truckee River flowing from Lake Tahoe, through downtown Reno, and terminating at Pyramid Lake.

General Arnold points at Lake Tahoe. "How can we warn the people out on the lake?"

"The Washoe County Sheriff's Department has some boats," says Pete.

"There's a United States Coast Guard Station a mile east of Tahoe City," Howlin' Mad says. "I launch my fishing boat right next to their base."

"Yeah," says Abel. "I see them yesterday 'fore I pick up Sherm and KB."

"Let's use *all* our resources," Howlin' Mad growls. "This ain't no time for holdin' back."

"Agreed," says General Arnold. "Chief Hamper, why don't you get ahold of the sheriff's department."

"I personally know Rear Admiral Joe Fontana," says Sherm. "He's commandant of the Thirteenth Coast Guard District at—"

Pete hands Sherm his cell phone.

The generals devise a plan for the most effective use of the National Guard's helicopters, trucks, jeeps, and troops as well as utilizing the Air Guard's Lockheed C-130 Hercules group of four-engined cargo planes.

"Hello, Joe?" says Sherm into the cell phone. "Sorry, matey, but we have an emergency here in Reno."

Governor Miller steps into the room. He wears a blue sweat suit, white tennis shoes, and a blue baseball cap boasting the great silver seal of Nevada.

Chief Hamper steps to the table. "I've notified the sheriff's department. What else can I do to help?"

"Chief," says Howlin' Mad, "call all the police agencies in this area and put them under our direction."

"You bet, General Clark."

"Doctor Oakes," says Howlin' Mad. "What'd you get from the Coast Guard?"

"I talked to Admiral Joe Fontana. Lake Tahoe's in the *Twelfth* Coast Guard District. He said he'd immediately get in contact with the commander and have him place the Coast Guard under the command of our senior officer—Major General Harlan Clark."

Howlin' Mad pulls the cigar from his mouth, and grins like a new daddy.

The Truckee River
3:35 a.m., Sunday morning

Pete's XJ6 Jaguar sedan heads west on Interstate Eighty, on their drive to Lake Tahoe. Rain and hail pelting the car sounds like spent buckshot. Thunder rolls down the mountain as the Jaguar twists back and forth alongside the Truckee River. The full moon peeks around the thunderheads.

"There is not much traffic at three in the morning," says KB. Heidi snuggles close to her mistress's leg and shivers.

"Aye," says Sherm, from the back seat.

Nearby lightning strikes turn the Truckee River into molten silver. On the craggy outcroppings stand black silhouetted pines.

"Everything is in place," says KB quietly.

"Aye, mateys," Sherm says. "Daylight'll break, in an hour."

"I got a kick out of Hamper," says Pete. "He even activated the local Boy Scout troops."

KB rubs little Heidi's head. "Yes, his heart must be aching, yet he throws his all into the task."

"Aye, that he does," Sherm says. "He's postponing the suffering for his loss until this crisis is over."

Pete steers the car around a basketball-sized rock in the road. "That's right, Sherm."

"Your Governor Miller pitched right in, as well," says Sherm. "He has the area's doctors and nurses standing by for the morning's onslaught."

"I guess," KB says, "that everything that can be done is being done."

"I hope we haven't forgotten something crucially important," Pete says.

KB pulls Heidi closer. "Pete. Could you maybe just turn on the heat a little?"

"Aye, matey," says Sherm. "Miss Bjørnsen and I are not correctly dressed for this early-morning adventure."

Pete chuckles and reaches for the heater knob. "What do you think of *my* outfit? This ensemble looked pretty sharp when I was on TV yesterday. Do you think a pinstriped suit is haute couture for warning skinny dippers off the nudy beach?"

Sherm chuckles. "If you average the two of us together, we come out about right."

Pete laughs. Beyond the windshield wipers he sees a deer fixing to dart across the road. He eases up on the throttle. The deer trots safely to the other side.

"I wonder," KB says, "how many deer and other wild animals have been attacked by female hags attempting to spawn? What if an infected deer makes it by the National Guard's quarantine line and escapes the Tahoe National Forest?"

For a few minutes, they drive on in silence.

"What is it, Pete?" asks KB. "Are you fearing that this may not be simply a local problem?"

Pete turns the windshield wipers on high. "Actually, it's Nicole. I'm *really* worried about her."

"Yes," KB says. "Of *course*, you are worried." She turns to the back seat. "What can we do?"

"You don't have any idea where she might be, is that correct, Pete?"

"That's right, Sherm."

"She's water-skiing, correct?"

"Affirmative. On weekends she spends lots of time with her friends. They camp and water-ski at various lakes and reservoirs."

"Hmmm. That considerably narrows down where we have to look, that is, if we're searching from a hundred-and-ninety mile per hour airplane—one that lands on water."

KB smiles. "You mean, Sherm, that you—"

"Yes, me little Danish flower. We'll crank up *The Gander*, take Pete along to guide us, and we'll quickly cover all the water-skiing hangouts until we find her. You think that'll work, KB?"

"Oh, Sherm. You bet. What do you think, Pete?"

Pete appears to be all choked up.

KB pats him on the arm, then leaves it there.

Lake Tahoe
4:30 a.m., Sunday morning

Lightning drills the sky—followed by a thunderclap. On the Jaguar's floor, Heidi shivers between KB's feet.

Pete wheels into Tahoe City. Windblown hail and rain flog the automobile's side. Pete turns off North Lake Boulevard and drives on toward the waterfront. He hears his tires making that slishing sound on the flooded asphalt.

The full moon maintains its sentinel between warring thunderheads, as it makes ready to set behind California's forested peaks. On the Nevada side, graying appears on the location where the sun is preparing to rise.

In the black-and-white landscape Pete spots the Grumman Goose. Dark and cold, it bobs on choppy water at the end of the Tahoe City pier.

Pete pulls up next to the boat-launching sling. The Jaguar's wipers labor to clear the windshield. Pete sips coffee from his Styrofoam cup; it'd grown tepid. His car's headlights shine on the lake water.

"Look at that, Sherm. There's whitecaps as far as you can see."

Sherm laughs. "Whoopee, at least *The Gander's* still afloat. That's a *good* sign."

Pete snorts and turns off the engine. He picks up his two-way radio. "Are you ready for this?"

"We will be soaked," KB says, "that is for sure."

Pete nods. "You got that right."

"Arrr. If KB and I aren't dressed properly for this mile-high mountain morning, we sure as to craperenski ain't dressed for this deluge."

"It's often like this in the summertime," Pete says. "The thunderclouds build up all afternoon, it thunders and rains at night, and then clears off to a beautiful blue sky in the morning."

"Uh hum," says Sherm, "truthfully, Pete, knowing that doesn't help one effing bit."

Pete cracks up.

"We can fly safely in this stuff," says Sherm. "It's just gonna be a smidgen tougher to locate our objective."

"I'm sorry I don't have any rain hats in the car."

"I got my straw hat," Sherm offers.

Pete snickers. "By the time we reach the end of the dock, Sherm, your straw hat will look like a dish of soggy shredded wheat."

"I am wearing the baseball cap you gave me, Pete."

Pete looks into KB's eyes and gives her an affectionate smile. "Are you ready?" He grasps the door handle. *"Let's make a run for it."*

The trio trots toward the seaplane.

"Come on, Heidi," KB hollers in the roar of the storm. "This airplane is leaving town."

Sherm opens the airplane's door. "Let's get in out of the rain," he hollers.

"Crawl in there, KB," Pete yells. "I'll hand Heidi to you."

KB sticks first one leg in and then the other. Rain soaks her T-shirt. She almost appears to be topless. "Ugh. What is that **stench**?"

"Here, KB," says Pete. "Here's Heidi."

KB's hands reach out.

"Whew," Pete says. "That smell would make a seagull retch. What happened? Did a sperm whale flop in here and die?"

"Aaargh," yells Sherm. "Yer close, matey. If you can't stomach it, stand aside, I gotta get in out of this fizzling drizzle."

"I'm goin' in, Sherm. I just hope you have a barf bag on board."

"Affirmative, Pete, that is, unless KB's used 'em all."

Pete crawls inside.

Sherm crowds close behind. As he pulls his head inside, his hat falls in the lake. "Didja ever have one of those blooming days?" To fetch his hat Sherm lays his belly across the door opening.

"Here," Pete says. "I'll hold your feet."

"Hold on *tight*." Sherm retrieves his hat, shakes off the excess water, and hauls the straw hat inside. "I'll have fungoidal extrusions growing on it by dawn's early light." He sets his hat on an ice chest. Then he stands up straight and reaches for the light switch. "You gotta weak stomach, Pete? Ain't you no swabbie?"

"I served in the Navy; did a little stint on the USS Ranger."

"Arrr, did ya ever get seasick?"

"Steaming around Cape Horn. What's the matter, can't you find the light switch?"

"Aaargh, we don't have any juice. Excuse me, I'll just get the flashlight off the bulkhead there."

"Here, Sherm," Pete says. "I'll just get—what the hell's that? I just stepped on something."

"Let me get this flashlight switched on."

KB screams.

"Oh, crap," Sherm says. "Hold on there, KB. Don't move. Here comes the light."

"Hurry," KB shrieks. "Something's hurting my toe."

Heidi barks.

The flashlight lights the deck. A medium-sized crab pinches KB's big toe. Sherm begins to laugh. The light beam swings to Pete's shoe. Little crab feet quiver from under his sole.

"Blazing bewildertoods." Sherm rolls his head back and stares at the overhead. "I'm immersed in clumsitude. It's like a recurring nightmare. I'm full tilt cracking up. I'm fixin' to bite a chunk outta this fricking aluminum wall. Hag'em high, me hearties. Hag'em high."

Floodlights, a mile and a half to the east, suddenly jump on.

"Look at that," says Pete. "That's the Coast Guard station. They must've just received their reveille call."

The seaplane's interior lights up. Then the outside red, green, and white boat navigational lights blink on—and lastly, the wingtip airplane lights.

"How'd you get lights, Sherm?" asks Pete. He glances at KB, who is just slipping her hip flask back into her purse.

"Ahum, the salt water in the bilge caused a minor short. I simply cleaned the corrosion off and we're back in business."

"I am sorry, Shermy. It is all my fault."

Sherm replaces the deck plate, "Not to worry, me little Danish dumpling, we'll be airborne shortly."

"Shermy. This bottle containing hagfish eggs is getting too warm in my purse."

"Arrr, drop it in the ice chest. It'll stay cool enough in the seawater."

Pete wipes his side window clear with his pinstriped suit coat sleeve. He bends down and attempts to look through the smeared window. "I think the rain's lessening."

Sherm peeks through the windshield. "Hmmm, I don't know, Pete. This boat's sure pitching and yawing."

"By golly, Shermy," says KB. "I think I got all the crabs into the ice chest, you bet you. There is enough salt water in there to keep them healthy until we get back to the lab. You should have seen them attack the little bottle."

"Ahhh, excellent work, me lass. Yes, those poor-starving crustaceans will eat anything. How many of the little scum-sucking decapods are still alive?"

"Twenty-eight, though I do not know if all of them will survive. There are quite a number of dead ones floating in the bilge."

Pete sniffs. "So, I noticed."

Sherm hollers from the cockpit. "Okay, KB. Get seated and let's start the preflight."

"Time to load up, Heidi," says KB. Heidi sits and waits to be picked up. KB hands Heidi through the narrow door opening and drops her on the copilot's right-hand seat. KB squeezes in, sits down, and then plucks up the list.

"Ahhh, Pete," Sherm says. "Would you be so kind as to stand by out there in the monsoon, and at the proper signal cast off the mooring lines?"

Pete throws Sherm a quick salute. "Aye, aye, Skipper." He grins like a little boy.

Reno
4:35 a.m., Sunday morning

From the Reno Police Department conference room, Howlin' Mad controls *Operation Save the People*. Upstairs, Chief Hamper coordinates the area's law-enforcement Officers.

Sergeant Goodnight pokes her head into the conference room. "General Clark. There's a Barnacle Bill on the phone for you."

Sitting at the table's far end in front of a powerful radio, Sergeant Mills stifles a grin.

Howlin' Mad glances up from his map. He scowls in General Arnold's direction. "This's no time for jokin' around. Who the goddamn hell is goddamn Barnacle Bill?"

General Arnold shrugs. Howlin' Mad shifts the cigar in his lips. He looks at Sergeant Goodnight and shakes his head.

Sergeant Goodnight retreats.

Three minutes later Sergeant Goodnight is back. "Sir, it's *Chief Warrant* Barnacle Bill Parker. He claims he's the head of the Coast Guard station at Lake Tahoe. He says he's *working for you*."

General Arnold chuckles.

Howlin' Mad shakes his head. "Whataya think, Nate?"

General Arnold grins. "We can use all the help we can get, Harlan."

Howlin' Mad waves Sergeant Goodnight in. She hands the general a paper, turns, and heads for the door.

"Thanks, Goodnight," says Howlin' Mad. He hands the paper to General Arnold.

"Sarge," says General Arnold. "Get ahold of, ah, Barnacle Bill there. Let's get 'im on board."

Lake Tahoe
4:40 a.m., Sunday morning

Rain soaks the two men on the dock. Pete stands by, waiting for the word to cast off. Sherm gives the seaplane the once-over, searching for dripping hydraulic fluid, frayed wires, loose nuts. Pete's stomach feels like it's full of butterflies, with the anticipation of zooming off Lake Tahoe's six-thousand-foot-high lake.

Through the tattoo of drumming drizzle, Pete hears Sherm tapping the airplane's aluminum skin. Sherm peers into the front of the port engine. He grasps the ailerons and pushes them up and down. He gives the strut holding the float a shake.

"Aye, me hearty," Sherm says, stepping around Pete. "I think the ol' bird just might make one more trip."

Pete gazes through the rain at the lit-up Coast Guard station. A cutter, lights aglow and flags a-flapping, accelerates away from the dock. The boat curves to starboard. Still gaining speed it settles on a course straight for *The Gander*.

From the open pilot's window, Sherm hollers, "*All clear.*"

On the seaplane's far side, the three-bladed prop jerks. The powerful four-hundred-fifty-horsepower radial engine begins to turn. It coughs and then blares into life. Nine exhaust pipes shoot fire and smoke. After running rough for several seconds, it smooths out and purrs like a sated Bengal tiger.

For a few moments Pete ceases worrying about his daughter. He gives Sherm a thumbs-up. Sherm returns the signal.

Pete glances at the lake. The fast-coming Coast Guard cutter is bounding across the waves.

Again, Sherm leans his face out the window. Pete points at the fast-approaching boat. Sherm squints. Pete sees KB get Sherm's attention and points to the preflight list. Sherm raises his hand and holds it there.

The heavy-built steel boat slows and curves in toward the dock. Pete steps to the dock's edge to help. The white-colored boat, boasting the international-orange Coast Guard racing stripe on the bow, comes off plane and settles into the water. Through the boat's rain-streaked windshield, Pete sees the coxswain's hand push the port throttle into reverse. A great bulge of water billows from the stern. The boat gently sidles up against the dock.

Pete hears Heidi barking inside the seaplane. As Pete steps forward to assist, a blue-uniformed young sailor wearing the three white stripes of a first-class seaman, steps smartly onto the boat's gunwale.

"Lash 'er down, fore and aft," commands a voice from the cabin's open aft door.

"Aye, aye, skipper," the seaman hollers back. He steps onto the dock and hustles to the cutter's bow. In two seconds flat he has the bow secured to the pier's cleat. He hurries to the stern and in a similar fashion ties down the after end. The twin powerful outboards idle. From the rear door emerges the driver.

A lean young man, boasting carrot-red hair and full beard, smiles up at Pete. He wears the bell-bottomed blue dungarees of an enlisted man, but the khaki shirt and commissioned officer's cap of a Coast Guard officer.

Grasping the handhold on the cabin's roof, the officer pulls himself onto the dock. Rain spatters his cap's bill. He sticks out his hand. "How do you do, sir? I'm Barnacle Bill Parker."

Pete spots the officer's bar on the man's collar that proclaims him a W-2 Chief Warrant Officer. "How do you do, Chief Warrant Parker?" Pete shakes his hand.

Barnacle Bill smiles.

"You the skipper of the Coast Guard Base?"

"Aye sir, I am."

"I'm Pete Ferrari, mayor of Reno. I'm damned glad to meet you, skipper."

Barnacle Bill chuckles. "Sorry, Mister Mayor. I didn't recognize you, with—"

"With my hair plastered to my face making me look like a porcelain pot." Pete laughs. "You can just call me, Pete."

"With all due respect, sir, I just couldn't do that, Mister Mayor."

Pete nods. He turns his head toward the seaplane. "Hey, Sherm. I've someone here you'll *love* to meet." Pete escorts Barnacle Bill to the open cockpit window. "This is the skipper of the coastie's base, Barnacle Bill Parker."

"Aye, matey. It's a pleasure to meet you, that it are." Sherm sticks his hand out the narrow opening. They shake hands. "Arrrbeedarrr."

Barnacle Bill grows a wide white smile.

"Skipper, this is Doctor T Sherman Oakes. He's a marine biologist from Newport. He's down here to help us with *the hagfish attack.*

"And there"—Pete presses on Barnacle Bill's back to invite him to bend down—"is Miss Kristian Bjørnsen. She's Doctor Oakes's assistant and an expert on the fishes that're attacking our citizens."

"Hello, Miss Bjørnsen," calls out Barnacle Bill. "It's indeed a pleasure to meet you."

"You got that right," Pete mumbles under his breath.

Heidi barks.

Barnacle Bill furrows his brow and stands up. He snorts to clear the stink from his nasal passages and pulls on his nose.

Pete, Sherm, and Barnacle Bill coordinate their plans to warn all boaters and swimmers off Lake Tahoe. The Coast Guard Base boasts two, twenty-four-foot Munson-built cutters. Twin two-hundred-twenty-five horsepower Mercury outboards power each boat. Even though the boat weighs a whopping fourteen-hundred pounds they easily accelerate to forty-five knots. They operate with a crew of two but are certified to carry fourteen.

Barnacle Bill steps down into the cabin of his boat. The young seaman stands by to cast off.

"All clear," hollers Sherm. The portside radial engine turns then catches. A cloud of smoke bathes the pier.

Barnacle Bill shakes his head, then grins.

"Cast off," Sherm shouts.

Pete unties the seaplane's after end, then the front.

"Cast off," hollers Barnacle Bill.

Pete watches the seaman release the forward end, then hustle to the stern and repeat the maneuver. The seaman gives the released cutter a nudge and hops aboard. Pete gives the seaman a little wave.

"Avast thar, Ferrari," Sherm yells. "Quit yer daydreamin' and climb aboard, 'fore you got to swim for it."

"*Oh, crap.*" Pete dives across open water headfirst through the door.

Within five minutes, two high-speed cutters, Coast Guard ensigns and pennants flapping, roar away from the north shore. The one commanded by Barnacle Bill heads east, the other cutter heads west.

The Grumman Goose accelerates across the chop and gets airborne. Rain streaks the windshield. The seaplane speeds east toward the Nevada side.

Reno
5:00 a.m., Sunday morning

At the Reno-Tahoe International Airport—twenty air miles east and two thousand feet lower—high-winged shapes hulk in the pre-dawn gray. The tarmac holds puddles; the last thundershower had passed thirty minutes earlier. Turbo-propped engines whine at run-up speed. Red and green navigation lights glow. Strobe lights flash.

Freshly printed leaflets fill four-dozen boxes. General Arnold has ordered his Hercules C-130 crews to dump the leaflets on all lakes, rivers, and streams. Squadron Two received instructions to form up at dawn over Lake Tahoe, fly down the Truckee River, and terminate on Pyramid Lake, after spreading leaflets along the entire shore. Special orders guide Squadron Three to bombard the towns of Truckee, Reno, Sparks, Fernley, Carson City, Fallon, Silver Springs, and Wadsworth.

The copilot on the first C-130 talks to the tower. *Miss Silver State* is painted on the side. The airplane begins to roll.

Biggest Little City follows, then comes *Battle Born*. They form a line, and then they trundle toward a solitary figure standing out on the tarmac. He wears an ancient flight suit and an Air Force general's cap.

Two more fat-bellied C-130s pull into line: *Viva Las Vegas* and *Cotton Tail Bunny Ranch*. Red sky reflects on their greenhouse fronts.

Miss Silver State comes abreast of General Arnold. The pilot slides his window open and snaps the general a neat salute, followed by a solid thumbs-up. General Arnold returns the gesture.

Miss Silver State makes its turn onto the runway.

Carson City
5:05 a.m., Sunday morning

The National Guard Armory, on South Carson Street in Carson City, disgorges a mile-long row of jeeps and trucks. Their lights create a white, amber, and red parade. The citizen soldiers don't insert loaded clips in their assault rifles on this mission. Howlin' Mad has ordered them to physically warn all fishermen, campers, hikers, picnickers, gold miners, swimmers, and sunbathers. Their orders are to search on, in, or beside the water, and inform the citizens to get off it, out of it, and away from it—*at once.*

Half the column turns left toward Highway Fifty, Spooner Summit, and Lake Tahoe's South Shore. Their orders are to warn citizens at the lake's south end and work their way north around both sides, being especially persistent at the several parks. Then, they are ordered to proceed down the Truckee River toward Reno.

The column's other half heads north on Highway Three-Ninety-Five straight to Reno. The soldiers intend to cover the parks along the river in Reno and Sparks, and then continue toward Fernley and Wadsworth, finishing at Pyramid Lake. This column figures to reach Reno by dawn.

Reno
5:10 a.m., Sunday morning

Chief Hamper has awakened Cliff Brown, the head of the Nevada Council of the Boy Scouts of America. Brown agreed to help by immediately driving to the Nevada Council's office on Mae Anne Avenue, where he called his area scoutmasters to call up their Boy Scout troops and Explorer posts.

"Get 'em in uniform so everyone'll know who they are. It'll be an hour 'for the National Guard gets up here so get 'em into the hobo camps at the railroad yard. Order 'em to search through the bushes for sleeping winos. Find the early-morning fishermen. Locate the illegal alien's camps down by the river. Instruct the scouts to tell 'em '*agua peligroso*'—there're fishes in the Truckee River that'll dine on your *piranhas* for a morning snack."

Chapter Eight

St. Mary's in the Mountains, Virginia City, Nevada

Reno
5:15 a.m., Sunday morning

Howlin' Mad sits at the conference-room table, chewing on his cigar. He's been staring at the contour map, for the longest time.

"Excuse me, General," says Sergeant Mills. "But you've been studying that map for quite a while."

"Yeah, sarge, I have the godamndest feelin' that we've left somethin' undone."

Sergeant Mills stands up from his station at the radio, and ambles over behind the general. "From Lake Tahoe to Pyramid Lake I see colored marks."

Howlin' Mad grunts.

"However, I don't see any marks here." Sergeant Mills points at Carson City.

"Yeah, sarge. That's on the Carson River drainage district. The scientists don't think the happy haggy fishes have arrived down there"—he glances up—"*yet*."

Governor Miller strolls into the room.

Sergeant Mills snaps to attention.

"Good morning, Governor," says Howlin' Mad, as he struggles to his feet.

"At ease. Hi, Harlan. Sergeant. How's things going?"

Howlin' Mad gestures at Sergeant Mills.

Governor Miller glances at Sergeant Mills and nods. "Carry on, Sergeant."

"Yes, sir, Governor Miller.

"General Clark, I suppose Virginia City's in the same situation. It's in a different drainage system?"

"Sure." Howlin' Mad waves his hand at the map. "Virginia City's in the, the ..."

Howlin' Mad positions his reading glasses on his face. "Wait a minute. I remember something from a meeting with the Army Corps of Engineers. What was it? Something about Virginia City not getting its water from pumping wells."

"Darn," Governor Miller says. "You're right. Don't they get their water from Lake Tahoe?"

"Yeah, that's it. They get their water through a big god-damned pipe. It goes all the way across Washoe Valley." Howlin' Mad's finger traces a path across the map. "It's this dotted line right here. It's underground."

"Son of a gun," Governor Miller says. "That means those doggone hagfishes could get into the Virginia City water supply."

"Damn," says Howlin' Mad. "Only it wasn't Tahoe the water came from. I remember. It's *Marlette Lake*. Looky here, Governor."

Governor Miller bends down.

"Marlette's fourteen-hundred feet *above* Lake Tahoe and drains directly into it."

"Ah hah," says Governor Miller. "The hagfish could swim upstream to Marlette Lake. Then ride through the pipe and arrive fresh as well-scrubbed little alligators, directly into the toilets of Virginia City's unsuspecting citizens."

Howlin' Mad nods his head and chuckles. "That was a good goddamn piece of work there, Sergeant Mills. If you hadn't been a little inquisitive, the poor people of Virginia City mighta lost their ... *assets*."

Governor Miller snickers, General Howlin' Mad roars, and Sergeant Mills smiles and shakes his head.

"Sarge," says Howlin' Mad, "call up the nearest Huey and order 'em to land here at police headquarters, immediately. Governor, do you wanta go on a chop-chop ride?"

"Ah. You want me to, what?"

"Look, Governor Miller. You're the boss around here, but still, I *gotta* stay here. If you can make the time, why don't you hop in that Huey and get up to Marlette Lake and Virginia City as fast as that goddamned eggbeater'll go."

"General Clark," says Sergeant Mills. "*Gutsy Lady* lands on the police department's roof in three minutes."

Governor Miller grows aware of the beating sound of an approaching helicopter. For that matter, it may've been there all along. He begins to grin. Then he remembers. "Holy cow, Harlan. I'd love to go. Unfortunately, I simply have too much going on. What about Ferrari's sometime chauffeur, the burglary detective?"

"Sarge," says Howlin' Mad, "call the chief."

"Yes sir, General."

After a brief telephone conversation, Sergeant Mills reports that burglary detective Abel Sanchez is on his way.

A minute later Abel steps through the door.

Howlin' Mad yanks the cigar from his mouth. "Detective Sanchez, hurry yer ass up those stairs to the roof. You've got the pleasure of going on a chop-chop ride with one of our finest, Captain Vickie Doolittle."

Sand Point
5:20 a.m., Sunday morning

Sherm hollers back through the door opening. "Ahoy there, Pete."

Pete uncouples his seatbelt and kneels between the two front seats.

"What're we looking for?" Sherm asks.

"Several of Nicole's friends own ski boats. The one most easy to spot is *The Undertaker*."

KB raises an eyebrow.

"That's Nicole's boyfriend's boat. It's a black flat-bottomed job with a big-block chrome decorated engine in the back. On the hull's side, in green, it says: *The Undertaker*. We may see it pulling a half-a-dozen skiers."

KB furrows her brow. "I did not know a ski boat could pull so many."

"Uh hum," says Sherm. "I don't suppose there's much water-skiing in the fjords."

Pete chuckles. "It's true. Believe it or not, that little boat cranks out five hundred and fifty honest horsepower and can make ninety miles per hour."

"God, I love it," declares Sherm.

"Of course," Pete says, "that's without skiers."

Sherm snorts.

The sun lights up the trees on the California shore. *The Gander* skims the lake's surface at one hundred fifty miles per hour.

Pete pushes himself back to his seat. He searches the shoreline. *It's early yet. Still, this is when the water's the smoothest.*

The Grumman Goose works its way around Lake Tahoe, past the charming California hamlets. It flies over the California-Nevada border, roaring by the north shore casinos. Pete sees no one along the water's edge.

They streak past Lakeshore Drive's mansions.

All at once the nose pulls up. The two mighty radials roar as they strive to hoist the seaplane higher into the air. Up and up. Then, the left-wing dips. The airplane starts a circle around a point.

"Uh," Pete grunts. He looks down and observes the Ponderosa Ranch where the *Bonanza* television series was filmed. Pete glances forward and sees Sherm talking in the mike, and KB nodding.

The seaplane completes its circle and dives for the water.

Pete feels his stomach rise in his throat. He notices KB searching from side to side and up and down for other aircraft. Incline Village's houses abruptly give way to pine trees and a sandy beach.

"We're at Sand Harbor," says Sherm checking his map.

They graze the lake's surface, flying like a fighter plane. For the moment Pete forgets the empty pit in his gut over Nicole. He sees early-morning walkers on a beach curving into the lake.

"Sand Point," says Sherm.

There's a low-slung dark-colored boat pulled up on the beach. Two-dozen figures mill around it.

Pete unhooks his seatbelt and plunges forward. "Sherm." He slaps him on the shoulder. "Look."

Sherm glances up from his chart and squints where Pete is pointing. He jerks his head at KB.

KB begins looking up and to the right. Abruptly, the seaplane performs a right turn. KB reaches over and flips the switches. The floats start down.

Pete fights his way back to his seat and buckles up.

The seaplane comes around and lines up on Sand Point.

The engine revolutions drop. The flaps extend. The seaplane settles onto the water. It idles up behind the group standing around the ski boat. Pete stares out his window.

Sherm shouts back. "Whataya think, Pete?"

Pete slowly shakes his head. "That's a *V-hull*."

KB points toward the south. A string of army vehicles advance up Highway Twenty-Eight. Their headlights flicker on and off as they proceed through the pine trees. Sherm moves two levers on the center console, reversing the pitch of the screws. Then he moves the two throttle levers forward. The big radials roar.

The spray blows *forward*. The seaplane ceases its forward motion. Sherm brings the engines to idle. At once, it is quiet enough to talk in a normal voice.

"Aye, me mateys," snarls Sherm. "It's good to see the Army's on the job."

"Yes, it is," Pete says. "That's likely the Nevada National Guard out of Carson City."

"Correctamundo," says Sherm. "Looky there."

Pete peeks out Sherm's window. Making their way through the low bushes on Sand Point is a line of young fellows wearing tan uniforms and red kerchiefs.

"Whataya think, Mister Mayor? A contingent of the Lake Tahoe Marine Corps Historical Battalion?"

Pete snorts. "Negative, I don't think that outfit's motto is 'Semper Fidelis.' More likely, it's 'Be Prepared.' I'll wager that's the Boy Scout troop out of Incline Village."

Lake Tahoe
5:25 a.m., Sunday morning

"Pete," says Sherm. "That ice chest has moved. Would you, please, shove it back in the corner and secure it?"

"Affirmative, Captain."

Pete lifts the lid. "How're you doing in there, crabbies? Sherm, KB, you better get back here and look at this."

Sherm unhooks his seatbelt. "Whataya got?"

"It appears a highly motivated crab pulled the cap off KB's little bottle."

Sherm and KB scramble into the cargo area.

"KB," Sherm says, "where's your egg cases?"

"Jumping Jiminy, *there* is one." KB points. "It has been ripped open." She reaches into the water and picks it up.

"Hmmm," Sherm says, "it appears the Decapoda have eaten an unfortunate hagfish egg."

KB kneels and searches around the crabs. "By golly, I think you are right. All three egg cases have been torn open." She looks up at Sherm.

"Arrr, let's keep this discovery at the forefront of our minds."

"Yes, Sherm, this may turn out to be a valuable break-through."

Pete grins. "It's about time something broke in our favor." Then he remembers Nicole. His guts knot up and he sighs.

A powerful megaphone blares out. "This is the United States Coast Guard. On the order of the Governor of Nevada, I'm warning you away from the water's edge. There are dangerous fish in the lake that *will* attack you."

Pete peeks out his window. Pounding around the point, at a blistering forty-five knots, speeds the twenty-four-foot Munson-built cutter.

The citizens on the beach freeze. The cutter pulls up to the small crowd. The water behind it boils up again, and the craft comes to a stop, bobbing up and down in place.

Pete sees Barnacle Bill step up onto the deck. After a brief exchange the crowd moves away from the beach.

The cutter idles out to the seaplane. Pete walks to the plane's rear and opens the door. Sherm kills the port engine and slides his window open.

The cutter swings its after end toward the Grumman and stops. Barnacle Bill steps out onto the fantail.

"Blow me down," growls Sherm. "If it ain't Barnacle Bill the sailor man."

Barnacle Bill grins. "How're you folks getting along?"

"Aye, skipper," says Sherm. "We thought we saw something, so we dove down for a closer look."

Sherm tells Barnacle Bill that after they finish flying around the lake, they'll hop over to Boca Reservoir, fly way down to Lahontan Reservoir, and then make the dash out to Pyramid Lake.

Barnacle Bill waves. "Good hunting."

Pete notices Barnacle Bill looking up to the southeast. He leans out the door and sees a Huey high over the mountains. "I wonder what he's doing way up there?"

Barnacle Bill shakes his head.

"Okay, Sherm," Pete says.

"Aye, matey," Sherm shouts. "Let's pull a vacuum on this beach. *Clear.*"

A billow of smoke and noise explodes out the port engine's exhaust pipes as it catches hold and revs up, cutting off all further conversation.

Pete salutes Barnacle Bill and closes the door. He makes his way back to his seat. The seaplane begins to move. Pete lashes himself in.

A voice sings from the cockpit. "God, I love this."

The seaplane picks up speed, gets on the step, and begins to hop across the waves.

"Whoopee." shouts Sherm.

The hull lifts out of the water.

"*Yeow.*"

Marlette Lake
5:30 a.m., Sunday morning

The helicopter that Pete and Barnacle Bill had seen is *The Gutsy Lady*. Captain Vickie Doolittle, Lieutenant Barnes, First Sergeant Smith, Sergeant Nguyen, and Private First-class Armbruster make up the crew of the craft.

Abel is strapped in the seat behind the pilot. Captain Doolittle hands a flight chart back to crew chief, Sergeant Smith. The sergeant lays it on Abel's lap. Captain Doolittle leans back and points out Marlette Lake on Lake Tahoe's Nevada side. Then she points toward the deck and twirls her finger.

Abel nods.

The Huey descends. Abel sees the tree-rimmed lake rise nearer and nearer. The east side remains in early-morning shadow. He spots a wooden rowboat floating close to shore.

To avoid chopping the alpine trees, Captain Doolittle brings the helicopter down *over the lake*. They hover near the rowboat. Private Armbruster pulls the sliding door open. Abel delights in the glacier blue lake, the green grass, and white granite boulders. Sergeant Nguyen and Private Armbruster continue to search the shoreline.

So delicately, that Abel isn't aware of the movement, Captain Doolittle maneuvers the Huey behind the little boat. The rotor wash begins to move the small craft toward the shoreline. After a couple of minutes, the boat bumps against the rounded boulders.

"This's Virginia City's water supply," yells Lieutenant Barnes. "That might be the water service's boat."

Abel nods.

Captain Doolittle flies the Huey around the mile-and-a-half-long lake, its belly hovering a mere ten feet above the water. Directly under the rotors, the lake's surface grows prickly.

The Huey returns to the boulders. Its landing skid hovers

six inches above the biggest boulder.

Captain Doolittle calls into the back. "Armbruster." She motions with her head while her two hands work to maintain position. Private Armbruster makes his way forward and kneels between the two front seats.

"Hit the ground and warn away any citizens who might be thinking of swimming or fishing in this—"

"Why, ma'am," says Private Armbruster, "ain't *nobody* gonna be swimmin' in *this* lake. It's as cold as a well . . ."

Captain Doolittle smiles behind her radio mike and raises a gloved finger. "Yeah, I know, Armbruster. Grab a pouch of rations and a radio. I'll have somebody relieve you in a couple of hours. Report in if you see any sign of the slime eels."

"Yes, ma'am."

"Make *sure* you keep everybody out of the water."

Private Armbruster nods. He grasps a ration pack and a radio. He steps out onto the Huey's landing skid.

Captain Doolittle hollers, "Oh, and Armbruster."

Private Armbruster turns his head.

"If you get thirsty and bend down to take a sip from the lake, be sure to keep your teeth together."

Grinning, Private Armbruster shakes his head and steps onto the rock. "Thanks a lot, ma'am," he shouts. He throws Captain Doolittle a sharp salute.

Captain Doolittle returns the salute and gives Private Armbruster a thumbs-up. He nods and smiles. The clattering chopper rolls away and beats its way back into the sky.

Silver Creek Campground
5:35 a.m., Sunday morning

The United States Forest Service pickup truck bounces off Highway Eighty-nine and into the Silver Creek Campground.

Granitic dust catches the early-morning sunlight. The pickup truck skids to a stop in front of the path leading to the public restrooms.

Dressed in their Forest Service uniforms, Donald Teeters and Bunny Bardot slide out. Bunny clutches posters. Donald reaches into the pickup's back and plucks out planks, a hammer, a can of nails.

They stride toward the dry holer.

From the campsite next door, a happy camper and his partner glance up at the Forest Service employees.

"How many more we gotta do?" Bunny asks.

"Well," says Donald, "we got to close down every one of these restrooms . . . today. We just have to keep workin' our way down Eighty-nine 'til we meet the team comin' up outta Reno."

"I was afraid you'd say something like that," says a smiling Bunny.

Donald drops his boards in front of the restroom. Bunny sets her posters down.

Donald holds a board across the women's door. Bunny holds out the nail can. Donald places several nails between his lips. He secures one end of the board with his shoulder; Bunny has the other end.

Happy Camper and his partner watch.

Donald pounds in a nail, then another. Bunny then nails up her poster:

This restroom is quarantined.
There is a mud-borne infestation
that has been determined to be life threatening.
Please use other facilities until further notice.
US Forest Service

Donald and Bunny hammer a pair of boards over the men's door. They pick up their materials and saunter back to their pickup truck.

Cradling a fresh roll of toilet paper, Happy Camper's partner walks up to the restroom. His face droops as he reads the poster. He scowls at the dust cloud that the departing Forest Service employees are stirring up.

Happy Camper's partner stares at a grove of trees. He shakes his head and heads for the bushes.

Reno and Sparks
5:40 a.m., Sunday morning

Three Bell Huey's work their way down the corridor where the Truckee River runs through Reno and Sparks. Early-morning sunshine reflects off their big greenhouse windows. Megaphones, attached to their landing skids, blast the message, *"Evacuate the area."*

Kermit and Lucille, a pair of joggers wearing astonished faces, stop and look.

"The water is dangerous."

Pat Hawkins, a fly fisherman, prepares to make his first cast.

"There's an infestation of hagfish."

Bubba, Gene, and Dexter—men of the road sleeping in the hobo jungle—awaken and blink their eyes.

"These fish cause injury and occasionally *death*."

Sleeping on the lawn at Wingfield Park, clutching a bottle-shaped paper sack, Nigel rolls over, putting his back to the chattering helicopters.

"Do not use ground-floor toilets within three hundred yards of the river."

Homeless couple, Jorge and Juanita, stand and peer up through the riverbank willows at the helicopters. Behind them they hear the snarl of the turbine-propped C-130s taking off from the Reno airport. They look at each other, then pick up their blankets, and begin to move away from the river. Their little black-and-white terrier, *Freedom*, scampers ahead.

Sierra Mountains
5:45 a.m., Sunday morning

Aloft in *The Gutsy Lady*, Abel takes in the view of his life.

After leaving off Private Armbruster at Marlette Lake, the Huey climbs to the top of the Sierra Mountain ridge.

"¡*Por Dios!*"

Captain Doolittle glances back and smiles.

The Huey shaves the ridge. The tree-covered slope falls away. In an instant, Abel's vision extends a thousand feet straight down. He beholds Washoe Valley. He gazes up the side of Mount Davidson.

The Huey descends, following the course of the water pipe. At the bottom the pipe moves eastward across Washoe Valley.

The Huey crosses Highway Three-Ninety-Five. The four-lane freeway boasts two lanes full of vehicles heading south. The northbound lanes remain deserted.

Just clearing the tops of the big cottonwoods, the Huey makes its way around the southern end of Washoe Lake. Captain Doolittle and her crew search along the shoreline.

Captain Doolittle guides her helicopter over Washoe City, a collection of homes broadcast over Mount Davidson's lower western slope.

Abel notes the Huey's engine beginning to work. They climb up Mount Davidson's side. Abel views whipping dry grass and blue-green sagebrush. As they gain altitude, Abel notes the dark-green Juniper trees.

The *Gutsy Lady* reaches the top and Abel feels his stomach lurch upward as the aircraft pitches forward. The skids just clear the Junipers. The Huey drops down the eastern side. The trees beneath the chopper whip as if in a cyclone. An old jack-rabbit hops away.

Abel sees a reservoir approaching. He points.

"Yes," says Lieutenant Barnes, "that's where the Marlette Lake water ends up."

The helicopter hovers over the reservoir and makes a slow three-hundred-sixty-degree turn.

"*Bueno*," Abel says. "No one here on Sunday morning."

Captain Doolittle aims straight for Virginia City, five miles ahead. The early-morning sun lights *Saint Mary's in the Mountain's* brilliant white steeple.

Within two minutes the Huey reaches the Virginia City limits.

They cruise above "C" Street, the main road. Abel observes crowded sidewalks. The crowds of tourists act as if they are cut off from Reno's troubles.

At the north end of town, where the attractive Saint Mary's in the Mountains Catholic Church beckons, Captain Doolittle turns the chopper 360 degrees over the old Masonic Cemetery on Boot Hill.

Captain Doolittle finishes her turn over Boot Hill. She glances at Lieutenant Barnes. She raises her eyebrows. Barnes shrugs.

Abel kneels between the two front seats. "Captain, at south end is waterworks building. Put me down there and I tell folks of danger. Okay?"

Captain Doolittle smiles and gives Abel a nod.

From high up over "A" Street, Abel sees the backside of Piper's Opera House and the hundred-and-twenty-year-old Storey County Court House.

"There," says Abel, pointing out the Huey's front window. "See big red barn?"

"Yes, sir," answers Captain Doolittle.

"That is the Virginia City Waterworks building. There big parking area in front."

The Huey exercises a tight left turn over the parking lot. Abel sees no vehicles. Captain Doolittle begins her descent.

"¡*Caracoles*! This Sunday. Nobody here."

When they drop below the barn's roofline, Abel sees that the bay doors stand open. As the Huey nears the parking lot, two men wearing coveralls emerge.

"¡*Caramba*! Someone working on Sunday?"

Behind the two men, with a trouble light lying underneath it, squats a carnival-colored dune buggy.

River Ranch
5:50 a.m., Sunday morning

Sherm's Grumman Goose has completed its circle of Lake Tahoe's shoreline. Pete reports in to Barnacle Bill.

The seaplane buzzes low and slow over the dam at Tahoe City. The Grumman then flies down the Truckee River over the Silver Creek Campground toward the town of Truckee.

KB turns in her seat and points down. The river remains in morning shade.

Pete hollers. "What is it, KB?"

"There are people in the water."

Sherm pulls the seaplane up and around in a tight left turn.

Pete knows it can't be Nicole's party. There isn't room to water-ski on the river.

"Kayakers," he shouts.

"Chrissake."

Pete grabs Sherm's shoulder.

"Sherm." Pete points down. "Kayakers. They're going to splash around in the water and collect a starving slime eel in their lap."

Sherm nods. He rolls the plane the opposite way, keeping

the kayakers in the middle of KB's window.

Pete struggles to hold on.

Sherm shouts. "There's no place to land."

Pete shoves himself back, and he secures his seatbelt. He plucks up the radio. "General Clark. General Clark, this is Mayor Ferrari. Come in."

"Mayor Ferrari," the radio squawks. "This is Sergeant Mills. General Clark will be with you momentarily."

Sherm brings The Gander G-21 sea plane around in a tight left turn. Pete grunts. He stares at the kayakers, trying to ascertain if any appear distressed.

"Yeah, Mayor Ferrari." The radio crackles. "Whataya got?"

"General Clark. Uh. Uh. We have some kayakers here at River Ranch. They appear to be paddling around as if they haven't heard of the danger."

"What's all that grunting? You in the Grumman?"

"Sure as to hell, General Clark. Doctor Oakes is attempting to shove my stomach right out through my butt cheeks."

Howlin' Mad laughs raucously.

"At any rate, General, there's no place to land here. We can't warn the kayakers."

"That River Ranch's just outta Tahoe City, correct?"

"Affirmative."

"Yeah, right. Don't worry yourself about it, Mister Mayor. I got an advance crew just arriving at Tahoe City. Hold on a second. Sergeant. Have the lead element divert immediately to River Ranch. All right, Mister Mayor. I'll guide them in from here. Carry on."

"Thanks, General."

"And good hunting to you, Mister Mayor. I got my fingers crossed."

"Thank you, General. Thanks a lot."

KB leans around the corner. With her middle finger touching her thumb, she gives Pete the A-OK.

Sherm straightens the seaplane out, dives to gain airspeed,

and aims down the Truckee River.

"Whew." Pete clutches his stomach. "Thanks a lot, Sherm, for returning my guts to my belly button area."

"Arrrbeedarrr."

Verdi
5:55 a.m., Sunday morning

Miss Silver State flies over the California-Nevada border and the mountain town of *Verdi*. Two additional C-130s fly on her right. Two others keep pace on the left. They form a V formation and fly low and slow toward downtown Reno. The five C-130s and their twenty turbine engines produce an earsplitting turbine engine whine. The rear cargo doors are hooked open. A snowfall of white paper flutters down.

Four-year-old Justin runs across his yard. He plucks up a sheet of paper, and rushes it back to Clark, his dad. Clark studies the paper and furrows his brow.

Dangerous!
Stay away from the Truckee River
It is infested with a fish that attacks humans.
Do not swim, fish, mine for gold, or boat in the river.
Do not use "outhouse" type toilets placed alongside
the Truckee River.
Hagfish burrow into mud and can make their way to
the toilet.
Hagfishes infest the Reno/Sparks sewer system.
Be cautious in using your home bathrooms.
If you have contact with a hagfish, please report the
incident to:
Brigadier General Nate Arnold at (775) 329-FISH

The Truckee River
6:00 a.m., Sunday morning

The Gander makes a quick revolution around the popular *Boca Reservoir* and returns to the Truckee River. Sherm tips the seaplane so that the river's shore shows up on its left side; then he rolls the plane to the other side.

KB points out the window. "The mountains and trees remind me of Norway." Sherm spins his finger in the air; KB returns to her vigil.

"We're approaching the Reno area," says Sherm. "From the increased radio chatter, we know there's heavy air traffic ahead."

KB nods at Sherm. Then she hollers back to Pete, "What is that cute little village?"

Pete says. "Why, that's *Floriston*, Nicole."

KB smiles at Pete.

"Oh, I mean, KB."

KB reaches back and pats Pete on the knee.

Sherm SHRIEKS—"Tally Ho."

The seaplane stands on its right wing. Pete grabs at the radio but it falls against the starboard bulkhead.

KB screams.

Earsplitting whines saturate the air.

"Holy kee-feckin'-rapp," Sherm shouts.

Pete peeks up through his side window and sees the underbelly of a Hercules, so close he could've inspected each rivet.

Sherm levels out just inches above the treetops. "We feckin' near drove right up his anus."

Pete leans forward and peers out the windshield. A C-130 passes overhead; its rear doors stand wide open. The two airmen stationed in the back are secured by belts. Their eyes are as big as snooker balls. Little Heidi shivers between KB's feet.

"KB," Pete asks, "would you be so charitable as to pass me a sick sack, please?"

"There." Sherm points his finger in front of KB's face.

"Yes, Sherm. A platform anchored in the river. I see it."

Equipment sits on the platform. Hoses hang in the water. A campfire smolders on shore. Beside the camp squats a 1975 F-150 Ford pickup.

"By golly, what is it?"

"That's a gold miner," shouts Pete. "He's working underwater in a frogman's suit. That compressor on the raft is sending him fresh air. Goddamn, Sherm. Did you see that?"

Sherm rolls *The Gander* onto its left flank.

"Something swirling in the water," says KB.

"Arrr," grumbles Sherm.

"Is the gold mining supposed to look like that, Pete?" asks KB.

"No. Uh. Uh. There's too many hoses in the water, and *they're jumping around.*"

"Aye, mates. Those ain't hoses. That poor mucker *is under attack.*"

Sherm's head swings from side to side. "I can't see a place to put 'er down either on land or water."

"Can the miner be protected with his rubber suit?" KB asks.

Sherm looks at KB.

KB slumps in her seat. "Pete," she calls out. "We can't set her down. Can you call on your radio?"

Pete pulls his face from the window. He locates the radio on the starboard side of the airplane and pushes the "talk" button.

"KB, my little Danish dumpling," says Sherm. "We've a lot more area to search and the sun's climbing in the sky." He levels out and aims the seaplane down the river. Sherm and KB pull their sun visors down.

Pete talks to Sergeant Mills.

University Ridge
6:05 a.m., Sunday morning

The Gander flies over Mogul. Pete is infatuated by the Reno skyline opening up before him, and all the different aircraft. It looks like somebody has just swatted a hornet's nest. Hercules C-130s drone in formation; leaflets flutter out their bellies like pollen blowing off ponderosa pines. Huey helicopters fly above the Truckee River, their megaphones barking into the willows. The Care Flight helicopter continuously shuttles back and forth across the Truckee Meadows.

Sherm glances from the air chart on his lap to the airways in front. Little Heidi has taken cover between KB's ankles.

"Sherm," begins KB. "It is so crowded over the downtown area. Let us circumvent it and fly directly to where the water-skiers are."

Pete yanks his face from the window. "I'll vote for that."

"Aye," says Sherm. "Yer right." Sherm tips the left wing up and takes a look. "All clear."

Then Sherm banks left. "I'll maintain a thousand feet above the north hills. We'll dash around the north edge of town and hurry on to Lahontan Reservoir."

Two minutes later, Pete's head begins to swing back and forth like a radar antenna.

"What is it, Pete?" asks KB.

"Oh, I live around here."

"You live near Madam Zho's place?" Sherm shouts.

"Affirmative"

"Let's fly over your house," hollers Sherm, "and see if Nicole's home."

"All right, Captain. It's in that cluster of houses right there on top."

"Aye, got 'er."

"Oh, this is much better, Sherm," KB says. "There is not an

aircraft in the sky."

"It's right there," says Pete. He kneels between the front seats and points. "I don't see her little blue Miata. If she was home, it'd be parked right in the driveway."

"Jumping Jiminy," cries KB. "I see Madam Zho's house. I think Mister Morley is placing luggage in the trunk."

Pete says, "Let's take a closer look, Sherm."

Sherm makes a right turn. Immediately, he banks left keeping Madam Zho's mansion in the center of the portside window.

"Arrr, you be right, KB. Mister Morley's throwing luggage in the back like they're departing on a six-month all-expenses-paid Caribbean cruise."

"Let us buzz them, Sherm," says KB. "Maybe we can scare them back into the house."

Pete laughs.

"Buckle up tight, ol' buddy," hollers Sherm.

Pete pushes himself back to his chair. He belts up and clutches the radio with both hands.

KB picks up Heidi and holds her tight.

"We're a thousand feet above the terrain," hollers Sherm, "so we'll be scorching the sky when we dive-bomb Zho's pink limo."

"Affirmative," Pete hollers. "*Let 'er rip.*"

The seaplane tips forward, and dives. Pete leans forward and gazes through the windscreen. He exhilarates in the crash-dive acceleration. Madam Zho's roof grows bigger and BIGGER. The screaming engines produce a shingle-shaking shriek.

Pete squints at the airspeed indicator. "Oh shit." The needle has disappeared beyond the two hundred twenty-five mile per hour mark.

Just when Pete thinks they might scrape off Madam Zho's weathervane, Sherm suddenly pulls the wheel back. *The Gander* rotates. Pete feels his belly push right down into his under pants. The stinking bilge water, dead crabs, and sea urchins splash toward the stern.

"Holy kee-rapp," yells Sherm. He slams the throttles full forward. He adjusts the constant-speed props for maximum bite. Blue sky fills the windshield.

The two big radials bellow under the strain, fighting to lift the waterlogged airplane back into the sky. The engines roar but the airplane still slows. All eighteen exhaust pipes blast on Madam Zho's roof. Pete imagines the decibels shaking the plaster off her ceiling.

"Holy kee-feckin'-rapp," Sherm screams. "All that weight in the stern—we're gonna feckin' *stall*."

Heidi barks and barks.

Now—as pent-up water is wont to do—it slams into the back – then the bilge water reverses course and cascades forward. Sherm jams the wheel into the dashboard. At the same time, he twists it to starboard as far as it will go. He stomps the right rudder pedal. With panic showing on his face, he pulls the two throttles back an inch and then pounds them forward against the stops.

The cotter key falls from the carburetor linkage. The right radial reduces to idle. The Gander turns violently to starboard and rolls on its back. The twenty-five ice chests tumble onto the overhead.

Heidi falls from KB's arms onto the instrument panel. Heidi's scrambling feet brush the starboard float toggle switch, and the float begins its rotation to the down—now up—position.

The Grumman Goose falls down University Ridge Drive, upside down, straight toward Reno's central gaming district.

"Holy feckin' shit, KB," *shrieks Sherm*, "get that aphid-powered hound off the feckin' instrument panel."

Sherm reduces the left throttle. The bilge water crashes forward into the cockpit, boosting the airspeed fifteen percent, forestalling a stall. Skimming over the rooftops at a mere two hundred feet, Sherm rights the seaplane. The left wing tears off a cottonwood branch. Seawater and sea creatures, alive and dead, rain on *The Gander's* deck.

Spanish Springs
6:25 a.m., Sunday morning

"Thanks, Chuck," says Sherm.

The seaplane had limped over to Spanish Springs and landed at Sky Ranch Park. Chuck Readen, the airport's operator, and licensed A&P mechanic has repaired the carburetor linkage with a wired pin that can't fall out. Chuck has also pulled the bilge plug and drained the stinking seawater onto the tarmac. Only the big chunks remain in the bilge. Sherm hands Chuck his credit card.

"I will take my sick sack to the garbage can," KB says.

"Here," says Pete, "will you take mine also, please?"

At the garbage can, KB pulls the flask from her purse and takes a swig.

"I called Chief Hamper, Sherm," Pete says. "He said they couldn't possibly spare the manpower to run Madam Zho down at this time. We'll have to snag 'er later."

Sherm nods. "Chuck said he almost charged extra for working on the ol' *Gander*. He claimed it smelled worse than a Soviet fish cannery ship."

Pete chuckles.

KB licks her lips. "This is your airplane, Shermy, and you did not know there was a drain plug?"

"Uh hum. Me lovely, how could I have possibly drained the bilge with the craft sitting in water?"

Pete laughs. "Or flying upside down at a hundred feet."

Sherm clenches his teeth.

KB picks up Heidi and holds her. "The saltwater drenched the dashboard, Shermy. Do you think it will affect the electrical connections?"

"Hmmm, it most assuredly will, my little Danish dumpling. However, after conferring with Pete, I think we only need two more hours to search the rest of the waterskiing spots. I've made arrangements with Chuck to have him steam clean the inside of *The Gander*, as well as clean and apply gel on all the electrical connections."

Pete spreads his hands. "The city of Reno insists on paying all of your airplane expenses, as well as all of your hotel charges, Sherm. We're grateful for your efforts."

"Aye, matey. I'm overwhelmed with your generosity. I think I'll take a couple of minutes and trot over to the pilot's comfort station and attempt to shower off this crustacean stew."

"Oh, Shermy, look at Pete's face. He is worried sick about Nicole."

Sherm drops his hand on Pete's shoulder. "I'm filled with remorse for the callousness of my selfish suggestion, my friend. Let's load up and hasten on our way."

"Very well, partner. After we return to Sky Ranch, we'll hire a ride to my place, take long showers, and steam away the sour sea smells."

"Arrrbeedarrr."

Lower Truckee River Valley
6:45 a.m., Sunday morning

The trio fly over Spark's Family Hospital. The Grumman Goose gains altitude to clear the eastern hills. The Truckee River meanders back and forth in the narrow Lower Truckee River Valley.

Sherm tips the plane to the right. "We better stay up outta there, Pete. No room for maneuvering."

"You ain't-a-lyin', Sherm."

The morning sun shines into the front windows. A column

of Nevada National Guard vehicles drives east on Interstate Eighty. Two jeeps peel off and take the Mustang exit.

"Sherm," KB says. "What is *that*?"

Sherm dips his wing. "Is that man fly fishing?"

Pete hollers, "There's always that ten percent who just don't get the word."

"No shit, Sherlock," shouts Sherm.

"Are you going to buzz him?" asks KB.

Sherm shakes his head. "I'm afraid to dive down into that canyon, citizens. Too much traffic and the canyon is awfully narrow."

"Not only that," Pete says, "but I don't think we could convince him to come out of the water by diving at him, anyhow."

Sherm guffaws.

"Fly on, Sherm. I'll call Sergeant Mills."

A Huey pulls up out of the Lockwood area and flies straight toward Sparks Family Hospital.

Pete talks on his radio. "Fly fisherman. Derby Dam Exit."

Wadsworth
6:50 a.m., Sunday morning

Pete uncouples his seatbelt and crouches between the front seats.

Sherm squints at the chart lying on his lap. "We're approaching Wadsworth, Pete. Do you wanta circle 'round Lahontan or would you prefer to fly directly to Pyramid?"

Pete peers forward. He sees far-off cottonwood trees growing between tan sagebrush hills. His guts feel like a knot. He licks his upper lip; it tastes like moribund clam chowder.

"Lahontan's smaller, Sherm, not too far away and wouldn't

take long to check. On the other hand, Pyramid's larger. There's a lot more water-skiers there."

Arching an eyebrow, Sherm looks back at Pete.

"Pyramid, Captain."

"*Whoopee.*"

Pyramid Lake
7:00 a.m., Sunday morning

Sherm immediately banks north, turning to port. The sun now shines in the port windows. Pete watches the airplane's shadow race across the sagebrush deck. Mighty Pyramid Lake lies just fifteen miles ahead.

Pete enjoys seeing the historical old ranches along the river. Their ancient buildings take cover under the cotton-woods. Irrigation spray creates rainbows.

Sherm points to starboard at a fast-approaching hamlet.

"Nixon," Pete shouts. "It's on the Pyramid Lake Indian Reservation."

The seaplane roars low over the Truckee River delta. They skim the ponds of the Paiute Tribe's fish hatchery.

In front of *The Gander* spreads the vast Pyramid Lake. It is ten miles wide and stretches twenty miles to the north—all the way to the horizon.

"Oh," says KB. "It is beautiful."

"Aye, me hearties. That it is."

"Where's the rest of 'em?" Pete shouts.

"It would appear," Sherm hollers, "we're the first ones here. Now, where's this *Undercutter*?"

Tamarack Bay
7:05 a.m., Sunday morning

Pete crouches between Sherm and KB. The Grumman Goose cruises at one hundred ninety miles per hour and fifteen feet off the lake's surface.

"I'm riding the ground effect," Sherm says.

Pete's eyes focus on the speeding beach. "Uh-huh."

The sun bathes the west shore. At Tamarack Bay, KB points at a cottonwood grove sheltering several vehicles, a dozen people, and three boats—including a dark-colored one pulled up on the sand.

"Hmmm." Sherm aims *The Gander* inland. Then he pulls it up and around in a tight turn, keeping the beach camp in the middle of KB's window.

"Do you see *The Undertaker*, Pete?"

"Uh. I don't think that's it, Sherm. That boat's too big. But look at *that*."

Pete points at a teenage boy a hundred feet from shore. The teenage boy reclines in a truck's inner tube. His rear end hangs down in the water. He slowly strokes and kicks, obviously enjoying the warm morning sun.

"Oh, golly," says KB. "Have the hagfishes reached the lake?"

"Do you think we ought to put down," asks Sherm, "and warn the poor bloke?"

"Cripe," Pete says. "I don't know. He looks like he's getting along all right—at least for now."

The teenaged boy's family waves at the Grumman Goose. Sherm straightens out and gives the wings a wigwag.

"Jiminy Cricket," shouts KB. "*Look.*"

The teenage boy is now beating the lake's surface. The water froths around him as if a great white shark is scavenging his bodily parts - the parts that are hanging below the water line.

The teenaged boy's companions exuberantly wave at the G-21.

"Chrissake, Sherm," hollers Pete. "They're attacking."

"Aye. Hit the float switches, KB." Sherm wrenches the seaplane around.

Pete falls against the bulkhead. "Uh."

"Full flaps."

KB places the flaps at forty degrees. The plane's nose pitches forward.

"Carburetor heat."

Sherm straightens the plane out and pulls back on the throttles. The seaplane settles for the surface.

As soon as the hull touches the water, Sherm roars over to the battling teenage boy. Pete makes his way back to the door. KB undoes her seatbelt and follows.

Pete opens the door and leans out. He sees a boat charging away from shore, driving straight to them. He unhooks the safety bar and latches it so they can lie on it.

The Gander floats up to the *screaming teenage boy.*

"Here," yells Pete, half hanging out the door. "Gimme your hand."

Sherm cuts the port engine. The teenage boy screeches as if suffering more bites.

Pete grabs hold of the teenage boy's arm. The teenage boy shrieks in agony. The other arm slaps at the water. Pete pulls him upward. Pete is strong. Nonetheless, the teenage boy is good sized. The teenage boy is more involved in fighting off something in the water, than escaping into the seaplane.

Heidi barks and barks.

KB leans against Pete and bends over the safety bar. Hagfishes make the water boil. One frantically attacks inside the right swimming suit leg. KB grasps the teenage boy by the top of his swimsuit.

"*Pull*," KB hollers.

KB's cry electrifies Pete. He yanks up on the teenage boy

with uncommon strength. KB grins. The two pull up so vigorously that the teenage boy's body jumps right out of the water. He yells in pain.

The head end of a big aggressive hagfish attempts to dine inside the teenage boy's swimsuit. Its rear end flaps against his leg.

"Let's get 'im in," bawls Pete.

Pete and KB drag the teenage boy over the transom. The aluminum edge scrapes his knees. He falls on the seaplane's deck.

The teenage boy lets out a loud cry, as if the hag has gone back for another helping.

Sherm yells from the pilot's doorway.

"*The ax*, Pete."

Pete squints at Sherm.

"Behind you," KB cries. "On the wall."

In one motion Pete spins around, yanks the fire ax off the wall, and chops the creature's end off—right between the teenage boy's thighs.

The hagfish drops out of his swimsuit. The teenage boy pushes away with his feet. Pete chops again, severing the slime worm right behind its faceless head.

Pete hears an outboard powered boat pulling up underneath the wing.

"Matthew. Matthew. Are you all right?"

KB leans out. She waves them up to the open door. "Come on," she says. "Come on in."

A young boy, from his facial features obviously the teenage boy's younger brother, crawls up on their boat's bow. He hands KB their rope and wrinkles his nose. KB holds the rope while the mother clambers into the seaplane.

"What's happened in here?" The mother pulls her sweatshirt up over her nose. "What's that *ghastly smell*?"

While the mother tends to her son, Sherm makes his way past them and leans out the door. He briefly tells the boat's driver about their danger.

The boat driver says he'll tell his people on shore. He steals a glimpse at the inner tube, still under attack. Slime globs float in the water. He assures Sherm that he will set out in his boat and immediately warn the other campsites along Tamarack Bay.

Pyramid Island
7:30 a.m., Sunday morning

The Grumman Goose flies north toward the shorefront town of *Sutcliffe*. Again, Pete kneels between the two front seats.

"Do you think Nicole's group could be on that big island over there," says KB, pointing out her starboard window.

"That's *Anaho Island*, KB," says Pete. "It's a bird refuge. Only scientists are permitted on it."

"Arrr. We're scientists, ol' boy."

"Yes," says Pete. "That you are. Maybe, when this whole affair's over, you can take me out there."

"What about *behind* the island?" asks KB. "Are those people or rocks?"

"Try the binoculars," says Sherm.

"Oh," says KB. "*Those* are *people*. One just came up out of the water. Look, she is . . . *waterskiing*."

The Grumman Goose heels to the right. Sherm pushes on the throttles. He adjusts the mixture.

Pete peeks at the gauges. He sees the tachometer needles push past their redlines. The airspeed crawls above one-ninety. one-ninety-five. Two hundred . . .

"Arrr," says Sherm. "Military power setting. Could be Nicole."

Pete nods. "Carry on, Captain."

Pete glances out KB's window at the starboard engine. He sees gray smoke puffing from it.

At this speed, they are covering three miles a minute.

Sherm pulls the plane up to four hundred feet. He aims past the bird refuge and straight for Pyramid Island.

Pete drops his hand on Sherm's shoulder. "Watch for pelicans, Sherm. They'll fly right in front of you; make you take evasive action."

The seaplane zooms over Anaho Island. Four hundred feet below, three white pelicans lift off.

Alongside the *three-hundred-foot-tall Pyramid Island*, a young woman water-skies behind a fast-moving outboard boat manned by a driver and accompanied by a spotter. The lake lies smooth as a glass table. The skier crisscrosses the boat's wake, producing a curlicue pattern.

Sherm glances at Pete and raises his eyebrows.

Pete squints at the skier. "I can't tell if it's Nicole. Let's try *shooing* them off the lake." Pete flexes his fingers in a shooing motion.

"Aye, aye, matey."

The Gander had, by now, flown past the skier. Sherm nudges back on the throttles. They bank left and then fly around the pyramid's backside. The airspeed needle drops from two hundred miles per hour to one hundred fifty. They reduce altitude to one hundred feet. The pyramid rock fills Sherm's port window.

The Grumman Goose flies from behind the geologic formation. The boat and skier appear directly in front of them. Sherm noses the plane down. He pulls back on the throttles, slowing to one hundred twenty. He aims just above the oncoming boat.

The Gander's hull clears the young woman skier by an enormous thirty feet.

Sherm brings the plane around to starboard.

"Oh no," screams KB.

Sherm pulls the plane around harder.

Pete falls against his chair. "Uh." He sees the boat pulling an empty bouncing rope.

"She is in the water," KB shouts.

Pete pulls himself back between the seats.

"Blazing bewildertoods," Sherm yells. "We'll put down at once, KB, and get her the hell outta that water." "Floats."

"Floats. You bet, Sherm."

"Cripe sakes," says Pete. "I guess that wasn't such a good idea, after all."

They quickly get on the water. The seaplane skips over to the skier.

The ski boat takes a tight turn and returns at full speed—ski handles bouncing on the wake.

The seaplane eases up to the skier. She stares with tangerine-sized eyes.

"Here," cries Pete. "Gimme your hand."

Pete hangs out at the seaplane's door. The skier stares. She maintains her hands well below the water's surface. The ski boat nears.

"You're in danger," shouts Pete. "Let me help you out of the water."

"What's going on here?" hollers the driver. The spotter turns and stares south toward the town of Nixon.

Pete sees the spotter point and say something to the driver. Pete bends down and looks. *"Holy bombing run."*

"What?" Sherm asks.

"Look." Pete points.

Over the horizon, in a V formation, fly five huge four-engined Hercules C-130s. Over the Goose's idling radials Pete hears their whining engines. He sees flashes of light behind the giant craft, as if a huge flock of arctic birds fluttered beneath them. "What're those flashes?"

"Leaflets," says Sherm.

The seaplane drifts past the downed skier.

Pete tells the skier, the spotter, and the boat driver that he is the mayor of Reno. They don't recognize him. He tells them that they are in danger. They wear skeptical faces. The driver glances again at the formation of advancing airplanes.

The Grumman Goose has drifted fifty feet past the skier. Pete yells for them to get her out of the water, *fast*. They look at each other. The young woman nods. The driver and spotter pull the skier from the water.

Pete motions the driver to approach the seaplane's door. He steps back and invites KB to lean out and explain the danger.

KB tells them about the teenage boy in the inner tube. The driver's head nods. He glances at the advancing airplanes. The driver thanks KB, cranks up his boat, and speeds for shore.

"Buckle up," shouts Sherm. "We're outta here." He shoves the throttles forward and both engines bellow. The seaplane accelerates. It gets on the step, then up, and away.

Pete peers out his window. "Hey," he yells. "Check it out."

KB and Sherm glance left. Clattering over the Truckee River delta approaches a squadron of Hueys. A column of National Guard jeeps hurries down Highway Thirty-Three's steep incline onto Nevada State Highway Four-Forty-Five, which is the highway rimming the left side of the lake.

"All right, Pete." shouts Sherm. "Let's find that daughter of yours."

Enchanted Beach
7:55 a.m., Sunday morning

Sherm flies back to the west shore. The Grumman seaplane makes a circle around the boat-launching facility at Sutcliffe. Pete searches for *The Undertaker*.

They fly north. Ahead, a point of land juts out. Sherm looks at his chart.

"Pelican Point," Pete says. He sees that the gauges indicate one hundred ninety miles per hour at four hundred feet altitude above the lake's surface. He searches the shoreline. He pushes on his stomach.

"Hang in there, matey," says Sherm. "At this speed we'll be at the upper end in seven minutes. Then we'll hunt the other side."

KB gives Pete another pat on the knee.

Sherm points at the next point of land.

"Warrior Point." Pete sees several groups of boaters along the beach.

A young man squats in the water holding his ski rope. His boat idles out, steadily taking up the towrope's slack. KB catches Sherm's attention and points down.

Sherm makes a quick search for other aircraft and dives to ten feet above the water.

At one hundred ninety miles per hour, he swoops across the ski boat's bow.

The boat driver *slams* his throttle to idle. The towrope goes slack. The young man's jaw drops as he sits back down in the water.

The Gander rockets back into the sky. They bank right.

"Pete, me man," Sherm says. "Any of that bunch Nicole's crowd?"

"Negatory, Sherm." Pete's nose touches the window. "She's not there."

The seaplane continues to turn and climb. KB points out her window. An armada approaches: C-130s, Hueys, and guardsmen driving jeeps.

Straight ahead, Pete sees light-colored spires growing in size. "That's *The Needles.*"

Within half a minute, they are there. Sherm pulls the plane up and around. Pete feels his heart race.

He's seen something. Their airplane comes around in a tight high-G turn. Pete strains to get a better look.

"It's her," shouts Pete. "Uh. Sherm. It's her. That's *The Undertaker,* and that is, most definitely, uh, Nicole waterskiing behind it."

Sherm pulls up to five hundred feet. He puts the airplane in a slow turn with Nicole at its center.

"Okay, Pete. Whataya want us to do?"

Pete feels his forehead sweat.

"Why not just fly slowly by?" suggests KB. "Far enough away so as not to cause alarm. Pete, you can lean out the door so that Nicole can see you. Motion her to ski toward the beach."

Sherm turns his head toward Pete.

Pete grabs them both by the shoulders and gives them a good friendly shake. Then he turns and makes his way back to the door.

Sherm sets up the plane's glide path so that it comes in from behind, parallel to the water-skier.

Pete opens the door. He lays his belly on the safety tube and leans out.

"Nicole." Pete waves. "*Nicole.*"

Sherm waggles the wings.

"Yes," Pete yells. "That's good, Sherm. No use scaring her last three meals out of her."

On her single ski, Nicole jumps across the wake. Pete sees her gawking at them. She appears to be distancing herself from the merlot-and-white flying apparition. By now, they'd flown half a football field beyond Nicole.

"I think she recognized you," hollers KB.

The plane comes around again, floats down, maximum flaps, and flying so slow it wallows in the sky. Pete leans way out. They approach on Nicole's right side.

"Nicole, honey. Get off the water." Pete waves his arms and firmly points toward shore. "Go to the shore." The seaplane flounders past.

"Yes, KB," Pete shouts. "She recognized me."

The seaplane comes around again. It lines up beside Nicole. It staggers through the air at ten feet elevation.

"Nicole." Pete emphatically points toward shore. "Sweetheart."

Nicole shrugs her shoulders. She prepares to throw her tow rope handles up in the air, preparatory to settling in the water.

"For God's sake, *don't drop the handles*," Pete yells as the airplane skews past. "Don't dump in the water."

Little Heidi stands behind Pete and barks and barks.

Now, Nicole grasp's both handles in her left hand. With her free hand she points toward shore. Immediately, Brad turns *The Undertaker* toward Enchanted Beach. Nicole gives Brad a spin up sign, followed by a more emphatic jab toward shore—*Put the Pedal to the Metal.*

Pete hears the powerful big-block 427 cubic-inch Chevy engine *put on a burst of unleashed horsepower*. In mere moments, Pete sees Nicole skimming so fast that her ski barely touches the tops of the waves, occasionally splashing the water.

"Jesus Christ, precious. Don't fall."

Now, Sherm lets the seaplane land in the lake. They slowly approach the water-skiers' camp. Sherm nudges the bow against the beach. The trio clamber out and wade to shore. KB carries little Heidi.

Pete scoops up his astonished daughter and gives her a really long hug.

Sutcliffe
8:35 a.m., Sunday morning

The Gander circles Sutcliffe.

"What time is it?"

"8:35."

Sherm shakes his head. *"Arrr, a lot has happened in a day and a half."*

"Congratulations are due," says Pete. "We've accomplished our first goal. *There shouldn't be any more human deaths.*"

"You bet you," says KB. "Let us declare victory."

"Affirmative," Pete says. "I'll publicly congratulate the individuals and organizations who participated."

"Very good, Mister Mayor," says Sherm. "Your confidence-building statement should go a long way to averting a panic-fueled stampede."

"If we had any *hotter air* in here," observes KB, "this airplane wouldn't need wings."

Pete laughs uproariously.

"Aye, me hearties," Sherm says. "Now for phase two. Let's figure out how we're going to annihilate these slimy worms."

"First," says Pete, "I'm going to go home and sleep for a week."

"Ugh," says KB. "I will have a shower first."

Sherm laughs. "Look alive now."

They begin their descent. Below them, a Huey moves north up the beach. Leaflets litter the shoreline.

The Gander settles into the water, and then idles into the harbor. It magnificently approaches the dock.

Pete talks on his cellphone to Abel.

KB makes her way to the plane's rear. Heidi follows. KB gives Pete a thumbs-up. He smiles widely and returns the gesture.

KB opens the door. The plane's hull nudges the dock. Little Heidi jumps out on the dock and runs for shore.

KB steps out and ties the craft down fore and aft.

Pete, KB, and Sherm saunter off the dock and walk to the beach. Heidi runs ahead.

Sherm places his arm around KB's shoulders. KB smiles and glances at her watch. "It's 8:50." Sherm chuckles and pulls her closer.

A gunmetal gray Camaro rumbles into the parking lot. Nicole and Brad crawl out of the Camaro and stroll to the beach.

"Hi, Daddy." Nicole waves. "Thank you for rescuing me." She trots up to the trio and gives them each a warm embrace.

"Eeew," says Nicole. "You could use a shower, Daddy. You smell like you could be associated with the dumpster at Fisherman's Wharf."

An approaching Huey drowns out further conversation.

"Jiminy Cricket. It is *The Gutsy Lady*."

"It's Abel," Pete shouts.

Sand and sagebrush branches begin to fly. Nicole picks up Heidi. The trio, plus Nicole and Brad, turn their backs to the stinging rubble.

Before the helicopter touches ground, Abel steps down onto the parking lot, then hurries to the beach. *The Gutsy Lady's* engine begins to wind down.

"Well done, everyone," Pete says, "especially you, KB. That was a brilliant plan that you proposed. We've been one hundred percent successful, and we now officially declare *victory*."

"Arrrbeedarrr, and right you are, Mister Mayor. My little Danish dumpling grabbed the bull by the horns and brought us to this historic triumph."

"Oh golly, Sherm. I only contributed a small part."

"On the contrary, me little chickadee," Sherm says. "And, in commemoration of this momentous occasion"—Sherm wrestles a small wad of tissue paper from his pocket—"I present you with this little gesture of my admiration."

KB grows a quizzical look. She takes the paper and unfolds it. "It's a beautiful charm for my bracelet, Sherm, but what is it?"

Everyone gathers around.

"Outta sight, KB," says Nicole. "It's a sterling-silver longhorn steer. It's, like, *beautiful*."

Sherm clutches KB's hands. "This silver bull celebrates your courageous decision to *grab the bull by the horns*."

KB wraps her arms around Sherm and gives him a huge hug. "Thank you, Shermy. This means so *much* to me."

"Pete has gift," says Abel quietly.

KB glances at Abel, then Pete.

Pete shrugs, then fishes in his pocket. He retrieves a tiny box and hands it to KB.

KB removes the top. She gasps.

Brad looks at Pete. "Totally awesome, dude, but—"

"It's a twenty-four-karat gold baseball bat, Brad," says Nicole, "with a little diamond on its end. It goes on KB's charm bracelet. It's totally rad, Dad."

"You saved the day, KB," says Pete. "When Reno was desperate for help you *stepped up to the plate and took a swing.*"

For *a long sizzling moment KB stares deep into Pete's eyes. "Thank you so much,"* she, at last, whispers.

Nicole grabs Brad's arm. "My dad's in a *swirl for the girl.*"

Abel smiles as if his favorite nephew has just announced his engagement.

Pete, KB, Sherm, Abel, Nicole holding Heidi, and Brad gaze out on Pyramid Lake. All at once, Pete points to movement, a hundred feet offshore.

It's a barely discernible wake, swimming north.

The end

Thank you

1. First, I thank Victor West of Pacific Literary Service in Richmond, California, who resurrected my ailing story by teaching me how, among other things, to develop authentic, stand alone, characters. Before starting over, I took each of the main characters and wrote what he or she did from the time they woke up until they went to sleep. I got to really know each individual character, at which point the novel practically wrote its self.

2. Alex Kale – Managing Editor at Atmosphere Press. She's a sweetheart, managing the business and keeping everybody on track.

3. Cameron Finch – Atmosphere Press Book Publicity Director. She is another sweetheart, helping to present the book in the best light for sales.

4. Dan Gutstein – Atmosphere Press Developmental Editor. Dan's a fabulous editor who's suggestions made the book more appealing to read, and much more attractive and interesting.

5. Ronaldo Alves – Atmosphere Press Art Director & his team in Rio De Janerio. They produced an absolutely amazing future iconic cover picture. This is gonna make people pick up the book.

6. The Proofreader Editors, Sharon Rutland and Chris Beale were undeniably marvelous rooting out the many blunders that I had made. Thank you, thank you, and thank you.

7. Thank you to the entire Atmosphere Press Team for being so darned helpful.

8. Thank you, Noah Goodman – who lives a few blocks from us in Florence, with a bachelor's in computing from the University of Oregon. He helps me with my swine computer plus putting together our splendid web page: Oregon Coast Pictures, Inc.

9. Lastly, but most importantly, is my immediate family: Nina, my wife, who helps me in so incredibly many different ways. Next, my daughter Kristian and granddaughter Kloee, who live with us. Kristian is a much-needed Drug and Alcohol Counselor. Kloee is a teen attending Mapleton HS, where she plays on the girls basketball team. They keep us young and are absolutely wonderful to have around. And we mustn't forget Coco Puff, our loving terrier dog.

About Atmosphere Press

Founded in 2015, Atmosphere Press was built on the principles of Honesty, Transparency, Professionalism, Kindness, and Making Your Book Awesome. As an ethical and author-friendly hybrid press, we stay true to that founding mission today.

If you're a reader, enter our giveaway for a free book here:

SCAN TO ENTER
BOOK GIVEAWAY

If you're a writer, submit your manuscript for consideration here:

SCAN TO SUBMIT
MANUSCRIPT

And always feel free to visit Atmosphere Press and our authors online at atmospherepress.com. See you there soon!

About the Author

BERNIE CHRISTENSEN lives in Florence on the Oregon Coast with his loving family - his long-time wife, Nina, daughter Kristian, and granddaughter Kloee.

Bernie was raised, for a few years, with his parents and grandparents on a coastal dairy farm outside of Bandon. Then they moved to the other grandparent's dairy farm between Junction City and Eugene. Bernie attended school in Junction City and then Willamette HS north of Eugene. He joined the Coast Guard Reserve while still in high school and served eight years, finishing as a petty officer second-class engineman.

After boot camp and a stint on a 300-foot-long coast guard cutter, he landed a job as a switchman on the Southern Pacific Railroad, and at the same time attended the University of Oregon for six years, earning a bachelor's degree. He then railroaded, as a locomotive engineer, in California, Nevada and Utah on the Western Pacific RR, which was eventually gobbled up by the Union Pacific RR, where he retired in Reno after 43 years of railroading.

Then he wrote a couple of books.

Milton Keynes UK
Ingram Content Group UK Ltd.
UKHW042221180324
439698UK00005B/374